YOUNGBLOOD

YOUNGBLOOD

SASHA LAURENS

RAZORBILL

RAZORBILL

An imprint of Penguin Random House LLC, New York

First published in the United States of America by Razorbill,
an imprint of Penguin Random House LLC, 2022

Copyright © 2022 by Sasha Laurens

Visit us online at penguinrandomhouse.com.

LIBRARY OF CONGRESS CATALOGING-IN-PUBLICATION DATA
Names: Laurens, Sasha, author.
Title: Youngblood / Sasha Laurens.
Description: New York : Razorbill, 2022. | Audience: Ages 14 and up. (provided by Razorbill.)
Identifiers: LCCN 2022011426 | ISBN 9780593353202 (hardcover) ISBN 9780593353226 (trade paperback) | ISBN 9780593353219 (ebook)
Subjects: CYAC: Vampires—Fiction. | Boarding schools—Fiction. | Schools—Fiction. Lesbians—Fiction. | LCGFT: Vampire fiction. | Gay fiction. | Romance fiction.
Classification: LCC PZ7.1.L3822 Yo 2022 | DDC [Fic]—dc23
LC record available at https://lccn.loc.gov/2022011426

ISBN 9780593353202

Manufactured in Canada

1 3 5 7 9 10 8 6 4 2

FRI

Design by Rebecca Aidlin
Text set in Garamond Premier Pro Medium

For the girls still figuring it out

1

KAT

I LEANED OVER the counter of the Snack Shack at the El Dorado Hills Country Club and stared out at the pool. The cool, bright-blue water would feel incredible against my sweaty, greasy skin. It was an early August scorcher and the pool had been packed with screaming kids all day. The lunch rush slammed us so bad, it ran into the snack rush, and I still had milkshake in my hair. Now, at last, the sun was edging below the trees and a cool shadow was creeping across the line of deck chairs. The lifeguards were herding the kids out of the pool and back toward their nannies and au pairs and stay-at-home parents.

"Kat, if I have to make one more Caesar salad with no croutons or dressing, I will scream," Guzman said from the sink. "Like, it's literally just romaine?"

I laughed, but my eyes were fixed on the pool. In the evening, a different set of club members came out. I'd been watching them emerge all summer: swimmers doing laps in the fading sun and well-dressed women who sipped white wine from the indoor bar. For these club members, the whole world seemed to relax to give them a moment of easy peace.

I wanted to be one of them.

Guzman blasted the inside of a blender with water. "Is Shelby flirting with that cute lifeguard—what's his name, Ryan?"

I cut my eyes toward the lifeguards' office in time to see Shelby, in their red lifeguard's rash guard with their sport sunglasses pushed up, thwack a shirtless dude on the arm with a pool noodle.

"Yup, Shelbs is definitely flirting." I yanked the gallon jug of ketchup through the service window. "Do you think before summer's over, the club management would let us sit out there, after closing?"

"What, let us have a swim, order some fries, lay out in the sun?"

It was impossible. I couldn't eat fries, and the sun tended to make me queasy. But still, something in me pulsed with longing. "I just want to feel what it's like to be a country club member, you know?"

"Uh-huh, I do know, I'm pretty sure my whole family knows, including everyone we left back in El Salvador. And no, I absolutely do not think they'll let us take an afternoon off to pretend like we belong. We wear the uniforms around here."

I turned back toward the dim kitchen, my vision throbbing after the brilliant light of the pool scene. "We'll have to become millionaires first. We could be members ourselves."

Guzman was rooting through the fridge. "I love the long-term vision, but as an immediate act of resistance, I'm making a quesadilla. This institution robbed us of our lunch break. You want half?"

The truth was, I hadn't skipped lunch because we were busy. I'd skipped it because Guzman had been there. Summer break meant I could work enough to have some savings left over for the school year. Guzman was planning to do the same, and we'd both applied to the Snack Shack. With Shelby lifeguarding, it had seemed like the perfect setup for a perfect summer—even if Guz and I would be spending it in a tiny, overheated kitchen.

There was only one problem: I'd forgotten to factor Hema into the plan. Having Guzman around all day meant that the human blood substitute I drank at breakfast would have to hold me until my shift ended. The first few days, I'd gotten so hungry by closing I'd caught myself looking a little too long at the bare wrists and exposed necks of the club members. I considered sneaking some Hema into the kitchen, so I could grab a sip when Guzman wasn't looking. But having to explain why there was a bottle of blood next to the burger patties was far worse than going hungry.

I pressed my hand to my forehead, slightly dizzy. Most days, I could manage. I was no stranger to self-control. But my mom and I often had only enough Hema to get by, and this morning we'd come up short. When we'd split the last bottle, both of us knew we'd be ravenous come dinner. Neither of us said anything about it. I'd have to pick some up tonight.

"I'm good," I told Guzman.

He slapped a tortilla on the flattop grill. "If I find out that you're on one of these clean-eating diets where you can't have any gluten or cheese or fun or happiness, I'm going to be so mad."

I turned off the fryer and tossed the last cold, salt-crusted fries into the trash. "My stomach has been acting up lately."

Guzman gasped dramatically. "Sorry, I *totally* forgot."

"Guzman, if I catch you being mean to Kat, I'm gonna write you up for violating pool rules." Shelby's blond head poked in the service window. They had a deep summer tan that made their teeth brilliant white when they smiled.

"It's nothing," I said. "Stomach stuff."

I pretended not to notice the glance Shelby gave Guzman.

At the start of sophomore year, I began to lose the ability to digest food—at least the kind my friends ate. It had been a hard, sad year, not knowing if I was tasting my last ice cream cone or ripe strawberry or slice of pizza. My mom put together paperwork from her clinic diagnosing me with a digestive disorder. By the time school got out, I was subsisting entirely on Hema, which meant to everyone else's eyes, I didn't eat anything. Ever. It was hard for people to accept, even if they knew my condition was medical. That didn't stop the school guidance counselor from passing me pamphlets about well-rounded nutrition—or my friends from shooting each other concerned looks that they thought I didn't catch.

I wasn't ungrateful for Hema. I was incredibly lucky that I've never had to sink my fangs into someone's neck, especially not now that one wrong bite could kill you. But the lying was exhausting already. I didn't know how I'd survive the two more years of high school, stealing sips from a thermos of lukewarm blood substitute crammed into my locker, right next to my gym clothes.

Not just two years. Not just the rest of high school. Forever.

Or however long vampires were supposed to live.

Shelby hopped up on the counter. "Gimmie half. I'm starving."

Guzman, brandishing a knife in one hand and an avocado in the other, looked at Shelby over his shoulder. "I bet you are, after a long day of *shameless flirting*—ow, shit!"

Shelby clicked their tongue. "Karma's a swift mistress."

I turned to Guzman. He was saying something like *can you believe this*, and holding his hand out to me. From a gash in his thumb, a crimson rivulet ran into his palm.

Blood.

Hunger shot from a dull dizziness to a head rush. My vision narrowed to that precious, dark red pool gathering in his hand.

"I'm gonna grab a first aid kit," Shelby said. "Kat, can you get him a paper towel?"

But I couldn't.

My mouth was watering, and before I could stop them, my fangs were pressing into the inside of my lip. Panic careened through me as I snatched my hands to my mouth. This *never* happened, I never lost control and let my fangs slip free. If anyone saw, my life here would be over. But even under that terror there was a pounding in my head—hunger—and a little voice whimpering that maybe just one little taste wouldn't hurt—

No. My palm still pressed to my lips, I backed away from him, until I was up against the counter, the farthest I could get from him in the tiny kitchen. What was I *thinking?* That I would *drink Guzman's blood*? That was horrible—it was wrong—and I would never do it. Even if I would, I *couldn't.* You never knew who was carrying the infection. A drop of the wrong blood, and just like that, immortality meant nothing.

"Earth to Kat?" Guzman yanked a paper towel from the roll, then wrapped it around his hand. With the blood out of sight, I took a fragile breath—steadying enough that I was able to draw my fangs away. A second later, Shelby was back, pulling a dozen different antiseptics and bandages from a first aid kit.

Shelby eyed me. "You good?"

My skin was clammy, my nerves jangly and raw. I ran my tongue over my incisors, checking them once, then again. "I've got, um, one of those blood phobias? I just see a drop of blood and I get nauseous," I mumbled. "Guzman, why don't you get out of here? You can't close if you're bleeding everywhere."

What I really wanted was to get myself out of there, but if I did, it would cost me an hour's wages. I couldn't afford that, not with how Hema prices had been recently.

"But we were gonna hang out," Shelby protested.

"I have to pick my mom up from work." I forced myself into a fang-free smile. "I'm sure you guys can manage to have fun without me."

Guzman drew his freshly bandaged hand back from Shelby, threw his apron in a corner, and squeezed me into a quick, french fry–scented hug. "You are officially my least fun friend, and thank you."

"Text if you can meet up later, okay?" Shelby said.

"For sure." I knew I wouldn't. The knot in my stomach didn't begin to loosen until they both were gone, the aborted quesadilla was in the trash, and I'd sprayed a thick mist of cleaner over the entire area—until the only trace of blood that remained was the slow, persistent throb of my own hunger.

I PULLED INTO the parking lot beside the Sacramento Shared Services Clinic and texted Mom. Fifteen minutes later, I gave up waiting and went inside. Mom was born in 1900 and turning 122 this year. Even though her vampiric body still looked like she was in her late thirties, she was always forgetting that texting was a thing.

As I pushed open the doors of clinic, that distinctive stomach-turning scent closed around me: disinfecting chemicals; the cloying synthetic odors meant to cover their smell; and beneath it all, the ever-present tinge of blood.

Infected blood.

The waiting room had an abysmal energy. The walls were hung with prints of watercolor swooshes, as if mail-order art could elevate the atmosphere. The patients waiting in the duct tape–patched seats had that distant look that I recognized as a sign of severe CFaD, even if it wasn't a symptom. Their minds were elsewhere, trying to manage their pain or their bank accounts. In the corner, an exhausted woman and her toddler slid wooden beads along wire tracks—the world's most depressing toy, found exclusively in depressing settings like this one.

This clinic served patients with clotting factor dysfunction—CFaD, for short. Since the virus was discovered in the 1970s, more than half the human population had been infected by the CFaD virus. Most of them got no sicker than they would from a regular cold. The patients who wound up in my mom's clinic were the unlucky ones whose condition was chronic. CFaD sent their circulatory system haywire. Their blood clotted too fast or too slowly or not at all, in the wrong places and at the wrong times, and they could die without treatment. CFaD was mostly harmless—until it harmed *you*.

Vampires had always understood that perfectly, long before the first severe cases. Any vampire who fed on a human carrying CFaD—symptoms or not—was dead within minutes. Vampires called it the Peril: as CFaD exploded in the human population, we'd nearly gone extinct.

Hema was the only thing that saved us from extinction.

Even if it hadn't been enough to save my dad.

"Hi, Kat," the clinic receptionist said. "Angela should be done soon. We were shorthanded today."

"Like every day, right?" I said.

The clinic never had enough of anything it needed. No CFaD clinic ever did. Even with insurance, a lot of my mom's patients cleaned out their savings to afford treatment, hoping to hang on until a cure was discovered. The Black Foundation for a Cure—the biggest name in CFaD research—had been working on it for something like forty-five years. If CFaD was curable, the Black Foundation would cure it. It was, after all, run by vampires.

Vampires didn't often find common cause with humans, but they'd make an exception where disease-free blood was concerned.

The other exception, of course, being my mother, who lived her life like she wanted to forget she was a vampire altogether.

As I settled into a seat to wait for my mom, I texted Donovan, our Hema dealer, with an order to pick up later, reacted to a video from Shelby, and then, more out of habit than anything, I swiped to the last screen on my phone, opened a folder of games I never played, and found the icon for an email app hidden there.

I should have deleted the account already. I'd promised myself I'd do it when school got out for the summer. Mom would be furious if she found out that I'd set up an email account in her name. But the end of school had come and gone, and the account was still there. In all of the several thousand times I'd checked it, the inbox had always been empty. Now it was practically the start of junior year and I had submitted the application in January. It was way beyond too late to hear—but how could I give up hope when I hadn't gotten any reply at all?

I peeked down the hallway, to make sure my mom wasn't coming, and opened the account.

Email account: AngelaFinn1900

Inbox: 1

Admissions@TheHarcoteSchool.edu—Admissions Decision for Katherine Finn

I went still, staring at the screen.
This is it.
I tapped to open the message.

Throttled by the clinic's crappy Wi-Fi, it loaded slowly. First, the header image, with the bat-and-castle crest that I would have known anywhere. Beneath it, curled Latin script reading *Optimis optimus*, which I knew translated to "The Best of the Best." I was barely breathing by the time the text finally appeared.

Dear Ms. Finn,

It is our pleasure to extend an offer of admissions to the Harcote School for the coming year to Katherine Finn.

I apologize that I was unable to send word of her acceptance earlier in the spring, as is our custom, but we have assembled a special financial aid package, which caused the delay. An anonymous donor will be supporting Katherine's enrollment. This generous offer is detailed on the following page.

The academic year begins in just over two weeks. We are ready to provide all assistance to ensure that Katherine is prepared. Please sign and return the attached document as soon as possible.

Let me be the first to welcome Katherine to the Harcote School in our twenty-fifth anniversary year!

Sincerely,
Roger Atherton
Headmaster

I'd gotten in.
I'd actually gotten in.
My skin went tingly all over, and my head felt dizzy, only this

time it wasn't hunger, but a head rush of excitement that didn't feel real.

The Harcote School was one of the very best boarding schools in the country. In the human world, it was known to be ultra-exclusive, with a single-digit admit rate. That was because humans didn't know Harcote accepted only one kind of student: Young-blood vampires, born since the Peril.

Not just any Youngbloods—the Youngblood elite, descended from the richest and most powerful figures in Vampirdom.

And now, also: me.

I read the letter again and again, trying to sear that feeling of satisfaction into my brain. If I marked myself with it deeply enough, I might carry it forever. Because when I scrolled to the financial aid offer, I'd have to give up the dream of attending Har-cote once and for all.

Tuition was tens of thousands of dollars a year, and financial aid was notoriously nonexistent, no matter what forms you sub-mitted with your application. That didn't matter to the kids who went to Harcote: they were the children of Vampire Captains of Industry and Vampire Zillionaires, and their fangmakers—the vampires who turned their parents—were probably legendary. I was the daughter of a Vampire Nurse Practitioner, and as for my dad, he'd made it through the worst of the Peril, only to lose his life feeding on a human when money ran too short to afford Hema. That put elite private school tuition pretty far out of reach. Even if we could have afforded it, my mom was convinced that I had no place at Harcote.

It didn't matter that I'd dreamed of going there since long be-fore my fangs had come in.

My mom and I had never fit in with Vampirdom. It wasn't just that she'd always sent me to public school, when most Youngbloods had private tutors, or that our bank account eternally hovered just above zero. We didn't have the pedigree that Vampirdom celebrated. Before the Peril, my mom told me, your fangmaker defined who you were in our world. Your fangmaker was an older vampire who selected you for the immortal life and passed along that gift by turning you. A true fangmaker taught a new vampire how to hunt and feed, how to glamour humans and use vampiric charisma, how to adjust to unending life. Basically, how to *vampire*. Fangmaker and fangborn shared an eternal bond. Now that new vampires were born, not turned, that tradition had been adapted: your parents' fangmakers were yours too. When other vampires asked about my pedigree—or used to ask, because I hadn't met one in years—I told them both my fangmakers had been lost in the Peril and steered the conversation to my dad's fangmaker; he really hadn't survived. My mom's fangmaker was entirely off-limits. The truth was, we didn't know if he'd succumbed to the virus or if he was still among the ever-living, never-dying. We didn't even know if he was a *he*. That was because my mom didn't know who her fangmaker was, period.

My mom hadn't been chosen for this life, and her immortality hadn't been given as a gift. Her fangmaker hadn't meant to turn her at all: he'd fed on her and left her for dead. For years she'd thought she was the only vampire in existence.

When she finally found others, she realized she'd been better off that way. They treated her like she didn't deserve to be one of them, like her immortal life was a mistake and the vampire that bit her should have finished the job. They wanted nothing to do with her.

That's why she'd begun to lie—lies I'd inherited, and always told too.

Except once.

It came back to bite me quick enough. I had plenty of time to think about my fuckup too, on the cross-country drive, as we left behind the life we'd had in Virginia for a fresh start in California. In Sacramento my mom promised (herself—I was not consulted) that she was done with other vampires. We'd been here three years, and outside of Donovan, I didn't know a single vampire in the entire state.

At first, I was happy to leave Vampirdom behind, after how I'd been burned. But as I got older and my vampiric features couldn't be ignored, the isolation started to grind me down. Maybe it was wrong to want approval from a world that had rejected me, but I couldn't help the diamond of ambition that hardened in my gut when I thought of Harcote. The school would obliterate everything that made me different, less-than. I'd truly *belong*.

It wasn't a feeling my mom was sympathetic to. At all. She said applying was out of the question. Anyway, we'd never be able to pay.

This year, I was done with asking permission. I filled out and submitted the application myself, in secret.

I blew out a sigh. Better to get the bad part over with. I scrolled to the financial aid offer.

Financial Aid

Funding provided per year, for two years (Third and Fourth), conditional on compliance with the Harcote School Honor Code:

—Annual tuition and fees: provided in full.

—Room, board, uniform: provided in full.

—Additional expenses, including textbooks, computing needs, costs related to clubs, sports teams, or educational travel: provided in full, at request, no limit.

—Travel stipend for relocation to Harcote campus and one home visit per term: provided in full.

—Incidental expenses, including new clothes and other necessary items prior to arrival on campus: provided in full, at request, no limit.

All funds furnished by anonymous donation.

Elation, bright and hot, surged through me, I pressed my lips between my teeth. It didn't feel right to grin in that dismal waiting room.

"What are you so happy about?"

My mom stood in the hall. She was pale and gaunt at the end of the long day, but she was wearing a curious grin.

I leaped up. "Mom, I'm going to Harcote—I got in!"

Her face spasmed with anger: her eyes bulged and her lips pulled back. Just as quick, she composed herself. She set her mouth in a firm line and tightened her fist around the strap of her purse and walked right past me, right through the waiting room and out into the parking lot. The door of the clinic swung shut before I could follow.

2

KAT

"DID YOU HEAR what I said?" I jogged after my mom. She was power walking through the parking lot and was almost at the car when I caught up.

Standing at the passenger side, she gave me a hard look, sucking in her cheeks so they looked hollow. "Kat, unlock the car."

"I got into *Harcote*," I repeated.

"I understood you the first time. Please unlock the car."

"That's all you have to say?" I held the car keys tight in my fist. "Not even like, 'Congratulations, Kat, my only daughter, for getting into one of the most competitive high schools in the country'?"

"Yes, Kat, congratulations on going behind my back to apply when I expressly told you not to. With a mind like that, it's no wonder they admitted you."

Her words stung—badly—but worse was the look in her eyes, a pointed anger that told me she'd only said a fraction of what she was really thinking. "I don't understand," I stammered. "I thought you'd be proud of me."

Heat radiating from the roof of the car sent ripples through her face when she looked back at me. "I'm always proud of you, Kat. But I'm not sending you to Harcote. Now, it's been a long day, and I'm tired."

Suddenly, a bolt of anger crackled through me, shearing away the hurt and confusion of a moment before. So my mom was tired? No shit. *I was tired.* I was tired of working at the stupid Snack Shack, serving people a hundred times richer than I'd ever be, when I could have gotten an internship or taken an extra class that would look good to colleges and eventually law schools; tired of worrying about money and Hema; tired of feeling like the only vampire under a century old in the entire state of California.

I was tired of wanting more and never getting it, and I was tired of being scared that my life would be like this forever—that for the rest of my immortality, it would never get better.

I ground my teeth, but I did as she'd asked. I drove us home in what I hoped was a scorching silence. It was a calculated prelude to the argument we'd have once we arrived. In my head, I played out a hundred different arguments, gaming out the best possible attack and how to parry her defenses. I waited until the door to the apartment was closed and she'd hung up her coat before I started in.

I was firm, rational, in control. "I know it's super late in the summer, but they gave me full funding. The aid package covers full tuition, room and board, *everything.*"

"That doesn't change the fact that you lied to me."

"Technically, I never lied. You never asked."

Her nostrils flared. "Silly me, never asking if you had secretly submitted any boarding school applications."

"Fine. I did go behind your back, and that was wrong," I conceded. "But now the situation is that I've been accepted and we can afford it. We might actually be able to save some money for once, if I was away at school and everything was taken care of."

"It's not just the money—or the timing, which is frankly

ridiculous. I don't want you in a boarding school, especially Harcote. All vampires, no humans. I want you to know a bigger world than that."

"Since when is Sacramento *a bigger world*?" Judging from her glare, this was a misstep. I switched tactics. "And I *am* a vampire, Mom. Living with humans isn't going to change that."

"Where's this coming from, Kat?" She held her hands out in front of her, like the *this* in question was an invisible presence in the room. "You have plenty of friends here."

"*Human* friends, who I lie to every single day about who I am. Do you ever think how hard it is for me to spend my whole life not knowing a single vampire my own age?"

"I didn't realize your life began when we moved to Sacramento, Kat. I seem to remember your spending quite a lot of time with a vampire your own age before we came out here."

It cut deeper than it should have. It was true: before the move to California, we spent four years living with a vampire family. Well, not *with* them, but in their guesthouse, which was a thing they had because they lived on an actual estate. Their daughter had been my best friend—until she betrayed my trust and we were out on our asses.

"That was different," I snapped. "We were just kids, not even really vampires yet. And you know I haven't talked to her since we left. I need to be around other Youngbloods *now*, when it really matters."

"You have me, and you're lucky to have that. Vampires have always lived solitary lives, Kat. That's the nature of turning."

"And everyone agreed that wasn't exactly a good thing. Why should I have to live like that when things are different now?" Before the Peril, vampires weren't interested in children—vampiring was an adults-only activity, and pregnancy was hard to achieve in an immortal body that healed superfast. It was only since CFaD made turning impossible that vampires started having children. "There's a whole *generation* of Youngblood vampires like me, and I'm out here, all alone."

She was massaging her temples again. I was wearing her down. "Why are you getting so much financial aid?"

"Because we're broke and the rest of them are rich. Because I deserve it."

She leveled a weary look at me. "The world doesn't work that way, and you know it."

She was right: I did know that. I had for a long time. The walls of the small apartment felt too close, the air too still and hot. I ran my hands over my face. For reasons I couldn't pinpoint, I'd lost the advantage. That was impossible, unacceptable, but I was so frustrated I couldn't find a way to get back on track.

"Harcote could *change my life*, Mom!"

"I've tried to give you the best life I could." Her eyes were glossy, and that set me reeling. She was *always* doing this, going frail and tragic, as if that was a legitimate way to win an argument instead of an embarrassing cop-out.

"Don't guilt-trip me when you're the one in the wrong! Just because you're happy pissing away your immortality here doesn't mean I am. *I'm not.* I can't live like this forever."

Forever.

A familiar tightness throttled my breath in my chest—the grip of panic that seized me whenever I let myself think about it.

Humans talked about immortality like it was some amazing gift. It sounded nice if you were planning to spend it in a castle, sitting on a mountain of cash, with all the time in the world to fritter it away, like vampires in movies and books. That life seemed pretty good to me too.

It wasn't the life I had.

Immortality looked a lot different when you were staring down decades of uncertainty. I had plans for the next few decades. Youngblood vampires aged like humans until the end of our teens; from then, the process slowed to a crawl. I might look like I was thirty by my hundredth birthday. That made it hard to make a life anywhere permanent. My plan was to do college and law school on loans, then scramble to make partner at a law firm. I'd spend a few years saving every cent I could, sneaking sips of Hema at my desk, until the fact that I still looked like a college freshman raised too many eyebrows. Then I'd do what other vampires had done before me: move somewhere new, set up a new life, and wait for the process to repeat itself. No lifelong friends, no watching anyone get old, no twenty-year high school reunions. It only went so far in getting what I really wanted: safety, stability, a life where I'd never worry about accidentally committing a murder-suicide if my bank account ran too low.

"I want to go, Mom," I said, my voice ragged. This had to be my trump card. "I think Dad would have wanted this for me too. To make sure I don't end up like him."

Two thin lines appeared between her eyebrows, like they usually did when she was about to agree to something she thought was a bad idea. This was it—my *yes* was coming. Then she said, "I don't agree that he would want Harcote for you. But he'd have faith you would find a way to get by without it."

My body went rigid, my mouth fallen open. The whole time we'd been fighting, I'd had this engine of anger steaming inside me, but now I had slammed, full-speed, into a wall. I couldn't argue with her about what my father would have wanted. He'd died before I was old enough to know. Most of the time I was okay with that, but right now, it felt like my mom was deliberately reminding me of what I'd lost.

"Believe me, Kat." Her voice softened. "This is what's best for us."

I couldn't even look at her as I grabbed the empty Hema bottles from the kitchen counter. "Donovan's expecting me."

THIS IS WHAT'S *best for us.*

Those words chased themselves in circles in my head as I drove to Donovan's.

Harcote was a world-class school, a place of power and privilege and excellence, with classes that were college-level hard. Harcote students *became* someone, if they weren't someone already. Every opportunity was at their fingertips, and the financial aid guaranteed that I would have the same.

How could my mom possibly believe Harcote wasn't best for me?

I had to admit, there was something too good to be true about the financial aid, but I was one of the best students at my high school, and I'd written a knockout admissions essay. I had the merit, and I definitely had the need. My grip tightened on the steering wheel. The only thing standing in my way—that had *ever* been standing in my way—was her.

I pulled into the strip mall where Donovan's was located and drove around back. From the front, Donovan's was a dive bar with a glitchy neon sign and blacked-out windows. Out the back, Donovan ran a distribution for Hema, and we counted on him to give us a good rate. I pressed the buzzer, then waited among the dumpsters and wood pallets and cigarette butts. It smelled like trash, with a rank undertone of urine. I knocked an empty beer can away with my toe.

I wished I felt nervous or scared in that dark parking lot. Or disgusted. Or out of place.

But I didn't.

Instead, all I felt was that familiar anxiety constricting my chest: *an eternity like this, an immortality like this.*

Forever. I was going to live forever like this.

The door swung open and Donovan poked his head out, the stub of a cigarette between his lips. "Hey there, Kat."

He stepped out and lit a fresh cigarette off the butt. Donovan had an ageless look, imbued with vampiric charm that drew humans to him, although they couldn't put their finger on why. Especially because he didn't take care of himself: his hair was greasy, and a century of consequence-free chain-smoking meant that the stink of smoke emanated from his pores.

"Two bottles, right?"

"Yep." I held out the two empties I'd brought.

"With a little discount for the bottle return . . ." He tapped at his phone with a nicotine-stained finger. "It's three hundred and ten bucks."

My stomach dropped. "That's twenty bucks more than normal!"

Donovan let out a cloud of smoke and jabbed a fingernail toward some itch in his scalp. "CasTech sets the prices, babe. I'm just the middleman."

"If I give you two hundred now, can you put the rest on our tab?"

Donovan grimaced apologetically. "You're going to have to pay that tab down one day, you know? But I'll do it for that pretty face of yours."

I forced myself to smile while I counted the money. My stomach was at my shoes by the time I got to the last bill. "This is only one ninety. I thought I had more."

"You're killing me, Kat." Donovan tossed his cigarette away. "Look, I do have some product I need to get rid of. I'll do it for one ninety, fair and square."

Donovan disappeared inside, then returned with two bottles. Inside, the Hema looked almost black. I tilted the bottle, watching how the thick liquid clung to the glass, then unscrewed the top of one and smelled it. I nearly spit into the street.

"This is already half rancid!"

"Beggars can't be choosers. The freshest stuff is going for five hundred a pop right now."

I wanted to cry or scream or both. I could almost see myself smashing the bottle on the ground, into shards of glass and sticky old blood—to let the Hema splatter on Donovan's feet and find out how he liked the smell then.

But I didn't do that. I couldn't.

What I did instead was screw the top back on the bottle and take the second one from him. I handed over the cash and thanked him for helping us out. Donovan winked and said it was a pleasure doing business, like he always did. Like it always did, it felt like an added humiliation. Then I got back in the car and headed toward home.

Five hundred dollars for a bottle of fresh Hema. Prices like that, it was a wonder any poor vampires managed to survive. I shivered. Would it come to that, someday, for us—for me? If Hema prices kept climbing, if the clinic's funding got cut. We were always only one wrong step away from slipping over the edge. Hunger made you desperate, and desperate vampires took unthinkable risks. Risks that cost them everything.

This is what's best for us.

Mom was wrong. I felt it, hard and true in the same place where the claws of my immortality scraped against my ribs. Maybe this was the best she hoped for, but I wanted more. Now, for the first time ever, I had it. Harcote was a way out, the path to something better, to a place where I could finally *belong*.

If she couldn't understand that, there was nothing left to talk about.

When I parked outside our apartment, I took out my phone and opened the message from Headmaster Atherton. Quick, before I lost my nerve, I signed the documents with my mother's signature, checked all the right boxes, and then hit send.

Junior year started in two weeks and when it did, I would be a student at Harcote.

3

TAYLOR

ON THE UP-CAMPUS hill, I sat on the portico railing of the library porch and pushed my sunglasses up my nose. The frames were huge and made me look like a bug, but they were also the darkest I'd found in my summerlong search, almost too dark to properly see. Unfortunately, they weren't dark enough to obscure what was happening down the hill below me: Move-in Day at the Harcote School.

My mouth dipped into a scowl, where it would probably be stuck until school got out in June.

I'd been through Move-in Day as a starry-eyed first-year and then as a jaded second-year, and this one was no different. The whole thing was a pageant, full of made-up traditions, like the way the faculty had to wear black ankle-length capes on the first day of school, even though it was so hot and humid in upstate New York that we might as well have been trapped in an armpit. As if Atherton was worried they wouldn't be recognizable as vampires without taking accessorizing tips from cartoons. The point of it all was to make overprotective vampire parents feel like they were entrusting their precious Youngbloods to a hallowed institution as old as they were—to make it easy to forget that Atherton had only gotten his hands on the school and vampirized it twenty-five years ago.

I bounced the heel of my sneaker against the wooden railing. I'd been here less than three hours and already I could feel my shoulders getting knotty, the tension in my jaw getting tight. It was hard to believe that as recently as this morning, I'd been a little excited about getting back to school. Now that I was actually on campus, it was obvious that three months stuck at home with my parents had damaged my mental faculties. I'd confused a desperation to get the hell away from them with a desire to return to Harcote.

Down-campus, among the vampiric family units sheltering under black silk parasols and enormous golf umbrellas, I spotted Radtke, the Vampiric Ethics teacher. She was dabbing her forehead with a lacy handkerchief. Radtke was one of those traditionalist vampires, an old-school Victorian bloodsucker—literally, she had been turned like 150 years ago. She still wore the same mourning gowns with corsetry and everything. Her skirts were dappled with bloodstains from back when you could still feed on humans. She visibly strained not to *tsk* at every girl who dared to wear a tank top at Seated Dinner, but of course, she didn't like my conservative button-ups any better. Radtke was also the steward of Hunter House, my residential house for the year. I already had reason enough to avoid my house, Radtke notwithstanding.

Around Radtke, the aides—glamoured human servants who barely knew what they were doing—dutifully unloaded luggage from luxury SUVs into the parking lot. Every year there were a few honest-to-god *Titanic*-era steamer trunks because vampires could never just leave anything in the past. Some of the parents were already getting emotional at the prospect of letting their darling baby monster out of their sight for a whole semester. My parents had been the same the first time around, although now I got myself to school without them—though when it was my little brother's turn, my mom would surely deliver a weepy goodbye at all four Move-in Days and drag our fangmaker to Descendants Day in November. One firstie was making the tragic mistake of clinging to his mommy right in front of everyone; I projected his reputation would not recover until, at very earliest, spring break.

The rest of Harcote's esteemed student body—the Best of the Best, offspring of the ever-living and never-dying, each of them a special and unique monument to our perseverance in the face of the Peril and a beloved classmate of yours truly—were acting like the feral goons they always were when left unsupervised. They were galloping across the quad and screaming out of residential house windows and leaping into each other's arms like they'd just Returned from the War, not three months of vacation. I could practically hear them comparing notes from their social media surveillance from here: Who just got back from modeling in Milan? Did you hear so-and-so went on tour with a K-pop band? Ever the true Harcoties, they wasted no time establishing who had gotten hotter or richer or cooler over the summer and who was going to be at the top of this year's social house of cards. They could smile and act friendly, but everyone, obviously, had fangs. They'd take each other down if they had to.

Or if it seemed like fun.

I sighed. I was so far past the point of caring about any of this. Any of *them*.

Behind me, the porch creaked with footsteps. "Moved in already?"

I swung one leg back to the other side of the railing and let the sunglasses slide down my nose.

"I practice a minimalist lifestyle, Kontos, precisely for that reason. Easy peasy."

Kontos's caterpillar mustache wiggled as he tried to smirk (he was too nice, he lacked the skill). He had his black cape slung over one arm and his shirt was damp with sweat. "Exactly how many pairs of sneakers does a minimalist lifestyle accommodate?"

"This year? Seventeen. There's always room for the essentials."

"Good to have you back, Taylor," he said, grinning.

I broke into a smile, hopped off the railing, and gave him a hug. Kontos was a science teacher and one of the few things—possibly the only thing—that I liked about Harcote. My first year, he'd taught Scientific Inquiry and I'd been assigned to his table for Seated Dinner. But we only got to be friends after I came out, because Kontos was gay too and Harcote was a certifiable homosexual desert. Kontos's fashion sense had stopped developing some point in the decades after he'd been turned, so he continued to rock a look that I thought of affectionately as Seventies Dad, complete with the thick 'stache.

"How's the roommate situation this year?" he asked.

My smile withered, crumbled into dust, and blew away into the sunset. "It's literally worst-case scenario, DEFCON 1, total catastrophe."

"It can't be that bad."

"I don't take the word *literally* lightly." I snatched off the sunglasses so I could glare at him more forcefully. "Evangeline Lazareanu."

Kontos's mouth opened and closed several times in false starts as he prepared to make the best of this. "That might not be ideal, but weren't you two friends once?" As if on cue, a high-pitched shriek echoed from down-campus. Both our heads turned in time to see the swish of long black hair as a girl ran across the residential quad and tackled someone to the ground with a hug. Giggles! Smiles! Girls being girls!

"Imagine living with *that*," I said. "Then add in a healthy dose of mutual loathing and her catty friends . . . It's a good thing I'm immortal, otherwise I'd probably asphyxiate on the fumes from her hair products. Don't laugh!"

Kontos made like he was smoothing his mustache to hide the fact that he was chuckling. His attempt failed. "I'm a teacher, I'm staying objective. Why don't you see if you can transfer?"

"You know they don't grant transfers for 'personal reasons.' How else will we learn to love the fellow members of our vampiric horde, if not by being trapped in a small room with them for nine months?"

"There's nothing wrong with making an effort. You're going to know these vampires for the rest of your life, and that's a very long time."

I shoved the sunglasses back on. Kontos might have been my closest friend at Harcote—as pathetic as that was—but that didn't mean I'd given him the full story of what went on with me and Evangeline. I jutted my chin toward his cape. "Aren't you supposed to be wearing that?"

He gave me a stern look. "I can't teach the youth to celebrate our traditions if I have heat stroke. Let's go," Kontos said. "We've got to get lined up for Convocation."

IF ONE SINGLE site could convey why vampires were so freaking stupid, it was Harcote's Great Hall. When Atherton decided to create a school just for Youngbloods, he was definitely after that Oxford-Harvard vibe. Whatever dinky chapel came with the boys' boarding school he bought wasn't cutting it. Plus, given that the school was going to serve fell creatures of the dark, a standard chapel didn't make a lot of sense. The problem wasn't crosses— those didn't even produce the mild allergic reaction that garlic sometimes did. It was that when you were expecting to live forever, a lot of the most impressive parts of Christianity, like the resurrection, weren't so interesting. Instead, Atherton built something twice as large and a million times as ornate and called it the Great Hall. From far away, it looked like a cathedral had been airlifted from Europe and dropped onto campus. Up close, you could see the stonework had all been made vampire-y, with carvings of bats and ravens and skulls and humans (mostly ladies with unignorable boobs) swooning into the arms of be-caped and befanged vamps who sucked the lifeblood out of them. The bright colors and thick leading of the stained glass windows made them look like they'd been copied from a comic book.

So basically, understated undead elegance.

In my opinion—which no one cared about and which I always shared anyway—Atherton could have designed something more exciting than a knockoff church. How could vampires really be *so super powerful and superior* if we were just reproducing the same types of power that human society relied on? But imagining something new wasn't at the forefront of the vampire skill set.

I left Kontos to re-robe and trudged up to the Hall. Five lines of vampires snaked from its wooden doors: faculty, fourth-years, thirds, seconds, and last, the barely pubescent firsties. As I found my place in the third-year line, a few kids from cross-country or theater tech threw head nods or waves my way, but no one was so overwhelmed with emotion at seeing me that they tackled me to the ground. No one even asked how my summer was.

Which was whatever. It was fine that they didn't pretend to care about me; I wasn't about to pretend to care about them either.

So when Carolina Riser, who'd stood in front of me in line for two years, spun around to chat, I almost thought she was looking for someone else. "Taylor! I heard you're in Hunter House this year?"

It begins. The major downside of these sunglasses was that no one could see me roll my eyes. I had a devastating eye roll. "Yep, with Evangeline. Who are you rooming with?"

Brazenly ignoring my attempt to make the conversation about not this, Carolina said, "Ugh, Evangeline is *so fun*. Isn't Lucy in Hunter too?"

Great. Perfect, actually.

Carolina's face held an eager little smile, waiting for me to incriminate myself. *You would not believe what Taylor said about Evangeline and Lucy.*

No joy for Carolina. Lips zipped, I shrugged.

It was not exactly unexpected that my and Evangeline's roommate assignment would get people talking. Roommate tension on Move-in Day was a gift. It could produce enough drama to carry us through the first two months of school until the Founder's Dance gave us a fresh hit. Evangeline was the kind of popular where half the school thought she was Marie Antoinette and the other half thought she was Mother Teresa, whereas I was pretty universally—and correctly—considered a gay weirdo and a bitch. Everyone knew we didn't get along. I couldn't quite imagine what would happen when me and Evangeline were trapped in a room together all year, but I could easily see her spinning whatever it was into some story that only made her more feared, more beloved, more powerful. To be honest, Evangeline's talent for manipulation was impressive (and a teeny tiny bit hot). That didn't mean I wanted to live with it. I cracked my neck, then my knuckles. Maybe Kontos could get the administration to make an exception and move me into a single room to spare everyone the trouble.

The lines began filing into the Hall. First the faculty, then the fourth-years, their chests all puffed out and proud. My line of third-years followed and took seats in the profoundly uncomfortable straight-backed pews (entirely unnecessary, given that the Great Hall had never actually been a church). The chamber choir sang the Harcote Song, "I Pledge to Thee, O Harcote," which was positively dirgelike. I slumped down in my pew, my knees digging into the bench in front of me and my head resting on the hard wood. I was just about to drift off when the Great Hall doors creaked open.

A few moments later, Carolina was whispering to the pew in front of us that there was a new girl sitting in the back.

That almost never happened at Harcote.

Interesting.

Maybe me and Evangeline wouldn't be the only source of entertainment this year.

KAT

BY THE TIME the glossy black town car finally drove through the gated entry to Harcote's campus, I was more than a little anxious. My flight had landed late, then my bag came out literally last at baggage claim. Not that I'd had a lot to collect. The Benefactor—that was how I'd been thinking of the anonymous donor funding my financial aid—had arranged for all the pieces of the Harcote uniform and most of the school supplies I'd need to be delivered to my room. The day after I'd sent back the enrollment papers, a Harcote representative overnighted me a debit card to pay for everything else, including my flight (minor traveling alone) and a brand-new laptop. In the end, all my stuff had fit in a single suitcase: some of my clothes, a few mementos. With all the delays, I was so busy apologizing to the vampire driver that the Benefactor had arranged to drive me the rest of the way to campus that it didn't even hit me until we were pulling onto the highway that I had actually been *met at the airport by a vampire driver.*

I wanted to text Guzman and Shelby about it, but of course, I couldn't. Anyway, they hadn't exactly understood why I was bailing on junior year. And I certainly wasn't about to text my mom.

Instead, I spent the ride feeling my pulse creep higher and higher as we drew closer to campus.

The campus gates parted for us—for *me*. As we made our way down a hill to the lower campus, it felt like seeing the set of your favorite TV show in real life: the buildings nestled among the broad oak trees and manicured lawns looked so familiar after the hours I'd spent on Harcote's website that I felt like I'd fallen through the computer screen.

The car stopped in a parking lot, and I immediately made the limo-amateur mistake of opening my own door. A vampire with a pointed face and deep-set eyes was waiting for me. He was dressed in a heavy black cloak and his long fingers skittered over a tablet.

"Miss Katherine Finn," he said in a nasal voice. "Welcome to Harcote. Convocation has already begun in the Great Hall. An aide will see to your bags—er, bag."

He gestured and a man in khakis and a Harcote polo took my bag from the trunk. There was something almost mechanical in the way he did it, with an unchanging, faraway look on his face, as if he were barely aware of us.

"He's a human?" I ventured.

"Naturally," the pointy-faced vampire answered. "We don't leave those kinds of menial roles to vampires."

I stiffened. Maintaining the facade of lies and deception that concealed vampires from humans was paramount, always had been. It was unthinkable that humans could be at a place like Harcote, unless . . .

"They've been *glamoured*?"

The vampire set his knobby hand on my shoulder. I guess he imagined I'd find it reassuring to be touched by a stranger. "Headmaster Atherton glamours the aides personally."

Glamoured. That meant they were under Headmaster Atherton's control. It wasn't just that they had to comply with whatever the headmaster asked of them; they weren't even capable of *wanting* to do otherwise. When they came out of it, they'd never know they'd been servants at a vampire high school.

A trickle of sweat ran down my neck. "Are they—how do they volunteer for this?"

"They're generously compensated," he said, which didn't answer my question. He squeezed my shoulder again. "If we hurry, time should be on our side—Headmaster Atherton's speech is about to begin."

If this was normal at Harcote, then it had to be okay. Didn't it?

I let the vampire steer me up a flight of stairs to the upper level of campus and toward a huge old church. Harcote's Great Hall. It looked straight out of a history book, but I didn't have time to appreciate it before the vampire was pulling open an enormous wooden door.

Inside, the whole of Harcote was seated in pews, listening to a choir that was just finishing singing. It was just my luck that as the final note trailed off, the wooden door slammed shut with a *thunk* that echoed up to the vaulted ceiling. Every single student must have turned to look as I tried to hide my burning cheeks behind my hair and slide into the last row of seats. My eyes stayed pinned to the floor until someone cleared his throat into a microphone.

This was Headmaster Atherton?

Standing at the lectern was a young man who looked so fresh-faced and ruddy-cheeked, he might have passed for a student. Unlike the rest of the faculty, he was wearing a light blue button-up, slightly rumpled from the heat, and khakis. His outfit only emphasized how obviously young he was. Or had been, when he'd last been able to age. He was absolutely beaming at us, rocking on the balls of his feet with enthusiasm.

"Boys and girls, welcome to another year at the Harcote School!" he cried. "Saying those words never gets old, and I've been doing it for twenty-five years. That's right, this is our anniversary year! For some of us"—he hammily pointed at himself—"twenty-five years is just a drop in the bucket, but a lot has changed in that time. When I opened Harcote's doors with just fifteen students, the worst of the Peril was over, but we weren't out of danger. Vampirdom was still a new idea. *Youngbloods* were still a new idea! We didn't know how they would develop, but we knew—we *hoped*!— that if everything went right, vampires would do more than just survive the Peril. We'd *thrive*. Vampirdom and the Youngbloods are linked, forever." Headmaster Atherton laced his fingers together to demonstrate. "That's why the Youngblood generation is so special to us all, and why it's such an honor for everyone at Harcote to prepare you young vampires to walk the earth until it is no more! Let's just take a minute to look around and think about how *lucky* we are to be here, surrounded by our kind. By vampires *just like us*."

I hadn't expected much of the Convocation—at my old school, we just went to class on the first day, no ceremonies necessary— but as I scanned the pews before me, my heart was filled with a strange, satisfied ache. *Youngblood vampires, just like me.* Not just one or two, but almost two hundred.

"Now, we have a lot of fun surprises in store this year for the anniversary—and yes, we're going to do some learning too. But let's remember that although your life may last forever, these precious years don't," Headmaster Atherton said with bubbly earnestness. "Now let us stand, and reveal our fangs, to recite the Harcote Oath."

Reveal our fangs?

I hurried to my feet, my hands balled into anxious fists. Fangs, I'd been taught, were something you kept hidden. If they slipped out by accident, you kept your mouth closed until you could retract them. When they first grew in, Mom had me practice every night, letting them free then forcing them away. She'd had to learn that all on her own, she'd remind me. I was lucky to have her to teach me to pass among humans.

But I wasn't among humans anymore. I was surrounded by vampires, and apparently all of them were used to popping their fangs out on demand, like they were an orthodontic retainer.

I tried to focus on letting them slip free: that feeling of stretching tight muscles, of letting out a breath you'd been holding. But all I could concentrate on was the feathery thrum of panic in my chest, the subtle hissing around me as the other students let theirs down.

I couldn't do it.

A chorus of voices began reciting the Harcote Oath. I'd made a special point of memorizing the words, but I kept my lips pressed closed. I couldn't risk anyone taking this as a misstep that was evidence that I was just a pretender here—that I would never fit in.

All at once, I felt like I was back in Virginia—that final day at the Sangers'. For the four years we'd been staying with them they'd been happy to help a single mom and her daughter get back on their feet. My mom hadn't exactly been stable after my dad died, and we moved around a lot. The Sangers' guesthouse was the closest I'd ever felt to having a *home*. Not that everything was perfect there, like how I knew to stay away from the main house when they had guests, to spare everyone the awkwardness of explaining what we were doing there. But it was good, safe. One gray December morning, everything changed. Ms. Sanger came over to talk to my mom the moment she got home from work. The look on my mom's face made the hair at the back of my neck bristle. We were leaving, right then.

I didn't want to believe it. I begged for an explanation—*What changed? What did we do?* As my mom crammed our things into suitcases, I followed behind her, dumping out whatever she filled them with.

Finally, she had looked me in the eye. "I don't know how, but they found out about my turning. They're worried about their reputation, especially with the kids. They've asked us to leave, so that's what we're doing."

That was the end of my complaining. Because I *did* know how the Sangers had found out our secret. I'd told one of them myself.

Bitterness flooded my mouth. The guilt, the loss, the *betrayal*— none of it had ever gone away.

I couldn't let the same thing happen here.

"If this year at Harcote is your first or your twenty-fifth, may no year be your last, but let each count as if it could be," Headmaster Atherton exclaimed. The sun streamed through stained glass behind him, filling the hall with a crimson-tinged light. "Let the school year begin!"

I FOLLOWED THE girls rushing out of the Great Hall to the Girls' Residential Quad. It was a series of four-floor brick buildings with white window frames, forest-green shutters, and at the top, windows protruding from the slope of the gray slate roofs. Hunter House was on the north side. In the little central garden, some parents and fangmakers were saying their final goodbyes. It seemed like *everyone's* family had come for move-in.

Ignoring them, I made my way to Hunter House, my new home. There was dark wood everywhere, paneling and molding on the walls, the floor scuffed from use. As I climbed the stairs to the second floor, I could hear the slamming of doors, the laughter of my new housemates, and the thumping of bags on the floor. I was double-checking my room number when the door opened. Two girls filled the doorway.

"Are you Katherine?" one of them asked. She was Chinese, with large round eyes and a heart-shaped face that felt familiar. "I'm Lucy and this"—she tipped her head toward the other girl, who was white—"is Evangeline."

Lucy and Evangeline flashed matching smiles at me, and all at once my brain short-circuited.

They were utterly, completely *gorgeous*.

Both of them were pretty in a way that belonged on TV or in a magazine, not in real life, where you could reach out and touch it. Lucy's eyes were warm mahogany, perfectly complemented by her thick lashes, just like the deep Cupid's bow of her lips was matched by a perfectly placed beauty mark. Sheets of glossy dark hair framed her face. Beside her, Evangeline had a cascade of thick black waves, luminous blue eyes that stood out against her pale skin, and round cheeks. These had to be the prettiest girls in school, maybe the prettiest girls in the whole state of New York, and they just stood there *looking* at me. Mischief glittered in Lucy's eyes and Evangeline held the edge of her thumbnail pressed against her soft, full lips, like they were both trying not laugh at me.

I almost wished they would.

After an awkward silence that lasted ten thousand years, I managed to say, "Actually, it's just Kat. My name, I mean."

Evangeline smiled like I was a baby who'd just said her first words. It was hard not to look at her mouth. "Okay, *Kat*, here's the thing: You're assigned to live with Lucy, but me and Lucy are best-best friends. We were *really* hoping to room together this year."

Lucy slung her arm over Evangeline's shoulder and pulled her close. "So we were super bummed when Evangeline got assigned to a room on the top floor. It would be so cool of you to switch with her."

"I'll be down here all the time, and it would truly be so annoying for you." Evangeline's face wrinkled into an expression somewhere between empathetic and irritated. "We'd be up all night talking when you were studying or something, and then you'd have to be quiet when we're studying. This would be *so* much easier."

"I heard they don't do room transfers."

"Oh, they truly do not even care," Lucy said, "as long as you arrange it yourself and everyone agrees. We already had the aides put your stuff upstairs and move Evangeline's stuff down here. Cool?"

The girls paused. Evangeline's lips had crept into a half-smile, while Lucy was drumming her fingers against the door, and neither one of them was entirely hiding the chaotic glee lurking right beneath the surface. I was missing something, I just had no idea what. Maybe it didn't much matter.

"That's totally fine. I like the top floor better anyway. No upstairs neighbors, right?"

This won me two blank stares—plenty of time to kick myself. These girls had never lived in an apartment building: they'd probably been raised in mansions. Or estates like the Sangers'. Or on private islands.

"You're the best," Evangeline said.

The door shut. Behind it, the shrieks of laughter I'd been wait-ing for finally broke free.

ON THE FOURTH floor, there was only one room. Like I expected, it was smaller than what I'd been assigned to downstairs. As the at-tic room, it had slanted ceilings on both sides that forced the two twin beds a little close together. There were two desks, two closets, a door that led to the bathroom. Sun from a large dormer window flooded the room and gave a beautiful view of the trees behind the building and, from one corner, the path up-campus.

My bag was set on the right side of the room. That was the only way I knew that that side was mine, because I'd never seen any of the other things there before: fresh sheets, pillows, and a Harcote-garnet duvet on the bed, notebooks and packs of pens on the desk, books I'd need for my classes, all arranged by the Benefactor's staff.

And in my closet—

The rack was hung with every imaginable piece of the Harcote uniform: gray and dark red pleated skirts, collared shirts in white, black, and gray, three blazers with piping in different variations of the Harcote colors with the bat-and-castle crest embroidered on the breast pocket, scarves, hats, and a dark gray peacoat for win-ter. Running along the floor were pairs of white tennis shoes, bal-let flats, oxfords, and loafers. I opened the drawers of my bureau: Harcote polo shirts, T-shirts and shorts for PE, sweaters whose purpose in life was to look completely appropriate, and one sweat-shirt that telegraphed, *My parents met in the Ivy League.* In the top drawer, there were two headbands (I'd never worn a headband in my life) and a range of approved socks and tights. It was like looking at someone else's wardrobe: the perfect Harcote girl.

It was hard not to remember what Shelby had said before I left.

When I told my friends I'd be coming to Harcote, Guzman moaned extravagantly that he was wounded to the core that I hadn't told him I'd applied to a different school and that he would absolutely die without me. He was over-the-top with everything, but this time, it was concealing actual hurt.

Shelby, who never pretended anything if they could help it, said, "Seriously? Schools like that are full of rich assholes."

"If I turn into an asshole, I'm sure you'll be the first to let me know, Shelbs."

Desperate to lighten the mood, Guzman pulled up the school's website on his phone. "Damn, is everyone at this place a *model*?"

He zoomed in on a guy in a slate-and-garnet Harcote jersey, a lacrosse stick slung across his shoulders. "If this boy is real, *promise me* you will find him and date him!"

I rolled my eyes. "You drool over anything with muscles."

Shelby grabbed the phone and swiped around. Harcote's website presented it as a typical prep school with an old-money conservative streak that obscured the fact that it was only twenty-five years old. The styling could have been the same in 1950 as in 2022—which was, undoubtedly, why vampires liked it. The points of collars stuck out from the neck of every sweater. It was all headbands and pleated skirts, peacoats and pearl earrings—the same things I'd just found in my closet.

"This place has an extremely cis-het energy," they said.

"Well, you're always calling me your favorite cis-het ally, right?" It was a running joke between Shelby and Guzman that I was their token straight friend. And usually it was funny—or funny enough—but Shelby wasn't smiling.

"None of this is *you*."

"It'll be *me* after I get there."

"My thing is like, why go somewhere that fitting in is going to be so hard?"

But that was the point of a uniform, wasn't it? Not every day of your life had to be a statement on your charisma, uniqueness, nerve, and talent. And anyway, I didn't need to justify myself to Shelby.

I fell to my knees and dug through my bag. I'd barely brought any clothes from home, but now I wished I'd brought nothing at all. None of it would work here, that much was obvious, and I didn't want it to. I didn't need reminders of home.

I pulled out a sweatshirt with frayed cuffs and a pair of basketball shorts from my old school, some thrift store finds I'd made with Shelby, a few T-shirts and jeans that had barely been cool enough for Sacramento, and shoved all of it into the corner of my closet. I shut the door with my back against it.

I faced my roommate's side of the room. Evangeline hadn't even told me her name. Her closet door was hanging open, offering a view of a truly excessive number of sneakers and a collection of button-ups. On the desk sat a nice laptop covered in stickers. Beside it lay a battered copy of *1000 Movies to Watch Before You Die*, the pages all dog-eared and papered with sticky notes. I flipped it open, and it fell to a page about a Hitchcock movie I'd never seen, the margins full of cramped notes. I looked closer at the handwriting—it looked sort of familiar.

"What are you doing to my shit? I swear, Evangeline, if you—"

"I'm sorry, I wasn't—" I whirled around to face my new roommate.

My guts did a U-turn, up to my throat, down to the floor, then back again. The girl standing in front of me was tall and slim and wearing jeans and a white T-shirt. She had a halo of curling hair that fell to her shoulders and the dark sunglasses she had on didn't hide the fact that she had the delicate boyish face of a fashion model, and I absolutely hated her.

"*Taylor*? What are you doing here?"

Taylor's mouth was hanging open. The sunglasses blocked her eyes, but her eyebrows had gone sky-high. Finally she managed to say, "What am *I* doing here?" Taylor gestured like she owned the place. *Of course* she did. "This is my room. What are *you* doing here? *You don't even go here.*"

I folded my arms. The horrifying power of this coincidence had hit me directly in the stomach, and I really did not want to throw up right now. Of all the vampires at Harcote, I had ended up rooming with *Taylor Sanger*. Taylor, whose parents had kicked us out to protect the family's reputation. Taylor, who had told them the truth about my mother's turning in the first place. We'd been best friends once, but after that horrible morning, I'd never heard from her again, which was exactly how I wanted it. "Weird that they'd let someone who *doesn't even go here* move into the dorms."

I retreated to my own territory on the other side of the room as Taylor stalked over to her bed and sank down onto it. She was rangy and slim like she'd always been, but taller now, and sitting on the low bed with her face in her hands, her long limbs were all angles. "I cannot believe I'm about to say this, but what about Evangeline?"

"I was assigned to room with Lucy and they asked me to switch. Obviously I didn't know whose room I was switching into." I shook my head. "How did I never consider that I could see you here?"

"Where else would I be?" Taylor pulled her sunglasses off, and

I saw her face for the first time since we were thirteen. She had cheekbones now, thicker eyebrows although they still ran almost straight across her brow. And though she wouldn't quite look at me, I knew under that scrum of lashes her eyes would be the same gold-flecked brown. "Harcote's the only vampire high school in the country."

"Some of us do actually go to school with the humans."

That shut Taylor up for a minute. She fell back on her bed, flung an arm over her head, and stared at the sloping ceiling above her. She'd tacked a rainbow Pride flag to it, I now saw.

"Are you . . ." I stopped myself. It wasn't that I was surprised—no one who knew her could have been surprised that Taylor wasn't straight, especially now. But there was a bristle of something like hurt that she hadn't told me. How many times had we promised each other, *no secrets*?

Then again, look where that promise had gotten me.

Taylor saw me notice. "If that's going to be a problem, you can fuck right off."

"I'd love to fuck right off, but that has nothing to do with it." I glared at her. Then, because I have manners, I asked, "What are your pronouns?"

She narrowed the one eye that peered at me from under her elbow, like this was some kind of trap. With every second that Taylor didn't answer, my mouth got drier, my palms sweatier. At home, people mentioned their pronouns all the time. If Taylor was offended by the question, then she could be the one fucking off. I turned back to my mostly empty bag. "Mine are she/her. In case you were wondering."

"Same," Taylor said. "She/her."

I forced myself to concentrate on organizing my shower caddy.

I didn't know what Evangeline had against Taylor, but I was sure of one thing: Taylor wasn't going to spoil a single second of my time at Harcote, not after she'd already spoiled so much in my life. "I'm just as miserable as you are about this situation. We're not going to be friends. All I ask is that you don't ruin this for me." I glanced at her over my shoulder. "Promise me you won't tell them anything about me."

"*Kath-er-ine Finn.*" Taylor drew my name out the way she always had when we were kids, lingering on the middle syllable that most people skipped entirely.

"Don't call me that," I said. "You know it's Kat."

"Don't worry." Taylor rolled off her bed, grabbed her sunglasses and headed for the door. "I'll leave you alone."

5

TAYLOR

I TOOK THE Hunter House stairs two at a time until I was out on the quad and legging it in the direction of the athletic fields for no good reason other than the burning desire to be *elsewhere*. The house meeting would be starting soon and Radtke would be in a snit if I was late, but I'd been born on Radtke's bad side anyway.

Right now, I needed to recover from the sucker punch that fate just caught me with.

Katherine *freaking* Finn.

At my school.

In my house.

In my room.

The prospect of living with Evangeline had been about as attractive as cohabitating with a scorpion wearing a human skin suit, but this was, impossibly, *so much worse.*

I found myself at the empty lacrosse field, its green grass offensively cheerful given the situation. I stomped up to the top row of metal bleachers and flopped down noisily on my back. The metal was hot against my skin.

There had to be some kind of law against this, like a statute of limitations. If it's been three years since your best friend disappeared without a goodbye, you would not be forced to room with her. If the last communication with that person was a text that said *I never want to speak to you again*, you would not be expected to spend nine months sleeping in a bed three feet away from hers. If you had no idea what had gone wrong but were willing to accept that it was probably your fault anyway, you would not have to revisit one of the shittiest times in your life.

Obviously we lived in a world without justice, because no such laws existed.

It wasn't that I'd never imagined Kat could show up at Harcote. I'd imagined that exact scenario approximately one zillion times, and I admit that on more than one occasion—okay, many times more than one—I'd been too weak to resist scrolling her socials. It wasn't as if I didn't know that she still wore her silky auburn hair long, and that in the right light it shone red, or that she had the same round cheeks that made the corners of her eyes crinkle when she smiled. But that had done nothing to prepare me for actually *seeing* Kat again, for how it felt when her hazel eyes, the irises threaded with green, blazed in absolute fury when she recognized me.

I'd seen her standing there and all of a sudden, I could feel the actual contours of my heart. It trembled in my chest like a frightened rabbit waiting to be killed. *This must be how humans feel*, was what I'd thought, *right before they're glamoured*.

I stamped my foot against the bleacher, releasing a *clang* that reverberated into my skull.

We met when she was nine and I'd just turned ten. From the beginning, we were inseparable. She was the only person I wanted to spend time with, and I know she felt exactly the same about me. Well, after a certain point, not *exactly* the same, but even I hadn't understood what my feelings for her truly meant. Then one day, she and her mom were just *gone*, up and vanished with all their stuff. No explanation and no goodbyes.

I'd never been that miserable before, like my chest cavity had been cracked open and the wound wouldn't close. When my mom told me the Finns had skipped town, I buried my face in my pillow and cried, and stayed there long after the crying ended. My moping must have been especially hard-core because my mom—a woman who had the emotional capacity of a three-hundred-year-old tortoise—actually tried to comfort me. I wasn't out to her yet, but I could have sworn that she knew what was really wrong.

I was heartbroken.

Approximately thirty-three months of total noncommunication had done nothing to change the fact that Kat held the dubious honor of Taylor Sanger's First Crush. Seeing her again— *standing in the middle of the room that we would be sharing for months*—drove that home with all the subtlety of a sledgehammer.

I pushed myself up onto my elbows and looked back toward the girls' quad. The house meetings might have already started. I resettled the sunglasses on my face and lay back down.

It's not like Hartline provided a lot of opportunities to replace First Crush with First Girlfriend. The only other actually queer girl I'd known at the school was a fourth-year when I was a firstie and way too cool to be aware of my existence; since her graduation, I'd reigned supreme as the campus's Token Lesbian.

Honestly, the position had some perks, in the form of girls who sneakily asked if I wanted to kiss them. They never literally wanted to know if I wanted to kiss them—they just assumed I did because I guess that's the Way of the Dykes—but this was their way of saying they wanted to try kissing me. Like they were doing me a favor. Some of them added a bit about how they were curious, if it was different with a girl. Not that I cared what they were after; I wasn't their therapist, or even their friend.

Obviously, I always kissed them anyway.

Why shouldn't I have a little fun? Yes, they were using me, but it felt good to see them recognize that I had something they wanted. Plus, it was hot to see the perfect little Harcoties scared that they were doing something they weren't supposed to—even though it was fucked up that they believed kissing girls fell into that category.

The clear downside was that none of these girls would be repeat customers at Taylor's Kissing Booth. They normally made that clear to me as soon as the kissing ended, and this made the afterward part not so much fun. There was an evil alchemy to those little reminders. They transformed a fun conquest into a rejection from someone I hadn't even wanted in the first place. Most of the girls were true to their word: one kiss and it was out of their system.

Except one. I couldn't imagine begging someone to take off your bra and then acting like they're the bane of your existence, but then again, there was a lot that Evangeline did that was beyond my comprehension.

But what if Kat could change all that?

Keep it together, I told myself as I sat back up fast enough for a head rush. Kat hadn't wandered out of a daydream to become my *girlfriend*. Even *thinking* the word *girlfriend* felt idiotic. In real life, Kat didn't even want to *know* me, let alone be friends. On top of that—I remembered this vividly—Kat was straight. My lesbionic sixth sense would have known if she weren't.

I let myself smile, just a little, thinking of her asking my pronouns. I had never heard a vampire ask that, although I knew that humans sometimes did. But all that meant was that Kat had spent a lot of time around humans. She might be different from the other Harcote girls for now, but that wouldn't last long. It would be stupid to assume otherwise.

And I wasn't stupid.

At least, I was trying not to be, starting now.

I cracked my knuckles, then stomped extra-hard back down the bleachers, so each step rang out across the field.

I wasn't about to get my heart broken, not at Harcote and certainly not by Katherine Finn.

KAT

UP IN MY temporarily Taylor-free room, I paced. I couldn't get used to the idea that I'd be sharing this space with Taylor for a year. I could be brushing my teeth: Taylor. Writing in my journal: Taylor. Studying for precalc: again, Taylor. It would be like being haunted by a ghost specifically engineered not to let me forget what I had come to Harcote to leave behind. All I could do was hope she would keep her mouth shut about my family and let me get on with my life.

Now, I'd run out of time for freaking out. The house meeting was starting in a few minutes, and right afterward, we'd be heading to the first Seated Dinner of the year. The dress code for Seated Dinners was "neat semiformal." I didn't know what that meant exactly, but it didn't matter. I pawed through the things in my closet looking for what the Benefactor had provided. What I found was black.

A lot of black.

I pulled the dresses out of the closet and threw them on my bed. There wasn't anything wrong with them per se. A few were perfectly nice, if you were a depressed librarian or really obsessed with tarot cards. I held up a wad of black lace and spent two minutes trying to figure out where the sleeves where before tossing it aside. Others were from a different era altogether. One with an actual corset screamed, *Ask me about my services as a professional mourner!* Another looked like I could have worn it to an audition for Elvira's stunt double.

I frowned at the pile of dark fabric. At home, I almost never wore black. How was I supposed to pick when none of these felt anything like *me*?

I grabbed one of the least-bizarre dresses, slipped it on, and stood in front of the mirror. I looked like a gloomy bridesmaid at Satan's wedding. Then I pulled back my lips and tried to ease my fangs down. The incisors were lengthening, almost imperceptibly, when the stairs creaked and I snapped my mouth closed. I wasn't about to let Taylor see me like this, uncertain and vulnerable. I waited for her to explode into the room, a whirlwind, as she'd done earlier that afternoon.

But no one was coming up the stairs.

All of a sudden, I missed my mom so badly, it was almost unbearable. I wanted to tell her about Taylor, about how scared and out of place I felt here, to hear her reassure me that I could do this

I just didn't trust her to do that anymore.

Things between us had been awful since the night I came back from Donovan's and told her what I'd done. I'd expected her to come around and accept my decision, but she never did. We'd barely discussed the fact that I was leaving. In fact, we hardly talked at all. She had never been that cold to me. After all, we were all each other had.

When we'd finally said goodbye at airport security this morning, it almost came as a relief. When she gave me that last hug, part of me hadn't wanted to let her go. But that resentment lingered, like an itch that couldn't be scratched. *She* was the reason I had to do this this alone. When I pulled back, she tried to tuck a loose strand of hair behind my ear and I brushed her hand away.

"Promise me you won't forget who you are," she'd said.

"People change, Mom," I'd said. Then I had turned and walked away.

What did it matter anyway if my mom thought I could do this? I was doing it anyway.

I forced in a deep breath, then squared my shoulders to settle the dress.

Harcote was my chance. I'd staked everything on it. I'd burned my friends and thrown a hand grenade on my relationship with my mom. I had to make this work.

I stared at myself in the mirror and concentrated on my fangs. With the twinge of a muscle long out of use, they slid down: barely long enough to reach my lower gumline, almost translucently pale and wickedly sharp. I couldn't tell if it felt unnatural or just unfamiliar. But it was proof that I'd hidden the fact of my vampirism for too long, that Harcote really was where I belonged.

I practiced again and again in the mirror until I couldn't see the discomfort.

HUNTER HOUSE'S FIRST-FLOOR common area was a series of cozy parlor-type rooms. The study was lined with bookshelves and held a long wooden table with green-shaded study lamps. At the back of the house was a more casual space with couches and a projector for watching movies. The main room had an enormous mantel surrounding a fireplace (bricked over—vampires are flammable) and was packed with cozy couches and armchairs. It was nice. *Really* nice. I could see myself curled up in one of the armchairs, doing my reading, or staying up late to watch a movie with my as-yet-unidentified new friends. Maybe I could just avoid spending time in my room altogether.

At the foot of the stairs I assessed the girls gathered before me in the main room. The residential houses combined girls from each of the four years. The fourth-years were piled on top of each other, trying to share one rolled-arm leather sofa that was clearly Senior Territory. The first-years were talking to nobody and wearing outfits picked out by their parents. The seconds and thirds were mixed in among them.

But each of them—*every single one of them*—was absolutely beautiful.

My mouth went dry.

When I met Evangeline and Lucy, I'd assumed that they had to be the prettiest girls in school. Rarity was the only thing that made sense for beauty like that. But now, looking around this room of girls, it seemed that Evangeline and Lucy were somehow *normal*.

Adult vampires were attractive in a distinctive way, but it was usually more of a charisma than something physical. Nearly all of them had been born human: turning could only improve what they'd started with. The students at Harcote were different: Youngblood vampires who had been born like that, and you could tell.

These girls were crushingly, achingly beautiful in a way that made it hard to think straight. Each of them seemed to possess her own form of perfection. Luscious hair, thick lashes, curving lips. Even their bodies—which I was really trying not to notice, because that was rude—were astonishing. I mean, they were *hot*. It wasn't that they all looked the same—some girls were thinner or thicker, muscular or curvy, just like the girls at my old school had been. There was just something graceful and specific and arresting about each of them, as if each girl was the fullest version of herself. It was like I'd stumbled into a meetup of Junior-Level Goddesses or Undiscovered Princesses, who had each come to Harcote from their own separate paradise islands, not the Sacramento International Airport like I had.

But I was here, I was one of them. I touched my fingers carefully to the curve of my jaw. Did *I* have that effect on people?

I'd always been told I was pretty. Truthfully, I hadn't needed telling; I'd always known it, like I knew I had four limbs and fangs, and I hadn't done anything special to acquire those either. That didn't stop total strangers from commenting on whatever part of my body they felt it was their right to call attention to. Even my friends teased me about how I'd never had an awkward phase. Being pretty—and a pretty white girl at that—carried privilege with it. But I still felt like every day of my life was an awkward phase, and the way I looked only made it harder to hide.

At Harcote, I wouldn't stand out at all.

A wall of washed-out black, reeking of mothballs, stepped into my path.

"You are Miss Katherine Finn?" the woman asked.

"I go by Kat," I answered.

"I am the Hunter House Steward, Ms. Radtke. It is a pleasure to meet you."

Ms. Radtke looked like she'd teleported right out of *Great Expectations*. Her hair was swept into a grand chignon pinned into place with bone combs, and she wore a floor-length dress with an actual bustle and a high-necked lace collar. The bodice was embroidered with beads carved into the shape of human skulls. Everything else about her, from the fabric of her gown to her hair to her skin, was the dull gray color of dust. It was impossible to guess her age: she felt like the Crypt-Keeper but her eyes showed only the barest signs of crow's feet.

In short, she was the gothest bitch I had ever seen.

"Welcome to the Harcote School," Ms. Radtke continued briskly. "Evangeline has registered a change in your room assignment, and you will now be residing in 401 with . . . Taylor Sanger. Is that correct?"

Ms. Radtke's voice curdled at bit Taylor's name. Evangeline and Lucy must not be the only ones she didn't get along with. I nodded, and she penciled a brisk check mark into her leather-bound folio. "I have asked Lucy to help orient you." Ms. Radtke beckoned her over.

Lucy had changed into a baby-blue halter top and a matching high-waisted skirt, with her sleek hair in a high ponytail. It was definitely extra, but she was more than pulling it off. I fiddled with the lace sleeves of my dress. Compared to Lucy, I looked like an off-duty mortician.

Lucy's outfit was having a very different effect on Ms. Radtke. "Miss Kang, must you insist on wearing such outrageous attire to the first Seated Dinner of the year?"

"Miss R, I would never! I'll put this on before we leave," Lucy held up a ball of fluffy baby-blue fur, then she grabbed my arm and pulled me away. The sweet smile slid from her face. "Fucking Radtke drives me bonkers. She's a total trav."

"What's a trav?"

Lucy shot me a side-eyed glance. "A traditionalist vampire? You know—old-school, haunted house–looking weirdos. They act like Nosferatu was a lifestyle guru and not a truly made-up fictional character."

Clearly this was something everyone but me knew. "Where I'm

from we, uh, call them something else. Listen, this might sound weird, but you look so familiar. Have we met before?"

"I get that a lot." Lucy caught the end of her sleek ponytail in her fingers and squinted one eye closed.

I froze. "Oh my god. This is so embarrassing—you're LucyK, aren't you?" Everyone at my old school, especially Guzman, was obsessed with LucyK. Her videos weren't really anything special, but people *loved* her. I had friends who wore the lip gloss LucyK used, who bought the sweatshirts LucyK wore in her clips, who copied the way LucyK posed in her photos. Guzman once told me he felt like she was actually one of his friends. It had never occurred to me that she could be a vampire. "I follow you like, *everywhere.*"

"That's so sweet!" Lucy pushed her lips into a pout. "My vampire followers are truly special to me. With humans I can never tell if the support is real, but with vamps you know it comes from the heart."

"What do you mean, if the support is real?"

"Vampiric charisma is a crazy good marketing tool." Lucy swished her ponytail back over her shoulder. "I was the first to use it for influencing. I've got it down to an art. All of my followers feel a *connection* to me." Lucy laughed. "Sometimes I think about the power I have over them, it's just like, aaah, so intense, right?"

Lucy wasn't doing a very good job pretending to be anything other than delighted by that idea. I was trying to figure out what to say when Ms. Radtke summoned us to attention.

"Welcome to Hunter House and, to our new students, welcome to Harcote." The front door snicked closed as Taylor slipped in. "The girls around you will be your family for the next year. You will study together, room together, eat together. We hope that these house friendships form so strongly they last throughout your immortal life.

"We expect very much of you at Harcote. You are the Best of the Best, and our standards are high—for your personal behavior as well as your academic performance. You are expected to adhere to all rules and policies at all times per the Honor Code. We observe curfew from ten p.m. to six a.m., the sole exception being weekend passes, which I personally approve. And with no exception, *no boys.*"

The room convulsed in whiny moaning. I stole a look at Taylor, who had contorted her long limbs so she could sit on a narrow windowsill that was not meant for sitting. She was smirking: being locked in a house full of girls wasn't the same kind of torture for everyone.

Ms. Radtke clapped and the girls quieted. "I expect each of you to act like young ladies at all times. If you cannot be convinced to avoid embarrassing yourselves, then consider that ill behavior reflects on your fellow members of the house, on myself and Harcote, and indeed on all of Vampirdom." Ms. Radtke tried gamely to achieve a smile. "Now, we have new students to welcome to the Harcote family, including a new member of our third-year class."

Oh no no no no.

"Please introduce yourself, Kat Finn."

Twenty-three pairs of eyes set in perfectly symmetrical faces focused on me.

My mouth went dry. Shouldn't I have been warned about this? Because I had *not* been warned about this.

"Hi, I'm Kat. I'm from Sacramento. I'm just really excited to be here." My brain was gently but definitively severing its connection to my mouth. "It's such an awesome opportunity and I can't wait to meet everyone. Um, go Harcote!"

The silence that followed was profound and disturbing. It gave me plenty of space to wonder if it was possible to pass out from blushing too hard. Although my back was to the window where she was perched, I was sure Taylor was struggling not to laugh.

Ms. Radtke put me out of my misery. "Lovely. And now the first-years. Recall that dinner begins shortly, so don't feel you each must give such a spirited speech."

AFTER THE HOUSE meeting ended, Lucy and I fell in with Evangeline for the walk to the Dining Hall. They steered clear of the other two third-years assigned to Hunter in addition to Taylor. Anna Rose Dent and Jane Marie Dent were identical twins who looked like Southern sorority sisters.

"Total weirdos," Evangeline muttered. "You know when twins get, like, *too close*?"

I didn't know what she meant, but I was happy not to talk to the Dent girls. They reminded me of the girls at my old school who'd *All lives matter* any conversation about police violence.

"Don't let Radtke and the Dents give you the wrong impression," Evangeline went on as we followed the neat brick paths that crisscrossed the campus. "Most of us aren't travs, not at all. Like, maybe the Dent girls dream about hunting humans—"

"*Horrible*, and so gross," Lucy added as we joined a line of students on the Dining Hall steps, waiting to consult the table assignments.

"—but my dreams are like going to Yale, you know? Most of my classmates would be human."

That was a relief to hear. "Before I came here, I actually went to, um, I guess you'd call it human school," I said.

"Seriously?" Lucy said. "Like a regular high school?"

"Like a regular public high school." I smiled, pleased that I'd said something to impress them.

Evangeline's aquamarine eyes sparkled. "But aren't those schools kind of shitty?"

"I mean . . . my old school wasn't as good as this one."

As Evangeline moved to talk to the girls in front of us, Lucy popped a smile that set warmth radiating through my chest. "I'm doing a terrible job orienting you! Seated Dinner is twice a week and you're assigned to the same table for the whole year. They mix up guys and girls from all the years plus one faculty. It is deeply lame. Other nights, you can eat whenever you want. Usually we go at seven, if you want to join."

"Thanks, that would be so great," I said. "I really appreciate everything you're doing for me."

Lucy leaned in close, her eyes narrowing "Pro tip, Kitty Kat, try rolling back all that *thank you so much* and *I'm so happy to be here* shit. No one wants to feel like you're a charity case, you know what I mean? Just relax."

I knew I looked mortified. I could feel the slackness in my face, the wideness of my eyes, and it felt terrible, like I'd jumped off the diving board and my top had come off.

"Yeah, totally," I stammered. "Thanks for saying something. It's just first day nerves."

"That's what friends are for," Lucy said, then turned to hug the girls Evangeline was talking to.

A charity case.

All of five minutes of conversation, and they knew I wasn't like them. I had to do better. *Be* better.

We'd reached the front of the line. Evangeline leafed through the list of seating assignments, then jabbed a pointed red nail at the paper. "Look who's at New Girl's table."

Lucy peeked over her shoulder and gasped, "*No.*"

"Who?" It had to be Taylor, Taylor again, always *Taylor*. The thought of sitting across from her at dinner twice a week, when I already had to share a room with her, made me never want to eat again.

Lucy leveled her eyes at me and said, with gravity, "Galen Black."

My gaze darted to the metal sign affixed to the building beside us: SIMON AND MEERA BLACK DINING HALL. "Galen Black like . . . like the Black Foundation?"

Without answering, Evangeline tossed the list back on the table. The two of them straightened up, tossing their hair around and adjusting their dresses. I looked for whatever had grabbed their attention.

It wasn't hard to spot: boys.

Loose packs of them were walking up the path from the Boys' Residential Quad. The first-year boys mostly still had the same overgrown in-betweenness of human fourteen-year-olds, but clearly, that didn't last long. The Youngblood boys striding down the path looked more like the men they cast as teenage boys in TV shows than the kids I'd been going to school with. They made me want to use a word like *striding*. None of them were gangly or gawky. Instead of acne or a few scraggly facial hairs, their skin was clear. A few of them were showing off that they needed to shave by not doing it regularly. A lot of hair product was in play, some of it holding together hairstyles that would have looked ridiculous on a mere mortal. Predictably, some of them were wearing hideous novelty ties or attempting a power-clashing aesthetic, but their clothes all fit correctly, showing off broad shoulders and biceps that pressed against the sleeves of their jackets. As they got closer, a fug of mountain-extreme-cool-rush-man scent slowly engulfed us.

"Galen hasn't changed at all from last year," Evangeline said.

I had no idea which one Galen was—maybe the lacrosse player Guzman had been thirsting after? Honestly, as good-looking as they were, the boys were hard to tell apart.

"He better not have." Lucy adjusted the fluff of blue around her shoulders; it had turned out to be a kind of shrug. "If that boy got any hotter he'd burst into flames—ooh, he's looking at us."

A dark-haired boy, a little taller than the rest and dressed in black, had turned his head our way. Evangeline was staring back at him, her lips pursed. "I'm going inside," Evangeline said, and pushed open the door, her heels clicking against the polished marble floor.

Lucy grabbed my hand and pulled me after her. "Don't get too caught up on Galen, Kitty Kat. He's ending up with Evangeline."

MR. KONTOS, A science teacher with glasses and a thick mustache, was the head of my table. He exuded unimpeachably dork vibes as he asked how I was settling in. I liked him immediately.

Instead of another old-school building like the Great Hall, the Dining Hall was modern, all windows and angles, white paint and blond wood. Across the room, my eyes snagged on Taylor's head of curls. She was slumped in her chair and fiddling with a spoon like she couldn't care less about any of this—the dinner, the other students, life itself. Taylor was biting her lip—all at once, I remembered that she did this when she was thinking too hard and when she was nervous. Suddenly she looked up and her eyes met mine, like she'd known exactly where I'd be and that I was watching her. I looked away as fast as I could.

"Who're you?" The seat across from me had just been occupied by six feet of dark-haired vampire-boy.

Mr. Kontos clicked his tongue. "Galen, would it kill you to be polite?"

"It wouldn't kill me, Mr. Kontos. I'm one of the ever-living, never-dying." Galen held me in his gaze. His lashes were thick and dark, and his eyes were an unusual smoky gray—beautiful in an obvious way. The corners of his mouth turned up slightly, but it didn't feel like he was smiling at me. More like he was smiling to himself. "I'm Galen Black."

"I'm Kat. I'm new, in the third year."

Galen arched a dark eyebrow. It was the platonic ideal of an eyebrow-in-arch. Galen had that classic vampire look: lush black hair that loosely curled, worn long enough that it threatened to tumble charmingly in his face. His skin was light brown but slightly darkened, almost bruised, under his eyes. It could have looked sickly but instead only emphasized his general air of condescension, as if he had just been awakened from a nap and would rather get back to it. His face was perfectly symmetrical, down to the square chin. Like me, he wore black; the two of us looked like we'd dressed for the same funeral.

"I like new things," he said slowly. The voice he affected was probably supposed to be sexy, but was in fact deeply gross. *This* was the guy they all wanted?

Just then, a human aide arrived at the table with a silver tureen. I went still. Before today, I'd never been around glamoured humans before. How were you supposed to act around them? From the expressions on my tablemates' faces when Mr. Kontos thanked the aide who served our Hema, it looked like even basic courtesy wasn't expected.

But I forgot all about that, because Mr. Kontos had removed the lid from the tureen and my mind went blank. The air filled with that distinctive smell of hot Hema: metallic, a little sweet, a little salty, with an undercurrent of something chemical that marked it as distinct from real blood.

He dipped a ladle into the thick, rich liquid, releasing a tendril of steam. That familiar dizzy feeling buzzed in my head as my stomach clenched. I hadn't eaten since that morning, an eon and several time zones ago. Mr. Kontos filled the bowls, and Galen and I handed them down the table. With each passing bowl, hunger sank its claws deeper into my ribs. The portions were so generous—would there be enough for all of us?

When the student to my right had been served, I dared to peek into the tureen. Surely there would be nothing but the last clotted dregs. My mouth fell open: the dish was still half full. It felt impossible: tens of thousands of dollars of Hema had to be steaming in these serving bowls. Our empty fridge, the trips to Donovan's, the funk of nearly spoiled Hema ran through my mind. Beneath it all, that fear of going hungry, and what you might do if you went hungry long enough. How many of these vampires had ever thought about that?

"Everything okay, Kat?" Mr. Kontos asked.

"It's just so much Hema." As soon as I said it, I regretted it. What had Lucy just warned me about? "I mean, hopefully the leftovers don't get wasted, with the crazy-high prices CasTech sets."

"Victor Castel donates Hema to the school directly," Galen told me, as if that had any relation to what I'd said.

My eyebrows pinched together. Surely with Harcote's tuition, the school could afford to feed its students without handouts. Galen's parents were the biggest philanthropists in all of Vampirdom. I'd expected he would have understood that. "It would be nice if he made sure all vampires had the same access."

"He does," Galen said flatly. "Vampires only have access to Hema at all because Victor Castel invented it. Our kind would have been wiped out by the disease if it wasn't for him."

I raised my spoon to my lips (after watching everyone else first—at home we just drank Hema from mugs) and felt that first swallow of warm liquid coat my stomach. I couldn't let Galen fluster me, even if he was talking to me like a child. "Every vampire left alive knows what Victor Castel did. I'm thankful for Hema. But an essential thing like blood substitute shouldn't be so expensive. He could make it more affordable."

"Is this some new reunionist thing?"

I had no idea what reunionists were, but from the note of scorn in Galen's voice, it wasn't something I wanted to be. "It's just my opinion."

"The price of Hema is completely fair." I doubted Galen even knew what Hema sold for. He didn't have the look of someone had to haggle for a bottle of blood in a piss-scented alley. "Victor Castel is generous, but he isn't running a charity."

"You just said he donates this Hema to Harcote. Isn't that charity? Sounds pretty hypocritical."

Galen darkened. "I won't have my fangmaker spoken ill of."

I nearly choked on my blood substitute.

Victor Castel was Galen's *fangmaker*? I, a total nobody, was arguing with someone whose vampiric pedigree ran directly to *the most important vampire ever*. Not only had Victor Castel invented the blood substitute sold as Hema, he was a hero for it. Vampires only survived the Peril at all because he and his company, CasTech, managed to get Hema distributed, just in time.

The fourth-year girl beside him checked her phone. "Nine minutes, thirty-four seconds. Nice, Galen. You just won me a hundred bucks."

I raised my napkin to my lips for a second to compose myself. I hadn't come to Harcote to fight for lower Hema prices. I'd come to Harcote so that someday, I wouldn't have to think about the price of Hema at all. The first step to achieving that was fitting in, and that clearly meant getting along with Galen.

"He's really your fangmaker?" I tried to sound impressed. "What's he like?"

Before Galen could answer, Headmaster Atherton rose from his table at the front of the hall and called us to attention. His cheeks were blotched red. I wondered if he was ever anything other than excited.

"I have a very special announcement, boys and girls." I narrowed my eyes. At my old school, no one ever said *boys and girls*, since it left so many people out. "As you know, the Harcote School is honored to enjoy the support of Mr. Victor Castel. You know him as the president of CasTech, the man responsible for the survival of our kind and the inventor of the very blood substitute we currently feast upon, and the chairman of our board of trustees. But this semester, to celebrate our twenty-fifth year, a very lucky student will get to know him in a different way: as a *mentor*."

A ripple of excitement ran through the hall.

"Yes, you heard me! The one and only Victor Castel will be mentoring a Harcote student this year. He wants to give back to our community. The mentee will have the chance to meet with Mr. Castel over the course of the year, get a look into his life as a leader of Vampirdom, and get a little insight into what immortality holds. I think that sounds pretty darn incredible! All *you* have to do is submit an essay about what Harcote means to you." He grinned. "I know our selection committee is going to have a bear of a time making its choice."

When I turned back to the table, Galen must have hoped that

the smirk he wore on his finely sculpted lips would pass as excitement. I wasn't convinced. His jaw was clenched so hard, every
muscle in his face seemed taut. His water-and-smoke eyes slid to
me. He arched that infuriating eyebrow.

"Maybe you'll get to see for yourself."

7

KAT

I HAD ALWAYS loved the first day of school: The fresh notebooks, an unblemished planner, the whole year was ahead of you. Of all the worries I'd had about coming to Harcote, the coursework hadn't been one of them. I had always been a top student, and my teachers loved me. I expected the classes to push me, but not more than I could handle.

But by the end of third period on the first day of classes, I was starting to think I'd overestimated myself.

I'd already been assigned more homework for one night than I'd had in a week at my old school. A French test every Friday, a precalc problem set every night, three days to read the entirety of Homer's *Odyssey*, and on top of that, the application for the mentorship with Victor Castel.

By the end of classes, my new planner was already packed with due dates. I was looking for the library when I ran into Evangeline. She was wearing soft brown riding jodhpurs that fit like leggings and tall, polished-leather riding boots. An English saddle was perched against her hip and she had a riding crop in one hand. Part of me couldn't believe that people dressed like that in real life, but then another part, insistent, wondered if I shouldn't start dressing like this, because wasn't it, actually, kind of hot?

"You're going riding?" I asked, because I was a brilliant conversationalist.

Evangeline shifted the saddle to the other hip and shook back her waves of thick black hair. "The stables are off campus. I'm the captain of the equestrian team. This is for our table."

"Your table?"

"For the club fair."

I twisted my thumb into the strap of my backpack. "That's today? I have a ton of homework already, and I haven't even started on the essay for the mentorship."

Evangeline waved this idea away with a swish of her riding crop. "I wouldn't waste too much time on that."

"I thought it was kind of a big deal," I said uneasily.

Her eyebrow quirked. "It is, for one of us. Galen is Victor Castel's fangborn. You knew that, right?"

I rolled my eyes. "I've been in the same room as him."

"Well, Castel doesn't have any Youngbloods of his own—actually, the rumor is that he *can't* have kids. That makes Galen his only descendant. So the mentorship is obviously for him."

I shook my head. "That's ridiculous. Victor Castel doesn't need to hold a contest to mentor his only descendant."

"Don't be dense. Galen's the Chosen One. He's going to lead the Black Foundation one day, and personally, I think Castel wants him to take over CasTech too. But he can't simply announce that he's going to give Galen special treatment. You're not the Best of the Best because of who sunk their teeth into Daddy's neck a hundred years ago. You're the Best of the Best because you worked for it."

"So they hold a competition to make it look like Galen beat everyone else out," I said slowly.

"Exactly."

That only made sense if the school's motto wasn't just an inspirational metaphor and the Youngbloods at Harcote really were the Best of the Best. With the tuition as high as it was, there had to be dozens of Youngbloods like me, who needed nothing short of a miracle to compete for the mentorship at all. Something told me that Evangeline wasn't going to be able to clarify that for me, so instead I asked, "If the mentorship is Galen's, then why is *anyone* bothering to apply?"

She gave me a wry smile. "We're all responsible for maintaining the facade, aren't we?"

It made sense. I'd already had enough good luck this year, with the Benefactor—no sense in pushing it and wasting my time applying for a mentorship I'd never win. But it was hard not to be disappointed.

We dropped the saddle off, then Evangeline toured me around the tables set up in the Dining Hall: Latin and Mandarin clubs, literary magazines, a philosophical debate society, and groups for students who were interested in Vampiric History or chess. At my old school, almost no one had the chance to become a nationally ranked squash player or discover a new planet at Astronomy Club or travel to France with the Gastronomic Society. Between my job and school, I'd barely had time for extracurriculars, but that was the case for almost all my friends.

Harcote was different. In addition to being an equestrian, Evangeline was a theater kid. She was planning a one-act play about Joan of Arc, starring herself; she'd been working on it all summer. Lucy was the president of Marine Biology Club and captain of the tennis team, Carolina Riser was allegedly good enough to be a concert violinist, and even the Dent twins were involved with some kind of entrepreneurship incubator thing. But as Evangeline talked, I couldn't get the mentorship out of my mind.

She hadn't had any trouble admitting that everyone performed for Galen so that Vampirdom itself could pretend he had worked for something he was born into. But the more I thought about it, the more it seemed almost everyone at Harcote benefited from the same thing. Harcote was *academically* elite, but clearly, that wasn't the only kind of status the school valued. If you wanted the chance to prove yourself as one of the Best of the Best, you had to be born with a fancy vampiric pedigree, social standing, and most of all, wealth. When you had all that going for you, why wouldn't you be successful?

"Are there any social justice–type clubs?" I asked Evangeline.

"You mean like a human rights club?" Her nose scrunched up prettily. "Last year, a senior tried to start a human rights club. I can't remember why it didn't happen—I think Atherton vetoed it. Truly, what's there to discuss? With CFaD and Hema, it's not like we hunt anymore. Human politics social-justice whatever isn't really a problem here."

I stared at her. Even if Harcote was an isolated bubble, social justice was a problem everywhere there was *society*. "I meant like—like Black Lives Matter? At my old school I was in Students for Racial Justice."

"Oh!" Evangeline scanned the room, a little uneasily. "There's the Students of Color Caucus, but that's not really *for us*."

I followed her eyes to a table that wasn't attracting much attention. It was manned by a Black fourth-year I knew was named Georges—George, but with an extra silent *s*—and a girl I didn't know who looked Latina. I glanced around at the other tables.

"Georges isn't the only Black student here, is he?" I asked.

"Of course not!" Evangeline listed a few names in each year. It couldn't have been more than seven.

"It's a little messed up that you can name them all. Vampirdom has to be more diverse than that."

"Okay, Little Miss Political, it's a small school. I can probably name *all* the students, period. And Harcote is plenty diverse. Lucy's Chinese and Galen's Indian."

"He is?"

"Well, half, on his mom's side. His dad is British," she said. "Oh, I forgot about Climate Action Now! Everybody's a member."

It was better than nothing.

THAT EVENING, I went to dinner with Evangeline and Lucy, and a few girls from different houses. We stayed long after we'd finished our Hema so they could go over the important gossip from last year. But now that the clock was hitting eleven p.m. and I still had approximately thirty million pages of the *Odyssey* to get through, the snap of my neck as I dozed off was the only thing keeping me awake.

"Is Operation Suck-Up that exhausting?" Taylor said. She was lying on her bed, watching something on her computer. It seemed to be her main occupation.

"Are you seriously dragging me for trying to make friends?"

"I'm dragging you for trying to make friends with losers when we both know you'd rather be studying, because you're a natural-born nerd."

"So you're dragging me for trying to make friends *and* doing my homework?"

"Yup, that covers it," Taylor said.

"So what if I am sucking up to them a little? I don't want to spend the next two years friendless." I would never have said this to anyone else, but if Taylor wanted to destroy my life—again— she had more than enough ammo. And anyway, I'd never been good at hiding things from her.

"Careful they don't hear you talking like that. They hate try-hards. We're vampires—gotta maintain that stone-cold exterior."

"Can I ask you something?"

"Sure." She hit pause and pushed herself up on her elbows.

"I was at the club fair today and the school is just . . . really white. Vampirdom has to be more diverse than seven Black students out of like, three hundred fifty."

"The problem's with your expectations," Taylor snorted. "What made you think Harcote represented all of Vampirdom?"

"That's how Headmaster Atherton talks about it. And—and I don't know. I just didn't think it would be so white."

"I seriously doubt Atherton cares about winning diversity points. Who would that impress?"

"It's not about impressing anyone, it's about doing the right thing."

Taylor shot me a lopsided grin, like I'd said something funny. "Look, the vampires behind Harcote—and the parents and fang-makers of our dear classmates—weren't exactly at every Civil Rights march, you know? Atherton's like four-hundred-something years old. And have our local Southern belles, Anna Rose and Jane Marie Dent, given you the speech about how their family *lost it all* in the Civil War? Why would Black vampires *want* to come here?" Suddenly she laughed. "You're making that face."

"What face?"

"Your *oh shit* face. Your eyes get all huge and buggy. You're so in over your head, *Kath-er-ine*."

Every muscle in my body seized in frustration. "I am not in over my head, and my eyes are not *buggy*! And stop calling me that!"

"Or, I keep calling you Kath-er-ine, and then you complain to

Evangeline, and you two *truly* bond over how much you both *truly* hate me."

Taylor stuck her earbuds in and rolled over to face the wall, leaving me grasping for some kind of witty reply, which was infuriating. "Great idea, thanks!" I finally said, when she couldn't hear me anyway. At least now I felt like I could read all night if I had to. But when I went back to my book, I'd lost my place entirely.

TAYLOR

VAMPIRIC MORALITY

Radtke scratched these words onto the chalkboard and under-lined them, in case anyone had missed the point. The papery sound of chalk dust between her fingers made the baby hairs at the back of my neck prickle. "What is the fundamental question of vampiric morality?" she asked.

The hands of all the major nerds and suck-ups shot into the air. I slouched farther down in my seat. It was so unfair that Harcote's classrooms were set up "seminar style" with a U of tables. No back row meant nowhere safe to nap.

Predictably, Radtke pointed to Dorian, an overeager Count Chocula wannabe who was always wearing incomprehensibly lame outfits. Today it looked like the upholstery of some innocent foot-stool had been sacrificed to fashion his gray-and-garnet waistcoat. Dorian loved bragging that he was named after *that* Dorian, Dorian Gray, because his father had been "a dear friend" of Oscar Wilde's.

Sounded gay if you asked me, but no one did.

"Can immortal beings act morally?" Dorian said.

Radtke nodded. "Human moral principles traditionally rest on the assumption that all beings die. Can anyone think of an ex-ample?" Radtke pointed to Evangeline.

"The Christian religion," she answered. "It's based on the idea that if you follow a set of moral laws while you're alive, once you die you'll be rewarded or punished. The system doesn't work for vampires because we don't die."

"Well said, Miss Lazareanu. Human morality rests on a system of rules that they must be trained to follow."

"Like training a dog!" Dorian added. It earned him a few laughs, and an eye twitch from Radtke. She hated speaking out of turn.

Across the room, Kat had paused her usually frantic note-taking and was holding perfectly still. Most Youngbloods didn't spend much time around humans. It was as if our parents were afraid that with too much exposure, we'd forget we were actually undead monsters. But Kat's mom had always sent her to the local public school, even though my mom—*so very generously*, she said—had offered to let Kat study with the same tutor who homeschooled me and my little brother. This had to be Kat's first taste of vampiric philosophy. She was in for a treat.

Radtke went on, "What does this imply for *vampiric* morality?"

Galen indicated that he wished to speak. The Prince of Good Hair Days never actually raised his hand like everyone else. Instead he kept his elbow on the table and held two fingers up, like Radtke was a waitress and he was asking for his check. "That vampiric morality exists on a higher plane because it's not based on the threat of death. We know that there is no life after death, because there is no death. We don't fear some future punishment. We can make choices by a higher logic."

And here I found my entry into this argument. "If that's true, then what is that higher logic?"

Radtke cut me off. Eye twitch. "In this classroom we raise our hands, Taylor."

I stuck my hand in the air to Radtke give the pleasure of pointing at me. "You make it sound like vampires don't have to think about the consequences of our actions at all, just because we can't die. But that's not a superior morality—that's no morality at all." That special *zip* of getting good argument started was fizzing through me. I leaned across the table toward Galen. "If vampires can't act morally because we're immortal, that would make us *inferior* to humans. Because humans are capable of morality and we aren't."

The flustered chatter this provoked was incredibly satisfying.

"That's the dumbest thing I've ever heard," Galen said. "You can't possibly think that humans are better than us. *We were born to suck their blood.*"

"So were leeches," I said with a grin. "And mosquitos. Vampires are parasites, and since the Peril, we can't even do *that* right anymore."

"We're *immortal creatures.*" Galen pounded a fist on the table. "The ever-living, never-dying!"

Now Evangeline jumped back in. Radtke's eye twitch-twitch-twitched, but of course she never called them out like she did me. "That's absurd. Thousands of humans work for my parents and we subsidize health insurance for most of them. Who's the parasite there?"

"That's capitalism, not morality, E. Besides, it's not true that vampires can't die. There's fire, staking, CFaD." As soon as I said this, I froze, and my eyes went to Kat. She had a grip on her pen so tight she could have snapped it in two. I noticed that, because I was deliberately not looking her in the eyes, which felt simultaneously pointless and extremely necessary. I'd already reminded her of how her dad died.

Radtke shocked us all by saying, "Taylor brings up an interesting point. Thoughts?"

Evangeline launched a hand into the air. "You know what I

think is immoral? Vampires who don't take precautions against CFaD and waste the gift of their immortality. And if vampires can act immorally, it stands to reason they can act morally, ergo you're wrong, Taylor, and vampiric morality exists." She topped this off with a self-satisfied grin that made me want to shove her into a corner and kiss her.

"So feeding on humans is fine, as long as you take *precautions*?" I said. Evangeline glared at me. I knew it was a point she didn't want to rebut; everyone had heard the rumors. Luckily, she was rescued by Galen's need to deliver a Black Foundation sound bite.

"Soon, vampires will be protected from CFaD. Our scientists are working every day to make sure that's possible. A vaccine or a cure is coming, I promise you that."

"I'm holding my breath," I muttered. "Good thing I can't suffocate."

Radtke wrinkled her brow at me—the old lady version of an eye roll. "This brings us to an interesting dilemma," she said. "CFaD has made feeding on humans incredibly high risk, but it has also greatly reduced the loss of human life at vampire hands. What if CFaD was cured and vampires could feed on humans without any danger?"

Dorian was so excited by that, he was practically drooling. "Then the natural order would be restored. We could live as vampires have for time immemorial!" No eyes were left un-rolled. Vampires had lived in all kinds of ways since time immemorial, and a lot of them were kind of shitty. Of course, actual history didn't stop the travs from idealizing a past that had only ever existed in *Castlevania*.

"You're all aware of the reunionists, correct? Vampires who believe that with a cure for CFaD and free access to Hema, vampires can live in harmony with humans. Any thoughts?"

"If Hema were free, Galen's fangdaddy would go broke," I said.

"Watch your mouth." Galen's voice was gravelly in a way that might have been intimidating, if you were the kind of person who was intimidated by lifelong smokers.

"Why should I?"

"Be respectful," Radtke warned.

"Reunionism is a fantasy," Evangeline said. "With much respect to the Black Foundation, CFaD keeps humans safe, and Hema keeps vampires safe."

"You don't trust yourself to keep drinking Hema without the threat of turning into black goo?" I said. "Just because we can feed on humans doesn't mean we should. If CFaD were cured, I'd keep drinking Hema no matter what. I know *I'd* rather not be a murderer."

"Look who's ready for sainthood," Galen said.

I couldn't help myself. Everyone at this school was so obsessed with Galen, with his fancy hair and his rich-boy pedigree, like they couldn't see he was just a jackass. "Don't be such a dickvein."

"*Taylor*," Evangeline said.

I crossed my arms. "Please, defend him. I can't wait."

Her lips parted in a contemptuous little sneer, her eyes flashing. "You're such a freaking lesbian," Evangeline ground out under her breath.

Not that a soul in the room didn't hear it.

For a sharp, clear moment, everything inside me stopped: heart and lungs, blood, every muscle was coiled and tight, like in one of those dreams where you're trying to run but you're frozen in place. It wasn't even a real insult—it was a factual description. It had no power to hurt me, therefore I wasn't hurt, especially not in front of all these idiots. I couldn't let Evangeline have the last word. But I just couldn't think of something to say—

"What *the actual fuck*, Evangeline?" My eyes snapped to Kat. Her cheeks were flushed, her eyes narrowed.

People gasped, literally gasped, and a crack reverberated through the classroom. Radtke had smacked the blackboard with a ruler, a wisp of hair pulled loose from her dusty chignon. "Enough!"

I stared at Kat, waiting for her to look at me, but her eyes were glued to her notes. She held her lip between her teeth and her breath was coming short and quick.

Radtke said, "Kat, Taylor, I will see you in my office after class. Evangeline, I will speak to you later."

KAT

WAITING IN MS. Radtke's office was like spending purgatory in an antique store. The lighting was dim old-style filament light bulbs and the furnishings were all brocade and fringe. Chalk dust and *dust* dust coated every surface. There wasn't even a computer on the desk, just a ledger and an actual fountain pen.

I sat on my hands to keep them still. I'd never gotten in trouble at school before. Now I hadn't even been at Harcote for two weeks and I'd cursed at another student in the middle of class. I wondered what archaic notions of punishment Ms. Radtke held. Hopefully it wouldn't throw my financial aid into question.

"What we did really wasn't that bad, right?" I asked Taylor anxiously. "Kids get in trouble for worse all the time. Someone got stabbed at my school last year. Compared to that, this is nothing."

Taylor was slouched in the antique chair beside mine with her legs spread wide, as if she'd popped by Radtke's office to play some video games.

"I've gotten in trouble with Radtke loads of times. It's no big deal. Can you stop fidgeting? You're freaking me out."

"Your *lack* of freaking out is freaking me out."

She slouched deeper into the chair.

I bobbed my knee more aggressively.

"You know, what Evangeline said was horrible and totally homophobic."

Her eyes darted to mine, then away. "I know."

I kicked myself. *Obviously*, she knew that. "I mean, that whole conversation was *so stupid*. Humans need to be trained how to behave, like dogs? It's not the Middle Ages anymore. They're not all Christian and—"

"Compelling points," a voice said from behind me. My back went ramrod straight. "I wish you had raised them in class."

"I'm sorry, Ms. Radtke, I didn't realize you were there."

Ms. Radtke settled herself at her desk, arranging her skirt so she fit in the chair, and leveled a stern look at the two of us.

"Harcote students abide by our Honor Code," Ms. Radtke began. "Miss Finn, you signed the Honor Code when you enrolled. Miss Sanger, can you remind us of the principles of the Harcote School Honor Code?"

Taylor cleared her throat. "The Honor Code requires us to act with respect to Vampirdom in all that we do: respect to ourselves, to the other vampires in our community, to Harcote." She dropped her head against her shoulder and gave me an insolent, sideways look. "Basically, instead of just telling us not to cheat on tests or steal or whatever, they want us to guess what they don't want us to do, and if we guess wrong, we get in trouble."

Ms. Radtke pursed her lips. "No editorializing, please. For example, Taylor's posture at this moment, despite the gravity of the situation, is highly disrespectful, and a potential violation of the Honor Code. Taylor, please sit properly." Taylor begrudgingly shoved herself up in the chair. "Thank you. Now, in class today, did you violate the Honor Code?"

"I didn't mean to," I said quickly. "I was just responding to Evangeline—"

"Me too!" Taylor jumped in. "I was just responding to Galen."

"Your responses were not respectful," Radtke replied. "Kat, I am unfamiliar with your former educational institution, but at Harcote, we do not use profanity and we certainly do not direct it to other students. We value the spirit of debate. Sometimes those debates may challenge us, but discomfort helps us grow."

I burned to tell her that what Evangeline had said wasn't anywhere near part of the debate, but I checked myself. Wasn't talking back against the Honor Code? "I should have chosen my words more carefully, and I am sorry. I'll do better."

"Please do." Ms. Radtke now glared at Taylor. "Let's not pretend you haven't found yourself in this position before, Miss Sanger. What do you have to say for yourself?"

"Honestly, when you consider what we *could have done*, I think we were being really respectful of Galen and Evangeline."

My stomach lurched. "Why are you saying *we*? There's no *we*."

Taylor kept talking right over me. "We could have *stabbed* them. That's how they settled things at Kat's old school, but we said, *No, let's use our words*. Really, we should be getting an award for our achievements in the realm of respect."

"We weren't going to stab them," I hurried to say. "We didn't have some kind of plan!"

Taylor shot me a pouty look. She'd managed to sink back into the same sprawling posture that Ms. Radtke had just told her was disrespectful. "Aw, Kath-er-ine, I thought we were partners in crime."

"Are you actually incapable of taking anything seriously?" I burst out. "And it's *Kat*."

"Miss Finn there's no reason to raise your voice, though I certainly agree that Miss Sanger can test one's patience." Ms. Radtke shook her head and quickly marked something in her ledger. "I won't have the young ladies of Hunter House engaging in wildness. You will meet here in my office tomorrow after classes to write letters of apology to Galen and Evangeline. You're dismissed."

We stood and grabbed our bags. Taylor looked back at Ms. Radtke. "What's going to happen to Evangeline?"

Ms. Radtke's face was taut. "That's none of your immediate concern," she said. "Now, please, get out of my office."

THE DOOR TO Ms. Radtke's office had barely closed before I wheeled on Taylor. "What the hell is your problem?"

Taylor shrugged as she typed something into her phone. "Last time I got tested, I was problem-free. *You* seem a little upset though." She set off down the hallway, forcing me to trail after her out into the stairs.

"Of course I'm upset. That's the appropriate response in my position!" I thought back to the pressure that had ballooned inside me as I tried to pretend I didn't care about that horrible discussion, and the sharp crackle of anger as that facade broke. "If it wasn't for you egging them on like that I would have never violated the Honor Code!"

"I'll make sure to consider your reaction to every comment I make in class from here on out," Taylor said. "The Honor Code is a scam anyway. They just want to teach us to think like them. Pretend there's a tiny Atherton or Radtke in your head watching you all the time, second-guessing your decisions. It's bullshit."

"So what? Those are the rules, which means we have to follow them. Is it really so terrible to think like them if it means staying out of trouble?"

Taylor stopped in the middle of the stairs and turned to face me. The look of disdain in her eyes was so unvarnished I flinched. "Yes, it really is that terrible, because thinking like them would kill me. You think it's my fault that I don't fit in here. But this school—all of fucking *Vampirdom*—only has room for a certain kind of person. If you weren't born that way, you better force yourself to change, fast. Maybe you're happy to do that, but I won't. I *can't*. Someone like Radtke is never going to understand me. She's like two hundred years old, and she's always on my ass for dressing like a boy. And you want me to let her into my head— give her more authority over me than she already has? No fucking thanks."

I was on the stair above her, which, with our height difference, brought us level. I opened my mouth, ready to tell her that I didn't have the luxury, that I was only here on the generosity of a stranger and I had to prove myself worth it. But then I saw how the flecks of gold in her irises seemed to glow. Her pulse was flickering fast, in her neck, and her chin was trembling, just a little. It was the first time since Taylor had walked into our room on Move-in Day that I hadn't heard a shred of sarcasm in her voice.

"Okay," I said.

A strange, soft look crossed Taylor's face, but before I could read it, she was bounding down the rest of the stairs. On the landing, she paused and turned back to me.

"Thank you for what you said to Evangeline. Just so we're clear, I don't need you to defend me, 'specially not from her."

I crossed my arms. "You're welcome. And so we're clear, I wasn't defending you. Evangeline was being a—a dick-vein."

Taylor kicked the toe of her sneaker against the bottom stair. "Yeah, all right. See you later, Kath-er-ine."

Taylor turned down the next flight of stairs and was gone before I could correct her.

TAYLOR

I TOOK THE Old Hill stairs two at a time.

Katherine *freaking* Finn.

I was almost dizzy, remembering the fierce snap of the words Kat lobbed at Evangeline, how it had electrified the room. No one ever stood up for me like that, except for myself.

No—I was reading too much into it. Kat was an ally to the queer community in general. That didn't mean she was an ally to me *personally*. She would have defended anyone—it was just the kind of person that she was. She'd told me on no uncertain terms that we were not going to be friends, and I had to take her at her word. Anyway, the heat of her judgmental glaring back in Radtke's office had practically given me a sunburn.

That was for the best. Kat and I might have history, but that didn't mean she could be trusted. The truth was, no one else could be trusted to love you, even to like you. Certainly not to understand you, and only in a few cases to respect you. If I forgot that and let myself get hurt, it would be my own damn fault.

The truth of this was cold and clean and steady and I clung to it like a life raft, even as I typed out a response to the text I'd just gotten.

Be there in five minutes.

Outside Old Hill, I yanked my sunglasses out of my pocket and smashed them onto my face. Instead of heading to the library or back down-campus to Hunter, I hung a right and made for the theater building.

The best protection from the judgment of other people was to be aggressively yourself, all the time. If you were constantly daring them to reject you, then obviously their rejection meant nothing to you. That won you back your upper hand. Sure, it had driven almost everyone at Harcote away, but I had a freedom that they didn't.

But the situation with Kat was different.

First, I couldn't entirely drive Kat away because no matter what happened, she could never get farther than the opposite side of that stupid little room.

Second, Kat had gotten to me before these defenses were in place. Actually, she was partly responsible for them. She was like a sleeper agent, behind enemy lines, lying in wait to hurt me all over again.

Third, and worst of all, I didn't *want* to drive Kat away.

Not at all.

The opposite, even.

And that was so completely, foolishly hopeless that even *thinking* about it made me want to lobotomize myself.

I didn't have the tools to perform a lobotomy right then, so instead I cut around the front entrance to the theater and headed to a side door that led to the backstage area. Only students in Advanced Drama Ensemble had swipe access to this door, and I would not be caught dead in Advanced Drama Ensemble. Conveniently, a piece of paper was jammed in the lock so I could shove it open easily. At the end of the darkened hallway, light spilled from under the door to the costume closet.

A familiar feeling tightened in my stomach—a delicious kind of dread. Wanting what you weren't supposed to want. Doing what you weren't supposed to do.

I pocketed my sunglasses, pushed a hand through my hair, and opened that door. Calling this room a *closet* was a little misleading. It was bigger than my room in Hunter House and filled with racks of costumes from past productions, some sections perfectly boring, others all razzle-dazzle-y. Along one wall ran a counter below a mirror studded with incandescent bulbs that lit the room golden. I locked the door behind me.

"That was *not* five minutes."

Evangeline was sitting on that counter, her feet swinging in the air. Her hair was swept over her shoulder in a luscious night-dark wave, her lips pouty with annoyance, and she had this awful look in her glacial eyes, a bored hunger like she was about to destroy whatever crossed her path.

She was, as usual, breathtaking.

I hesitated. I wasn't going to apologize for not coming faster when I'd already come when called. But then I said, "Sorry. I got held up. What do you want, E?"

Evangeline hopped off the counter. Her pleated skirt *swished* against the lino. I could have listened to that sound all day. As she closed the distance between us, it was all I could do to stop myself from biting my lip. Evangeline could tell. She was smirking at me. "Come on, Taylor. What do you think I want?"

"Had enough humiliating me in public, now you want to do it in private?"

She tilted her head. I could see a triangle of her gorgeous neck, which I was not touching. "Are you mad at me?"

Yes, I was, but I kept my mouth shut.

She licked her lips. *Fuck.* "I liked it when you got all upset in class."

"I don't care what you like."

This was the correct thing to say. It was true—or it had been true at some point in the past, maybe even as recently as five minutes ago. I wasn't sure if it was true right now. At the end of school last year, I swore I wasn't going to have anything to do with Evangeline come fall. This had been a Decision that I'd made for Reasons, but now it felt very far away. Whereas Evangeline was right here, the living embodiment of an argument *for* that outweighed every argument *against*.

Against: this was never going anywhere. For: neither was anything else.

Against: hooking up with mean girls just because they demanded it of you wasn't topping the list of Ways to Respect Yourself. For: Evangeline's lips.

Against: I'd feel terrible afterward. For: *afterward* was a problem for later. Right now I could feel great.

Evangeline was standing very close to me and doing this irresistible thing where she gently hooked one of her incisor over her beautiful lip, and she was looking at my mouth, and then up at my eyes, and then back at my mouth again—like she was imagining us kissing. "It was such a long summer," she sighed.

An undeniable fact that my body was intensely, insistently aware of in that moment.

"Please?" she whispered.

My breathing went raggedy. Evangeline was *flirting* with me. Evangeline wanted me bad enough to *try*, to look at me the way she looked at those idiot boys.

My lips were on hers so suddenly that she gasped, and then we were kissing, full and electric, our bodies pressing together, Evangeline's back against that mirror haloed in golden light. I was kissing that pale triangle of her neck, and her breath was on my ear, and it felt so infuriatingly, stupidly *good* that it was almost cruel, and I wanted to disappear into that horrible feeling forever.

LATER, I HUNG around awkwardly near the door and pretended like I wasn't watching Evangeline tuck her polo back into her skirt. Now that we were done, the badness was setting in quick. The wondering why I let her have so much power over me, and why I let her convince me, when we were alone together, it was me who had power over her. I wanted nothing more than to wash the smell of her from my hands, but for some reason I never left until Evangeline dismissed me.

"Are you going to give Kat shit for what she said today?" I asked to break up the silence.

"I haven't decided." Evangeline looked at me through the reflection in the mirror. "Why?"

"No reason."

She turned, her hands on her waist and her eyes glittering awfully. A Goddess of Chaos. *"Taylor."*

"What?" But to my total horror, I could feel it—could see it, in the mirror across the room: I was blushing.

"You do not have a *crush* on your *roommate*!"

"No, I—that's not what I said. I just—because I know her from before. And you're such a bitch. I know how you are with people."

It was too late. Evangeline was looking at me like I was a wounded puppy: a perfect candidate for torture. "Aw, Taylor. That's truly the most pathetic thing ever."

The words hit me in the chest, right in the vicinity of my heart. I tried to keep my expression casual as I grabbed my backpack. No way was I going to let Evangeline see I was hurt. Because I wasn't. I was actually angry—although not at Evangeline. It was her nature to sink her fangs into any soft place you left exposed. No, I was furious at my own idiot self for mentioning Kat at all, for meeting up in the first place, for the fact that even now—right at this second—I *wanted wanted wanted* the barest scrap of a kindness from Evangeline. Some little sign that she cared about me outside of hooking up. That she was sorry she'd seen the truth about me so easily.

I was *truly* the most pathetic thing ever.

"I'm getting out of here, if that's cool," I managed to say.

Evangeline had turned back to the mirror to apply gloss to lips swollen from my kisses. "Don't let anyone see you leave."

KAT

THAT NIGHT, AS I lay staring at the slanted ceiling in that dark room, my mind wouldn't quiet. There was nothing to distract me from playing a highlight reel of the day, again and again. I'd have given anything for the racket of a car alarm to break up the silence. What I had instead was the quiet creaking of the old house and the occasional rustle of Taylor's sheets.

I rolled over to the cooler side of the pillow. A few feet away, Taylor was lying on her back, her chest slowly rising and falling and her mouth a little slack. Seeing her at ease like this made it obvious how tightly wound she was during the day.

The more I tried to fit in, the more obvious it was how little Taylor did the same. She didn't have any close friends and she didn't waste any effort trying to correct that problem. I rarely saw her in the library or the Dining Hall or in the Hunter House common areas. In the room, she was distracting even just sitting there. She barely needed to say anything to make it clear she was judging me, like the way she'd said *"A cappella?"* when she saw the flyer for tryouts on my desk, or how she called me "Kath-er-ine" when she knew I hated it.

That wasn't the Taylor I remembered.

Because she strutted around campus in her sneakers and her sunglasses and called out bullshit wherever she saw it and generally acted like no one on Earth had the power to tell her what to do, people thought she didn't care about anything.

But that wasn't true.

Taylor had told me as much that afternoon. She didn't follow the Honor Code because she didn't want to let Harcote and Vampirdom control her. I'd never thought about rules that way before, like they were a path you could choose to go down or not. Taylor even knew she'd be punished for it—by Ms. Radtke, by people like Evangeline and Lucy—but she did it anyway. I didn't have to like her to admit it was brave.

I rolled back onto my back and watched the moonlit shadows of the nearby trees shift across the ceiling.

Maybe I didn't want to follow the rules either. I didn't love the idea of learning to think like Ms. Radtke—*letting her into my head*. But I wasn't like Taylor. She could get in trouble a thousand times and never really bear the consequences like I would. Her parents would find a way to stop the school from expelling her, and even if Taylor did get kicked out, she had a home to go back to.

I didn't. Not anymore. I had my financial aid to worry about.

A forever-long future that turned on what I did and how hard I worked right now, at this place, with these people. I kicked the blanket down, then pulled it back up again, and it was still impossible to get comfortable.

Harcote and Vampirdom were the same. If I wanted to rise within them, I had to follow its rules. Taylor made everything more complicated than it was.

Finally, I rolled over again to face the wall.

"Jesus, Kat," Taylor groaned. "If you're gonna masturbate at least wait until I'm asleep."

I froze. "I thought you were asleep. I mean—I wouldn't—I'm not doing that, I'm just trying to get comfortable."

"That's what you call it?" Taylor's mattress squeaked as she shifted her weight.

I couldn't help but grin at that, and suddenly, it was as if I had let out a breath I'd been holding all day. I listened as Taylor's breathing slowed into a sleepy rhythm, and soon I was drifting off too.

KAT

CLIMATE ACTION NOW! held its first meeting during clubs period on Friday. Evangeline hadn't exaggerated: half the student body was crowded into the auditorium. That made sense. Given that we were immortal beings who didn't tolerate hot temperatures well, vampires had a lot to lose in global warming. Still, I knew who I had to sit with.

It wasn't that I regretted what I said to Evangeline. Evangeline couldn't go around calling someone a *lesbian* as if that were an insult and not like, something to celebrate. Taylor claimed she was fine, but someone *trying* to humiliate you was only a little less humiliating than when they actually succeeded. If the Youngbloods at Harcote had been anything like my friends in Sacramento, Evangeline would already be socially excommunicated. But here, if anyone was going to face consequences for what happened in Ms. Radtke's class, apparently it wasn't Evangeline. It was obvious that she was going to be important at Harcote, and in Vampirdom, for a long time. As long as that was true, I needed her to like me.

And that meant a real apology, not just one of Ms. Radtke's letters.

Evangeline and Lucy were both scrolling through their phones when I walked up. Before they could freeze me out, I sat down and plunged right in.

"Evangeline, I'm sorry about what I said in class. It came out totally wrong, and I hope you weren't offended."

Evangeline's ice-water eyes watched me over the edge of her phone. I felt that same sensation I'd had the day I met her, like she had considered crushing me, but decided it would be more fun to play with me first. Suddenly, she smiled and put her phone down. "Oh, that? It's fine. No hard feelings."

"Seriously?" I said.

"It was kind of funny, truly," she said.

I couldn't tell if she was lying.

The meeting started, and Evangeline and Lucy resumed whatever they were doing on their phones. Actually, it seemed like nearly everyone in the auditorium was doing homework, or chatting, or even taking selfies. I was about to ask if the group held protests on Climate Fridays, but before I could, the three student leaders started arguing over how much responsibility vampires bore for anthropogenic climate change, because humans were really at fault for it—after all, it wasn't called *vampirogenic* climate change for a reason.

Evangeline leaned toward me, her chin resting on her knuckle. "Everything worked out okay with the room, right? Things are cool with Taylor?"

"Totally," I rushed out. I didn't want to know if she was asking if I was freaked that my roommate was queer. "I actually already knew Taylor. We were friends, as kids."

"So random," Evangeline said, fascinated. "Were you guys close?"

It was a simple question, but it made my chest ache. Long ago, I'd shoved the memories of my friendship with Taylor as down deep as I could. I wanted to forget how she'd hurt me and what she'd done—I wanted to forget her altogether—but seeing her again was like opening a time capsule. I hadn't forgotten anything: how often our stomachs hurt from laughing, her knack for getting in trouble, the way a single glance between us was like a whole language, that feeling that bloomed in my chest when we promised each other, *No secrets.*

I shrugged. "I haven't seen her in forever."

"Like how long?"

Two years, nine months. "I'm not sure. A few years? What's her deal, anyway?"

Evangeline sat back in her chair, a snakelike smile on her face. She nudged Lucy with her elbow. "Luce, Kat wants to know what Taylor's deal is."

Lucy blinked as her eyes adjusted to looking at something more than ten inches from her face. "Taylor's just got a bad energy. Last year, she literally quit Climate Activism Now! because she thought we weren't getting anything done. Like, no shit, we're not solving climate change, we're in high school? But she made a big thing about it, then everyone else felt bad for not quitting, *and then* a bunch of people really did quit because they hated the drama and that's Taylor for you."

"No fun," Evangeline said. "The total opposite of fun."

Lucy was looking at her phone again. "Thinking you're better than everyone else isn't a substitute for a personality." They both laughed.

It was craven, but I laughed too.

THAT NIGHT, AS I was leaving Hunter House for Seated Dinner, wearing a dress fit for an actor at a boardwalk haunted house,

Ms. Radtke stopped me at the door. "Kat, I have not received your application for the mentorship with Mr. Castel. Remember, it's due tonight."

"Right, that. I actually wasn't planning to apply."

"Why is that?"

"I just thought . . ." My fingers knotted together. Ms. Radtke had to know that applying was a waste of time, that the whole thing was a setup for Galen. I already had more homework than I could handle, all those clubs, and what Taylor had called Operation Suck-up. It didn't make sense to write an application essay for a mentorship I'd never win.

"I cannot bear the suspense," Ms. Radtke said. "What did you think?"

"Another kid is better for it."

Ms. Radtke's granite gaze was focused on me in a singular and entirely unpleasant way. "I did not realize you sat on the selection committee with me."

"I . . . I don't."

"And yet you presume to tell me that you're not a qualified candidate. That another *kid*"—from Ms. Radtke's mouth, the word sounded more likely to refer to a baby goat than a teenager—"would be a superior choice. Please let me know who we should select and you'll save us a great deal of time."

"That's not what I meant. You can pick anyone you want."

"Precisely. Very generous of you. This is an excellent opportunity, and you are an excellent candidate. You have a unique perspective that the other students here do not." Ms. Radtke straightened, her long strands of pearls clattering against each other. "Remember, Kat, a closed mouth won't be fed."

I caught up with the girls for the walk over to the Dining Hall. They were talking about a movie night they had planned for later in the common room, but I was barely paying attention. At dinner, I ignored Galen, who was dressed entirely in black again and brooding in my general direction, like he'd just wandered in off some windswept moor. I didn't have time for entitled glowering tonight. I needed to think.

Ms. Radtke was right: the feeling that I wasn't good enough to win the mentorship wasn't a reason not to apply. It might be a long shot, but I hadn't let that stop me in the past. After all, I had managed to get into Harcote, with full funding, against the odds.

I *did* want it. I wanted my name to be called. I wanted to shake the hand of *Victor Castel*. Being picked for the mentorship would prove that I really belonged, not as a charity case, but because I was the Best of the Best like them.

I tilted my bowl and watched the last bead of Hema draw a crimson line across the china.

It would prove it to my mom too.

I looked around me. At every table, students were slouched in their chairs, stressed or bored or being lured into awkward conversation with their faculty member. An outsider couldn't tell, just by looking, that I was different; that some of their last names were known worldwide, while mine meant nothing; that their fangmakers were celebrated while mine were mysteries. I might not have what they had and maybe I never would, but I was still here. The Best of the Best. I didn't need anyone else's permission to act like it.

The idea flickered in my chest. *That* was what Harcote meant to me: this place could make us equals, if I let it.

I checked the time. I could give the girls an excuse and sneak off to one of the Old Hill study rooms right when dinner ended. If I worked fast, I could make the deadline.

TAYLOR

It was Friday night and I was sitting in a dark classroom in Old Hill with my chem teacher. Kontos was a lot cooler than anyone else on campus, and besides, it wasn't my fault no one wanted to join French Cinema Club. Actually, so few people had wanted to join that technically it wasn't a club, just me and Kontos. Which meant that when I lost interest in French cinema and we started watching *Killing Eve* instead (it partly took place in France so it technically counted), there was no one to object.

Even if it was a little weird to spend Friday night with my science teacher, what else was I supposed to do? Chill at Evangeline and Lucy's Hunter House movie night? No fucking thanks. The mere idea of being in the same room as Kat, under Evangeline's gaze, struck real terror into my heart. Since yesterday, I'd cursed myself ten thousand times for mentioning Kat, and then ten thousand times more for letting Evangeline get a glimpse of my true feelings. I wasn't afraid Evangeline would tell Kat—although that would suck incredibly, and I definitely didn't want it to happen. It was that Evangeline didn't actually have to tell anyone to make me feel bad. All she had have to do was shoot me one of those looks when Kat was nearby, and the message would be clear: *I know your secret.*

It was incredibly unfair that liking girls made them torture to be around.

I cracked my neck. On the screen Villanelle was murdering someone with extraordinary flair, but somehow I'd missed who it was. Stupid Evangeline, stupid Kat, distracting me from one of my favorite shows, and they weren't even in the room.

I'd teased Kat about Operation Suck-up, but really, I hated that she hung around with Evangeline—and not because I was jealous. Kat didn't know how to handle Evangeline's twisted mind. Evangeline was the kind of person who could make you lose yourself before you even noticed your grip was slipping. Kat already spent every minute of the day here trying her hardest. She might be good at hiding it from everyone else, but not from me. I knew the pressure of trying constantly and in a million microscopic ways to be someone other than yourself. It could splinter you, if you let it, and it was exactly the kind of thing Evangeline would try to exploit.

I didn't want Kat to get hurt.

"What did you think?"

I snapped out of my reverie. Kontos was turning the lights back on.

"Oh, um—great! Great episode." I rubbed my eyes.

"Great episode?" Kontos said. "That's all you've got? You usually pick these episodes apart."

I scratched an eyebrow. "Did you not think it was great?"

"I did. A great episode." Kontos drummed his fingers against the desk. "You want to talk about the show or do you want to tell me what's bothering you?"

"That depends." I tilted my chair back onto two legs. Me and Kontos were close and he was my only gay friend, but he was still my science teacher, a dude, and like seventy-five years older than me. He knew only the G-rated version of the situation with Evangeline, and I wasn't about to run my mouth about my feelings for Kat. "Are you going to sit backward on a chair, so I know you're a Cool Teacher?"

"I'm a Cool Teacher no matter how I'm sitting," Kontos

protested. "I heard about what happened in Ms. Radtke's class this week."

I rolled my eyes. "I know dick-vein wasn't my best work insult-wise. It was just something new I was trying out." Kontos wasn't amused. "Radtke already gave me the respect talk, so if that's what this is, I'm gonna head—"

Kontos held out a hand. "It's not."

I slouched back in my seat, shaking my head. "I should've known Radtke would rat me out to you."

Kontos *tsk*ed. "She mentioned it because she knows you and I are close. She's really not that bad."

"That means nothing coming from you. You like *everybody*."

He pressed a hand to his chest. "Stake me in the heart, Taylor! You really are losing your edge if you think that's an insult. I could say the same thing about you."

"That if I hate everybody it doesn't mean anything either? There's where you're wrong. There's people I dislike, people I hate, and people I *loathe*, and I *loathe* Radtke. She probably believes women shouldn't be allowed to ride bicycles or wear pants." Anger was simmering inside me now. Better to be angry than to feel anything else. "She punished Kat for talking back to Evangeline because *the ladies of Hunter House can't run wild*. But what happened to Evangeline? Fucking nothing."

"Evangeline was disrespectful to you too."

Figuring out why I wasn't half as mad at Evangeline as I should have been was more than my brain could handle. It was definitely more than I wanted to explain to Kontos. I shrugged. "So she called me a lesbian, what'll she do next—call me an undead bloodsucker?"

Again, Kontos didn't laugh. "You don't have to joke about it."

"Don't tell me what to do," I said with a sudden fierceness. My breath was coiled tight in my chest, my heart beating quick. I hadn't meant to say that, not at all. I'd meant to make another joke, prove again that Evangeline couldn't hurt me—no one could. "Don't tell me how to feel. If I say it's no big deal then it's no big deal."

"I'm sorry, Taylor." He said it gently, like I was some fragile creature, and it absolutely made me want to die. "I want you to know that she was wrong to speak to you like that and she's been talked to. She'll be writing you an apology."

I couldn't wait to put that note directly in the trash. I stood. "And you're here to talk if I need to. Is that it? It's almost curfew."

"That's not it, no. Sit." He gestured toward my empty chair.

I didn't like the tone this was taking, but I sat.

"I heard in Ms. Radtke's class, you said that if there was a cure for CFaD, you'd keep drinking Hema—you wouldn't feed on humans."

"Something like that. She wanted to have a discussion about whether vampires could live with humans."

"The loudest voices in Vampirdom want us to feel different from humans, but we're the same in so many ways. Personally, I wish we were working toward more openness, a shared community."

"Radtke would probably get you fired if she heard you talking like that. It's Vampirdom 101: doesn't matter what you eat, what matters is that we're better than humans. The Best of the Best, right?"

"Forget about Ms. Radtke for a moment. What do *you* believe?"

I didn't follow much of Vampirdom politics—I got my fill of hypocrisy at Harcote—but I'd definitely thought about the idea of integration with humans. I remembered Kat asking my pronouns and how I'd barely been able to answer. It had been exciting and surprising at the time, but the more I thought about it, the more it just made me sad. Hell, there were more than a few vampires who were still using the word *gay* to describe a pleasant afternoon in a park. If vampires wanted progress—which I definitely did—humans were our best hope.

"I think if vampires could be closer to humans it would be good. But I don't see how that could happen."

"Why not?" Kontos leaned forward, his elbows on his knees. "If you think about it, now that we have blood substitute and don't need to hunt, what's really stopping us?"

"You sound like a reunionist."

Kontos spread his hands and grinned. "Well, if the shoe fits!"

My mouth fell open. "If the shoe fits *what*?"

"I'm a reunionist," he said. I'd never heard anyone call themselves a reunionist before. It was understood—at Harcote, at home, in vampire society—that reunionism was talked about the way one talked about stepping in dog shit. Hated by all, kind of disgusting, almost embarrassing. "I believe vampires can live in harmony with humans, with a cure for CFaD and free access to Hema. It seems like you believe in some of those things too."

I didn't know what to say. I *did* believe those things, but when he strung them together like that, it added up to a conclusion—reunionism—that didn't sound like me. At least, I'd never thought it had. All of a sudden, I had hesitated a beat too long and Kontos looked at his watch. Just like that, everything felt normal again. "Shoot, it's nearly curfew," he said.

I stood and fixed the collar of my jean jacket. "Great. Don't want Radtke on my ass again."

Kontos grimaced. "Can you try, for my sake, to watch your language?"

I looked out into the dark hallway. "Sorry, bud, but I don't fucking think so."

THE HALLS OF Old Hill were dark. I checked my phone and cursed under my breath. Kontos's watch must have been slow. It was already five minutes past curfew, and the building was technically closed. I considered going back to ask him to walk me back to Hunter, as an on-hand excuse for being out late, but I couldn't let the whole residential quad see our science teacher escort me home on Friday night.

I took the East Stairs down then headed toward the Headmaster's Office. Whoever designed Old Hill, long before Atherton bought the school, had wanted to make sure no one would get lost on the way to the Headmaster's Office. The East and West Stairs converged on the first floor into a single wide stairway that connected the Headmaster's Office to the building's entry. Basically, anyone coming in or out was funneled past Atherton's office. Some mornings he stood there, flanked by human aides, so he could smile upon our sleep deprivation. He'd also let whoever did Harcote's interior design go wild on vampiric symbology down here. The lower floors of Old Hill were chock full of dark wood carvings that riffed on the bat-and-castle theme, columns and railings carved with creepy little gargoyles, and alcoves that displayed school memorabilia and pre-Peril antiquities, like the fancy chalices that were basically giant sippy cups for the bloody life force that sustained us.

I was about to hit that last set of stairs when I spotted a sliver of
yellow light on the parquet floor outside the Headmaster's Office.
It widened as the door opened. I didn't wait to hear voices before
stepping into the shadows of one of the alcoves. It was a good
thing I did, too, because once I got to listening, I recognized that
voice: Radtke.

10

KAT

WHEN I FINISHED my essay, I spent a long moment staring at the email. Galen might have been the designated winner, but the essay I'd written was *good*. Everyone at Harcote claimed we were here on merit, because we were the Best of the Best. I was going to give them a chance to prove it. I hit send.

Then I checked my phone and my stomach leaped to my throat. Curfew had completely slipped my mind. I needed to get back to Hunter House fast. I couldn't get in trouble twice in a week, inside my first month at the school. Radtke wouldn't be so forgiving a second time. I shoved my stuff into my backpack and hurried out of the study room.

I looked down the unfamiliar, dark halls—and nearly jumped out of my skin as a human aide pushed a custodial cart into view. I didn't know if the aides reported things like students out past curfew, but even if they didn't, their glamoured, vacant stares freaked me out. I didn't want to be caught by one of them at night. I took the East Stairs two at a time and shoved open the first-floor door.

The light coming from the Headmaster's Office was unmissable. The door was open, casting the shadows of two bodies into the hall.

I was completely, utterly screwed.

I needed to hide or get away or make any kind of attempt at self-preservation, but how? My legs had turned to jelly.

The door to the East Stairs whined as it swung closed behind me. The voices shifted in tone—*What was that?*—the shadows moving, and all I could think was that Harcote had been nice, for as long as I'd had it.

Someone—something?—grabbed me from behind. My eyes bulged and I nearly screamed, but a hand pressed tight over my lips. On instinct, my fangs slid free and sank into the flesh clamped over my mouth. Another sharp burst of panic: had I just bitten a human aide—a CFaD carrier? I strained against whoever was holding me, but their grip was solid and they were pulling me into the dark space between the wall and a case of Harcote memorabilia. My back was pressed to them, but I could swear the person smelled strangely familiar, a scent I could nearly place.

Like new sneakers.

"Stop thrashing around and *be quiet*," Taylor breathed into my ear.

I went still. Taylor released her grip on my mouth, and I wedged myself around to face her, ready to demand what the hell she was thinking—when the snap of heels on the hardwood floor sent another jolt of fear through me, and instead I found myself pressing up even closer against her. My arm braced against the wall, and Taylor's encircled me: the two of us hiding in a shadow only big enough for one.

It had been ages since I'd touched her.

From Headmaster Atherton's office, a voice was saying, "This has gone too far . . . Vampirdom is better than this."

"Ms. Radtke?" I whispered. My eyelashes brushed against

Taylor's jaw, that's how close we were. I felt it as much as saw it when Taylor nodded, her face tense as she strained to hear more.

". . . I won't stand for it any longer and I'm not alone . . ." Ms. Radtke's voice faded.

"You can't make demands like this, Miriam!" Headmaster Atherton's voice quavered like pouty child throwing a tantrum. I wondered again how old he'd been when he was turned.

"What he's doing threatens all of us . . ."

Suddenly, I was scared—a rounder and fuller fear than the anxiety of breaking curfew. We were eavesdropping on a conversation we were definitely not meant to hear. My breathing was so shallow, my chest barely rose and fell at all. I crowded myself closer to Taylor. She was hardly breathing either.

A brief pause, then Atherton released an incredulous laugh. "Leo Kontos is not a threat."

At his name, Taylor's body went rigid against mine.

The sound of heels on hardwood again, and now Ms. Radtke's voice was clear. "If he refuses, we will take drastic action. That's the final word."

The door to Atherton's office slammed. Radtke's shoes struck the steps, and the door to Old Hill whooshed open, then closed again.

We both let out a breath. I sagged against Taylor's shoulder as the adrenaline ebbed. She laid her cheek against my forehead, her arms still across my back—

Suddenly, my body flushed with heat. What was I *doing*?

Taylor must have had the same thought, because all at once she was shoving me off her and we were wriggling out of the alcove, putting space between ourselves. Taylor waved me after her, and she led us out of Old Hill and into the darkness around the side of the building.

"You fucking *bit me*?" Taylor's voice was a harsh whisper. She held out her palm in the dim light. The strip of flesh between her thumb and first finger bore two red-smeared punctures.

"*That's* what you have to say?" I wiped my mouth: Taylor's blood was on my lips. "What were you even doing here?"

"Saving your ass, for one. What were *you* doing here? I thought you were at movie night."

"I was finishing my essay for the mentorship application, in one of the study rooms."

"You've got to be the first Harcote student in history to miss curfew to do *homework*."

"If I'd written it in the room, you'd've been bothering me the whole time!"

"You could have asked me to leave you alone. You've done it before."

I flinched. Of course, I knew what she was talking about: the last message I'd sent her after she blew up my life. Two weeks living together, and this was the first time she'd mentioned what happened. I wasn't holding my breath for an apology, but I certainly hadn't been expecting her to *guilt trip* me.

"We have to get back before Radtke does check-in," I said. "Let's go."

WE HURRIED DOWN-CAMPUS. Ahead of us, Ms. Radtke's rustling skirts against the brick path made it easy to keep an eye on her. Once I stumbled in the dark and Radtke's head whipped around, looking right in our direction, but we managed to duck behind a tree just in time.

Finally, I followed Taylor around to the back of Hunter House. Our fourth-floor room was impossibly far away.

"The window's unlocked," Taylor whispered.

"And how exactly do you think we're going to get up there?" It came out harsher than I'd meant. Even if I resented Taylor in general, this exact situation wasn't her fault. Actually, I was more than a little lucky that she was there. I swallowed hard, remembering how she had pulled me into the shadows, saving me, and here I was making her feel bad for it. "I'm sorry, I just can't get in trouble again."

"Same, I hate trouble," Taylor said, and I couldn't help it—I smiled. Taylor pointed at a gutter that ran from the roofline down, affixed to the brick. "We're climbing that."

"We're vampires, not spider-men."

"Do you have a better idea?"

I frowned at the pipe. It didn't look like it would hold the weight of a squirrel.

"Come on, *Kath-er-ine*." Taylor drew out my name, slowly. "I dare you."

When Taylor smiled, it came out crooked, one side higher than the other, and the cool blue moonlight seemed to snag on the white of her teeth. Her eyes met mine and they were bright against the dark fan of her lashes—somehow too alive for the night. She looked, all at once, like the girl I used to know, who'd felt like I'd found a missing piece of myself.

My heartbeat quickened.

I grabbed the gutter and began to climb.

11

TAYLOR

I WOKE UP on Saturday to Kat combing out her hair after a shower, and thoughts of last night flooded my mind—the way she had pressed against me, my cheek against her hair. Most of all, the way she looked at me when I dared her to climb the gutter. It was like I could feel it physically between us in that moment—the connection we had.

Used to have.

I'd barely swung my legs out of bed when she said, "So have you decided what you're going to do? Because I know you're going to do something about the Mr. Kontos thing, and I just hope it's not something stupid."

"Wow, I'm feeling really judged right now."

Kat paused combing out her hair and glared at me over her shoulder, which absolutely did not give me heart palpitations. "So you're going to do nothing?"

"Jesus, who do you think I am? We can't let Radtke go after Kontos!"

She looked back to the mirror. "I'm not even convinced that's really what's happening. Ms. Radtke was talking about someone who's a big threat and Mr. Kontos is—he's just so *nice*."

I chewed my lip. A day ago, I would have agreed with Kat, but that was before Kontos had confided in me that he was a reunion-ist. I wasn't about to share that with Kat, but if Radtke knew, it would explain a lot. "Radtke's a trav. They still feel threatened by the invention of electric light. Kontos . . . isn't a trav," I said. "Maybe it's about that."

"What do the travs even want? I thought it was just a really ter-rible fashion sense."

"They're vampire supremacists," I told her. "Not that that's so unusual in Vampirdom, but travs are especially jazzed on it. They think that since CFaD made it impossible to feed on humans, vampire culture is being lost. Youngbloods need to know that there was a *before* time, when dressing up in bat cosplay was not an immediate dealbreaker and vampires were fell creatures of the night who slept in mildewy coffins." Since Kat hadn't had the plea-sure of two years of vampiric education, I added, "The stupidest part is, that's basically a fantasy pieced together out of Bela Lugosi movies and Anne Rice novels. As far as I know, before the Peril, there *was* no vampire culture. Vampirdom didn't even exist. A solo vampire could go decades without even running into a fellow bloodsucker, so it was literally impossible for stupid aesthetic trends to emerge."

Kat's brow was furrowed. "I've never heard that before—the Peril brought vampires together?"

"The vampires it didn't kill, yeah. If you survived, it was because you had regular access to Hema. That meant, for the first time, vampires started clustering together, talking to each other. That's the recipe for Vampirdom. The travs popped up as a nostalgic thing."

"So that's why Ms. Radtke teaches Vampiric Ethics, to make sure the Youngbloods stay vampirey," Kat said. "Not that that has anything to do with Mr. Kontos. He's just a chemistry teacher. He's not exactly corrupting the youth."

"Right." Of course, the conversation we'd had last night sounded a little like he was trying to recruit me into a reunionist cult, but we'd been close friends for nearly two years before he mentioned it. He was nowhere near launching an on-campus insurrection.

"Whatever's going on, it's definitely none of our business," Kat said. "So when you get involved in it, leave my name out of it, okay?"

"'Course. Most of the time I barely remember you."

It was Tuesday afternoon before I finally managed to corner Kontos in his office attached to the chem lab. It was probably the least-nice office Harcote had to offer. The desk was piled sky-high with papers and beakers full of the clicky pens he loved. He had an oversized bookcase that stuck out from the wall, making the room feel even more cramped. On the windowsill, a family of potted cacti eked out a meager existence.

He grinned at me under that bushy mustache. "Taylor, greetings!"

I didn't sit down. A stack of books was already sitting in the sole chair. "I need to talk to you. You're in trouble."

I told him everything, leaving Kat out of it: that I'd overheard Radtke trying to convince Atherton that Kontos was some kind of a threat. As I spoke, Kontos was bouncing his thumb off his chin, like he was *bemused* that one of his colleagues was trying to destroy his life. "Atherton was real angry at her, but it didn't sound like she was going to take no for an answer," I finished.

He blew out a sigh. "Thank you for sharing this with me, Taylor, but there's nothing to worry about. Miriam Radtke and I are on great terms. If she has something to discuss with me, she'll bring that to my attention."

"*Drastic action*, Kontos! Those were her exact words."

"I'll keep an eye out for anything drastic, then. Seriously, you've got nothing to worry about."

I scowled at him, and continued scowling as I headed to my next period. I felt zero percent better about the situation. Kontos might have been sure it was a harmless misunderstanding, but he was too trusting—too *good*—to believe otherwise. I wasn't about to let him go down like that, especially not at Radtke's hands.

Something was going on, and I was going to find out what.

KAT

THE TINNY, SWEET scent of Hema filled the room at Tuesday's Seated Dinner. It still set off a particular, frenzied feeling inside me, but the spike of desperation was gone. I was slowly getting used to the fact that there would always be enough Hema—as much as I wanted, whenever I wanted it.

The firstie sitting next to me caught a fang on his spoon and sent a streak of red down his shirt. I gave him a reassuring smile. "It took me a while to get used to Hema too, but eventually you don't even miss human food."

He shot me a sour look. "I've been drinking Hema since I was a *baby*. Human food's disgusting."

Galen observed this scene from across the table. He was wearing another black-on-black outfit that should have made him look like a waiter, but instead made him look like he'd spent the afternoon drinking espresso and reading poetry in a Parisian café.

"It's not my fault no one ever gave that child a Cool Ranch Dorito," I said.

An elegant divot appeared between Galen's brows. "A Cool Ranch what?"

Headmaster Atherton brought the room to order for announcements. Every time he did this, the sheer emotional impact of a roomful of Youngbloods threatened to overwhelm him, but today his cheeks were ruddier than usual. "I have some very exciting news to share with you this evening, boys and girls," he said. "I know you are all eager to hear who has been selected for the mentorship with Mr. Victor Castel. It really says something about this school that so many of you applied—that get-after-it-ness is one of the vampiric virtues that distinguishes our Harcote students!"

As Headmaster Atherton carried on, Galen was twisted elegantly in his seat to face the front of the room, his arm slung over the back of his chair. He kept his expression politely blank, almost bored. I wondered if he'd ever in his life wanted anything he wasn't sure he could have. Was he even aware that every student and teacher in the Dining Hall was pretending to believe a lie, just for him?

"I am pleased to announce that the recipient of the mentorship is . . ."

Headmaster Atherton paused for dramatic effect, which no one appreciated.

In that brief moment, Galen raised knuckle to his lips and pressed his teeth against it. It was a subtle thing that would have come off as casual, if I hadn't seen the tension in his hands, or how a small muscle flickered in his jaw.

He *did* care about this, even though it was a sure thing that he'd get it.

"Galen Black!" Headmaster Atherton announced.

Galen dropped his hand instantly, a confident smile spreading across his face, that damn eyebrow fishhooked into an arch again. Polite applause filled the room, almost loud enough to drown out the disappointed groans. Galen half stood and gave an easy little bow—like he'd had enough occasions to bow in his life that he could calibrate it exactly to let people know he appreciated their support, without making too big a thing of it.

I clapped along with them, pretending that disappointment wasn't flowering in my chest. *A closed mouth won't be fed*, Ms. Radtke had said. But you could open your mouth and still go hungry. People like me were supposed to be happy to have the chance to be considered. Actually winning it was left to the Galens of the world.

"That's not all!" Atherton continued. "The applications were *exceedingly* strong, so strong, in fact, that Mr. Castel has agreed to mentor *two students*. I have a second name to announce!"

All at once, my disappointment vanished and butterflies swarmed my stomach—no, butterflies were for good things, and this was going to be a bad thing. Thrashing squids of dread swarmed my stomach.

"And that second student is . . ."

The squids thrashed.

"Oh, what a lovely surprise. Our new third-year, Katherine Finn!"

The squids vanished. It was quiet for what felt like an eternal second. I was frozen in my seat, my mouth hanging open.

But then Mr. Kontos was squeezing my shoulder and the rest of the table was telling me to stand up. I knocked my chair back into the table behind me as I got to my feet.

The first face I saw was Taylor's. She stared right at me when the rest of the Dining Hall was still wondering where this new girl was seated. She wasn't smiling. Instead, there was a strange, bitter expression on her face, almost like disappointment. I knew Taylor was one of the few students who hadn't applied to the mentorship—she'd called it a circle jerk and said her time would be better spent napping than hanging out with a five-hundred-year-old sleazebag in a suit. Maybe Taylor went about her life trying to prove she was better than everyone else, but I was here to prove something else: that I was just as good as the rest of them, not better or worse. I was one of them. The same.

A closed mouth won't be fed.

I raised my chin at her.

"Can you believe this?" Kontos was saying as I took my seat again. "When they said the Best of the Best, they must have been talking about Seated Dinner table twelve! Cheers to Galen and Kat!"

12

KAT

I WAS BUZZING with excitement when dinner ended. Galen and I were personally congratulated by Headmaster Atherton, who'd informed us that our first meeting with Mr. Castel would be the next day. I hadn't even minded walking back down-campus with Galen, who'd kept mostly quiet while I babbled about the mentorship. For all the (completely unnecessary and show-offy) defending that Galen did of Victor Castel, he hadn't seemed even a little pleased, not since Headmaster Atherton had called his name. But then again, all of this was inevitable for him. For me, it was a dream come true.

Back at Hunter, the girls were sprawled out on the downstairs couches.

Lucy raised her doe eyes from her phone. "How does it feel to be the Chosen One, Kitty Kat?"

"Sorry you guys didn't get picked." I wasn't really, but it felt like the right thing to say. "I know everyone wanted it."

Evangeline snorted. "Like *I* need help from Victor Castel? Everybody's been talking about it and we think we know why they chose you."

"It was a contest," I said warily. "I wrote a good essay."

Lucy went back to tapping something into her phone. "We just want you to know what people are saying."

"Right . . . I appreciate that," I managed. "So why did I win?"

Evangeline's clear blue eyes locked onto mine. Her face was expressionless. "Because you're a nobody. We looked you up in the directory, and none of us have heard of your mom. Your dad's not even *listed*."

"My parents aren't together." It was technically true, just not very accurate. I didn't owe Evangeline and Lucy the story of my dad's death. "I don't see why that matters."

"It matters, because your parents don't have any connections. Maybe your fangmakers pulled some strings, but we don't even know who they are," Evangeline said.

"It's honestly kind of weird," Lucy added.

I felt myself go very still.

Lucy raised her eyebrows. "Now's the part where you tell us who your fangmakers are, Kitty Kat."

She was right. I'd hidden from it long enough, and they wouldn't stop wondering until they knew. At least if I told them outright—by which I meant *lied* outright—I could control, just a little, what they were saying behind my back.

"Um, actually, neither of them survived the Peril. They both died before I was born. But you're right, I guess, that they weren't anyone super important. I mean, my fangmakers were never the consort to a Chinese emperor or an advisor to Vlad the Impaler or anything like yours were. They were nobodies like me."

"Wow, that's even better than we thought," Evangeline said, her lip curling. "You *really* make it all look equal opportunity."

My cheeks burned. Evangeline was right, of course. The optics were perfect: the golden boy and the girl from nowhere. Galen would look so good standing beside me.

"Nothing's ever really fair, right?" I said.

"That is so true," Evangeline said with a commiserating smile.

I did not scream at her. I did not cry. I gathered the storm of my feelings into a fist and kept it closed tight as I left the common room. I did not give them the satisfaction of watching me rush up the stairs. But to do it, I had to hold my breath until the door to my room was closed behind me and I was slumped against it, on the floor.

Hot tears of frustration streamed down my cheeks. It shouldn't have hurt as much as it did. After all, I wasn't under the impression that Lucy and Evangeline were *nice*. It was just that I'd been playing my part here the best I could. I'd convinced myself that at least sometimes, that had been enough to allow the girls to forget that I didn't come from the same world they did. But the second I won something they all wanted, they didn't waste time reminding me what I did and didn't deserve.

Even worse was that they'd jabbed me exactly where it hurt most: the vampiric pedigree I didn't have, the personal history I didn't know. The fact that my mom's fangmaker wasn't a good person—he'd tried to leave her for dead, but accidentally turned her instead—didn't stop me from wondering who he really was. What if he was actually on the level of the other Harcoties' fangmakers? How would my life be different if he'd stuck around and been a true fangmaker to my mom and to me? The weird part was that since I *did* know who my dad's fangmaker was, I didn't have to imagine anything about her, and that made it easier to accept that she wasn't around. But when I thought about my mom's fangmaker, it felt like a half-finished sentence. Part of who I was as a person—as a vampire—was missing.

On top of that, what truth I did know about him I had to keep a secret. Vampire custom, especially since the Peril, placed a lot of value in knowing your pedigree. Your fangmaker was the one who guided you through life as a new vampire, who taught you how to hunt or how to cope with leaving your human life behind. Of course, since the Peril and the Youngblood generation, vampires didn't need to be taught those things, but that didn't matter. It was a tradition, and the fact that it was irrelevant only made some vampires cling to it more tightly.

Vampires like the Sangers.

Taylor and I had always promised each other *no secrets*. It should have been an easy promise for a ten-year-old to make, but from the first moment we linked our pinkies together and kissed our thumbs, I knew I couldn't keep it. I had made another, far more serious promise to my mom: that I would never tell the truth about her fangmaker. It wasn't anyone's business, she said, and that made it a white lie.

But the older I got, the more it felt like dishonesty. My mom had woven a whole story about her fangmaker, but every time I repeated it, I was lying about *myself* too. I'd lost count how many times I'd repeated those lies to Taylor.

I told Taylor the truth around the time she was applying to Harcote—the winter we were both thirteen. We were in her room, allegedly doing homework, but really just talking. I remember we were lying on her bed, she had her head on my stomach, and we'd been laughing about something I can't remember now. She turned on her side to look at me.

"I can't believe they're making me go to that stupid school without you."

"Me either." I twined one of her curls around my finger. "But I'll be here when you come home for break."

She grinned at me, a little lopsided. "Maybe I'll sabotage the application. You know I have to write an essay about an important lesson passed down from one of my fangmakers. Maybe I'll just tell them I don't have any."

My hand stilled in her hair.

She sat up. She knew something was wrong. "No secrets," she whispered.

Still, I didn't *have* to tell her the truth. I wanted to. I was so close to her. I knew in my bones I could trust her. I wanted to confide in my best friend that I didn't really know who I was.

I've tried to forgive myself for those mistakes.

I haven't forgiven Taylor. She didn't waste any time telling her parents. And they didn't waste any time getting us out of their lives.

Suddenly I missed my mom so much it was hard to breathe. Our life in Sacramento might have made me feel trapped sometimes, but it still made sense in a way that Harcote and the vampires here never would. Since I'd arrived at Harcote, I'd only texted her enough to provide proof of life.

I had my phone in my hand. I could call and tell her the good news about the mentorship. She'd be happy, wouldn't she?

But what if she wasn't?

I pressed my elbow over my face and squeezed my eyes shut tight to seal in the tears. I really, really didn't want to cry. I wanted to go downstairs and have my new friends tell me I deserved this, to stand beside Galen Black and not feel like an idiot baby. And I hated my mom just then, because I could have pretended my way through all of that, if she could only have managed to be proud of me.

Just then—*of freaking course*—Taylor was trudging up the stairs. I could not let her find me on the edge of losing it entirely. I jumped up and managed to make like I was doing something at my desk before she flung open the door.

For some horrible reason she was *singing*. *"She is beauty, she is grace, she is corporate Vampirdom's teenage face."*

I didn't look at her. "Can you not be a dick to me right now?" My voice was thick, but at least it wasn't trembling.

"Such a gracious winner." She shucked off the blazer she'd been wearing for dinner. "I thought you'd be happy."

"I am—" My voice broke.

Shit.

I hid my face in my hands, tears catching in the creases of my palms.

"Oh, no, hey—what's wrong?" Taylor's voice was soothing. Her hand was on my shoulder, squeezing with a reassuring pressure, and that only made me cry harder, because how could *Taylor Sanger* be the one comforting me right now? I couldn't possibly tell her what was wrong—but what did it matter, if she was pretending to care about me when I needed someone to do it? "Were the girls mean to you? Because they're awful when they're jealous. It means they like you."

My hands covered my face—somehow it still felt important that she didn't see me cry. But I turned toward her, and she put her other hand on my arm, her thumbs rubbing circles on my shoulders a comforting rhythm. "Everything here is so . . ." I began, but I couldn't say more, because of the crying. I sniffed dramatically to prevent a river of snot from running down my face.

"I know," she said softly. "It sucks here sometimes, doesn't it?"

I drew in a raggedy breath. "It does."

Gently, Taylor eased my hands away from my face. I let her. She peered at me, her eyebrows pinched together and her lower lip jutting out.

"Hi," she said.

"Hi," I said, almost in a whisper.

"Can I give you a hug?"

I sniffed and nodded, and then Taylor's arms were circling me, strong and sure, and mine slid around her. Somehow, even though I was still crying—even though I hadn't even told Taylor what was wrong—I felt more solid, more like myself.

When Taylor pulled back, I almost didn't want her to. But I stepped away too. "Thanks. I'm sorry, I just—"

"Are you seriously apologizing for crying?" Just like that, that softness vanished. Taylor was already across the room, setting the sneakers she'd been wearing in their designated spot in the closet. It was the only part of her side of the room she kept anywhere near organized. "What's next, you're sorry that your fangs are too pointy?"

"They *are* too pointy. I could kill someone with these things." Taylor laughed, but there was something jittery in it. The room felt off-balance, full of an unresolved energy.

"Who's the note from?" Taylor cocked her head toward my bed.

There was a cream-colored envelope sitting on my pillow. I hadn't noticed it before. My name was lettered on the front. I ripped it open.

Dear Kat—I had not planned to reach out to you directly, however I am gratified that you have excelled during your first weeks at Harcote. My investment in you was not misplaced. Congratulations on winning the mentorship with Mr. Victor Castel. Use this opportunity to challenge yourself.

The note wasn't signed or on letterhead of any kind, but I knew who it was from: the Benefactor. He must have known about my selection before it was announced. Of course he did—he was obviously some kind of friend of the school, maybe a friend of Headmaster Atherton's. If my mom didn't understand what I was doing here, at least the Benefactor did.

"Who's it from?" Taylor asked again.

I shoved the note into my desk drawer. I'd learned that lesson already: Taylor didn't need to know about things that were none of her business.

"Congratulations from the admissions office." I changed the subject. "Are you done studying for precalc?"

Taylor sank down onto her bed. "I'm just gonna wing it. I suck at math."

"As a woman, you're not allowed to say you suck at math. They actually made it illegal, because it's internalized sexism. Are you internally sexist?"

"No . . . or I hope not," Taylor said.

I dug through my backpack. It wasn't exactly that I *owed her* for that hug; I just wanted to do something nice in return. "And you almost certainly *do not* suck at math, because I never see you stressing or studying, yet you haven't failed out. I can only conclude you're a genius with a terrible attitude."

Taylor scratched her ear. "I thought everyone loved my attitude?"

I held out a notebook to her. "Look at my study guide and then we can go over anything you don't understand. Okay?"

Taylor took it. "Okay."

TAYLOR

WHAT WAS I supposed to do—just stand there and let her cry?

13

KAT

THE NEXT DAY, after classes ended, there was a helicopter on the lacrosse field.

An actual *helicopter*.

And it was waiting for me. Well, me and Galen. The pilot fastened our seat belts and handed us headsets, and then we were heading up, up, up. My face was glued to the window. As the buildings and trees of campus grew small below us, the other students turned toward the noise, their hair blown back, their eyes following us as we rose.

"Can you believe this?" I said to Galen. Through the headset, I sounded a little breathless. He glanced at me, as composed as ever. Had Galen ever been excited by *anything*? "Of course you can. You probably fly around in helicopters all the time."

"Yes, you could say I've been summoned before." His eyes were fixed on the window again. I didn't know what that meant—we hadn't been *summoned*, Victor Castel wanted to meet with us— but Galen didn't elaborate. Soon, we touched down on an estate, the wind from the helicopter flattening the wide green lawn and thrashing the nearby bushes.

Some kind of vampire butler led us past a tennis court, what looked like a hedge maze, and a huge pool fed by a fancy fountain, to a house so enormous that calling it a house wasn't fair. We went down one the marble-tiled hallway after another. I'd already lost track of how we'd traveled and how many rooms we'd passed when we took an elevator to the second floor—what kind of a house had an *elevator*?—and were shown into a library. Galen, more withdrawn than ever, didn't sit, so I didn't either.

Bookcases ran to the ceiling, filled with books that looked legitimately ancient. On one wall hung a painting that looked like it belonged in an art history textbook. I looked closer—maybe it was *already in* an art history textbook.

It was one thing to know I was poor and the other students at Harcote were rich. It came across in everything they did, not just the way the mailroom was always overflowing with things they'd ordered online or how they'd replace a phone the instant the screen cracked. It was a confidence they took for granted, a sureness they'd been born with and never even had to think about. I'd thought I understood where they came from, because of the years I'd spent with the Sangers, but Victor Castel's wealth was on a scale that made the Sangers look humble. That Galen could see all this and be unmoved, think it was *normal*, made it clear that there was a whole world of wealth that I knew nothing about. And for some reason, this felt like another test I'd failed.

Then the door opened, and Victor Castel walked in.

At first glance, he wasn't remarkable: just an older man with deep-set eyes in a shawl-collared sweater, someone I might have served back at the Snack Shack. Yet at the same time, the energy he radiated filled the small library to bursting. It was the smooth, forceful energy of quietly expensive suits and traveling by helicopter to avoid traffic and the authority to say things like *It's taken care of* and have it be true. An energy that could cut through the problems of my life the way a sharp knife sliced the fat off meat.

He strode directly toward me. As he did, he smiled, revealing long, grooved fangs. "You must be Kat Finn," he said as he extended his hand to me. "What a pleasure to meet you."

As I reached for his hand, I remembered what Lucy had told me. I couldn't let him see how excited I was, or how my pulse was racing so badly I was practically trembling. I let my fangs down as smoothly as I could and parted my lips enough so he could see them. "Thank you, Mr. Castel. It's an honor to be here."

He gripped my hand. But as he did so, he was looking very intently at me, as if searching me for something—some kind of flaw, I was sure, that would prove I didn't belong here, or tip the scales in a comparison to Galen. I straightened my shoulders under his gaze. Finally, he broke away. "Please, call me Victor," he said, then gestured to the rolled-back leather sofa and commanded, "Sit."

We did. Victor himself sat in an armchair opposite us and studied us over steepled fingers. He still hadn't even acknowledged Galen's presence.

"Congratulations on your selection for this mentorship. The competition was very high caliber, so this is quite an accomplishment. Galen, we know each other well, so Kat, I'd like you to tell me your story."

My eyebrows popped up. "My story?" I didn't want to tell him anything he wouldn't like, anything that would emphasize how little I belonged with him and Galen in a house like this. "I'm sure it's not that interesting to someone like you."

Victor sat forward, focused on me. "Never say that about yourself, Kat. I'm here. I'm listening."

"Right. I'm sorry." I swallowed hard and began. I sketched the outline of my life, how we'd moved around a lot until settling for a few years in Virginia, then moving to Sacramento. I was surprised that once I got talking, Victor seemed genuinely interested in listening. His eyes stayed fixed on me, and he asked questions about my mom's work in the CFaD clinic, what it had been like going to school with humans and growing up without other vampires. I found that I wanted to answer him. An adult had never listened to me like that before.

Then he asked, "What about your father?"

"He passed away when I was little." I felt Galen tense beside me. I shot him what I hoped was a devastating side-eye. I wanted him to know that I was saying this to Victor. Galen just happened to be there, able to overhear. "It was CFaD."

Victor shook his head. "It's a shame that some vampires continued take unnecessary risks when the alternative of Hema is so readily available."

"It wasn't an unnecessary risk," I snapped. I could taste bitterness on my tongue. "When I was born"—I couldn't believe I was about to say this to Victor Castel, and in front of Galen Black—"my parents couldn't always afford Hema. My dad wasn't feeding on humans for fun. He was hungry."

Galen was staring at me now, his mouth slightly agape. Victor sent him a cutting look and I felt Galen's posture straighten.

I wanted to say more, to ask about the price of Hema, but then Victor said, "Surely your fangmakers could have intervened."

I drew in a quick breath and dropped my eyes to the pleats of my skirt. Hopefully if I looked upset enough, he'd change the subject out of politeness. "They died early in the Peril," I whispered.

Victor reached over and squeezed my hand. "It isn't right that you've grown up without your father, and your fangmakers. What a tragedy that you lost them on both sides."

I looked up at him. He was wearing that droopy look of pity

that every adult face melted into when they heard about my dad, and, if they were vampires, about my fangmakers. It always made me bristle, but for some reason now I felt this sudden, plummeting sadness—that my father was gone, that I didn't have fangmakers, that there were people who should have been there for me but weren't. It *wasn't* right, and not just because it made me stick out at Harcote. I rarely felt it, but I was missing part of myself.

"I'm so sorry, Kat," Victor said. "And I'm so glad you're here. I want you to know that I'm here to help you however I can."

Even after he'd sat back in his chair, I could feel the warmth of his touch on my hand. *Victor Castel*, the most powerful vampire in the world, had reassured me—had promised to help me however he could. What if this mentorship could make up for some of what I'd lost? The thought of that raised a lump in my throat so big, I wasn't sure I could speak. Thankfully, Victor moved the conversation back to the mentorship.

"I'm going to be very direct. I am not really looking for a student to mentor. I'm looking for a junior partner. Someone who can represent the Youngblood generation." My heart sank. It was just like Evangeline said: the whole thing was a setup to crown Galen as vampire royalty. Galen was even more composed than usual, with his back very straight and his hands resting lightly on the arms of the chair. I wondered if he'd known that this was coming.

Victor went on, "In the history of Vampirdom, there has never been anything like the Youngblood generation. A cohort of vampires, with no experience of humanity, spared the trauma of turning. The Youngbloods are only just beginning to come into their own, and already, a third of the vampires in this country are Youngbloods. Vampirdom is entering a new era. It's time for the Youngbloods to have a seat at the table."

"A seat at what table?" I asked, because I was an idiot.

Victor riveted his eyes on Galen. "What do you think I mean by that, Galen?"

Galen shrank into himself, just a little—as if that veneer of confidence he always wore was thinner than usual under Victor's assessment.

"Vampirdom is a living thing," Galen began. He sounded like he was answering from memory, repeating someone else's words—maybe Victor's. "It's a society of vampires that grows and changes, thrives or fractures. Its health is shaped by the choices of its leaders. Victor thinks it's time that we had representatives among those leaders."

I'd never thought of Vampirdom as having leaders before. "It sounds like you're talking about, like, a vampire *government*. Shouldn't there be an election, to give everyone a say?"

Victor smiled at me in a way that managed to be only slightly patronizing. "You have an active mind and a unique perspective, Kat. That's why I selected you for this mentorship—I see myself in that—but you cannot expect those around you to think the way you do. What I've learned, over hundreds of years on this Earth, is that people need leaders. But they're happier if they don't feel led."

"And that leader should be you?" I said before I could stop myself.

"It could be *you*."

I bit my cheek. It couldn't be me. I knew that, but my pulse had quickened all the same. I couldn't help it: I wanted Victor to see that potential in me. The way his attention was pinned on me, with the little muscles at the corners of his eyes tightened and his brow low, made me feel that he might.

"Think about your immortality, how long you have to live. Try, very hard, to understand that. What world would you build, if you had the power to make it happen?"

A closed mouth won't be fed.

"I'm giving you an assignment for our next meeting. I want you to identify where the next big threat to Vampirdom will arise from, and be prepared to present it to me."

A threat to Vampirdom. Wasn't that what I'd overheard that night with Taylor—Ms. Radtke saying that what Mr. Kontos was doing was a threat to us all? I'd never seriously thought about Vampirdom as a thing that could be threatened, as the living thing that Galen had called it. "Galen, I don't want to see you slacking off. I expect the most out of you. I don't want to tell your parents I've been disappointed."

"Don't worry, sir," Galen said. "I won't let you down."

"Me either, sir—Victor," I said. "I won't let you down. Thank you so much for this opportunity."

The warm spotlight of his focus shifted back to me. "Don't thank me, Kat. You deserve this."

I knew in that second that I would do anything to prove that he was right.

GALEN SPENT THE helicopter flight home elegantly glowering. I had to try very hard not to let it blot out my own enthusiasm. As we walked from the lacrosse field toward the residential quads, he finally spoke.

"You should watch what you say around him," he said tentatively. "When you asked if he should be a leader, I mean. Victor doesn't like that kind of thing."

I scowled. I needed Galen's advice about as much as I trusted it:

not at all. "He told us he's interested in the perspective of the Youngblood generation. That means he wants to know what we think."

A cold wind blew down the hill, kicking up leaves around us.

"He likes to control what's his," Galen said. "Be careful, Kat."

14

TAYLOR

KAT WAS POSITIVELY effervescent after her meeting with *the* Victor Castel. Helicopters, the enormous house, special alone time with special Galen. I kept waiting for her to get to the part where she realized that Castel was skeevy as hell.

I'd met him once. He'd come by our house to see my parents for some reason. I remember it was the same winter Kat and her mom skipped out, because in the three minutes I'd been left alone with him in the living room, he'd asked if I was applying to Harcote and told me he was proud of me for it—as if that was any of his business. He'd been looking at me like was sizing me up, assessing me as one of the treasured Youngblood generation. Sometimes you can just tell when someone isn't right, and I knew in my gut that Victor Castel wasn't.

I faced the window while Kat changed out of her uniform and into Harcote sweats. I knew they'd be Harcote sweats because Kat never wore her clothes from home.

Out the window, I spied a gloomy figure in decrepit crinolines sweeping down the up-campus path.

"Hey, Radtke's on the move."

"So?" Kat said. "Curfew isn't for two hours."

"*So*, she never goes up-campus this late." After I'd talked to

Kontos, I'd done a quick inventory of my Radtke-related knowledge: she liked hassling me, she had no problem enforcing the stupid Honor Code whenever the mood struck her, and her favorite perfume was mothballs.

There was next to nothing about her online. She'd created exactly one social media profile that I could find, apparently so she could join a group for families of people who'd died of CFaD, but she'd never posted. I had no idea what to make of that, to be honest. I'd resorted to looking at twenty-five years of Harcote yearbooks to confirm that she'd been here since Atherton had taken over the boys' boarding school, kicked the old students out, and converted it into a cozy incubator for Youngbloods. All that time, she'd been living in the Hunter House Annex. Making sure I got in and out of the Harcote History section of the library before anyone caught me being lame was my first trial run on sneaky spy shit.

I needed more.

So that was how I'd been reduced to low-key following her, hoping that she'd do something incriminating.

She usually went on walks after dinner, so I'd wait for her to leave Hunter House—she had to take the same door as the students—and then I'd tail her around campus. So far, this had been a total waste of time: she really was just taking a walk, the kind of thing that passed for entertainment in 1850. But she never went out this late. I stuffed my feet into sneakers and grabbed my jacket.

"What are you doing?" Kat asked.

"Following her, obviously."

"You are *not*!"

I reached for my keys. "Are you coming or what?"

She glared at me. "Obviously."

———

Radtke had a bit of head start so we had to hustle to catch up, but one advantage of sneakers, which Radtke had yet to discover, was that they didn't clack out an announcement of every step you took. She never once turned around.

I shoved my hands in my jacket pockets against the chilly evening. But I got goose bumps anyway because it was immediately obvious that Radtke was deviating from her usual route and heading toward the up-campus academic buildings.

"Is she going to Old Hill?" Kat whispered. "Maybe she's going to talk to Headmaster Atherton again."

But at the top of the up-campus stairs, she click-clacked right past the path to Old Hill and walked toward the Science Building.

The Science Building—technically the Victor Castel Science Building—was only ten years old and was offensive to architects everywhere. It had been designed to look like a molecule, which meant the layout made no sense and the classrooms were octagonal. The second Radtke pushed open the (also octagonal) door, I knew where she was going. Kontos's classroom was on the first floor.

We snuck down the hallway after her, which was more difficult than I expected: not a ton of places for two people to hide in a hallway, and even sneakers squeaked on the linoleum floor that the aides kept polished. Kat and I pressed ourselves up against the wall—definitely not touching this time—as Radtke approached Kontos's classroom. She didn't even test the door to see if it was locked before fishing a key out of her pocket. The doorknob turned easily in her hand, and she was inside, closing the door behind her.

"The lights are off," I said. Kontos was probably back in his own house annex in the boys' quad, doing something Kontos-y like bidding on vintage pleated khakis on eBay or thinking about the general goodness of people in the world. He had no idea that Radtke was breaking into his office—had *stolen herself a key.*

We crept over to the door. Kat gently tried the doorknob. Locked.

"You want to follow her in there?" I hissed. I was kind of impressed that she would consider doing something so risky.

"How else are we supposed to know what she's doing?"

I pointed toward the ceiling. Above the door was a window that let light from the classroom into the hall. "Better than nothing."

I found a chair, carried it over, and stepped up. This was perfect. We'd just need to haul ass before Radtke finished whatever trouble she was causing. I was just cupping my hands to the glass when I felt the chair rock and Kat was standing up next to me, fitting in her feet around mine on the seat. My mouth went dry as I shot her a *What-are-you-doing?* look. She jabbed her elbow into my arm.

"I want to see too."

So the two of us peered into the classroom. Radtke was out of sight, in Kontos's attached office. The door was open just enough to show that there was a white light illuminating part of the room. I knew the layout of Kontos's office, and the shadows that light was casting looked all wrong.

Suddenly, my phone buzzed, the *zzp-zzp* way louder than it should have been. I almost lost my balance as I yanked it out of my pocket.

Lucy's out till curfew, come by my room.

Fucking Evangeline. I clutched the phone to my chest, hoping Kat hadn't seen the message.

"Could you not put your phone on silent for this?"

"It *is* on silent."

"If I can hear it vibrating, it's not silent."

I wriggled around on the chair so Kat couldn't see me texting back. Kind of busy.

I chewed my lip, then added, Maybe later, then pressed my face back to the glass. The shadows in the room were weird, but none of them were moving around. Maybe Radkte was in there holding perfectly still?

Then all of a sudden there was something touching my leg—someone *holding onto my leg*, their firm hand closing around my right calf. My heart slammed up to my throat so hard it felt like it was going to keep going and shoot straight out of my cranium. I looked down.

An aide stared back at me. The aides' eyes were always distant, but this one's face was even blanker than usual—like the lights were on but someone else was home.

Kat yelped and tumbled off the chair, but I was trapped in his grip, his fingers digging hard into my calf muscle.

I couldn't let myself scream—that would get Radtke's attention. But maybe that wasn't such a bad thing? The aide's vacant face was freaky beyond words, like he was some kind of robot. Atherton controlled all the aides, but could this one somehow be . . . possessed?

"This building is closed to students after five o'clock," he said.

Screw sneaky spy shit. I flung myself backward off the chair, landing opposite the aide and nearly crushing Kat. The aide lurched forward, losing his grip on me and slamming the chair into the classroom door. We stumbled to our feet and we were barreling down that hallway toward the exit like bats out of hell.

We ran until we got back down-campus.

"What the hell was that?" Kat panted. "Why did that aide—"

"I don't know! They're not supposed to be able to touch us at all."

"Headmaster Atherton controls them. Does he use them for, like, *surveillance*?"

That had never occurred to me. The truth was, I rarely noticed the aides most of the time. Which was pretty stupid on a number of levels, now that I thought about it. "I hope not."

Back in our room, we sat at our desks in an awkward diorama of Harcote Students Casually Studying until Radtke knocked on our door to check curfew.

I sat motionlessly in front of my precalc book as Kat opened the door. "Just doing our homework, Ms. Radtke," Kat said woodenly.

"Don't forget your beauty rest, girls," Ms. Radtke said.

KAT

LATER THAT WEEK, I skipped clubs period and met Galen and Headmaster Atherton at the library. I'd been worrying for days that Headmaster Atherton would say something about what happened in the Science Building, but he was his usual ruddy-cheeked self in a grass-stained rugby shirt and soccer shorts. He was heading to an Ultimate Frisbee scrimmage after meeting us.

It always made me a little uncomfortable that Headmaster Atherton hardly looked older than a high school student himself. He was tall, but in a scrawny way like he'd never finished growing. His face was pitted by a scattering of acne scars that couldn't fade. It didn't seem as if he could grow a beard, but the way his lips were so strikingly pink against his parchment-pale skin made me wish he could have. My brain glitched thinking about how this was the same Headmaster Atherton who had founded Harcote in the middle of the Peril, who'd spent a few hundred years before that sucking human blood. He was powerful enough to control every one of the human aides, even as he bounced through the library's quiet room, speaking at full volume about the Ultimate team's next game. He squired us toward a neglected corner, to a door fitted with a swipe-access lock. A plaque beside it read ROGER ATHERTON EXTENDED COLLECTIONS.

Headmaster Atherton's tongue darted out to moisten his lips, like an eager little lizard. "The Harcote library that you've had access to so far, what you see behind you, is just our educational collection. There's so much more to it!" He swiped his ID in the scanner. "Welcome to the Extended Collections."

As he opened the door, cold air burst forth from the dark space. Galen's brows rose slightly, only enough to convey that he didn't have any idea what was going on here either. Then we both followed Headmaster Atherton into the dark.

On the other side, we stepped onto a metal catwalk that ran into a stairway that descended—I looked down—four floors. Though we'd entered from the first floor of the library, we were actually near the ceiling of a space that descended underground below the library. It was almost unlit, save for footlights running to light our step. In the center of that black cavern was a massive glass cube. Four floors of archival materials, enclosed in glass, sank into the ground beneath us, lit an eerie red by the occasional exit sign. It felt like we'd been admitted to some kind of book-powered nuclear reactor.

We crossed the catwalk that connected to the top level of the glass cube. Headmaster Atherton paused at a second door. "As the foremost institution of Vampirdom in the country, Harcote houses the most extensive archive of vampirology in North America. Our archive covers ancient folklore"—he air-quoted that—"to medical research from this year. How does the Honor Code say we should conduct ourselves here?"

"With respect," Galen said automatically.

Headmaster Atherton punched the air. "That's it! With respect, at all times. The items from the collection do not leave this wing: you conduct your research within the Stack."

"The Stack?" I asked.

As he pulled open another door, there was the suctiony sound of a seal being broken and another small rush of air. He ushered us through, then resealed the door behind us.

Motion-detecting lights blinked on overhead. It was so profoundly silent that my palms began to sweat.

"Welcome to the Stack," Headmaster Atherton said. "These doors must remain closed. The Stack maintains a lower concentration of oxygen in the air to mitigate decay of the collection. Generally speaking, we don't want human aides in here outside of emergency circumstances."

"Because they'd suffocate?" I said.

"Every human life meets some end, Kat." He turned on his heel.

We followed him down a flight of stairs and past a few dark alleyways of shelves, fluorescent lights blinking on overhead. The fact that we were in a glass box, in a bigger concrete box, descending deeper underground was hard to put out of mind. Galen was raking his fingers through his hair a bit more than usual, but if he was uncomfortable, it didn't read on his face. Nothing ever did.

"I've arranged for you to have swipe access with your ID cards at Mr. Castel's request. The whole archive is available to you, but this section may be of particular interest—the CasTech Collection." He came to a stop and gestured to a series of shelves and file cabinets. "Here, you'll find every book and article ever written, by human or vampire, about Victor Castel personally—biographies, magazine profiles, and so on—and studies of CasTech from a business perspective, the discovery of Hema, and the history of its manufacturing, including documents from its production during the Peril."

"What tremendous resources," Galen said respectfully.

"Tremendous, yes!" Headmaster Atherton rose up on his toes in satisfaction. "History is our connection to the past. Vampires, as eternal creatures, are the living embodiment of that connection. You'll feel just as at home here as I do."

With that, Headmaster Atherton turned and left us, the squeak of his sneakers again dustless floor fading away until we were alone in the silence.

Galen had his arms crossed, his black curls rakishly tumbled across his forehead. Even in the harsh fluorescent light, he looked like he could have walked right out of a painting by a Renaissance master. I knew we'd be spending a lot of time together for the mentorship. I just hadn't expected it would be in a windowless, fireproof below-ground parking garage for books.

"*Living embodiment of the past*," Galen grumbled as he surveyed the shelves. "If I'm the living embodiment of anything, it definitely isn't this."

"We're in an archive devoted to your fangmaker. All of this is literally part of your past."

Galen rubbed the bridge of his nose, like this was some great inconvenience. "My fangmaker isn't the most interesting thing about me."

"Which is why you try so hard never to mention him."

"It's what people expect. They look at me, and they think of Victor Castel. It doesn't matter what I do."

"That must be a real hardship," I said. "Especially considering how much he freaks you out."

Galen tried to scoff but didn't quite manage it. His gray eyes were uneasy. "Why would you say that?"

I shrugged. It felt good to catch him off guard—he hadn't even denied it.

Galen raked his fingers through his hair. "It's complicated. Victor expects a lot from the people he's invested in. If you knew what that was like—" He stopped himself and that blank expression settled over him again. "It's an honor to have his attention."

"It actually *is*. This opportunity really means something to me." My chest felt tight, sheltering the warmth I'd felt when Victor's eyes were on me. "I don't get to be around someone like Victor Castel every day. My fangmakers are—are gone. I want to know what it's like to live as long as he has, or how he managed to come up with Hema when the survival of all vampires was on the line."

"That's not how it happened," Galen said. "He'd already developed Hema. Ten years before the Peril."

I was so wildly annoyed by this I thought I might actually cry. "See?" I said, but I couldn't finish. *See*, I don't know anything about our history. *See*, you already have everything I want.

Galen sighed and unshouldered his bag. "I know Victor has us set against each other with this competition, but if we're going to be stuck together, let's make the best of it. I'm not your enemy, Kat."

"You want to work together?"

"I was thinking more like being friends." Then he smiled. The curve of his lips looked even more perfect when he wasn't frowning. I didn't like Galen, but that smile made it easier to see why everyone else did.

I swallowed hard, hoping I wouldn't regret this. "Being friends would be nice."

AS IT TURNS out, when you're the only two people in an enormous, low-oxygen sarcophagus of books, you get close, fast.

Since we couldn't take books out of the Stack, and both of us were too creeped out to go down there alone, Galen and I started spending a lot of time together in the Extended Collections Pit of Despair. We didn't know when Victor would ask us to report on the threats to Vampirdom that we'd identified, so we both wanted to be as prepared as possible. So far we'd just done a lot of background research. Galen had read through firsthand accounts from early in the Peril, in the 1970s. I'd started with the history of CasTech and how Victor had developed Hema. Galen had been right: Victor started working on Hema almost two decades before. The decision was a little bit mercenary: if I had no hope of actually winning, I could at least try to impress Victor with flattery.

Galen didn't like reading stories of the Peril any more than I enjoyed skimming books that could have been written by the head of the Victor Castel Appreciation Society, but he did relax a little whenever we were alone in the Stack. And when he relaxed, I was surprised to discover he wasn't that much of a dick: his shoulders un-hunched, he didn't run his hand through his curls every thirty seconds, and his eyebrow, for the most part, stayed un-arched.

"What do you think Victor is looking for in a leader of the Youngbloods?" I asked.

Galen's dark eyebrows came together pensively. "I've never been quite sure. He said he wants someone who can lead them, without making them feel led."

"He should have picked Lucy or Evangeline. Lucy literally has thousands of people who call themselves her followers. I don't know why he picked me."

I'd forgotten, for a second, that I *did* know why he picked me; the girls had told me. Galen and I had never acknowledged the fact that the whole mentorship had been set up so Galen could officially ascend to the role of Crown Prince of Vampirdom. I was just window dressing. Somehow, it felt important that we never mentioned it. Like it might hurt Galen's feelings if I called out the effort others spent for him to move smoothly through the world, and if Galen's feelings were hurt, then it had all been for nothing.

I changed the subject. "Threats to Vampirdom," I said. We were both keeping a running list. "Ready?"

"Ready."

"Go!"

"Hema distribution network failure," he said. "An accident or disaster could make it impossible to get Hema to the distribution points, and vampires would starve or turn to human blood."

"Or the Hema supply could become infected with CFaD. That might be possible, right?"

Galen looked a little alarmed. "CFaD could mutate, so vampires could catch it as easily as humans do."

"An asteroid could hit the Earth, killing us all." I skimmed my list, but none of the catastrophes felt right. "There are a million scenarios that could kill off vampires. But he wants threats to *Vampirdom*, not to vampires. It's different to him, isn't it?"

Galen nodded. "Vampirdom is the community. It's bigger than the individual vampires."

"What about the facade?" I suggested. "If the facade fell and humans found out about us, then there could be integration . . . But that doesn't mean Vampirdom would end. We'd still be a community of vampires—just a different kind of community."

"Victor wouldn't see it like that. He doesn't like humans very much, and he *hates* reunionists."

I tapped my pen against my notebook. "Maybe reunionists are the biggest threat. They literally want a world without Vampirdom, right?"

"They do, but they're nowhere near to making it happen. At least that's what my parents say."

Galen's parents, who ran the CFaD Foundation.

My pen clattered to the table. "The cure! If CFaD were cured, vampires could feed on humans again. We wouldn't need Hema, so they wouldn't need to live near distributors. And Victor would . . ."

"My fangdaddy would go broke?" Somehow he managed to repeat Taylor's words without animosity.

"You've thought about that before."

He broke into a charmingly ironic smile. "Have I thought about what it would be like to live in a world where I wasn't completely dependent on Victor Castel? All the time." Suddenly he dropped his gray eyes, like he'd just realized he wasn't making a joke, at least not one that anyone else would understand. "Victor is very invested in developing a cure, you know. He's the biggest donor to the Foundation, and chair of the board. My parents update him monthly on our progress. We're all working toward the same goal—a world where vampires are safe from CFaD."

"And humans too, right?"

"Of course, humans too," he said earnestly. "We're the good guys, Kat."

"I know," I reassured him. Just then, like a switch had been flipped, it was awkward again. He felt it as well, because he was checking his phone—although there was no reception in here.

I pulled the next item off the stack of materials I'd been working through. Today, it was documents from the early days of CasTech, when Hema was still in development. We both knew one of the problems Victor had run into early on, before the first vampire death from CFaD, was communicating to vampires that Hema existed as an alternative to feeding on humans. Vampires weren't exactly congregating in Facebook groups in the late fifties, when he first discovered it. I thought studying those early troubles might be revelatory, or at least impressive to Victor. So far it has just been *boring*.

I leafed through a magazine article from 1957 profiling Victor's research into a potential blood substitute for humans. This had been one of CasTech's earlier marketing initiatives. CasTech had never really tried to create a blood substitute that could be transfused into humans—that was more complicated than what vampires needed to feed on—but they'd promoted the company that way as an attempt to get the word out to vampires about Hema. The hope was, vampires would come to them. From what I understood, it hadn't quite turned out that way.

I turned the page to a spread of color photos of the lab. There was Victor, wearing black-framed glasses he didn't need, holding a vial of Hema to the light. Then there was a photo captioned "The research team at Castel Technologies." In the photo, eight people in lab coats circled a lab table, Victor at its center.

Galen reached across the table and tapped the page. "That's my dad, to Victor's left." Simon Black was white, tall, and broad-shouldered under his boxy lab coat, with sharp facial features that Galen's were the softer echo of. Galen pointed to a small woman with golden-brown skin, black hair, and striking pale eyes. "And that's my mom."

I peered at the photo of Meera Black. "You have her eyes."

"Her eyes and her hair," he said. "Otherwise, everyone says I look like my dad."

"She's Indian, right?"

He nodded. "My dad was involved with the British East India Company back in the day, so that's where they met."

"You mean the British East India Company that colonized India?"

He winced. "It's not as messed up as it sounds. My mom doesn't talk about it much, but she's from a wealthy merchant family in Gujarat, and he spent years pursuing her until she agreed. He didn't just make off with a helpless girl from some village. Anyway, it was a long time ago."

"Not *that* long ago—I thought the British only got out of India around the time this picture was taken."

"That was ten years earlier, in 1948. I meant that he turned her a long time before that." He looked up at me. "No one here ever asks me about this stuff. Between my dad and Victor—even though we're not related by blood—everyone sees me as white."

Hadn't I been doing that too? Galen seemed to have every possible privilege on his side, but I'd completely ignored the fact that he might feel out of place at Harcote too.

"That sounds really hard," I said. "Are you in the Students of Color Caucus?"

"Georges's thing? That's not really for me."

"What do you mean?"

"I guess I don't feel the need to spend my clubs period talking about being a vampire of color. That's fine for them, but I have too much other stuff going on." He pulled the magazine back toward him. His brow creased as he studied the photo again. "Oh, interesting! Meredith Ayres is in this photo."

"Who?"

He flipped the magazine back toward me. He was pointing at the only other woman pictured, standing on the other side of the group from Galen's mom. Suddenly I could feel my heartbeat thudding in my ears.

"Meredith Ayres. She's this kind of legendary figure—in my opinion, at least. She was part of the founding team, right at the beginning, and made some of the critical discoveries that Hema's based on."

I swallowed hard. "She did?"

"Victor would love to have done it alone, but she was essential. Then she disappeared before Hema became successful. Victor was clearly very upset, because she's basically been erased from the records and she's definitely not talked about."

"What happened to her?"

He shook his head. "She probably died in the Peril."

"Too bad," I forced myself to say. I flipped the magazine closed, catching my finger at the page of the photo. "I'm going to stick this back on the shelf."

A dull buzzing filled my head as I walked into the Stack. I was holding the magazine tight enough that even within its protective covering, the pages were wrinkling under my grip.

Far from Galen, I opened it again. I stared at the face of the woman that Galen said was named Meredith Ayres. I took off my sweater and balled it up around the magazine. Then I walked back to our desk and shoved it into my backpack.

In all the research we'd done, I'd never seen that name before, but I knew the face.

Staring up from the page was my mother.

15

KAT

ALL THE WAY back to down-campus, the magazine felt like a hundred-pound weight in my backpack. I'd taken it on impulse, and now I needed to hide it before I got caught stealing from Headmaster Atherton's special archive. But Evangeline and Lucy were downstairs doing homework on a couch.

"Hey, pretty girl," Evangeline said. "Come say hi."

Evangeline grabbed my hand and tugged me down onto the couch beside her. There wasn't really room for me, so my body was half-crushed against hers. My backpack—with the magazine in it—slipped to the floor. She shifted a little to make room, but we were still pressed up against each other, my face just inches from her huge blue eyes and full lips. I felt like I should pull away. I didn't normally get so *physical* with my friends. But Lucy and Evangeline were always putting their arms around each other or hugging when they had to separate for an afternoon class.

"So you and Galen are getting really close," she said.

Internally, my systems moved to high alert. My new friendship with Galen was a crucial status symbol, but I had to be careful. The girls might have pretended that they didn't want the mentorship, but they weren't capable of pretending they didn't want Galen. It was the one extracurricular they all had in common. Lucy had started dating one of Galen's closest friends—Carsten, the lacrosse player Guzman had slobbered over—and even she hadn't completely stopped talking about Galen.

At the same time, Evangeline had some special claim to him that everyone recognized. Every girl who began a sigh over Galen finished it with *But Galen and Evangeline are going to end up together.* I knew they had dated for a few weeks as firsties, but that was hardly enough to make them star-crossed lovers.

"We're spending so much time together. It's kind of inevitable," I said.

"Are you into him?" A tantalized smile played on Evangeline's lips.

"I mean, he's insanely hot," I hedged.

"Ugh, I know," Lucy agreed. "He's so *mysterious*, like he would rather get staked than let you see him get emotional."

"Truly, sometimes I look at him in class and I totally forget what I was doing," Evangeline said.

"Imagine how I feel spending all that time alone with him in the library," I said. The girls groaned sympathetically.

From across the room, a textbook slammed closed. I twisted around to see Taylor drumming her fingers against her precalc book. I hadn't realized she was there, and suddenly I was embarrassed that she'd overheard what I'd said about Galen. "Can you keep it down? Some of us are actually trying to study."

"That's what the library's for," Lucy said.

Taylor grabbed her stuff and stomped upstairs. I wanted to follow her, but Evangeline was winding her fingers through my hair.

"I don't know what that girl's problem is," Lucy said, as if Taylor had a terminal disease. "Anyway, the Founder's Dance is coming up. Do you think Galen will ask you?"

The girls had been talking about the Founder's Dance almost since Move-in Day. It sounded like homecoming and prom rolled up into one, and was held on Halloween night—although, Taylor had explained, that didn't mean costumes. The Dance was High Dress: formal wear, but make it vampire, she'd said.

"Galen *truly* doesn't see me like that," I said. "If he's going to take anyone, he'll take Evangeline."

Evangeline gave a little self-effacing smile that at once thanked me for recognizing that she deserved the hottest boy in school and made it clear that my recognition was irrelevant, since she had been born knowing she deserved him. With one tilt of her shoulder, she could remind everyone that she would get what she wanted eventually and this waiting period, where he wouldn't take her to the dance, was merely an inconvenience.

So I added, "But I'm just guessing. I don't want to give you the wrong idea. He hasn't said anything about you. Like not even once."

Evangeline's expression went brittle. *Good.* On the other hand, Lucy looked like her eyes were about to fall out of her head with fiendish delight.

"Kitty Kat, you're coming on Saturday, right?" Lucy said. "Party at my place in the city. It's an overnight thing. I cleared the permissions with Radtke, so you just have to put your name on the list." Lucy cocked her head toward the stairs. "It's just a few close friends, so keep it quiet."

As if Lucy needed to worry about me dragging Taylor to her sleepover party in New York City. It would probably be easier to drag her directly to hell.

"I'm in," I said.

IT WASN'T UNTIL Friday afternoon that I found a few moments in the room alone (Taylor was forced to take a break from streaming movies in bed for a cross-country meet) to look at the magazine again. I pulled it out from where I'd stashed it behind my bed. It was a stupid hiding place. If Taylor or one of the aides who cleaned our room found it, it would look completely suspicious. But it *was* suspicious. *Suspicious* wafted off this thing like fumes off spilled gasoline. It made me lightheaded to look at it.

I opened the booklet to the picture. There was no doubt that the woman in the photo was my mother. She literally hadn't aged a day since it had been taken, although her hair was different and, like a few others in the image, she was pretending she needed glasses.

Meredith Ayres.

What was my mother doing at CasTech?

Galen had said she was one of the founding employees, that she'd made critical discoveries, only to disappear. There was no way I could get that to square with what I knew about my mom's life—or what I *thought* I knew. She'd always said she had had to get by on her own, a vampire alone without even a fangmaker, until she met my dad. A few years later, they'd had me, and then he had died. Working for Victor Castel wasn't my idea of getting by on her own.

Maybe she hadn't worked at CasTech long, or she really had feuded with Victor, as Galen had suggested. But even if I rationalized it like that, it didn't explain why she had lied to me.

She'd lied to me my whole life about who she was.

I didn't even know what my name really was, I realized with a jolt that made the room seem to sway. What if I wasn't really Kat Finn at all, what if I was Kat Ayres?

I flipped the magazine closed, slamming my hand against the desk hard enough to send pain radiating up my arm. I shoved it back behind the bed, not caring if the pages creased. My mom was a liar and a hypocrite. She'd preached that we were better off away from Vampirdom when she'd been at the heart of it once, working beside Victor Castel and Simon and Meera Black. She'd guilt-tripped me for wanting to go to Harcote when we couldn't afford it, when she'd left a job that could have given us the financial stability I always wanted. She'd made me feel like trash for applying behind her back, when she'd been lying to me for *my whole life*. She'd broken my trust in more ways than I could comprehend.

Coming to Harcote was the best decision I'd ever made. If I'd been at home, I'd have had to sit across from her while we drank our Hema pretending I wasn't furious at her or faced the argument of a lifetime. But at Harcote, I could go to a party in New York City with my rich and glamorous new friends and forget my betrayer of a mother even existed.

LUCY'S PLACE IN New York City was in a neighborhood called SoHo. I got a ride into the city with Evangeline. The drive was two hours, but her SUV was *ridiculously* nice, and we spent the whole ride blasting music and singing along. It was so fun that I only thought about my mom to make note of how *little* I was thinking about her.

Even if I hadn't recognized it from her social media posts, Lucy's apartment would have been the coolest place I'd ever been. The main room was a huge open space with twenty-foot ceilings and polished concrete floors. Everything in it looked expensive: fluffy sheepskin rugs, two enormous couches, a huge glass coffee table, and in one corner, a real palm tree. A huge neon sign hanging on the wall lit the room up with pouty red lips and long white fangs.

Lucy showed us into the bedroom to change. I was nervous too. That was Taylor's fault: the way she'd been sullenly glaring at me the whole time I was getting ready to go—like having fun with my friends was the worst thing in the world—had set me on edge. "Make good choices, *Kath-er-ine*," she said, as if making good choices was something she had any expertise in.

On top of that, I hadn't brought any outfits worthy of partying with a major influencer to Harcote, and the Benefactor certainly hadn't included any in my wardrobe. If I wanted to dress up I was left with my clothes from Seated Dinner. Evangeline saw me wriggling into the *least* black black dress I had and said, "You are *not* wearing that."

"I kind of have to. I grabbed the wrong thing out of my closet," I lied.

Evangeline dug through her bag—she'd brought dozens of outfits—and tossed me a ball of green fabric. It was one-shouldered, with a cutout on the side, and it showed *a lot* more skin than I was used to. I cringed a little when I looked in the mirror: the tight dress, my loose hair that looked redder than usual against the green, the dark lipstick Evangeline had promised would look *to die for*.

I bit my lip. There was that familiar anxiety again, that I was being tested and about to fail. I tugged the dress down over my hips. "It looks okay, right?"

"You look *fucking hot*." She raked her gaze over my body, a fierce glint in her eyes that made my cheeks burn. "We're Youngblood vampires, Kat. You've never looked *just okay* for a day in your life." She skimmed her hand over my bare shoulder, then nestled her chin there, so our faces were next to each other in the mirror. "I bet Galen will love it."

Part of me wanted to pull back from her. But another part of me, the part I wanted to listen to tonight, liked the way the two of us looked in the mirror. And anyway, she had me cornered: I had nowhere to go.

"The boys just buzzed!" Lucy yelled. "You bitches better get out here."

16

TAYLOR

SATURDAY NIGHTS HAD a way of reappearing that really grated: a regular reminder that I didn't have plans, or friends, and I was supposed to have both. Instead, I had Kontos. This week Kontos was doing me a solid and holding French Cinema Club on a Saturday to make up for canceling our last meeting. In fact, Kontos had been pretty hard to get a hold of recently. I hadn't even found time to tell him that Kat and I had seen Radtke breaking into his office.

I barely waited until the door to the Old Hill classroom we'd reserved for the movie was closed before I blurted it out. At least this time, Kontos didn't take it so lightly. On the other hand, the main thing he was displeased with was me.

"You can't be doing things like this, Taylor. You're going to get yourself in trouble, and I won't be able to protect you."

"I'm not the one who needs protecting. And anyway, one of the aides caught us—me—but nothing happened."

Kontos's eyes widened. "An aide saw you following Miriam to my office?"

"Technically an aide saw me looking through the window into your classroom, while Radtke was in your office. I thought I'd be in trouble with Atherton for sure, but nothing ever happened.

But if I *did* get in trouble, it would be worth it because—" *because I care about you* was what I had wanted to say, but the words stuck in my throat. "Because it would make a great story. Boarding school hijinks and all that."

Kontos scrubbed a hand over his face, then smoothed down his mustache. He looked tired.

"Just tell me what's going on," I said. "Why is Radtke so upset? Is it just that she's a trav and you're a reunionist?"

"I'm going to ask you something and I want you to answer honestly. Can you do that?"

He was looking so exceedingly serious that it made my insides crawl. It took every bit of willpower in my body not to crack a joke. "I'll try."

"Have you even considered that Miriam might be right—that I really am doing something dangerous?"

I was a little stunned. "No. I didn't need to. Radtke completely sucks, and you're—you're *you*."

"Well, she isn't wrong," he said quietly. "The truth is, I'm part of a reunionist network. We're working for change. A world where vampires and humans aren't so separate. Where we can live together, bonded over our shared humanity."

I gaped at him. "You're talking about dropping the facade?" I asked. "Vampires everywhere, coming out to humans?"

"Not right now, no, but we want to be able to have that conversation someday in the future."

"Like, lightyears into the future? Vampires and humans have *always* been separate."

"That sounds like something a trav would say," Kontos said, casually wounding me to my core. "As an immortal, you learn that a lot of what you once thought was eternal is actually temporary.

I've spent most of my life living among humans. Not just to feed—as part of a community. Friends, boyfriends, a regular job. It's possible."

"Then you left all that behind to live in a dorm full adolescent Youngbloods?"

"The Peril changed everything. Some of us—vampires who were more sympathetic to humans, younger ones, like myself—realized that Hema and CFaD created an incredible opportunity: true integration was possible. Hema replaced the need to feed on humans, and CFaD provided some extra insurance. But in the early days of Vampirdom, that wasn't the idea that won out. CFaD made a lot of vampires scared of humans, and so many had already died that the threat of extinction was real. No one likes to be afraid. Another faction managed to channel that fear toward this idea of vampire supremacy over humans. The idea had been around for a long time, but after the Peril, it really took hold, and then the Youngbloods arrived.

"Before the Peril, vampire pregnancies had been extraordinarily rare. I'm sure you know they're very difficult, and often aren't successful. Frankly, most of us felt they weren't worth the trouble when you could turn anyone you wanted and put your mark on them forever, as a fangmaker. But with the Peril, turning became impossible, and by some estimates, there were fewer than two thousand of us left in North America. 'Natural-born' vampires were the only hope for our survival. The idea began to circulate that the new generation would be superior to turned vampires because if vampires were naturally superior to humans, then a vampire with no trace of humanity would be the best of all. The Youngbloods needed to be protected, kept separate."

"You sound like Atherton: *I believe the children are our future*," I said.

"Exactly. We want to see if we can change that future."

"No offense, but that seems pretty fucking difficult."

"Difficult, not impossible." Kontos sat forward in his chair, his elbows digging into his knees. "The reunionist movement needs three things. First, free, universal access to Hema or another human blood substitute. Second, a cure for CFaD—"

"I'm sorry, a what? You just called CFaD an insurance policy for humans. Nothing would stop vampires from slurping them up."

"Do you have any idea of the toll that CFaD has taken on the *human* community? We need to be free from this disease, it's in our mutual interest. Vampires have always practiced self-control. Which brings me to point three: we need the Youngblood generation on our side."

I felt vaguely dizzy. What Kontos had been saying was increasingly fantastical and I'd just hit the end of the beanstalk. I thought of the party at Lucy's that night and the rumors of what went on there. Would Kontos even be considering this if he had heard them too? "Half of them are, like, desperate to be murderers. You think you can convince them of a new vampire world order?"

"You said yourself that the children are the future." The fact that he'd tried for a joke, for my benefit, when he was being so serious, made me feel horrifically embarrassed. "The Youngbloods have a special role in Vampirdom, and they have the numbers—already a third of the population. If they can lead the way toward progress, others will follow. Others who might be too scared to do it alone."

I crossed my arms. "Kontos, this is the worst plan I've ever heard."

"Can you come up with a better one?"

"This is *your* thing!"

"It could be *your* thing, Taylor. That's why I'm telling you this. I thought you might be interested in joining us."

He held a hand up before I could answer.

"You see things differently, Taylor. A lot of the Youngbloods haven't woken up yet. But you have. If there can be a better world, we have to be the ones to make it a reality. I won't spend my immortality waiting patiently for it. I don't think you want that, either. And I . . . I hope you won't take this the wrong way, but it's okay to care about something."

His words felt like a hand plunged into cold water, searching for a grip on me, to pull me back to the surface. It was viciously uncomfortable. I understood what he was offering me: the chance to be part of something greater than the petty dramas of Harcote. He'd seen something in me—something that I thought I carried alone, that had never marked me out as good or special or worthy before, something no one else had understood. That anger, that negativity, that loneliness. I wasn't just some outcast bloodsucker gay weirdo—or I was exactly those things, and that's what he was telling me, now, made me worthy of this.

But that didn't mean I was.

There was no way in hell that I was the best person to help him. I wasn't even the best person to have a casual conversation about it with. If I said yes, I'd only end up disappointing him. I wasn't at all sure that was something I could handle.

I raised an eyebrow at him. "I might be down to join your secret society. How weird are the initiation rites? Any kind of naked stuff is gonna be a hard pass for me."

As soon as I said it, I regretted it. I'd fucked up the moment, just like I always did. In an instant the distance between us had reappeared, and I was alone on my island again.

Kontos rubbed his hands together, smoothed the creases out of his lame khakis. "Take some time to think about it, okay?"

"I will." I got up to leave. It felt like the right thing to do, although we hadn't watched a movie. "For real. I can be a shit sometimes, but you can trust me."

He tried for a smile. "I know."

17

KAT

THE MUSIC WAS turned up, and the whole space was lit with the red glow of that neon sign. The party wasn't big, a mix of third-years and fourth-years dancing and taking pictures and vaping. I was sitting on the arm of the sofa talking to Carsten, Lucy's boyfriend. He was drinking a forty of malt liquor. All the boys had shown up with them, and Carsten was going on about how forties were so legit, better than champagne. It seemed like drinking nothing at all would be better than drinking malt liquor sold at gas stations. But then again, I had no way to know, since I hadn't visited the Champagne region of France, like Carsten had. Most people who drank forties hadn't.

He took a slug then held the warmish bottle out to me. "You want?"

"No, I had some of that Everclear that Lucy's passing around." The alcohol was making my head feel light and fuzzy, my limbs loose and breezy. It wasn't a feeling I was used to. Vampires couldn't ingest food, but alcohol wasn't really food. It was a molecule that your blood carried to your brain, and our blood was perfectly capable of doing that. The purer the alcohol, the less it was like food, the better for vampires. That's why I was drinking Everclear, although it burned from my lips to my stomach. The boys' guts would be in knots tomorrow, but I guessed slumming it was worth it.

Back at home, I rarely drank. I was always afraid of letting my guard down. Admitting that I was a vampire or slipping my fangs down could ruin my life. Actually *biting* someone had consequences I didn't want to think about. Anyway, I didn't have time for much partying, with my classes and work, and Guzman and Shelby liked that I was always down to drive.

But here, now, none of that mattered. I didn't have to hide that I was a vampire from the other Harcoties, even if I still had secrets I wanted to guard. Alcohol made everything about the party easier. It uncoiled that knot of tension in my chest. I had posed for a selfie with Lucy right after that first shot of Everclear, and in the picture, I saw the girl Evangeline had told me I should be: hot, confident, no fucks given. I posted the picture with the caption "felt cute might delete later . . . jk @lucyk"

I checked the likes while Carsten talked about how he couldn't wait for ski season to start. Guzman had already commented, "are you kidding me???"

"Carsten, are you trying to bore Kat out of her mind?"

Galen was standing over me. There was a slight flush to his cheeks, his dark hair tumbling into his face, and he was wearing a flannel that made him look like he'd been cast as the bad boy love interest in a '90s movie. I smiled and pushed myself up off the couch—stumbling only a little bit. The alcohol buzzed in my head.

"You look nice," he said.

I pulled one shoulder up and batted my eyelashes at him. "Thank you. So do you."

He broke into a wry grin, his gray eyes shining. "This is what drunk Kat's like? You're a flirt."

"I'm not *flirting* with you, Galen." I laughed. "*You're* flirting with *me*."

He leaned closer to me, or maybe it was me that swayed. "Oh, really?"

"But it's not gonna work. 'Cause I still think you're an asshole."

His smile faded. "Oh. Okay then. Not flirting, I guess."

Shit. "I didn't mean it like that."

"Was it supposed to be a compliment?" He ran a hand through his hair. His black curls fell perfectly back into place. "Don't drink too much."

I pushed through the dancers toward the kitchen. I had this sick feeling like I'd done something terrible, but I hadn't—had I? It was a joke, and Galen didn't get it. And maybe it wasn't *hilarious*, but what did Galen care what I thought about him anyway?

I grabbed the bottle of Everclear and took a gulp.

Lucy swept into the kitchen and swiped the bottle from me. "Don't forget to leave room, Kitty Kat." She winked at me.

"Stop calling me that. You're worse than Taylor." I followed her into the living room. "And leave room for what?"

Lucy turned the music down. "Okay, boys and girls, we all know why we're here," Lucy said. Someone wolf whistled. I shifted nervously. I had no idea what she was talking about. "Let's bring them out!"

There were footsteps in the hallway, and then four people walked into the room.

Humans.

They were heavily glamoured. Empty smiles on their faces and a dazed, unfocused look in their eyes, worse than what the aides at Harcote usually wore. They didn't fidget, didn't look nervous. They had no idea what they'd just walked into.

"Meet the lucky winners of the chance to party with LucyK!"
There was a horrible, sinking feeling in my stomach. Lucy often
ran contests where her followers could spend a weekend with her.
Followers whom she'd admitted to manipulating with her vampiric charisma.

"Boys, meet Kayla and Vanessa." Lucy gestured at the two human women beside her. They weren't that much older than we
were, college-aged or just past. Kayla was white, with straw-colored
hair. Vanessa had light brown skin and loose brown curls, and she
was wearing an NYU sweatshirt. "And for my girls: Eric and
Clark." Lucy made a show of running her eyes up and down them.
Eric was Black, with short hair and a muscular build, and Clark
had an olive complexion, tattoos covering his forearms.

"They were all tested for CFaD this afternoon, and they're
clear." Lucy clasped her hands and tilted her shoulders—it was a
cute pose she used all the time in her videos. "You know the rules.
Don't drain them dry: we're not here to turn them or kill them.
Take a break if they pass out. And if you get blood on the couch,
I'll fucking stake you. Have fun!"

There was wolf whistling and whooping from the guys, who
didn't waste any time in descending upon the human women—but
the girls had awful, hungry looks in their eyes too, a laser-like focus,
and they weren't far behind, pulling the boys toward the couches.

The haze of alcohol, the impossibility of this situation, the revulsion roiling my stomach had ground my brain to a halt. *This cannot
be happening.* I told myself this again and again, even as I saw
Carsten push Vanessa onto the same seat on the couch where he'd
just been talking with me and sink his teeth into her wrist. Her
blood welled up—Harcote garnet—staining his lips. Vicious pleasure etched itself across his face. Across the room, a fourth-year girl

was practically straddling Clark to gain access to his neck. Beside
her, Evangeline had her lips pressed against his wrist. Blood drib-
bled from the corner of her mouth, but she didn't notice: Evangeline's dark gaze was riveted on the older girl, who was lowering the
sharp points of her fangs toward the pulse point in his neck. Two,
three vampires had their fangs in each human at once now. No
one had turned the music up again, and the apartment was full of
savage sucking sounds.

Beside me, Lucy was snapping pictures with a satisfied smirk
on her face.

"Get in there!" Lucy said. "When was the last time you had *real*
blood?"

"We can't let them do this," I blurted out. "Lucy, we have to
stop this."

"Don't worry, Kitty Kat." Lucy cupped my cheek. Her palm
was warm and sticky against my skin. "They're clean. Someone
would have died already if they weren't."

"That's not what I meant." My head was swimming. I couldn't
find the right way to explain it. "These are *people*. You can't just . . .
feed on them."

Lucy's face went hard, her gaze piercing. "I know they're people. That's the fucking point. They're people, we're vampires, we
feed on them. We're not going to kill them. It's *harmless*."

"But—"

"I am *so* not having this conversation right now," Lucy said.
"You're being a shitty guest."

Lucy shoved past me, catching me by the shoulder, and briefly
the room spun. I steadied myself against the counter as it righted
itself. They weren't going to kill the humans, but that didn't make
it anywhere near okay.

Across the room, Carsten raised his head from Vanessa's wrist.

His tongue snaked out and caught a drop of her blood from his lower lip. Her head was lolled back against couch cushions, her face ashen. Her body was limp. Carsten saw it too—I watched him—but there was a delirious look in his eyes, and he was panting with pleasure. Instead of stopping he pushed her head to the side and leaned into her neck.

"Stop!" I cried as I lurched over to him.

"Oh shit, new girl goes for female blood?" one of the guys said.

Carsten didn't hear me. His head was bowed over Vanessa's neck. I grabbed him by the shoulder—thick with stupid sports muscles—and yanked him back as hard as I could.

I didn't expect him to let go so easily, or maybe I had more strength than I'd expected. But as Carsten fell toward me, I lost my footing. We both went careening backward and crashed straight through the glass coffee table, shattering it into a million shards. I felt my brain bounce as my head collided with the polished concrete floor below, and everything went dim for a second.

For more than a second.

One of the girls was screaming. Maybe a few of them. My head was underwater—it was hard to tell.

Carsten's weight was on top of me, crushing me like the lid of a coffin, and then it wasn't, and he was standing over me, cursing me out as I struggled to sit up. His lips were rimmed in the residue of Vanessa's blood.

I shoved myself up to look at her. She was keeled over on the couch. The wound from her wrist was bleeding directly onto the cushions. But she wasn't safe—none of the humans were safe. I had to get them out of here.

I crawled toward her. Something was grinding under my knee-caps, but I ignored it. I tried to pull myself up on the arm of the couch.

"Savage!" someone yelled. "There's glass, like, stuck in her head!"

"What the fuck is wrong with you, Kat?!" Lucy shrieked. "You're bleeding all over my fucking apartment!"

I looked at the floor under me. It was covered in glass, and there were great bloody smudges where I'd just been kneeling. But that didn't explain the round red blots that were still dripping onto the floor. I put my hand to my hair. It was wet where it shouldn't have been. My fingertips found something jagged and hard. I pulled it free. A hot trickle ran down my scalp, my neck, my shoulders.

I let the shard of bloody glass clatter to the floor as the room began to spin—

Then my stomach heaved for real.

IN THE BATHROOM, I picked glass from my knees and back and scalp. Each fragment dropped with a *plink* into the trashcan. Then I got in the shower and stood under the water until it ran clear. Afterward I had no choice but to put on the shredded, blood-stained mess of Evangeline's dress. No one had brought me my stuff.

I sat on the toilet with my head in my hands.

The cuts would heal. Already they didn't need bandaging, although they still stung and were seeping blood. The terrible headache I had from colliding with the floor would be gone soon enough. But that sick, clawing feeling wasn't going away.

They were feeding, on people, just a few feet away from me, and I couldn't stop them. My brain swam with thoughts of my friends at home, of the four people out there with no idea what was happening to them, of my dad, reduced to feeding on humans to avoid the pain of starvation. These Harcoties had never even contemplated a decision like that. For them, human blood was a party game, another luxury they could throw money at without a care for the consequences.

I'd come to Harcote looking for other Youngbloods like me. But they weren't like me at all, and I didn't want to be like them, not anymore.

There was a knock on the bathroom door.

"Kat?"

I cracked the door. Galen stood there, his face drawn. He had my bag in one hand. "You okay?"

I didn't—couldn't—answer.

"I know you probably want to go back to the party, but Lucy asked me to drive you back to school."

"Are you sober?"

"I don't drink," he said tightly.

"Then please, get me out of here."

GALEN SPED THE whole way back to school. We barely spoke until Galen pulled his BMW into the parking lot and the purring engine fell quiet.

"Thanks," I finally said. "Sorry you're missing the rest of the party."

"I didn't want to stay." He fiddled with his keys, not looking at me. "Why did you do what you did?"

"You have to ask? You know my dad died from CFaD. Not because it was a fun party game. Because he was *starving*."

"Lucy's always really careful about CFaD."

"Because she can be!" I cried. "Because this is a risk she takes for fun. For some of us, it's still life and death."

"I get that." He said it in a way that gave me no idea if he actually did. "If it's any consolation, they never drain them. Lucy makes sure of it."

"So?"

"So, it's harmless, right?" It was the same word Lucy had used. He didn't sound entirely convinced. "They won't remember anything, like it's a bad hangover from partying with LucyK. And she always pays them."

I don't know what kind of look was on my face—outrage, disgust, anger that I hadn't realized that of course the Best of the Best still fed on humans—but it made Galen jump. "What makes that *harmless*? They've been glamoured so they'll agree to anything, and they'll wake up tomorrow with no idea that a bunch of rich assholes were crawling all over them, sucking their blood from their veins. If you think a few dollars would make that, in any way, even a little bit okay, that's fucked up."

"You've really never done it before?" he asked.

"*No.* I can't believe I have to explain this to you, but the humans that Lucy tricked to coming to that party are people like we are. They have *names* and lives and things they care about and people they love. They're not *less than us*. They're the same. How would you feel if someone scammed you into letting them *eat* part of your *body*?"

Galen was quiet. It was time to get out of the car. I'd probably already offended him beyond hope. I could just see him turning around to his friends and bitching about driving the crazy new girl home. But I had to know one more thing. I looked at him, his skin smooth and pale blue in the light.

"Did you do it?" I asked.

Galen's Adam's apple bobbed. He was staring down at his keys, pressing the pad of his thumb into the sharp edge. "Not tonight," he said carefully.

That anger flared hotter in my chest. I was supposed to thank him for his honesty or for pretending to see my point of view or not laughing in my face. But I couldn't bring myself to celebrate him for being a decent person for a few hours. What did that count for, when he'd done things he could never take back, things he probably never even thought to regret? For all I knew, I'd just lost my shit tonight before Galen had gotten his turn.

He was still talking. "To be honest, it never sat right with me. What I mean is, it's wrong. Feeding on humans is wrong. I thought it was really cool, how you stood up to them."

I shook my head, my mouth actually hanging open. "Galen, you have more power than everyone else in that apartment combined. If that's how you felt, *why didn't you help me?*"

He looked stricken, his pretty lips parted, his pretty eyes wide. It was the first time I'd seen him look even a little bit ugly.

I got out of the car and slammed the door behind me.

TAYLOR

THE LIGHT CAME on. I yanked the covers over my head. Kat wasn't even *trying* to be quiet.

"What happened to Lucy's?" I moaned, my eyes squeezed shut.

"Change of plans." That rough edge to her voice—something was wrong. I pulled the covers down to look at her and an instant later I was bolt upright in bed.

"What happened?"

"It's blood. I'm fine," she said without looking at me. She

unzipped her dress—what was left of it—and I forgot I was supposed to look away. Even her bra and underwear were stained a browning red, and her long hair was wet and frizzing, hanging in clumps down her back. Kat scooped the dress off the floor and hurled it into the trashcan.

"*Whose* blood?"

"Mine. Mostly."

She yanked open her underwear drawer and I looked away while she changed. When I turned back, she was just standing by her bed, flexing her fingers and her eyes shifting around the room, like she couldn't figure out what to do now. Her feet were bare. She looked cold.

"Are you . . . okay?" I ventured.

Her focus narrowed to me. There was a naked fire in her eyes, and it made me shrink back onto the bed.

"You knew, didn't you?"

"I've never been to one of those parties. But there are rumors."

I hadn't actually known if they were true, not until this moment. I thought of Kontos's plan—convincing the Youngbloods that we could live alongside humans. As if that could be possible when we were feeding on them for fun.

"Why didn't you tell me?"

"I didn't know I needed to. They're *your* friends. For all I knew, you were *excited* for it . . ."

"You thought I was . . . that I would . . ." She was wearing this awful look of bleak, unconcealed horror. Like she'd lost her footing on the world beneath her. For a second, I was filled with the thought of going to her, that maybe my arms could steady her.

But then her hands tightened into fists, her eyes bright. She didn't need comforting.

"How fucked up is this place?" she cried. "Any other nightmares you want to tell me about?"

"I don't know, man. I just go here."

She rolled her eyes at me. "Just like the rest of us, right?"

"What's *that* supposed to mean? I'm not like your stupid friends."

She shot me a dark look. "They're not my friends anymore. I lost it when they started feeding on the humans. I tried to stop them and . . . let's just say I'm not expecting any more invitations."

A spark lit in my belly. "You tried to stop them?"

"Well, I couldn't just stand there doing nothing, could I? I'm not *Galen*."

"What about Galen?"

"He made a little confession after he drove me back here. Apparently he thinks feeding on humans is wrong too, but it never occurred to him to try to stop it. I can't believe I'm in a situation where that actually seems redeeming and not totally fucked up on its own."

"*Galen* thinks it's wrong?" I knew *I'd* never feed on a human. But that was me. I'd never had much hope that other vampires would do the same. But if Kat, if someone like Galen thought that way . . . maybe Kontos's ideas weren't so crazy.

Kat collapsed onto the edge of her bed, her head heavy in her hands. She looked small and scared and alone. "What am I going to *do*?"

It crashed through my brain like an incoming tide, pulsing and trapped against my skull: *Go to her, go to her, go to her. Put your arms around her, rest her head on your shoulder.* The voice in my head was so loud I wondered if she could hear it.

"Worry about it tomorrow," I forced myself to say. "Can I go back to sleep now, *Kath-er-ine*?"

She looked at me through her fingers, her lips turned down in a beautiful, perfect glower, which did nothing to weaken that throbbing in my brain. "Why do you say it like that?"

"Say what like how?"

"Like *Kath-er-ine*. Three syllables. You know everyone else calls me Kath'rine, just two."

"I thought everyone else called you Kat. One syllable."

"They do." Kat sighed as she turned out the light.

18

TAYLOR

WHEN KAT WOKE up late the next morning, I'd already been at my desk for an hour, pen in hand. I wasn't the journaling type, so it felt unusual, even exciting, to be filling notebook pages.

I pointed at the tumbler on her nightstand. "Got you some Hema."

She rubbed her eyes. "Thanks. I'll probably never be able to set foot in the Dining Hall again."

I chewed on the end of my pen.

What Kontos had told me was burbling in my brain space all morning. Last night, I'd doubted him. I'd doubted *myself.* I hadn't known what I wanted or what I believed, and I didn't think I could be a part of what he was asking.

Then Kat had come home looking like a zombie princess. She'd seen her friends sucking human blood straight from the juicy source, and she hadn't thought twice. She didn't stand around wondering what she believed in or if she was ready to commit to it. She *acted.*

I loved her for it.

Kontos had taken a chance to show me that he thought I could stand for something. I knew without a doubt that if he'd done the same to Kat, she would have said yes on the spot. Even if she didn't feel worthy or understand exactly how she was supposed to help. I had done a lot of regrettable things, but passing this up wasn't going to be one of them.

There was, however, a sticking point: my new mission was trying to turn the Youngbloods to reunionism. I didn't know if it could actually be done. Kat was just one person. None of the other vampires at Lucy's party had done anything but laugh at her.

"Do you think the Youngbloods are a lost cause?" I asked Kat.

"What do you mean?"

"Remember that debate in Radtke's class, the day Evangeline called me a—"

"I remember."

"—a lesbian. We were talking about what would happen if CFaD were cured. What do you think they'd do if that happened?"

She let out an exhausted sigh. "Probably something a lot worse than what they're already doing. I'll admit that you were right. They call themselves the Best of the Best, but they're absolute monsters."

"But maybe they could, like, evolve? Change their minds?"

"Since when do *you* care about changing anyone's mind?" She flopped back against the pillows and pulled the covers back up over her head.

You would have thought that proof that my peers were sucking the life juices from human veins would have convinced me that Kontos's mission was irredeemably flawed. Youngbloods were doing the exact thing we hoped that they never would. But weirdly, the confirmation that it was not just a rumor galvanized me. At least we knew what we were up against. And it was too important not to try.

I tore out the page from my notebook, tossed it toward the trash, and started a second draft.

———

KAT WAS FULFILLING her own prophecy about never setting foot in the Dining Hall again—even though that was basically letting the enemy win—so when dinner rolled around, I was still on Hema delivery duty.

That was fine with me. It wasn't that I was happy to see Kat sad, but all day, it had been just the two of us. To cheer her up, I made her watch *Twilight*, a movie so heterosexual that even Lesbian Icon Kristen Stewart comes off as straight. But it got Kat laughing at the vampires' sparkle-skin and weird fetish for high-speed baseball. Seeing her smile hit me with the jolt of a drug, stronger than the buzz of sitting next to her on my bed, our shoulders pressed against each other and our knees knocking together and the jasmine scent of her shampoo filling my nose.

It had felt like it used to—like maybe it would be from here on out: me and Kat against the world. The other girls making fun of those freaks up in the top-floor room of Hunter House and neither of us caring, because we freaks had to stick together. If we had each other, who gave a fuck what the others said?

But now I was not in the safety of our room. I was in the Dining Hall, on business both personal and official. I grabbed two tumblers of Hema to go, then scanned the room. My stomach dropped. Evangeline, Lucy, and Galen were sprawled out at a table cluttered with empty red-rimmed dishes. Evangeline looked right at me, then at the tumblers, and a psychopathically smug look spread over her face.

I willed her not to, but Evangeline called out, "Is that for Kat? How's her head?"

Everyone turned to see Evangeline's gorgeous pout: a face that expressed *I truly care!* and also *I'm one of those serial-killer nurses.*

If Kat had been human, Evangeline's comment would have been rich-bitch passive-aggressive. But Kat was a vampire, a creature whose injuries—even concussions—healed with miraculous speed. Evangeline wasn't just reminding everyone of what had happened at the party: she was suggesting that Kat wasn't quite like us. Evangeline didn't know the truth about Kat's maternal fangmaker, but if Kat heard her talking like this, she might lose it all over again.

Alas, the presence of teachers in the Dining Hall meant I couldn't tell her to fuck off, and the presence of Hema in my hands meant I couldn't use a gesture to convey that message either. "Kat's none of your business," I said.

I immediately regretted it. The look of devilish delight—the slant of an eyebrow, the slight curl of a lip—that flashed over Evangeline's face was meant just for me. I knew what it meant: that I was *truly* the most pathetic thing ever.

Maybe, but at least Kat was on my side now.

I didn't have time to decode any more of Evangeline's facial twitches because just then, Max Krovchuk entered the Dining Hall. He had a pencil stuck behind his ear. Editor of *The Har-Notes* was an identity Max wore at all times.

I jogged up to Max as he was grabbing some Hema.

"Hey, Max, just the guy I was looking for!"

He grimaced. "I don't like the sound of that, Taylor."

"Hear me out! I've got something interesting for *HarNotes*."

"Write me a pitch and I'll bring it up at the next staff meeting."

I rolled my eyes. Max acted like editing Harcote's newspaper was only slightly less prestigious than editing *The New York Times*.

"Trust me, you'll want it in tomorrow's issue."

"Tomorrow? We're going to press in two hours."

"I promise, you'll want this. You've heard what everyone's talking about today?" Max's brown eyes narrowed hungrily. He was a gossip as bad as the rest of us, he just got to pretend it was for professional reasons. "I have an op-ed about it."

"If I agree to this, Taylor, you only have an hour to get me the copy."

"It's ready to go! But there's one more thing. It needs to be anonymous."

"You know I can't do that. Honor Code."

The Honor Code did indeed forbid—or appeared to forbid, since it didn't actually involve a fixed set of rules—the publishing of anonymous works. Hiding behind anonymity was, according to Atherton, disrespectful, and opened the door to bullying. I guess Atherton believed that door was currently very tightly closed.

"Just put your name on it. You love controversy," Max said.

"I can't. I didn't write this. I'm just helping a friend out—a friend who has something to say but doesn't feel safe." At the word *safe*, Max's eyes narrowed even further. "Come on, what about real journalism? Protecting your sources! The voice of the people! Telling stories that need to be told!"

"Okay, enough catchphrases."

"Everyone will be talking about it," I said. "Wouldn't it be nice to publish something that people gave a shit about?"

"Fine. Get me copy in the next hour."

"No problem."

Back in the room, I sent the op-ed to Max, then cocked an eyebrow at Kat. "Ready for *New Moon*?"

KAT

IT WAS UNBELIEVABLY cruel that on Monday, I was expected to get out of bed, leave my room, and actually go to class. In spite of the disaster of Friday night, the weekend had turned out almost nice. Taylor had talked me into marathoning the Twilight movies, which were a lot more fun to watch with another vampire, but it wasn't just that that made me feel better. It was that when we were curled up in her bed together, cracking jokes and wailing every time Kristen Stewart kissed one of those boys, it felt like how it used to be.

Before she broke my trust.

Taylor said I was wallowing, and she wasn't wrong. It was hard to express exactly what I was wallowing *about*. I didn't regret trying to protect those humans; I only wished I'd done a better job of it.

But if I didn't regret it, how could I regret ruining my friendships—with the exact same people who had been doing the blood-sucking? I'd totally humiliated myself in front of the coolest kids in school, covered in my own blood and shards of glass sticking out of my skin. The way whispers—and outright conversations—followed me around campus, I guessed they'd be talking about it long after graduation.

First period had been fine. I showed up to chem exactly on the hour, so I wouldn't have to sit through any chatter before class.

When I walked into Radtke's classroom for second period, the room fell entirely quiet, a sure sign that they'd just been talking about me. I could practically hear the three letters of my name crackling on their lips: *Did you hear what Kat did?*

Copies of *HarNotes* were strewn about, one in front of almost every student, like they might pretend they were talking about the schedule for Descendants Day—a weekend for parents and fangmakers to visit campus—that had just been announced.

The only empty seat was my usual spot next to Evangeline.

Given how she was glaring daggers at me, she was very well aware of that fact. Panic jittered through me.

Taylor was in the corner by the window, leaning back in her chair with her bright-white sneakers propped up on the desk. I locked eyes with her. There must have been a real look of terror on my face because the instant she saw me, her chair was on the floor and she was hooking her foot around the leg of an extra that was sitting in the corner to pull it up to the seminar table.

"Thanks," I mumbled as I slid into the seat.

She slid a *HarNotes* in my direction. "You read this yet?"

"I've got bigger things on my mind this morning."

She tapped the paper insistently. "Back page editorial."

The headline read VAMPIRES AND HUMANS HAVE A SHARED FUTURE.

I used to think that because I'd never killed a human (and never would) that meant I wasn't hurting them, I read.

I glanced up at Taylor. She raised her eyebrows as if to say, *I know, right?*

It's time we talked about an open secret. There are students at Harcote who feed on humans. It's not because they don't know it's dangerous, or because they're starving. They're doing it because it's fun. Because they can.

It doesn't matter what precautions you take or how nicely you treat them. With Hema, there is no excuse for feeding on humans. It is wrong to take the blood from their bodies. It is wrong to glamour them so they can't resist. Most of all, it's wrong to not to think about how our actions affect the world around us.

We have been hearing our whole lives that the Youngblood generation is so different our parents or fangmakers, how we're so special to Vampirdom.

This is how we're different: They had no choice but to drink blood, even if it killed the human they were feeding on. We do have a choice.

We can do better than the vampires that came before us. We don't have to be monsters or hypocrites or murderers. We don't have to give up our humanity.

One day, we might not even have to hide ourselves from humans at all. We already listen to their music and play them in sports and read their books in English class. I want a world where those connections go deeper, where vampires can learn from humans. A world where we don't need Vampirdom anymore and instead, it's just people, humans and vampires, living together.

I dropped the paper. My stomach twisted with nausea—but the good kind, the excited kind. In the last few days, I'd given up hope for the Youngbloods. Now one of them was advocating for reunion in the school paper.

"Bold move, Kat," Carolina Riser said from across the seminar table. "It wasn't enough to ruin a party, you had to call Lucy out to the whole school?"

"I didn't write this," I said. "I only just *read* it."

"Sure," Carolina snorted.

"Don't act so innocent," Evangeline said.

"Writing an op-ed isn't a crime," I said.

"An *anonymous* op-ed is a crime. At least an Honor Code violation. You're supposed to stand by your ideas," Carolina said.

"Which I would do, if I had written an op-ed."

I skimmed it again. It was easy to see why everyone thought that I had written it. It read like a manifesto from someone who'd just pulled the lacrosse team captain off a girl's jugular.

The realization burst over me like shit from a flock of seagulls. I knew exactly who wrote this.

She was sitting right next to me.

"Taylor, you did *not* . . ." I hissed through my teeth to her.

"Kat, I would *never*," she hissed back.

She was trying very hard not to smile as she spun a pen over her knuckle. I wanted to be annoyed at her for violating the Honor Code, for prodding this hornet's nest of the school, but to my surprise I wasn't. Instead, pride swelled in my chest. Taylor at Harcote was an antagonist. She dropped scathing insults and poked fun and stirred up trouble. She tore things down, leaving a border of protective rubble around her. This was the first time I'd seen her stand up for something, even if she'd had to do it anonymously.

Ms. Radtke walked in, a cloud of chalk dust trailing her and settling into the swirl of hair atop her head. It was already a little past the hour, which was unusual. She was never late, and what's more, she was flustered. It took her several minutes to set up the clip we were supposed to watch from *Interview with the Vampire*. It was the part where Lestat turns a little girl. Every time one of the vampires melodramatically sank their fangs into a human's neck, my stomach clenched. The edges of my memories of Saturday night were fuzzed from alcohol but I could still see them, gleeful and ravenous, descending on those poor humans. Ms. Radtke would probably follow it with a debate with a completely obvious answer, like whether it was immoral to turn five-year-olds into vampires, since they wouldn't age like Youngbloods did. This would be the second time Ms. Radtke has warned us not to turn under-eighteens into vampires, but I hadn't once heard her talk about racism and white privilege among vampires, or the patriarchy, or inequality. I'd asked Taylor if those topics ever came up and she'd rolled her eyes and said, *Like people at your human school really talked about that kind of stuff.* It took some convincing before she really believed that they had—that *I* had.

The lights came back on. "Ms. R, you should give us trigger warnings," Evangeline said, affecting a sad tone. "Some of us are so sensitive about seeing humans get bit."

Ms. Radtke's whole face was pinched as she said, "I'd hope you all would be."

Was there was any point in trying to get Harcoties to think about their moral responsibilities when, at the end of the day, morality was a set of rules? If you didn't believe that rules applied to you, morality would never matter.

But Taylor thought there was a point. If she believed it, maybe it was true.

19

TAYLOR

AT LUNCH, THE Dining Hall was buzzing over the editorial. I made an effort to sit with the cross-country team, then checked in with some folks from theater tech, and my suspicions were confirmed: *everyone* was talking about it.

I couldn't stay and chat. I needed to find Kontos.

Since Saturday, I'd been thinking about what I was going to say to Kontos. The world we had was completely fucked up, but I believed, like he did, that something better was possible. At least, I wanted to believe it. I was willing to try. I'd written the editorial to prove that to him. That's what I was going to tell him. Parts of it at least.

I found him in his office, staring into his computer and clicking his clicky pen.

"Taylor, I was hoping you'd come by." He sounded not especially happy to see me. It was very un-Kontos of him. "Close the door."

"I've been thinking about what you said the other night," I began, but he interrupted.

He pointed at the copy of *HarNotes* on his desk. "I assume you're the one behind this?"

"What did you think?" I grinned.

He sucked his teeth, then blew out a breath. "I wish you had talked to me first."

"But this is what you wanted. Agitating for revolution! Everyone's talking about it. The timing was perfect—after what happened at Lucy's."

He winced. So he knew about that too.

"Who knows you wrote this?" he asked.

"No one, I promise. Max thinks I'm covering for a friend who wants to stay anonymous. He was into protecting our sources. He even said he thought the ideas were really good."

He tapped the newspaper. "This is too public, Taylor. You're drawing a lot of attention to us."

"We can't exactly change people's minds in secret, can we? You said that you were waiting for the Youngbloods to wake up, but Radtke and Atherton are brainwashing them every day."

"If it comes out that you wrote this, you'll be in serious trouble."

"Don't worry. Everyone thinks Kat wrote it anyway." I did feel a little bad about that, although I hadn't set it up that way deliberately.

Kontos pressed down the corners of his mustache. "We need to be extra careful for the next little while. This might be hard for you to believe, but this editorial is making waves in places you can't see. You can't talk to anyone about this, even if they ask."

"So I should lie? What about the Honor Code?" It was another joke, but in truth, it felt strange to have an adult—especially Kontos—encouraging me to lie.

"This is more important than the Honor Code," Kontos said. "Frankly, Taylor, what I've asked you to get involved with could be dangerous. I can't say I haven't second-guessed myself, for your own safety. Are you sure you want to do this?"

I was not, actually, completely sure. "Definitely," I answered.

"I need you to promise me you won't do anything else without talking to me first."

I raised my hands in surrender. "I promise. I'll be extra super careful. What's my next assignment?"

"Your primary next assignment is not to do anything else without talking to me first."

"Come on, I told you, I'm ready!"

He took an external hard drive out of his desk and handed it to me. "Your *secondary* assignment is keeping this in your room. You don't need to hide it—that looks suspicious. Just keep it somewhere safe."

I turned it over in my hands. "What is it?"

"It's an external hard drive."

I shot him a black look. "I meant, what's *on* it."

"It's a backup of some data I've been collecting. Don't ask about what. But your editorial has put some heat on us and we need to store an extra copy out of harm's way, until things quiet down. That's all I can tell you. But it does have a few of my favorite movies on there too, so it will look like—"

I tapped the tape on one side, where FRENCH CINEMA CLUB was lettered in his blocky writing. I was proud of him for being sneaky. Kontos was like the anti-sneak, exhibiting Disneyland-tour-guide levels of helpfulness and honesty.

"You can count on me," I said.

I DID AS Kontos asked. I hid the super-secret hard drive not-so-super-secretly in my desk drawer and I didn't stage any more demonstrations of my devotion to the reunionist cause. Still, things didn't exactly quiet down.

First, Atherton tried to launch a mini-Inquisition over who

wrote the editorial. It stalled before it really got off the ground. Max was his first and last lead. Not only did Max not actually know who'd written the editorial, since I'd lied to him about that, he took Atherton's pressure as a chance to put his journalistic ethics on the line. He didn't give me up as his connection to the editorial. As punishment, Atherton called Max before Honor Council—a committee he chaired with Radtke, made up of two of the most suck-uppy students from each year—and suspended him for three days. Rumor was, Atherton had overridden the Council's recommendation for one day of detention to do it. After that, I definitely felt like I needed to keep an eye out for trouble. I didn't even risk thanking Max for what he'd done. At least he was wearing it as a badge of honor.

That wasn't the end of my problems. Even though Atherton never questioned Kat, the entire student body believed Kat had written the editorial about what happened at Lucy's. And of course, Evangeline wouldn't let anyone move on. Fanning the flames of the bonfire of Kat's social life was Evangeline's new number one hobby. It had been a week and Kat still couldn't go anywhere near Evangeline without hearing a snarky little comment. I was beginning to regret that we'd wasted all the Twilight movies in one marathon. I had underestimated how much cheering up Kat would need.

Not even the drama of the upcoming Founder's Dance could move the gossip cycle on. Kat and I had been forced to sit through Carsten's nightmarish a cappella–fueled promposal to Lucy at dinner earlier that week. Afterward, Kat had announced she definitely wasn't going to the Founder's Dance. I wasn't either, but to hear her say it made me sad. I didn't want to go to the Founder's Dance because I was Taylor Sanger: dances were obviously not my thing. But Kat *wasn't* me. She'd probably have a good time in spite of it being stupid.

Then, things got even worse. Atherton finally started looking into what happened at Lucy's parties. He didn't find anything incriminating, since none of Lucy's special chosen party guests wanted to give up their status as Cool Kid to be a rat. Still, Atherton banned everyone from off-campus overnights for the rest of the semester. When that happened, someone (Evangeline) anonymously posted a picture of Kat from the party, a look of terror and a lot of blood on her face, and I was back on Hema delivery duty.

That was the final straw.

After classes ended, I stalked down Evangeline. She was in the theater, working on the blocking for her one-act play. The theater was where this thing between us had gotten started. She'd been picked to stage manage the musical at the end of freshman year. I was doing tech, running the light board. Ever the control freak, she made me run the whole show, no one on stage, just the two of us up in the box and her calling the cues. I was barely out then, trying not to read too much into how her knee was grazing mine—not until she was leaning in so close, the only thing that made sense was to kiss her.

Today, the theater was empty as I stomped down the aisle: just Evangeline standing in the spotlight on stage. She had her hair pulled back, her script in one hand and a pen stuck behind her ear. Her lips curved into a perfect sneer when she saw me, and it made me want to eat her alive.

"What are you doing here?" she asked. "I'm not ready for tech yet."

"We need to talk." I took the side stairs to the stage and met her in the glow of the spotlight. "About what you're doing to Kat."

"I'm being perfectly civil to Kat."

"You're not. You're a bully, E, and you know it."

"How *dare* you? That's like, character assassination."

I kept my voice firm. "Stop making fun of her. And get Lucy to stop too."

Evangeline rolled her shoulders. The gesture pulled her button-up tight across her chest. Not that I was looking. "It's cute that you want to protect your little girlfriend."

"Says the girl I've been fucking for months."

Quick as anything, Evangeline grabbed my arm hard and hauled me offstage, away from the rows of empty seats, to where black velvet curtains would muffle our voices.

"What is *wrong* with you? Anyone could have heard," she snapped. "And we're not *fucking*, we're just hooking up."

"How do you think girls have sex?"

A look of genuine confusion crossed her face. Jesus, Harcote really was the straightest place on Earth. "I—I'm busy, Taylor. Tell me what you want and let me get back to work."

"Stop making Kat's life hell. If you don't, this is over."

"I've heard that before. *I'm done with this, E.*" She moved closer, giving me one of her flirty, sleazy smiles—which, in her defense, usually worked on me because it was *extremely hot*. "I know you, Taylor."

She was right. I'd said that it was over a few times out loud, and said it in my head far more times than I was capable of remembering. But those times had been about me. This was different. I stepped back, putting distance between us. Only a few inches, but it felt like more.

"But you still think I don't know you," I said. "You think I don't see the pathetic way you stare at Galen, or how you make the girls here love you just so you can hurt them, or how you're always all over Lucy—who is, by the way, the straightest person I've ever met in my life. None of them can give you what you want, and they never will. You're so lonely, you're an emotional black hole, E. And without me, you're alone." Her face had hardened into a mask of concentrated rage. "So be nice to Kat, okay?"

Evangeline ran her tongue along her teeth and readjusted the pen behind her ear. "Whatever," she said, stepping back on stage. "Find me in the costume closet in an hour."

20

KAT

I STOOD ON the cold, rickety catwalk looking into the glass cube of the Stack. I'd come here without Galen to see if I could dig up any other information about my mom's past. That, and to get away from the whispers and stares. The week had been overwhelming and lonely, and to cap it all off, someone (probably Evangeline) sent that awful picture around. After all the worrying I'd done about whether the truth about my fangmaker or my dad's death or my background would bring down my social life, I'd managed to do it the old-fashioned way, by making a fool of myself at a party. I felt totally friendless—other than Taylor, of course, who I'd come to depend on more than I wanted to admit.

I wasn't as alone as I'd expected. Through the glass, I could see that the desk we'd claimed as a workspace and the shelves around it were the one illuminated point in the cubular voidspace. Galen had one knee flexed, his black pants tight against his thigh, the other long leg kicked out. He was lost in thought, with one thumb pressing gently into the swell of his lower lip, those dark curls cascading into his face.

Even though I'd been hoping to avoid him, I was struck again by how beautiful he was, even in the all-black permutation of the school uniform that he preferred. He wasn't beautiful in a way that made you long for him, the way Evangeline was so pretty you wanted to put your hands on her, just to make sure she was real. Or even the kind of beauty that Taylor had: her features were like a map you couldn't learn, no matter how long you studied it. Galen was beautiful in a way that made me want to avoid touching him—to examine him from every angle, then store him in a preservative box. Which is to say, although he was the sole life-form inside the underoxygenated Stack, he looked like he belonged.

I swiped my ID card and the seal on the door *shhhnocked* open. I claimed the chair across from him.

He pushed himself up out of his slouch. "How are you? I mean is everything..."

"Shit? Basically." I didn't quite manage to sound lighthearted. "You've heard them talking."

He smiled softly. "Like *you* really care what they think."

But I *did* care. I cared more than I should, and I wanted to stop, but I couldn't. Every time Evangeline or Lucy made some cutting comment, part of me wanted to die. That part was not at all consoled by the fact that Evangeline and Lucy were sentient slimeballs.

Galen was looking at me with something like admiration. "I can't believe you wrote that."

"Except I *didn't*."

"All those ideas are yours."

"Then they're somebody else's ideas too."

He winked at me, conspiratorially. "Anyway, I thought the editorial—which was written by someone else—was really good. It got me thinking, the Foundation is going to cure CFaD some day soon. We should be talking about what kind of world we want to live in once that happens."

This time, I bit my tongue. I needed to stop being angry that he hadn't come to these realizations earlier and focus on being glad that he was having them at all.

"So what kind of world do you want it to be?" I asked.

His brow wrinkled. "I guess . . . we would have to protect Vampirdom, first and foremost."

I flung my pen at him. It thwacked him in the shoulder and he fumbled to catch it. "I didn't ask for an impression of Victor Castel. What do *you* think?"

He tossed the pen back at me. "I don't really know. Sometimes I wonder if Vampirdom isn't too—too *small*. Too rigid. Victor and Atherton talk about Vampirdom like it's fragile. Like we could destroy it, if we do the wrong thing. But it doesn't feel like that to me. You know that fence that runs around campus—the wrought iron one?"

I nodded. The fence marking the edge of campus was even topped with spiky finials when it ran through the woods, and the only gate I knew of was the one I'd driven through on Move-in Day.

"Most of the time I don't think about that fence at all. I usually only see it when I'm at the lacrosse field, and even then, it doesn't always bother me. It's not a *wall*. I can see right through it. But other times, I think about that fence and there's this *pressure*, like claustrophobia. Like that fence is caging us in here as much as it's keeping the rest of the world out. That's how I feel about Vampirdom sometimes. They drew these boundaries around it and now we're all kind of trapped by them." He ducked his head. "I know that sounds really stupid."

"It doesn't sound stupid," I said forcefully. "Not at all. I think I might feel that way too, actually."

Suddenly I realized he was looking at at me differently. His gray eyes were warmer, almost tender, and his lips had slightly parted. A tingling sensation swept up the back of my neck and spread to my cheeks. I didn't want him looking at me like that— so *intently*—anymore, so I pulled out my laptop. "I should get to work."

His hand shot across the table to stop me from opening it. "Go to the dance with me," he said.

"To the Founder's Dance?"

His eyebrow arched. "That's usually what we mean by *the dance* around here."

"Honestly, I wasn't planning to go at all, after everything that's happened. It'll be super awkward."

"Not if it's the two of us."

A bright feeling fizzed through me. The most desirable boy in school was asking *me* to the dance. I was supposed to say yes, but I found myself shaking my head. "What about Evangeline?"

He grabbed the pen back and started toying with the cap. "What about her?"

"She's already making my life hell. And I thought you would go with her, if you went with anybody."

"Where'd you get that idea?"

"You have to know what people say about you guys."

"They'd say that whether or not she's my date." He raked his fingers through his hair. "I'm always under a microscope here. And it's not even about me—it's Victor, my parents, stuff that's beyond my control."

"Is that why you don't date?"

"It's easier that way." He shoved the cap back on the pen and fell back in his chair. "Look, forget I said anything."

I pretended to work, but I couldn't stop thinking about his offer. If I was going to stay at Harcote and become the leader that Victor Castel believed I could be, I couldn't spend the next two years lurking in a corner, hoping Taylor would show up to sit with me at dinner.

A closed mouth won't be fed.

I'd been foolish to think that I ever could have been friends with Evangeline and Lucy. Anyway, friendship was no protection from their wrath. But I couldn't spend the rest of my ever-living, never-dying life hiding from them either.

I'd seen how they treated me differently after I won the mentorship with Victor, once they were done trying to convince me I didn't deserve it. To do that again, I needed to make myself impossible to ignore.

Right in front of me was another the prize Evangeline wanted, but hadn't yet won.

"Yes," I said.

Galen raised his head from his computer. "Yes, what?"

"Yes, I'll go to the Founder's Dance with you. On one condition," I said. "We keep it a secret up until the dance. You say you're going alone, and I'll pretend I'm not going at all, then we show up together. That'll keep Evangeline off my case. And it might be kind of fun."

He hesitated, his gray eyes half hidden through the filter of his thick lashes, as if he was looking at something he couldn't have and wanted very badly. For some reason, I wasn't at all sure it was me.

"Never mind," I said. "Dumb idea."

"No, it's perfect, actually."

Galen's smile, broad and true, was almost bright enough to illuminate the dingy archive.

———

THAT NIGHT, WITH the lights off, I listened to the wind whip through the trees outside our top-floor window and ran my tongue over the sharp points of my teeth and couldn't sleep. My mind was moving in circles, endlessly going over the events of the day until they were worn and smooth.

This was good, I told myself. Galen liked me, and even if I didn't see in him quite what the other girls did, I would, once I knew him better. But when I imagined myself at the dance, side by side with that group, all I could see was their lips smeared with blood. I had this heady, detached sense that it would be someone else who was there, who would be Galen's date. The dance was still a few days away—the coming Saturday—but already there was a knot in my stomach the size of a fist.

Across the narrow room, Taylor's bedding rustled.

"Taylor?" I whispered. "Are you awake?"

After some incoherent mumbling, Taylor's rumpled head poked up from the covers. "'Course. What's wrong?"

"Nothing's wrong. I just wanted to ask you something."

"Yeah, anything." In the cool moonlight filling the room, I could just see the brightness in her eyes, the subtle parting of her lips.

"Would you go to the Founder's Dance?"

"Like, as your date?"

"Oh no, no—that's not what I meant," I said quickly. "Just, would you be there?"

She propped herself up on her elbow. "Last I checked, you weren't going to the dance. Are you planning some kind of Carrie-style massacre?"

"No—it's hard to explain. I am going, but no one can know. It's sort of a surprise."

"Which involves me how?"

"It doesn't—I just—" I couldn't explain why I wanted her to go. Maybe I didn't know, myself. "Don't you kind of owe me?"

Taylor fell back. Her eyes were fixed on the ceiling, and her curls fanned out against the pillow. I didn't look away. It was too dark to see clearly, but I knew her face well enough to make out the pattern of grays that marked the rise and fall of her cheekbones, the jut of her jaw, the ripple of her throat. She looked eerily beautiful, like some kind of mystical creature. Which I guessed, as a vampire, she was.

After a long silence, she said softly, "Okay. I'll go."

As the tension in me began to melt, I whispered, "Thank you."

21

TAYLOR

WHEN I WOKE up the next morning to the sound of Kat getting into the shower, it took me a second to realize why I was so tired. Then I rolled over and moaned into my pillow.

Like, as your date?

How could I have really thought that Kat had asked me to a dance in the middle of the night?

Although that kind of *was* what she had done. Platonically. As friends.

And worse, like the absolute ding-dong I was, I had actually *agreed*.

I grabbed the other pillow and smashed it down over my head, creating a pillow-head sandwich, but even that suffocating situation couldn't alter the undeniable truth:

I was going to the Founder's Dance.

I'd promised myself I would never go again. Last year, Kontos had talked me into it: dances were awkward, but they were a rite of passage! But after an hour I slunk back to my room (technically a violation of the Honor Code). I was used to feeling like I didn't belong at Harcote. I just didn't expect it would feel that much sharper—almost painful—to stand among all those all glitzed-up boy-girl couples.

The dress I had worn had not helped. It had looked perfectly nice on the hanger, but once I put it on it just felt . . . wrong. I looked like someone had wrapped a plastic fork in a cocktail napkin. When I got back to my room, I kicked it into the deepest corner of my closet and left it there on Move-out Day.

I didn't know how I was going to do this, but I did know I wasn't going to let Kat down. I was riding high on doing the right thing, being a better person, someone who cared about things, and one thing I cared about was Kat.

Plus, I did kind of owe her. She'd taken a lot of flack for the editorial.

I launched myself out of bed and pawed through my closet. This was an utter waste of time because I knew nothing in there would work. It was one thing to get by with button-ups and pants for Seated Dinner. That didn't mean I had a full wardrobe of baby butch formalwear.

When Kat shut the water off. I kicked the heap of clothes back into my closet and jumped back into bed.

"You're gonna be late for first period," Kat said. She looked like an absolute angel, wreathed in steam from the shower.

"Two more minutes," I groaned, as I grabbed my phone.

I wrote out a text: *Emergency! Can you meet me after classes?*

No, that would freak him out. I edited it to say Fashion emergency!

And sent it to Kontos.

WHEN I GOT back to the room that evening, Kat was standing straight-backed and still. She was staring into a large box on her bed. The fallout of a tissue paper explosion was strewn across the room.

"Is that for the dance?" I set my backpack on my chair—the

outfit Kontos had helped me buy was stuffed inside. I'd hang it up later, just not in front of Kat. "I thought you were going to wear something you already had."

"I was." Her voice had a faraway sound that kicked my pulse into high gear. "But now I guess I'm going to wear this."

Slowly, Kat held the dress up. It slithered free from the tissue paper, rustling like a scaled thing. It was stunning: strappy and slinky, completely covered with crimson-red sequins, the kind of dress that would hug every curve.

"Wow," I said. "It's a lotta look, but I think you can pull it off."

But Kat was holding the dress like she'd never seen it before, like it might bite her. The hem pooled in a glittery red puddle on the floor.

"I feel like I'm missing something," I said. "When did you order that?"

This seemed to break the spell Kat was under. She threw the dress unceremoniously onto her bed.

"I didn't."

She fished around in the box and pulled out a note on cream-colored paper. She held it out to me.

Dear Kat—Consider this gift a reward for your hard work. The Founder's Dance is a time-honored Harcote tradition, and you should appear worthy of it.

"Who sent this? It has icky guy energy all over it."

"It's from the person funding my financial aid."

"You're on financial aid?"

"You don't need to pretend you didn't know."

"Yeah, because I actually didn't. I didn't think Harcote gave financial aid. That's why the school is full of jackasses."

Kat crammed the excess tissue paper back into the box like she was punishing it for escaping in the first place. "Come on, you really think me and my mom could afford this place?"

The back of my neck prickled. Talking about money made me uncomfortable. It was like taking your underwear off in public—you just knew you weren't supposed to do it. "So what? You're here now."

"*So what?*" Kat stared at me, her mouth hanging open. "*So what*, I can't afford the life that you and everyone else here take completely for granted? So what, we don't have the money to pay for a new pair of sneakers every week or car repairs or even enough fucking Hema keep us alive? Forget all of that. I'm here now, right?"

I stepped back, my hands up. "I meant, I don't think about that stuff when I think about you. Money doesn't really matter to me."

"You say that because you have it. Just because something doesn't matter to you doesn't mean it doesn't *matter*. Have you ever though how lucky you are that you can pick and choose what you care about?"

"You think I'm just like the idiots running around here?" I said.

"I think if you only compare yourself to the assholes at Harcote, then it's easy to think you're some kind of angel. You know, if Headmaster Atherton blames me for that editorial, I could lose my financial aid, and I'd be completely screwed."

"I didn't think about that. I didn't *know*."

She dropped the dress back into the box and gave it a kick. It slid halfway under her bed. "What do you care anyway? You probably want me to leave."

There was ice in my veins—I'd been stupid, so stupid, to assume all that all those moments we'd had together these last few weeks could be pieced together into a friendship. That those moments meant something to her like they had to me.

"How could you say that?" I wanted desperately to be not-here, to be anywhere else—to vanish into the ether. But I didn't. I grabbed her by shoulders. Kat's cheeks were bright, her breathing quick.

I tried to push all the honesty I had into my voice. "I'm sorry about the editorial. I should have thought how it looked—that everyone would think it was you. I can't explain why, but it has to stay anonymous." Kat's eyes were searching mine and I forced myself not to break her gaze. I didn't know how long I could stand being so close to her when she was like this: a fury. I swallowed hard. "I don't want you to leave. Not at all. Having you here—the two of us . . . I mean, it's been okay, hasn't it?"

"Yeah," she said hoarsely. "It's been okay."

Carefully, I let her go and stepped away. I was blushing furiously. "I can't believe the admissions office sent you a sex-bomb dress."

Kat almost laughed, and my heart performed a perfect somersault. "The funding isn't really through Harcote. It's an anonymous benefactor—or that's how I think of him. It's not just tuition. He paid for my computer, all these new clothes, my flight, everything. But he never did anything like this."

A scholarship for your education was one thing. Letting some unknown zillionaire dress you for special occasions was entirely different.

"You're not going to wear it, right?"

Kat frowned at the box sticking out from under her bed. "As long as it fits."

"But—"

"You read the note. I have to. He wants me to *appear worthy* of Harcote's traditions."

"Which means wearing a dress that makes you look like a blood popsicle."

"He's never asked anything of me before. And I have to wear something to the dance, right?"

I wrinkled my nose at the dress. "'Course. Small price to pay."

TAYLOR

ALL OF SATURDAY was determined by the dance: the countdown to getting ready, and then the countdown from getting ready to the dance itself. When Kat asked if I wanted help with my makeup—"It's cool if you don't want to wear any, but you'd look really great with a little mascara and eyeliner"—I said yes. The delicate brush of her fingers against my cheek, her lips pursed in concentration, made my ribs feel too tight. Hopefully Kat chalked that up to Big Dance Excitement. Then I stepped into the bathroom to change.

I checked myself in the mirror. The suit was royal blue and I wore it over a white tuxedo shirt that I'd found in the boys' department, the top button undone, no tie. I'd never worn a suit before, and I wasn't sure how it was supposed to fit or feel. But Kontos had told me he thought this was the one, and miraculously it didn't need altering. I copied what I'd seen people do in movies: I shrugged into the jacket, stretched my arms to shoot the sleeves, checked the buttons on the cuffs. To my surprise, I actually felt good.

When Kat saw me, and I saw the look on her face, I felt even better.

Kat was grinning, a sparkle in her eyes that I hadn't seen in a while. That little voice in my head, almost too quiet to hear, reminded me, *It doesn't mean anything.*

"You look fantastic," Kat said.

"Really?"

"Yes. *Really* really." *Don't be stupid, Taylor*, the voice pleaded. "I wish I was wearing something like that."

I went to my closet to choose a pair of sneakers. "But you're so girly."

"I'm not *that* girly," she protested.

I pulled out a pair of unblemished white high-tops and sat on my bed to lace them. "Kath-er-ine, have you seen your closet?"

"Those are just *clothes*." The frustration in Kat's voice made me wonder if I was missing something. Uniform notwithstanding, Kat's closet was so full of dresses and skirts, pleated and frilly and swishy, it could have belonged to Goth Barbie.

"They're *your* clothes."

"Only sort of. The Benefactor wanted me to have a wardrobe *befitting a young female vampire.*"

I looked up from my sneaker. So it wasn't just tonight's outfit.

Kat was worrying her red-varnished thumbnail against her lip. To some people, clothes might not seem like a big deal. Harcote's dress guidelines were pretty traditional, and some girls liked wearing that stuff anyway. But it wasn't just about looking nice. It was about making you *be* a certain way, about teaching you how to be a boy or a girl. Making sure that the way you looked expressed what they wanted it to, instead of anything about yourself.

Suddenly that sadness welled up in me. The sadness of having lost the chance to know Kat outside of this place. And sadness *for* her too, for everything she was putting herself through for this stupid school and its toxic people, for feeling like she didn't have a choice but to dress herself up like a doll every day.

"You would be phenomenal in a tux," I told her. "You should wear one next year. But tonight, you're dressing like a tall glass of hot sauce, and it's going to be amazing. Now get changed, or we'll be late."

Kat stepped into the bathroom, the red dress in hand. Once the door was closed, I was right back in front of the mirror. Checking the angles, making sure everything was sitting right and the toes of my sneakers poked out from the sharp creases of the bright-blue fabric. A tremor wobbled through my guts. I'd been trying to ignore that nagging anxiety all day, pretending like I wasn't worried about walking into the dance in a suit. My parents would lose it when they saw the pictures. They'd probably call me up for another chat about how they loved and supported me as their daughter, and they were really fine with *my choices* (yikes), but did I have to attract so much attention to myself?

The awful thing was, they honestly thought they were being supportive. Once my mom had congratulated herself on *being really very modern about the whole thing*. But there was nothing modern about the fact that they had never said the word *lesbian* or how they hoped that no one could tell I was gay just by looking at me. Still, I was lucky not to have it worse, given that both my parents were born before the Constitution was written.

But they weren't here tonight. I crammed my thoughts about them down deep in Basement Brain Storage and assessed myself in the mirror again. The longer I looked, the more the gut-tremor

steadied into something solid and right and true. I ran my fingers
down the lapels, brushed the jacket back to slide my hands into
the slashed pockets of the pants. I unbuttoned one more button of
the shirt—who cared what Radtke would say about dressing like
a lady—shook my curls out, and smiled. Fuck what *anyone* had to
say: I felt like myself in that suit and no one could take that from
me. Kat and I were going to walk into that dance together and
blow their minds.

Then Kat stepped out of the bathroom and my own mind was
blown. The dress—it was a lot when it was just lying in the box,
but on Kat, it was *incredible*. It hung loose off her shoulders, the
smooth bow of her clavicles, then skirted her body, coming in
close in all the right places, the red sequins catching the light and
playing up the auburn in her hair, which she'd twisted up into a
loose bun.

"Wow. You look—um, great," I mumbled. The dress really was
nothing like the fussy clothes this Benefactor had given her for
Seated Dinner. It left nothing to the imagination. As gorgeous as
she was, she also looked cold and uneasy. "Do you feel okay?"

Kat put her hands to her shoulders, like she wanted to hide. "I
just keep thinking . . . why *this* dress?"

"You don't have to wear it. There's time to change." She tried to
give me a look. "I know what you're going to say, but he can't take
away your financial aid because of a stupid dress."

"I'm wearing it," she said in a firm voice. She slid her feet into
sharp-looking heels, then knelt to fasten the straps. The light
caught on her cheekbone, the curve of her ear, the line of her neck,
and in spite of all that beauty, she still looked nervous.

"It's not just for him, is it?" I said slowly. "It's for *them*. I thought
you were done with those girls . . ."

Her gaze shifted toward me. She didn't deny it.

"What's tonight really all about? You asked me to go to the dance and I said I would, although I didn't want to. I promised I'd let everyone believe you weren't going. But to be honest, I'm not totally comfortable going into this blind."

She stood and adjusted her dress. "I'm going with Galen."

A fist of ice hit me in the stomach. "You're *what*?"

"Galen's my date. We planned it in secret, to surprise everyone."

"Galen?" I stepped back. "You don't even like him!"

Kat started. "You don't know that."

I glared at her. "I thought when you saw what those idiots were really like, you'd stop wasting your time trying to fit in. But here you are again, climbing a social ladder to hell."

"I'm not doing this to be friends with them."

"You expect me to believe that after Operation Suck-up?"

"I swear, sometimes you're the most judgmental person in this whole school, Taylor."

I was forced to admit, that one smarted. "This isn't *you*."

"Like you would know."

My heart was racing, my blood too hot. I clenched my hands into fists so Kat wouldn't see that they were shaking. "Then why did you want me to come? Just so I could see the *real you*, on the arm of the school's biggest asshole? Or are you going to fuck me over somehow? That would really make Evangeline happy."

"No! I'm not going to fuck you over. I just—I don't know, I was nervous and I wanted you to be there, okay?"

"Bullshit. You're probably planning to use me somehow to get back with them."

"I would never do that."

"Oh, *like I would know*?" I spat.

"Skip it then. If you want to. I didn't mean to hurt you. I'm sorry."

Before I could say anything else, Kat was through the door, picking her way down the stairs in her heels, to the common room where the other girls would be waiting, ready to gawk at her—to watch her pull off some coup that would hurt me more than it would ever hurt them.

KAT

MY HEART WAS racing so badly, I almost couldn't keep my balance heading down the stairs of Hunter House. Below, the girls were tittering with pre-dance nerves. They'd gathered in the common room, waiting for the boys to call on them—another old-school Harcote tradition. I had to focus on them, on Galen, who was probably walking the path toward the girls' quad right now, on keeping the spike of my heel away from the long swoop of the horrible red dress.

But all I could think about was Taylor.

Taylor sitting alone in our room, seething with anger because she didn't know how to just feel hurt. I almost didn't have words to describe how it had felt seeing Taylor wearing that suit. Something like pride, like exhilaration, like envy. Taylor had looked radiant. Her smile had been a rare thing—a smile that nothing and no one, not even Taylor herself, could suppress. I could have looked at it all night. For a minute I had caught myself thinking that we really were going to the dance together, not just as friends.

And then it all came crashing down.

I paused on the first-floor landing, clutching the banister.

I should go back up. I should see if Taylor was okay. I should apologize—but what for, exactly? For doing something Taylor didn't agree with? Taylor didn't agree with most of what I and everyone else on Earth did. Her standards were impossible to live up to, left no room for understanding or compromise or someone else's perspective. Taylor thought that I wasn't being myself and she was right.

That wasn't an accident or a weakness. It was a choice.

But standing next to Taylor in that suit, wearing this dress that crawled against me like someone else's skin, waiting for the date I'd secured just to impress girls I didn't respect, it didn't quite feel that way.

Downstairs, the front door swung open. The thumps of boys' dress shoes filled in the entryway.

I pressed my lips together tight against a burst of nausea. The lilting sound of Galen's name floated up the stairs to where I stood.

You don't even like him, Taylor had said.

I'd almost laughed when she said it. Not because it was funny, but because she was right. Somehow Taylor had managed to see what everyone else—Evangeline and Lucy, Galen himself, maybe, just a little bit, me—had missed: I had only ever pretended to like Galen as more than a friend.

I couldn't turn back now. My future was at the bottom of these stairs.

Not in the little attic room I'd just left.

So I adjusted the dress one last time and forced myself to go meet it.

I stepped into the common room. For a second, it felt like that first day: dozens of gorgeous vampire eyes trained on me, taking me in, sizing me up.

But this time was different. This time I was studded in ten thousand sequins, and I knew that, if looks could kill, everyone in that room would be dead. Across the room, elegantly leaning one shoulder on the fireplace mantle, was a boy waiting just for me. As Galen saw me, his usual wry composure melted into astonishment, his perfectly bowed lips parted and his gunmetal eyes wide. Then all at once he collected himself: un-notched his shoulder from the mantle and stood up straight, his face settled back into that elegant look. But his cheeks stayed flushed pink.

So what if I didn't get butterflies when I saw him? Real life wasn't a rom-com. I liked when he looked at me in that way, and that when he did, it made everyone else see me differently. Wasn't that enough?

As I crossed the room to him, my breathing was quick and shallow, but I don't think anyone heard it over the rustling of my dress. Lucy—Carsten's arms circling her waist—gave a low whistle. Evangeline was beside her, dateless. There was a smile located in the area of her mouth, but it didn't distract from the increasingly freaked out look in her eyes as they shifted from me to Galen and back again.

Evangeline laid her hand on my arm. "Kat! What a fun surprise— I thought you weren't coming."

"I changed my mind." I brushed her hand aside and went up to Galen.

"Hi," I said to him softly. With everyone watching us, the butterflies felt real enough—even if they weren't for him.

"Hi," he said, his voice a little husky. Then he leaned in and kissed me on the cheek. "You look beautiful, Kat."

I dropped my eyes and I bit my lip as a wave of awkwardness surged through me—but everyone would see how happy I was to be with Galen. The room hummed with subtle whispers passed from mouth to ear behind cupped hands as I nestled my hand into his.

Ms. Radtke, who was monitoring us a little less sternly than usual, announced that if everyone was accounted for, we had better move toward the Great Hall. I glanced toward the stairs. Was Taylor really not coming? Did she honestly think that I was going to make her the butt of some horrible joke? But it was too late to worry about that now—too late to stop what I'd set in motion.

As we walked the October-cold path to the Great Hall, Galen's and my hands stayed laced together, a faint film of sweat between our palms.

"Do you think they were surprised?" I asked.

He gazed down at me, his curls tangled with darkness and his face illuminated a chemical kind of gold by the path lights. "I don't care what they think. The only person I care about tonight is you."

He was being honest, I could tell, and suddenly our hands felt too close. I gritted my teeth. I was just getting used to being like this with him, I told myself. Once we got to the dance, I'd relax. "Come on, they're all getting ahead of us," I said.

The entry to the Great Hall was swarmed with students. Everyone saw us, noticed us, said something about us: The golden boy no one could have, the new girl they just now realized they wanted. The Vampire King and Queen of the night. This was what I wanted, I reminded myself. I said it again and again in my head as I climbed the stairs to the Great Hall, careful in my heels, holding my skirt out of the way. Then Galen was there gallantly beside me, holding my arm as if I couldn't manage it myself.

At the top of the stairs, I couldn't help it. I turned back and looked back at the path we'd just come down.

"What are you looking for?" Galen asked.

"Nothing," I said.

The other students stepped out of our way as Galen and I passed through the doors. Not one of them said a word to us.

22

TAYLOR

I SAT ON my bed with my head in my hands, my fingers poking up into my hair, for longer than I wanted to admit—for long after the strike of Kat's heels on the stairs had ended, and the frenzy downstairs had crested and burst out the front door, and Hunter House was quiet again. I was moping and I hated moping and my face was smeared with that godforsaken eyeliner I let her put on me, but I couldn't stop myself.

I was such a fucking fool.

My every wall should have been fortified against her, but she'd gotten through, wormed her way into my heart. I'd allowed myself to believe that the hot-air-balloon feeling I got when she looked at me was at least a little bit because she didn't want to annihilate me. That she wasn't like the rest of the students at this school, who were walking evidence for the theory that vampires had sold their souls to the devil for immortality. So here I was, again, like always: alone and cursing myself for giving two shits about Katherine freaking Finn.

But in my—admittedly fragile—defense, it had made sense to think that things would be different after Kat had come home from Lucy's party shattered and covered in dried blood. The person I knew Kat to be, the old Kat I couldn't completely let go of, would never have talked herself into being okay with that. But now, not only was Kat going to the dance with the biggest dick-bag of them all—with his stupid swoopy hair and hot cartoon character face, he looked like a young French alcoholic, like someone who would give half his NYU class chlamydia and deny it—and she was doing it to win over the exact people who'd set the whole party up in the first place.

I ran my hands over the blue fabric stretched across my thighs. I wanted to claw my own eyes out thinking about how stupidly happy I'd been just a half hour earlier. How I'd convinced myself that if we couldn't go as dates, we could go as friends, and that would be enough. That I lived in a world where I could walk into the Founder's Dance, wearing this suit, and things wouldn't just go totally to shit—that it mattered how I felt and that for once, I felt good. That this fucked-up universe would let me have that, for a few short hours.

If I was anyone to Kat at all, it was another person to crush as she stomped her way to the top.

But vampires were like that—they couldn't change their nature, and their nature was selfish. I had always known that, yet these last few weeks, I still allowed myself to believe—to hope—that something different was possible.

I raked my fingers through my hair.

I was going to the dance. Not for Kat—not for any of them.

KAT

THE GREAT HALL had been transformed: the pews gone to make way for a dance floor, its chandeliers lit with colored lights that cast strange patterns on the Gothic ceiling, the bass of pop music throbbing against its ornate carved walls. Despite everything, I still felt that rush of possibility as we walked in, as I had for dances at home. Our group did a quick tour of the space so Lucy, who was on the Founder's Dance Committee, could point out this or that decoration that they had agonized over. From the moment Galen had kissed me on the cheek, the girls had acted as if the last two weeks hadn't even happened.

We huddled into one of the dark chapels and Carsten passed around a flask he'd been hiding in his jacket. He hadn't spoken to me tonight—or actually ever—since I'd hauled him with me through a glass table at Lucy's party. As I took the flask from Evangeline, Galen shot me a questioning look, but I tipped it back. The alcohol was warm from Carsten's body heat and hit my mouth like acid. My stomach turned a little, remembering the last time I'd felt that burn on my tongue, the chaotic sound of the glass shattering under me, the hot flow of blood down my back.

But the alcohol made everything a little softer, a little easier to handle. I was grateful for it. Evangeline and Lucy were pretending I didn't know they'd spent the last two weeks being total assholes to me, and I let them. We all clung to each other, complimenting how hot we all looked: "Truly gorgeous, these boys don't deserve us"— "You *literally* slay"—"This is almost too hot to post." We pulled each other into selfies, cramming together to get in one shot.

"Fangs out, girls!" Lucy cried and let her incisors elongate, their tips so sharp they were almost translucent. Knowing what those fangs had been used for sent a wave of revulsion through my stomach, but I made myself ignore it. More than ignore it. I let my fangs slip down too, copying how the other girls smiled with their mouths hanging open in a sexy sneer, to avoid messing up their lipstick. I stuck my tongue out when they did. I copied how they posed, stuck my chest out, angled my shoulders. And I didn't feel bad about it—not really—because this was what I was here for.

Evangeline was even more stunning than usual. Her lips were painted bright red, and her hair was pressed into Veronica Lake–style waves, and the black column of her dress made the pale skin of her shoulders and the swell of her cleavage hard not to look at. On anyone else it would have been campy, over-the-top vampiric. On Evangeline it made you want to get down on your knees and beg her to suck your blood.

Everyone at Harcote knew Evangeline wasn't afraid to be mean, even cruel, even to her friends. That was why her opinion mattered: she set a bar most couldn't clear, which made people grovel for her approval. I was done groveling.

I put on a confident smile and opened with a classic: "I *love* that dress."

"Please, everyone's looking at you tonight." She ran her eyes over my body. "Truly, where did you get it?"

"I decided to come last minute, so I didn't have time to buy anything. Lucky thing, I had this lying around."

Evangeline's gaze shifted. She was watching the boys watching Galen, really. I kept my spine stiff, waiting for an attack I'd have to parry, some attempt to cut me down that I'd need to dodge. But then she said softly, "How did you get him to go with you?"

In that moment, Evangeline looked younger than I'd ever seen her, her brow wrinkled and her lips gently pursed. It was an earnest look of confusion, and beneath it, a kind of melancholy. It wouldn't take more than the truth to hurt her.

"What do you mean? I didn't *get* him to do anything. He just asked me. Out of the blue."

The tender look was gone from Evangeline's face. "That's so sweet."

"I know." I smiled. "I had a crush on him from that first day, but I'm just the new girl and everyone says the two of you are going to end up together. So I never even tried. I guess he wanted it bad enough for the both of us."

Evangeline turned to face me. Her arms were folded and, her long red nails resting against her pale white skin. "Did he tell you? Before he *just asked you* to the dance?"

She'd caught me off guard, and she knew it.

"There's a reason people say Galen and I will end up together." Her eyes shifted over my shoulder. "Watch yourself."

Suddenly, I felt hands running along my waist. I jumped.

"Hey, it's just me," Galen said. "Want to dance?"

I let him lead me onto the dance floor, leaving Evangeline alone.

TAYLOR

WHEN I STOMPED up to the Great Hall, it was bursting with sound, not just the beat of whatever stupid music they were playing, but laughter, screaming, the energy of the undead at a Halloween formal. As I climbed the steps, the hard drive in my pocket slapped heavily against my leg. Then I gritted my teeth and shoved open the door.

Whatever was going on inside could not have been less important to me. Trav Dorian wearing a high-collared cape and an honest-to-god top hat, dismally regarding the dance floor like he was disappointed they weren't playing organ music. Anna Rose and Jane Marie Dent, both of them looking like young widows who'd lost their husbands in the War of Northern Aggression, whispering into each other's ears. Party lights! Flashes from the selfie booth! Girls rubbing their formalwear-clad asses on boys who didn't deserve them! In other words: typical dance shit.

I wished there was a way I could look for Kontos without having to bear witness to this orgy of Youngblood vampire hormones, but alas.

Then, like in a scene from a movie, the crowd parted. There was no way I could miss them: Galen and Kat, in the middle of the dance floor. The lighting was perfect. They were right under one of the lanterns that hung from the cathedral ceiling, illuminating them in their own spotlight. It lit Kat's red dress up like wildfire, the sequins hugging her body and the low back showing her spine. My heart launched straight to my throat. Galen's stupid arms were around Kat's waist, hers slung around his neck. He was just the exact right amount taller than her that she had to look just slightly up at him, and he had to look just slightly down, his stupid mop of curls pomaded back and just a little loose from the heat. It would look to anyone who was watching them—which was definitely more than just me—like they were a heartbeat away from a kiss.

I had to hand it to Kat. With that glassy-eyed, moony look she had trained on Galen, I could hardly even see the lie.

But then they turned, and I saw where her hands met, behind Galen's neck. Kat was digging her fingernail into the cuticle of her thumbnail, hard enough to hurt.

"Caught you staring," a voice said behind me.

I faced Evangeline, specifically so she could see my eyes roll. "I was looking respectfully."

Evangeline arched her eyebrow, her lips in a slick red pout. I gave her a quick once-over: she looked absolutely killer, a vampire pinup in a tight black dress that skimmed the floor.

In return, she raked her eyes over me. "You're looking very Gay Pride Parade."

It sounded like an insult, but her tone and the glint in her eye said otherwise. "You look like Morticia Adams with a perm, so I guess we're even." Evangeline did something I didn't expect: she smiled, actually smiled, at that. I'd seen Evangeline arrange her lips in all kinds of ways, condescending little grins and manipulative pouts and derisive curls. But this—her real smile—I hadn't seen since we were firsties. I quickly said, "I'm just here looking for Kontos. Have you seen him?"

"He's by the Hema." Evangeline inclined her head toward a table on the far side of the room, a bubbling fountain of Hema sat in the middle of it, a human aide ladling it into fancy cocktail glasses. Kontos was bopping dorkily to the beat, every now and then leaning over to listen to whatever Radtke was saying— probably pointing out girls whose dresses she thought missed the turnoff for Acceptable Femininity and gone straight to Slut Town. I left Evangeline and circled the dance floor over to where they stood.

"Kontos, we need to talk," I yelled over the music.

"Taylor!" he beamed. "Wow, you look great!"

I fought the urge to cringe, although my guts definitely clenched up, as Kontos waved Radtke over to take a look at my suit. Another candidate for surprise of the night: Radtke assessed me and issued a tight-lipped smile with a curt nod—not an endorsement, but not the opposite either. Well. That was a nice change of pace.

"Can I talk to you outside—alone?" I asked.

"We can talk tomorrow! Have some fun tonight. I saw Kat was

here with Galen. They're both at my table for Seated Dinner and this completely slipped under my nose."

"*Kontos.*"

His mustache drooped, then he shouted something to Radtke and I followed him outside.

Away from the music, the night felt eerily quiet, packed in cotton. I led Kontos around the side of the building. I didn't want anyone interrupting us.

"I'm out," I said.

"You're out? Out of what?"

"Of your big secret plan!" I said. "I don't want anything to do with it."

"Taylor—what's wrong?"

I rubbed a knuckle over my forehead. "Why does something always have to be wrong?"

"You're obviously upset about something."

"Yeah, I'm upset that I bought into your bullshit."

His face fell. I pushed on.

"The whole project is just a big fucking waste of time. If you can't see that, I can." My voice was shaking a little, the words brutal, but I couldn't stop myself. Fuck him, fuck everything—I was so angry, and that anger needed a target, and maybe Kontos didn't deserve it, but he'd wandered into my crosshairs at the wrong time. "Vampires can't act morally. The Youngbloods especially. It's impossible. And even if they could, they wouldn't do it. Without that, your whole plan collapses into a literal bloodbath. It's a lost cause."

"I have faith that won't happen."

"How could you?" But all of a sudden, I wanted him to answer me truthfully. After everything he'd lived through, he still believed in goodness. I wanted that too—to have faith in things, to believe in people, to look at the unending immortal future that stretched out before me and imagine it could be anything other than total shit.

"People can surprise you, if you let them," he said earnestly.

"Surprise you with a stake in the back," I muttered.

"There are humans and vampires out there who need our help. I can see that. I know you do too. If there's the two of us, there are others."

I could still see the horror and disgust on Kat's face that night she came back from Lucy's. It was a distant memory from how she looked tonight, sucking up to the same people she'd called hypocrites.

"You're wrong about me," I said flatly. "I don't see it."

As his face crumpled, I realized that I would remember this moment for a long time. Because that look was worse than disappointment—it was heartbreak. "If you change your mind . . ."

I couldn't stand him looking at me like that—like I'd failed him. It wasn't my fault he wanted something from me that I couldn't give. The worst part was, I knew that he wouldn't give up on me, even after this. He'd still do French Cinema Club, he'd check in on me, he might even ask again if I'd join the reunionists. Kontos would forgive me and forgive me and forgive me when I didn't deserve it, because that was the horrible, beautiful way he was: forgiving people who hadn't done a single good thing in their entire immortal lives.

"I won't change my mind. I never really believed this would work. It was always a lie." To seal the deal, I thrust the hard drive toward him. "You can take that back."

"Taylor . . ."

I needed him stop looking at me like he was trying to figure out what was wrong with me.

"What?" I said viciously. He didn't continue.

"I'm going to put this in my office. Maybe we can talk about this on Monday."

"There's nothing to talk about."

He smiled sadly. "I hope you can still enjoy the dance. The suit looks perfect," he said, then walked toward the Science Building.

I just stood in that shadow at the edge of the Great Hall, burning with a feeling I didn't understand at all. I was heart-racingly, furiously angry—at Kontos, at Kat, at myself, at the whole of fucking Vampirdom—and for some incomprehensible reason there were tears in my eyes, even though I had banned tears from the vicinity of my eyes anytime I was in public. It was as if I'd wrenched myself in two. Half of me wanted to run back to my room and bury my head in my pillows and try to forget this night ever happened. But if I did that, I'd be alone with this pukey swirl of emotions until Kat came back and made me feel worse.

Or I could go back into the dance, where it was too loud to think about anything. I could pretend to be just like all of them, someone who didn't give a shit about anyone or anything other than myself.

Fuck it. I looked great in this suit. It would be criminal if I didn't show it off. I wasn't going to let Katherine freaking Finn stop me.

KAT

OF COURSE, RIGHT after we started dancing, a slow song came on. Galen slid his hands to my waist and pulled me close, like it was the most natural thing in the world. I set my hands on his shoulders, my fingers meeting at the base of his neck.

Only to me, it didn't feel natural.

It felt *wrong*. Like the world was out of alignment. Like it shouldn't have been the two of us like this, his hands weren't the ones that were supposed to be pressed against the bare skin of my back, my eyes weren't the ones he was supposed to be staring into with that soft look. But then he was looking at me with such gentleness, with a hopeful smile playing on his lips. I should have fallen in love with that look. I should have returned it. I *wanted* to return it.

But instead it made me feel small and lost.

"I have a surprise for you," he said, pulling me closer.

I took my hand from his neck and brushed my hair back, even though I knew perfectly well it didn't need brushing. "I don't need any surprises, Galen."

"I think you'll like this," he said. "You remember the humans, from Lucy's party?"

A knot tightened in my throat. "Of course."

"I know you were worried about them. So I tracked them down—"

"You *tracked them down*?"

"I have a lot of, um, resources?" he said awkwardly. "I thought you'd want to know that they're all okay."

"That's good." I didn't know what else to say. Those people weren't okay, no matter what Galen thought, or wanted to believe. They'd been glamoured out of their minds, then traumatized by hungry teen vampires. That had to leave a pale ghost behind, even if you didn't remember it.

"But that's not the surprise. You said I had the power to make a difference if I wanted to, and I couldn't stop thinking about that.

So I sent each of them some money. Anonymously, of course. I gave them each five hundred dollars."

My chest tightened. "You gave them five hundred dollars?"

"It was important, you know, to do something. It's like you said, feeding on humans isn't harmless."

Behind his neck, I dug a fingernail into the cuticle of my thumb. I could barely breathe.

Five hundred dollars.

Not even a month's rent. It was nothing, it meant absolutely nothing—especially from someone as wealthy as Galen, who could plunge into their lives and change it with money. Like the Benefactor had done for me.

No amount of money could make up for the way the way those people had been violated.

And Galen—I could barely look at him. When we'd first met, I'd thought he was in love with himself. Now I saw that wasn't the problem at all: it was that the whole world was in love with him and he hadn't yet understood that. People listened to him, caved to him, anticipated his needs so he'd never have to feel them too sharply. The world responded to his power in a million ways so subtle that he had never had to see them. It was exactly how Victor Castel would pick him as the voice of the Youngblood generation, a role he'd been born to play, and at the same time Galen could believe that the best he could do to stand up for humans was secretly handing out cash.

Suddenly the Great Hall felt cramped and close, the air sizzling with the heat of the bodies on the dance floor, the pounding thud of the music, flashing lights. The Youngbloods with their polished shoes and painted eyes, *harmlessly* sinking their teeth into any clean vein.

I wanted to light a match and watch all of them go up in flames.

Galen was looking down at me like an eager puppy, waiting for me to tell him that he'd been a good boy.

And what did I do?

I tipped my head up like he was my hero. I ignored the black slime coating my insides. I just dug my nail deeper into that cuticle, let the tiny burst of pain ground me.

"That was really great of you." I heard my voice say it. But I was far, far away.

TAYLOR

I STALKED BACK into the Great Hall like I was Keanu Reeves in *The Matrix* or Keanu Reeves in *John Wick*. I left the Taylor who felt bad about the conversation with Kontos outside; this Taylor was high on being an ass to the one person whose opinion mattered.

Obviously, I noticed instantly that Kat was still clinging to Galen. It produced absolutely no reaction in me whatsoever. Actually, an inverse reaction: it caused me to feel less. He was a dick-vein, Kat was a dick-veinette, none of that was my problem.

Evangeline was on the dance floor too, winding her hips in a circle of girls. Lucy was in the center, showing off her "twerk skills" (she had not shut up about this for weeks). Not even the totally heterosexual act of watching her gorgeous best friend competently shake her ass brought a smile to the face of Evangeline Lazareanu tonight.

She was still sulking that her Vampire Prince had chosen a new Princess.

That made me optimistic about what I was about to do.

I'd told her I wanted her to treat me better as many times as she'd told me she wasn't really into girls. Neither of those statements had ever made any difference in what we actually did. Evangeline was always the one who ran the show—who texted me, who snared me in the costume closet. All I ever did was go along with it, just so I'd have the chance to feel her body against mine and pretend it was affection.

Not tonight.

Tonight I was free: free of any fucks given about Kat, about Kontos's delusional hopes, about this whole idiotic excuse for school.

I slipped my hands into the pockets of my suit and circled the dance floor. I stopped exactly where Evangeline would see me. Normally, I wasn't very good at flirting—I rarely got to practice—but in that moment it came natural. Evangeline looked up and saw me, our eyes met, and something happened involuntarily: there was a fire in me, a fire that demanded feeding. That demanded *her*.

Evangeline's eyes widened, her lips parted. Almost in the same instant she was making some excuse to Lucy, rolling her eyes about it because everyone knew Taylor Sanger was the ultimate nuisance. I didn't hear what Evangeline said when her friends asked what business she had with me. The only thing that mattered was that as I walked toward a darkened chapel at the back of the Great Hall, she followed.

KAT

WHEN TAYLOR WALKED into the Great Hall, she was hard to miss—as usual, she was like a sparkler in the dark. I always seemed to know where she was.

So I saw it when she gave Evangeline that *look*. Like she was done undressing her with her eyes and was ready to do it with her hands. She jutted her jaw toward one of the chapels and Evangeline went right after her.

They couldn't be . . . they couldn't actually—Taylor hated Evangeline, and Evangeline couldn't stand Taylor. It was impossible, completely *unthinkable* that they'd sneak off together. Evangeline was a snake, and she'd hurt Taylor the second it was in her interest. She had to be planning some kind of scheme, something to get Taylor in trouble or worse, humiliated, and it was my fault that Taylor was even at the dance in the first place.

I considered going after them, grabbing Taylor and warning her, but they disappeared into a shadow.

Another slow song came on and Galen pulled me in again. Automatically now, I slid my hands up the front of his tux to rest on his shoulders. Just like that, I couldn't even see where Taylor and Evangeline had gone anymore.

I couldn't stop thinking about what would happen when they were alone, what Evangeline would do—what she might be doing, right now . . .

Evangeline's hands on Taylor, sliding under her jacket.

Evangeline's fingers twined in Taylor's curls.

Taylor pressing her up against the wall.

Their mouths, their lips colliding in a hungry kiss that they'd resisted for too long—

Galen slid his hand up my side. "Hey, where'd you go?"

I jumped, breathing sharply, and snapped my eyes up. It felt like they were open too wide, like I could see too sharply all of a sudden—my senses attuned to whatever was happening in that dark corner.

"I'm right here."

I tried to push the image of Taylor and Evangeline out of my head. But of all the things I'd forced myself to ignore in the last few weeks, this wouldn't leave me. My whole body felt too hot, wound too tight.

"You just seemed distracted."

He drew me closer—he was always *drawing me closer*, no matter how I tried to maintain the few inches between us. He'd been doing it all night—touching me in this gentlemanly way: his hand on my back guiding me through the crowd, his arms around my waist as we danced, a touch on my bare shoulder when he spoke to me. He did it with a confidence that would have been attractive if I'd been watching him treat some other girl this way. But instead I felt small, diminished, like I was vanishing into nothing. All night I'd been ignoring that feeling, but now that I was suddenly burning, I wanted his touch less than ever.

I pulled away. "It's a hot in here, isn't it?"

"Should we step outside?"

Fresh air would fix things. Whatever Evangeline and Taylor were doing, it was none of my business. There was a 100 percent chance that nothing was going on, it was all in my head.

But why was *that* in my head?

"Outside sounds good," I said.

Galen slipped his arm around me and it was all I could do to stop myself from flinching.

TAYLOR

EVANGELINE BARELY WAITED until we were out of view to smash her face into mine, cramming her tongue into my mouth, pressing her pointed nails into my neck. It was shocking in the best possible way: Evangeline never kissed me like that, like I was water and she was dying of thirst. I smiled hard against her lips.

This. This was exactly what I wanted.

Evangeline pulling on the lapels of my suit, tugging me forward until her back pressed against the stone of the chapel walls.

Evangeline curving against me when I breathed into her ear, "What if someone sees?"

Evangeline trembling as she said, "Fuck this dance and everybody here."

That might have made me tremble too.

I kissed her again, harder this time, running my hands over the bare skin of her shoulders, then lower. Her body arched against mine.

Evangeline wanted me. She wanted me even though she pretended sometimes that I didn't exist, and she didn't care who saw. *I* had that power over *her.*

She broke the kiss when we were both gasping for air, my leg pressing at the place between hers. With the pad of her thumb, she wiped away the lipstick she'd smeared across my lips.

I was considering taking her thumb into my mouth when she said, "You look so hot in that suit, for a second I thought you were a guy."

I froze. "You *what*?"

"I almost thought you were a guy. Hey—"

I pulled away, but Evangeline grabbed my arm. There was only so far I could go before we had no privacy at all. I had to settled for wrenching her hand off me.

"Don't say shit like that to me," I hissed at her.

"Come on, Taylor. It was a compliment."

"*You* come the fuck on. If you want to make out with a guy, why don't you go find one?"

She darkened—I almost felt bad about it. But when Evangeline was hurt—really when she felt anything at all—that's when the daggers came out. "Let me guess what comes next: *I'm done with you, Evangeline, this is the last time.* But we both know it's the last time when *I* say it's the last time."

I wanted to press her back against that wall and kiss her until she couldn't talk anymore. I wanted that almost as much as I wanted to walk away from her and never look back. But I guess more than anything, I wanted to stand there and let her hurt me.

Because that's what I did.

"You don't have a chance with Kat." Evangeline trailed a finger along the line of my jacket, the ruby-red nail catching the light from the dance floor. "But you don't need me to tell you that. You saw her with him."

It made me want to puke that Evangeline even knew enough to mention Kat precisely now. But I also knew that, in her own fucked up way, Evangeline was sympathizing. The two people we wanted, wanted each other instead. It would almost have been tragic, if it had happened to nicer people.

"There you are!" two voices said at once. "We've been looking for you!"

I sprung back from Evangeline, scrubbing my mouth with the back of my hand. Just as fast, Evangeline had her arms crossed, a bored stare on her face, like with the power of her impatient gaze alone she could vanish Anna Rose and Jane Marie Dent, the way some kids burned up ants with magnifying glasses.

"What do you want?" Evangeline demanded.

"We're not looking for you," Anna Rose said.

"We're looking for Taylor," Jane Marie said.

I'd already edged over to the far side of the chapel, en route to getting the hell out of there. "For me?"

"It's Kat," they both said at once.

23

KAT

I LET GALEN lead me down the steps of the Great Hall and out to the grass, far enough away that the chaperones could still see us. The cold air stung, but it did nothing to release that tightness in my chest or the tension in my stomach.

Galen swept off his jacket. "You must be cold."

He settled it around my shoulders before I had a chance to say anything, as if he'd wanted to go outside precisely so he could do this, not because I was feeling anxious. It smelled like his woodsy cologne and beneath that, the tang of his sweat.

I made myself focus on him. I used to fantasize about someone who looked like Galen—not exactly, but right in the way that he looked right, like he'd stormed in off a moor or out of an ad for men's cologne. He was handsome in a way that was flawless, exquisite, and it felt nearly bloodless. But the way he was looking at me—had been looking at me all night—I knew he'd be mine if I let him. At Galen's side, life at Harcote would be easy. I'd have a place in Vampirdom. I'd never be forgotten or left behind.

But as much as I had longed for that, I couldn't bring myself to long for *him*.

"Are you having fun?" he was asking.

"Yeah," I said faintly.

"I'm really glad we came together. Everyone was shocked. It felt really good to see them like that."

Taylor's face in our room earlier that night, when I'd told her I was going with Galen. The quick burst of disappointment, of hurt that she'd tried to hide.

Was slipping away with Evangeline some kind of revenge?

No, that was ridiculous.

Galen's knuckles grazed my chin as he tipped my head up. "Hey, you sure you're okay?"

I scrambled for an excuse. "I—I was thinking about home, actually. I just realized I'm not going to get to go to winter formal or prom with my friends this year."

Unexpectedly, I could see it so clearly: Taylor in the gym with me and Guzman and Shelby; Taylor and me dancing together, her hand in mine; Taylor actually smiling, laughing, that hardened frown she never let up at Harcote gone.

Galen arched that eyebrow. "Don't tell me there's a guy at home?"

"Oh no. That's not what I meant."

"Good." His voice was rougher than it had been a second before. I realized he was standing closer than he had been all night, his face hovering near mine. I knew what was coming. I let him do it. His fingers tilted my chin up, and then his mouth was on mine, and he was kissing me.

My eyes stayed wide open as his fluttered closed, and there was a voice screaming in my head, *be normal, think of what a normal person would do in this situation, and do that.*

Slowly, my lips moved against his.

I forced my eyes closed.

Galen slid his hands under the jacket, his icy fingers pressed against the bare skin of my back. Pulling me closer. His tongue in my mouth. Mine in his.

I didn't feel any kind of rush or heat or excitement. The only feeling surging through me was a hopeless kind of numbness. It was as if I was outside of myself, watching a beautiful girl kiss a beautiful boy, like it was a movie and I was sitting in the red velvet seats, my sneakers stuck to the floor, watching some starlet who wasn't me, who I didn't know at all.

But I wasn't outside of myself.

No one ever was.

My eyes flew open, and just like that, the fragile scaffolding of the last weeks shuddered and collapsed and the ground rushed up toward me: sucking up to Evangeline and Lucy, kissing Galen, leaving Guzman and Shelby's texts on read, how badly I missed my mom, all the things I used to be. What was I doing to myself?

I realized I was crying.

Then it was more than crying. I was shaking all over, pushing him away, and my shoulders had crawled up toward my ears—his jacket on the ground—I was saying "I'm sorry, I'm sorry, I can't" over and over. He was asking me what was wrong, with real fear in his eyes—"It's nothing, I'm sorry, I'm sorry." I said it again and again and again until I could barely breathe around the words, it was just the gulp and hiss over my lungs struggling for air. Was I dying, was I literally actually dying at a school dance? I fell to my knees, the grass wet against my palms and the sequins of the stupid red dress cutting into me, and I didn't think vampires could suffocate, but could we? *Could we?*

"Get Radtke!" someone yelled.

Then somehow I sitting on the steps, the stems of dozens of legs crowded around me, and Ms. Radtke was sitting beside me. "In and out," she was saying. "Slowly, slowly now."

How to breathe. Another thing I'd let go of in the last few weeks.

"Jesus, Galen, what'd you do to her?" someone laughed.

Galen's fist connected with his cheekbone and then chaos was erupting all around us. Ms. Radtke stumbling to her feet to pull them apart, yelling, "Where is Mr. Kontos?"

I stared down into my hands, smeared with mascara I'd wiped from my cheeks. The tears wouldn't stop, even as my breathing steadied. That feeling wouldn't leave me—like I wasn't anyone, like I could disappear completely. Like I already had. Like maybe that was a good thing.

Something blue slid into my vision. *Taylor* was crouching on the grass in front of me.

"Hey," she said. She didn't ask what was wrong or if I was okay. Just *hey*—but I understood. It meant, *I'm here*. It meant, *I've got you*.

I needed her. And she was here.

Just like that, that horrible feeling of nothingness was gone.

"So I know you're probably having a lot of fun," she said. "But I actually injured myself on the dance floor, and Radtke wants you to take me back to our room. Her hands are kind of full judging this toxic masculinity pageant." Taylor cocked her head to the left. Ms. Radtke had several boys lined up so she could scold them. Galen was shaking out his hand.

"You injured yourself dancing?" I said quietly.

Taylor nodded somberly. "Looks like a case of prom ankle. It could happen to anyone." She stood and held out her hand.

I took it.

TAYLOR

THE WALK BACK to Hunter House was slow, and cold, and the only sound was the wind blowing leaves off the trees and the tap of Kat's heels on the bricks. I kept watch on her from the corner of my eye. All Anna Rose and Jane Marie had said was that she'd gone outside with Galen and had some kind of panic attack. People were saying they'd been kissing. When I heard that, I'd wanted to kill Galen, although it was way too early in my immortality to become a murderer. But now that the sounds from the Great Hall were fading, I started to wonder if this wasn't part of Kat's plan. Everyone at the dance was talking about Kat and Galen. If Harcote had indulged in anything as trashy as the human tradition of prom queen, she'd have won by a landslide. Now they were watching us walk away, like Kat was a little wounded bird. Was the ragged breathing and mascara-streaked face part of her act?

Was *I* part of it? Kat had claimed she'd left me out of it. I'd sworn that I didn't believe her and sworn again that I was over caring about her. Still, I'd literally run through the Great Hall to find her. I'd never stopped caring about her. I never could. That was my problem. Like being in love with Katherine Finn was the stone I'd spend my immortality pushing up a hill, just so it could roll back and crush me again, and again, and again.

We closed the door to Hunter House behind us. With everyone at the dance, it was silent and still. Kat shucked off her heels and climbed the stairs. I followed her.

In the room, Kat went straight to her closet and started digging for something at the back.

I paced from my desk to my bed, waiting like an idiot for her to explain what happened or say she was okay or reveal that she really was a sociopath. I could still taste Evangeline on my lips, feel the cruelty in her words. The longer Kat was silent the easier it was to believe that she'd tricked me, that she had treated me just as badly as Evangeline did, and by a logic I couldn't quite follow, both of them were right for doing it. When Kat pulled the straps of that stupid gorgeous dress from her shoulders and let it fall with a *fwump* to the floor, I spun around and hung my jacket in the closet, just to have something to do.

When I turned back, she was wearing an oversized sweatshirt from her old high school and a pair of basketball shorts that hung past her knees. They were *her* clothes, not Harcote's or the Bene-factor's. Clothes I hadn't seen her wear since Move-in Day. She still looked shaken and a little sad, but a little more at ease. Actually, she looked a lot like the girl I remembered. The girl I'd imagined she still was.

Finally, I said, "If you're not going to tell me what happened, at least tell me if he hurt you."

"It was nothing like that." Her voice was heavy.

I set my hips against the edge of my desk. "You did a good job of making it look like it was."

"What do you mean?"

"That was your plan, right? Go to the dance with Galen, then cue the panic attack and you'll get sympathy points for the rest of the year. Honestly I'm all for pulling one over on Galen, since he completely sucks. I have to hand it to you. That's, like, Evangeline Lazareanu–level devious. I didn't think you had it in you."

"That's not what happened." I forced myself to ignore how exhausted she sounded.

"That's why you wanted me there, right? So your exit really popped."

Suddenly, she whirled on me. "Wow, you cracked my plan, Taylor. I *made* you to show up to the dance. Then I got you to make out with Evangeline, for extra added drama."

I froze. "I wasn't . . . doing that."

"I saw you go off with her."

"You didn't see anything else," I said. "You don't know what happened."

She folded her arms. "Then what happened?"

"We . . ." I began, but good lying is all in the timing and I was too late. Kat was shaking her head at me. "Oh, like you can judge me when you were making out with *Galen* in front of the entire school!" The name tasted rotten on my tongue.

"Exactly! And I hated every second of it." She'd hated kissing Galen—had she hated it so much she'd almost stopped breathing? "I thought you were better than Evangeline."

"What do you care who I kiss, *Kath-er-ine*? You don't know what it's like for me. How lonely and isolating it is to be the one queer kid in at a school like this. Everyone thinks I'm some kind of freak because I'm not exactly like them—"

"You're not a freak—"

"Thanks, but I fucking know that, okay?" I said. "I don't need any more of your little attempts to validate my identity. I can take care of myself."

"Or let Evangeline take care of you," Kat sneered. "When she's not busy insulting you in front of the whole class."

"What do you care about her anyway? Last I checked *you* were the one thirsty for her attention, not me. Are you jealous? Because she's a total psycho once you get to know her and—"

But there was no *and*. The *and* vanished into the ether, because all of a sudden, Kat was kissing me.

Kat was kissing *me*.

I didn't even clock her closing the distance between us. It was so sudden that my hands were still curled around the edge of the desk, clutching the wood laminate edge, my elbows locked. Kat's lips were warm and velvet and sweet against mine. Her hair fell against my face and it smelled like that jasmine shampoo. Her palm cupping my jaw, her fingers light against my cheek. I almost didn't manage to kiss her back—until I did. Her eyes were closed and her nose pressed into my cheek, and it was somehow gentle and frantic at the same time, like the way it feels just before you finally let yourself cry.

She pulled away. Her eyes full-moon wide, cheeks bright. Her lips were parted in something like shock, or disgust, or confusion. I had no way to tell, and no time to figure it out before she raised her hand to her mouth—probably she didn't want me looking at it anymore.

"Oh my god," she said.

My pulse thundered in my ears. I was frozen in place by that look on Kat's face. My hands were still tight on the edge of the desk, knuckles starting to ache. That stone was poised to roll back down the hill and obliterate me. The whole room, the whole universe, seemed to be paused, waiting, stretching this moment thinner and thinner. It felt like my whole immortal life had passed, though it was probably only a second before Kat said, "I'm so sorry."

24

TAYLOR

I WAS RUNNING.

The second the bracing air hit my face, even before the door to Hunter House swung closed, I was running.

If anyone saw me I'd look like a fool, if anyone caught me I'd probably get written up for some kind of Honor Code violation, but I didn't care, because as long as I was running, I couldn't be crying.

Or that was how it was supposed to work.

I didn't know where I was heading, but if I was going to cry or collapse or disappear off the face of the earth, at least I could do it alone. By the time I reached the lacrosse field, the tears were streaming down my face—like the only thing running had done was redirect energy away from my anti-tear defenses.

It wasn't even that I was thinking about the kiss. I *couldn't* think about the kiss. There was a black blot on my brain that obliterated everything except a voice that kept repeating, *I'm so sorry.* With each fall of my foot on the soft turf: *I'm so sorry, so sorry, so sorry.* That moment when she realized the mistake she'd made. I already knew that when she asked me, later, to keep it a secret, I'd say yes. Pretend like it never happened. Never mention it again. Nothing would have to change.

"Taylor!" *Shit.* "Come on, I can't run as fast as you!"

Of all things Kat could have said, that should not have worked to slow me down, but it did. Kat could not run as fast as me, not anywhere near it, and the fact that she'd somehow managed to chase me all the way out onto the lacrosse field was just surprising enough that I stopped. I didn't turn around—not while my chest was heaving and my face was streaked with tears.

Why had she come after me at all? As if I didn't know better than anyone how little kisses could mean, especially when those kisses involved me. I rubbed the heel of my hand over my cheeks, smearing away the tears.

The kiss *had* to mean nothing to her. How else could she have just crossed the room and kissed me, simple as day? She could do it because she hadn't spent years agonizing about it, dreaming about a lost cause like I had. She didn't care enough to wonder if she had waited for the perfect moment, if it would be just like she'd imagined, if I'd be completely disgusted and tell the whole school what she'd done. Whatever little crushed-up part of my soul that still survived should have been happy about it. But instead I felt cheated somehow, and used. And really, pathetically sad.

"Will you look at me?"

Her voice was more distant than I'd expected. I was just past the midfield line, but when I turned, slowly, she was still walking up from the goal.

The field looked different at night, the trees ringing us like black lace, and each blade of grass visible in the gray light of the full moon. The white lines on the field seemed to shine in the dark. In that light, Kat looked more ghost-girl than vampire: her skin silver and her hair loose and free, basketball shorts and bare feet, the sleeves of her sweatshirt swallowing her hands.

I wanted to go to her and kiss her. That I knew I *could not*, that I *never would*, made me want to disappear completely.

Kat stepped toward me slowly, like she was approaching a wild animal she didn't want to spook. Fair enough. She stopped a few feet away. Her hands balled into fists inside the cuffs of her sweatshirt. "Are you okay?"

I crossed my arms tight over my chest. The cold had long since seeped under my untucked shirt. "*That's* what you chased me out here to ask? I'm fucking peachy. Best day of my life."

"I chased you because you *ran*. Was I supposed to just let you wander the night when you're obviously upset?"

"I'm a freaking vampire. Nothing bad's going to happen to me."

She pressed her lips together before she said, "And I wanted to apologize. I shouldn't have done that—"

"I get it. Don't worry. It didn't change my life either."

"No, I—" Kat almost didn't, then did, step forward across the midline. Her bare feet streaked marks through the dewy grass. "Okay. What I meant was, I shouldn't have kissed you without asking first. That was wrong. And now I'm realizing that if I had, you clearly would have said no, and so I shouldn't have kissed you at all." Her voice wobbled. "I never thought I'd do that kind of thing. I'm really disappointed in myself. But mostly I'm just really, truly sorry, Taylor."

My mouth went dry. What was I supposed to say to *that*? That I wanted to say yes to kissing her a million times. That I probably would have said no if she'd asked, because I couldn't have admitted otherwise. In all of the scenarios I'd imagined where we kissed, after all the times straight Harcote girls cornered me to request a session at Taylor's Kissing Booth, I'd never once considered I could just flat-out ask Kat myself. Just the thought of it made me want to puke from the awkwardness.

She said, "I can ask Radtke to move me to a different room tomorrow. Or like you said, just pretend if never happened. If that's what you want."

"If that's what *I* want?" I said slowly. The six feet between us seemed like six hundred, and like none at all. "You know what I really want? I want to know why you hate me."

The little divot in the center of Kat's forehead announced she was dismayed. "I don't hate you, Taylor."

"Bullshit."

"But I used to." She shifted her weight from side to side, her toes sinking in to the wet grass. "You really want me to say it?"

No. "Yes."

"When your parents kicked us out, my life got completely turned on its head. It took a long time for me and my mom to get back to a . . . a stable place."

"My parents didn't kick you out. You up and left."

"*That's* how you want to be about this?" Her voice was hard, like I'd disappointed her in exactly the way she'd expected me to.

"I'm not being any kind of way about it."

"Then admit what actually happened." She worked her jaw, glaring at me. That anger that I'd seen in her eyes when I walked into our room on Move-in Day, like she wanted to scorch the earth, and me personally. "You knew about my mom's turning. I told you and you promised you would keep it a secret. The next thing I knew, your mom kicked us out because she didn't want her family associating with vampires like us—especially you and your little brother. As if we were going to rub off on you."

There was a strange buzzing in my ears. I remembered the day Kat confided in me about her mom's fangmaker. That winter, as I filled out the Harcote application, it had hit home for both of us that I'd be gone the next fall. It had made us somehow ravenous for each other. We were together so often, it made the idea of going away to school even harder to imagine. One night I'd made some stupid joke about sabotaging my application by saying I didn't have any fangmakers. Kat had stilled. Something was wrong.

"No secrets," I'd said.

Then she'd burst into tears.

She told me everything: how her mom's fangmaker hadn't meant to turn her and had left her for dead. I got why she'd had to lie, how she felt sometimes like she didn't know who she really was. So much of Vampirdom revolved around your pedigree, your parents, your fangmakers. My mom had often commented that it was such a shame that Kat had lost her fangmakers in the Peril. But to not even know who her maternal fangmaker *was*? The fact that he'd left her mom to die? It was something vampires didn't usually talk about directly, but it was pretty clear how they felt: without a pedigree, you were *less-than*.

Kat and I had pinkie-sworn on our immoral lives and our friendship that I'd keep her secret. I remember thinking it wasn't necessary. I'd already have rather died than break Kat's trust. But we tangled our fingers together and brought them to our lips anyway.

I said, "I kept that promise."

She shook her head. "Don't lie to me, not now."

I stepped toward her, close enough to look her straight in the eye. "I'm not. I never said a word to them."

I could almost feel how her lips had been so gentle against mine, the brazen confidence of her palm against my jaw. I forced myself to ignore whatever heat I was imagining existed between us. It was more important to let her search me and find a way to trust me instead.

"But all these years, I thought . . ." Her voice was half a whisper. "How did they find out?"

"I mean . . . are you sure they did? They never said anything to me about it."

"Then why did you think we left?"

I swallowed hard. What had been the truth until a second ago was now something strange and sour. "My mom told me you guys had moved on. Just up and gone in the middle of the night, like *all our charity* meant nothing. I wanted to message you. I should have. But I waited. I guess I was . . ." I meant to say I was pissed. That's how I liked to remember myself: if I cared enough to feel anything about it, it was anger. But when I really thought back to that place, that time—my face buried in my pillow, seeing Kat's bike left behind and rusting behind the garage, then that text she'd sent—it wasn't anger. "It felt like you abandoned me."

We were standing so close now, I'd had to let my eyes wander away as I said that—the abandoning thing. When I looked back, her eyebrows were nudged together.

"I thought you betrayed me."

It made sense that Kat hadn't written, that she hadn't trusted me. But if my parents had just kicked them out, then it didn't have anything to do with me, or with me and Kat. That felt too big to understand right now. I'd believed a different version of the story for so long. Whenever I missed her or whenever I felt alone, that thought, the story I'd told myself felt true now, a stone worn smooth, the grooves worn down by years of use. In that story I was someone to run from, someone worth leaving—and it was a story I'd invented for myself.

"I'm sorry," I said. A better person would have already thought to say that. "I wish none of this had happened. They should never have kicked you out and we'd still be . . ." I trailed off. We'd never talked about that time before. I couldn't assume I'd been anyone worth missing to her.

But then she said, "Best friends."

I didn't have anything to say to that except, "Yeah."

"Thank you," she said. "For the apology. For everything to-night."

"Oh, *Kath-er-ine*." I sighed. "Tonight was nothing. Don't thank me for apologizing. It's not like it makes a difference."

"Maybe it doesn't make a difference to you, but I'm sorry too."

The moonlight slid along her temple, the curve of her ear, the line of her jaw. The way she was looking at me, with her eyes soft and pressing her lips together just a little, it was easy to imagine kissing her. Easier than it had ever been. I could close the space between us, lean into her and slide my hand against her cheek, my fingers into her hair, and kiss her. I was barely breathing thinking about it.

But I had used up all my uncomfortable points for the day. One instant it had made sense that it was me and Kat standing in this field, her in pajamas and me in formalwear, the next, she and I were both shifting back and forth on our feet, wondering how we'd gotten there.

"Um, should we get back?" Kat asked.

"Wait." I bent to unlace my sneakers, pulled them off, and held them out to her. She slipped them onto her own feet. We walked back to the girls' quad like that, her in my sneakers, me in my dinosaur socks.

HUNTER HOUSE WAS still blessedly empty when we got back. As I was turning the light off, we heard the door downstairs bang open. We lay there in the dark listening to fifteen girls kick off their heels and stomp up to their rooms.

I didn't want to look at her, but I did anyway. I couldn't stop myself.

Kat was looking at me too.

25

KAT

MY FOOTSTEPS TRACED circles through the Extended Collection. The greenish motion-detecting lights switched on in each aisle as I passed.

I'd woken up that morning and seen Taylor passed out on her bed on the other side of the room and gotten out of there as quick as I could. Giving Taylor some space was the decent thing to do, and anyway, I needed to think too.

But now that I was alone in the Stack, all I could think about was her.

About the relief that bled through me when she knelt in front of me on the steps at the dance.

About the way she'd looked standing in that field, her white shirt like a beacon in the moonlight and her chest heaving, and something in me felt sure that she was lost, that I'd caught her in time—even though I was the one she was running from.

About *that kiss*.

One minute we'd been arguing, anger absolutely steaming off of both of us, and suddenly it felt like the only thing that mattered was the slant of her lips, that Evangeline shouldn't have been kissing those lips, and I couldn't *think*. I don't even remember deciding to do it before I was kissing her. The brush of her curls against my cheek, the gentle pressure of her mouth, that moment when she kissed me back, the way her body leaned into mine. Goose bumps prickled my skin—more than just my skin, deeper than that, like a hunger, something deep inside me pulling toward her. Like I wanted to cry but I couldn't, I wanted to laugh but I couldn't. I could have kissed her forever. Even right now, I felt like I could *still* be kissing her.

I shook my head to clear my thoughts.

It wasn't right. I should never have just forced myself on her like that, without any idea if she wanted it. I wasn't that kind of person. I cared about consent. But somehow, in the moment, I didn't wonder how she felt. I was so sure that she felt what I did. But she hadn't. She'd *run away*.

My phone buzzed. Hey party girl come to the dining hall we're drinking breakfast, Evangeline texted.

Suddenly the Stack felt too underoxygenated for me to breathe. *Evangeline.*

Of course, Taylor didn't want me. She had someone, even if that person was a nightmare with a human face who would never make her feel that way she deserved to. A person I'd been so jealous of last night, I'd practically fainted.

How could I be obsessing over *Taylor Sanger*, who had sold me out and broken my trust? No, I reminded myself, she hadn't. She'd told me last night, and I believed her, that she'd never said anything to her parents. Which made her Taylor Sanger, my ex–best friend and roommate. That felt like something else entirely.

Really, it didn't matter. Because I wasn't queer.

I would have known if I was queer.

I definitely would have known.

I thought about calling Guzman or Shelby. They'd completely lose their shit when I told them.

When I told them *what* exactly? How could I explain something to them that I didn't understand myself?

The thought of explaining this to my friends was so completely mortifying, I could have puked in the middle of the Early American Vampires section of the Stack.

I needed a distraction, something else to concentrate on. It was the first time I'd been alone in the Stack without Galen. I should have been tracking down info about my mom's time at CasTech.

My mom had been going by *Meredith Ayres*—Galen had called her that, and the magazine caption said the same. It wasn't that unusual for vampires to change their names, but my mom had never mentioned it. The Stack didn't have a digital catalog, so I had to go downstairs to the actual card catalog to search for the name.

Nothing. Of course.

I kicked the card catalog in frustration.

I hated not having answers. I hated *not knowing*.

If I was queer, I would have known.

But I didn't know. Which meant I knew that I *wasn't* queer.

I had no reason to be afraid to be who I was. It wasn't like I grew up in a place like Harcote, where Taylor's was the only rainbow flag in a five-mile radius. My old high school had a million queer, nonbinary, and trans students, with student organizations to represent them and all kinds of trainings about diversity and acceptance. I wasn't worried about what my mom would think (even if Harcote was apparently past the limit of her tolerance). Both my best friends were queer. We went to Pride and drag shows and all-ages club nights together, and they called me their number one cis-het ally. Even *they* were certain that's what I was.

I'd asked Guzman once how he knew he was gay, and he scowled. "I hate this question. How did you know you were straight?" When I couldn't answer that, he said, smug, "See? Straight people always assume it's something you have to *discover*, but I was born this way." Shelby was the same: they'd come out to their parents as trans at nine years old, then started using they/them pronouns a few years later. Guzman and Shelby made it seem like that was something every queer person had in common: you always knew your identity, and you decided when and how to share it.

That wasn't how I felt at all. If I was born this way, had I been lying to myself? Or was I actually just straight and last night had been some kind of fluke?

Giving up on the card catalog, I went back to the CasTech section. Maybe there were other documents from those early days that a woman named Meredith Ayres would be in.

I chewed the inside of my cheek. It was true that I'd never been quite as interested in boys as I was supposed to be. Not that I *was* supposed to be, but ever since I was a little kid people had been telling me that I would drive the boys crazy, that they wouldn't leave me alone. Even Guzman and Shelby made comments like that, as if the way I looked meant I'd been designed to attract boys.

I'd hooked up with guys at my old school and it didn't feel *bad*. It was more like I kept waiting for it to feel good. I never really got into it, but if I lost control, it could have been a bloodbath. Or at least, that's what I'd always thought. Maybe it was a sign of something that I never really got that turned on. But then again there were nerves, inexperience. Physically existing on the same plane as another person was awkward when you were fully clothed, and suddenly you were supposed to know what to do when you were partly naked?

I opened another magazine to see Victor's face staring up at me. I flipped it closed. I thought of how perfect Galen looked in his tux—how perfect he *always* looked. Galen was a Greek statue: undeniably, empirically exquisite. But I could never quite feel how Evangeline and Lucy did about him. It was the same at home—Guzman or Shelby were always pointing out hot guys to me, but I could never spot them on my own. But girls . . . I didn't need anyone's help to see them. Lucy and Evangeline were beautiful in a way that made me want to kneel at their feet. I'd felt it the first moment I'd met them, when they'd opened their door and my chest went tight. They burned in a way that made Galen seem like he was already ash.

But *everyone* thought girls were beautiful. The word was basically invented to describe girls. It wasn't gay to melt into a pool of jelly when a pretty girl looked at you.

Unless it totally, absolutely was.

I pulled a book off the shelf of materials about the founding of CasTech.

I couldn't be queer. I was a person who knew myself. I knew what I wanted. I might have spent my whole life wondering about my pedigree and searching for a place in Vampirdom, but this was deeper than that. If I was queer then I couldn't be the person I thought I was. And who would I be then?

It made my head spin. I shoved that book back on the shelf and tried another one.

Maybe it was just Taylor, something about her specifically. Our old friendship, all those feelings. The craziness of last night.

Taylor.

Even thinking her name made my chest seize up with a kind of craving.

But hadn't it always been that way with us? Like the world would stop turning without her in it, like she was the light in every room. Even when I hated her, that had still been true.

But we were friends—or we weren't—or I wanted something more from her—or maybe I didn't. It was just *her*, with her crooked smile and inappropriate jokes and the way she could always see right through me.

It had always been her.

It had always been the two of us.

I'd never kissed anyone the way I kissed her last night.

I gave up on the books and wrenched open a file cabinet.

That strange nausea from last night was coming back, that sickness in my stomach as Galen walked me into the dance. It was too much to untangle. What we were. Who I was.

One night—one kiss—couldn't change everything.

My hand stopped on a personnel list from 1979, about five years into the Peril. It registered every CasTech employee, their role, and the dates they were with the company, and had a column marked "status." She was right at the top: Meredith Ayres, research and development, 1944–1975, unknown.

Galen had been right: Meredith Ayres had started at CasTech the year the company had been founded. I skimmed down the page. Even Galen's parents hadn't worked there until 1947. They'd left CasTech to start the Black Foundation in 1975 too, almost as soon as the first vampire CFaD death was discovered. My mother had worked there for *thirty years*, then disappeared.

I took the list back to my desk and scanned the other employees' start dates. The only one, other than Meredith Ayres, who had been there in 1944 was Victor himself. His status was "living." The hairs at my neck prickled as I focused on the status column. Most of the vampires who'd worked at CasTech before the Peril hadn't survived it, their status marked "deceased." How was that possible? The Peril killed thousands of vampires, but these people had helped *develop* Hema. They should have had the easiest access to it when the Peril struck.

Meredith Ayres was the only one marked unknown. Galen had said that she'd disappeared. Why? How different would our lives be if she had stayed? And why had she never told me she spent twenty years working with the most important man in Vampirdom?

Of course, I couldn't just *ask* her about it now. This was a massive lie, a whole alternative life story. I didn't trust her to tell me the truth.

"I thought I'd find you here."

I nearly jumped out of my skin. There was a tall figure standing behind me, shoulders hunched up. Galen looked like he'd hardly slept, his curls tousled and the skin under his eyes darker than usual.

"Can we talk?" he asked.

I shuffled the list into my stuff. The last thing I wanted to do right now was talk to Galen. "Of course."

"I should never have asked you to the dance," he said.

"Okay. Yeah. I didn't mean to ruin it for you."

"No, that's not what I mean at all. You don't need to apologize." He took the seat opposite mine and pressed his hands against the desk. "Let me explain. Everything I do is scrutinized. I knew it wasn't fair to expose you to that, but I wanted to have one night to pretend I was normal. And I thought I could have that with you. But I couldn't."

I swallowed hard. *Normal.* The girl from nowhere. Galen only wanted me for the same reason I'd been given the mentorship.

I started gathering my stuff. "I get it. It's cool."

He reached across the table and stilled my hand. "I mean, I couldn't have it *because* of you." His gray eyes searched my face. "Who are you, Kat?"

TAYLOR

I STARED AT the Pride flag tacked above my bed and gently gave myself permission to think about last night. I would think about the kiss just this once, then never again. I'd forget it, like Kat wanted. At least she hadn't started a whole conversation about it, like some of the girls who visited Taylor's Kissing Booth, who wanted it extra clear that it was just an experiment, and I'd have to sit there and nod, sure, I understand. Tried kissing a girl once, didn't like it, happens to everyone—except me.

I could banish the kiss from my brain, but there was one thing about last night I wouldn't forget: what Kat had said about how she left Virginia. All these years, Kat thought I'd broken her trust, while I'd been thinking that she'd abandoned me. Now we knew that neither of those things was true, and the stories we'd been told didn't match up. What had really happened?

There was exactly one person on Earth that I trusted to help me figure this out. He was the same person I'd told to go screw himself last night.

I should never have talked to him like that. Kontos was my queer godfather. He deserved my respect, and I wanted to earn his. I vowed to tell him everything: about Kat and how she'd tricked me into going to the dance, even what had really been going on with Evangeline. I could only hope that in exchange for my honesty, he'd forgive me.

It would be very un-Kontos of him not to.

FINDING KONTOS, EVEN on a Sunday morning, didn't exactly require detective work. He was always in his office.

My sneakers squeaked down the Science Building's mazelike hallway. I wrinkled my nose. There was a weird smell, like a dissection specimen had been left out. And it was getting stronger.

The door to Kontos's classroom was open. But the smell was unignorable now. Maybe one of the fridges in the bio lab had kicked it and the frogs and fetal pigs in their little formaldehyde baths were starting to turn.

"Kontos, how are you working with this stink—"

But then I wasn't saying anything, just this weird half-throttled wail that didn't sound like me at all. It sounded like how running felt in dreams, stuck and dull and unreal but the urgency made it horrifying, the inevitable realization that it would never be enough.

There was a pool of blackened, half-dried blood. The toe of my sneaker was in it: half of my foot in his blood.

Kontos's blood.

He was on the floor, collapsed on his side. His chest had sunken in, like the bones inside weren't strong enough to hold him up. His shoulders were jammed up at a weird angle that pushed his face into the floor—into the blood. That blood had come from everywhere, his mouth, his nose, even his ears and eyes, running out of any orifice it could.

Next to him—dead beside him—was a woman. She had a tattoo on her shoulder that looked too bright and colorful against her bluish skin. Eyes clouded over and empty. Blond hair made duller by the linoleum it was fanned across. Two puncture wounds in her neck had leaked a crusted trail of blood onto the floor.

I was still making that noise, that ghastly droning scream I couldn't turn off, as I backed into the hallway. Then I remembered the smell, what the smell really was—it was Kontos, dead from CFaD, and the woman he'd gotten it from, dead next to him. The Hema I'd just had for breakfast came heaving up then, splattering the shiny floor of the hall with a garnet red, a jet of fake blood launched across the floor and it was *so fucked up*, that's what I was thinking, that it was so fucked up that these three kinds of blood were all mixed together, and I just had to leave it all there while I went for help.

The hexagons from the sole of my sneaker patterned the floor, my own red footstep chasing me down the hallway.

26

TAYLOR

THEY TOOK ME to a physics lab upstairs. Someone gave me a blanket because I guess I was shivering—rattled, I never thought it meant literally. The blanket sat next to me on a stool. I couldn't figure out what to do with it, where had the Science Building blanket come from, who even had brought it?

I wanted to go back to my room and crawl into bed so I could wake up from this bad dream.

Kontos.

His ridiculous mustache and pleated khakis, his clicky pens and earnest good intentions. His dumb faith in Vampirdom.

How could Kontos have died feeding on a human? It went entirely against reunionism. The core of their dream was that vampires could be *good*, we could restrain ourselves, we could live with humans as equals.

He'd almost convinced me. But I'd had it right last night: vampires couldn't be trusted. No one could be. No one but myself.

I scrubbed my hands against my face, then tore them away. I stared at my hands, searching the creases of my palms and the beds of my nails searching for blood. I hadn't touched anything. But I felt like I had.

Atherton arrived with Radtke. Radtke looked even more desiccated than she usually did, except for her nose, which was pinkish and running. The skin around her eyes was tight like the muscles had finally twitched too much and were now frozen in place. Her hair was down. I'd never seen it like that before, even in Hunter House. Seeing her like that made me a little scared: this was enough to undo someone as stone-cold as Radtke.

Instead I looked at Atherton, who was coping a lot better. The news of Kontos's death had interrupted a gym sesh. His aspiring-frat-bro face was splotchier than usual, and he wearing some kind of skin-tight exercise top. Through it, I could see the nubs of his nipples, which I wanted to erase from my brain and then couldn't stop looking at.

He grabbed a stool across from me.

"You had a real shock this morning, Taylor." He said it in a way that made the worst day of my life sound like an unfortunate hic-cup. "That had to be really upsetting."

"He's dead." I'd meant it as a question, but it wasn't really. I knew he was dead.

Atherton nodded. "We think it happened during the dance last night."

"During the dance?" I stammered. "But he was *there*. I talked to him—"

And then he'd gone back to his office to put the hard drive somewhere safe.

The hard drive I'd given back to him.

"I know this is difficult. But I—we all—" Atherton gestured around the room, although Radtke was the only other person there. "Think that it would be best if you kept the details to your-self. We don't want the other Youngbloods hearing about this dis-turbing news through gossip."

As if the Youngbloods weren't doing the exact same thing that had killed Kontos.

"Can you do that for me?" Atherton asked.

I nodded.

"I know this is hard to accept." He seemed to think he knew a lot of what I was feeling. "But Mr. Kontos had been struggling with this behavior for some time."

"You mean, killing humans?"

Something in me pushed back against this information, the oil-and-water-ness of it with my knowledge of Kontos. How could he have told me he believed Vampirdom could be better when he was the worst of it?

"We were trying to get him help." Atherton pulled a look of concern that seemed copied from a kid's cartoon: frowny face, googly eyes. "Unfortunately, it was too late."

I glanced at Radtke. She still had that look. Hollows in her cheeks, lips pressed so tight together you couldn't barely see them, clutching herself at her elbows. She was doing a great job of pretending to be upset, when this was probably exactly what she'd wanted that night we overheard her and Atherton in Old Hill. She was probably happy Kontos was dead.

"Why are you telling me this?"

Atherton's eyebrows did a little dance that meant he was trying to understand the young people. "You were close with Mr. Kontos. It's natural to be curious."

"He was my science teacher, that's it. Shit happens." The blanket took that moment to slide from the stool to the floor. I didn't pick it up. "Can I go back to my room now? I have a lot of healing to do."

Atherton looked uncomfortable. He was probably waiting for me to cry. The only thing men hated more than girls crying was when we didn't cry exactly when they expected. "You may."

I hopped off my stool and walked out of the Science Building.

The sun had come out and was shining on the wet campus. It looked like it had been staged for an admissions office photoshoot, and it made me feel like I was floating. As if I was in a dream, and none of this was real, not even Kontos's corpse still lying on the floor in the Science Building behind me, the insides liquefied from CFaD.

I didn't feel sad or upset or anything like what Atherton said.

Just tired. It felt like three years had passed since I'd left Hunter House. Back in the room, I unlaced my sneakers—the same ones I'd worn to the dance—and shoved them into the trash. I got into bed and lay there like vampires lie in their coffins in movies, my legs out straight and arms crossed over my chest and staring straight up at the ceiling, and I let my mind go blank.

KAT

"WHO AM I?" I repeated "I'm nobody."

"You're somebody to them," Galen insisted.

"You're not making sense."

"When you suggested surprising everyone at the dance, it wasn't just the other Harcoties I was trying to hide from," he said carefully. "My parents and my fangmaker have a lot of expectations for me. It's important who I'm seen with—"

"I'm sure Victor doesn't care who you take to a high school dance," I huffed.

"But he *does*. Everything's a statement for them." He said it in a way that made me feel stupid and young. "This is Harcote. We're the Youngbloods. The future of Vampirdom is in our hands, and for me, the future of the Black Foundation for the Cure, maybe even CasTech." He'd never admitted that to me before. "My parents have always been very clear that who I associate with reflects on them. It's my duty to respect that. By the time they were leaving on my first Move-in Day here, I knew there was one girl they preferred for me."

"Evangeline." I rolled my eyes. "What does everyone see in her?"

"It's *what* she is, not who she is. Evangeline comes from one of the oldest vampire lines in Europe. She doesn't even really have a fangmaker on her father's side because he's so old, he might be one of the originals—vampires made without a fangmaker. He lives in an actual castle in Romania. She barely knows him—she was raised by her mom and nannies—but that doesn't matter when she has his name and his blood. And there's something about Evangeline too . . . she's always felt like what she has isn't enough."

"She's rich, she's gorgeous, she's *vampire royalty*. What more does she want?"

His eyebrows lifted. "Power, of course. Her *own* power. Evangeline and I started dating right after school started. Everyone was pleased. But after a few weeks, I just—I couldn't do it. Even thinking about her could bring on a panic attack." He hesitated. "Have you ever felt like you were going through your life like an actor, reading out lines someone else wrote?"

I nodded.

"That's how being with Evangeline made me feel. I broke up with her. They were furious at me. I'd never felt like such a disappointment. My parents and Victor still think Evangeline is the perfect match. That we'll—"

"End up together. Everyone around here thinks that too."

He nodded. "That's Evangeline's personal PR machine at work. She's always spun the breakup like we're star-crossed lovers. The greatest romance of the Youngblood generation. At this point, I don't know if she hates me or loves me or both. But she might not be wrong."

"That you'll get back together?"

He raked his fingers through his hair. "We might. If they decide we should. Evangeline very much believes they will."

"Oh Galen, I'm so sorry."

He gave a tepid smile. "There are worse fates. After it ended with Evangeline, I promised myself I wouldn't date anyone else. I didn't want to put anyone else in that position. I convinced myself it was like my own private rebellion. But rebellion isn't *supposed* to be private. I realized that when I met you. This stuff with my family is nothing compared to what you've been through. Not having enough money for Hema, growing up all alone. You made me wonder if I could stand up to them. I knew you weren't the kind of person they'd want me with. No one knows what your pedigree is. You're a mystery—an outsider."

I bristled at that.

"You're exactly what they *don't* want for me. I guess that's why I fell for you." His dark lashes fluttered. "My parents called me this morning. I was expecting them to be angry that I'd taken you to the dance. But they weren't. It was like all those times they'd spent screaming at me about this—"

"They *screamed* at you about this?"

"—never happened. They said you seemed nice. My father said, *Good choice, son.* He's literally never said that to me before in my life, about anything."

"Maybe I made a good impression on Victor. It could all be about the mentorship."

"But why were you picked for that?" Galen said. "There was only supposed to be one slot."

"It's *because* I'm an outsider," I said. "I'm their rags-to-riches story, a nobody who grew up around humans."

"Whoever you are, I like you." A note of shyness crept into his voice. "I like you a lot, Kat. You've already met my fangmaker, but I was wondering if you'd want to meet my parents at Descendants Day next month."

I had to bite my tongue to keep from saying something stupid. Meet his *parents*? Galen and I had been on one date that was 50 percent disaster.

I knew I didn't like Galen as much as he liked me. But then again, the more time we spent together, the more I had come to care about him, and it was impossible not to feel bad for him after what he'd just shared. I ruined the dance for him. Didn't I owe him another chance?

Whatever I was feeling about Taylor, it was just that—a feeling, not something real. Taylor had Evangeline, and we were just beginning to repair our friendship.

But buried under all that confusion, like nuclear waste that never stopped pumping out radiation to taint everything around it, I had one desire that was absolutely clear: revenge. If I said yes to this, I'd basically be Galen's girlfriend, halfway to vampire royalty myself, and that would drive Evangeline up the wall.

"Sure," I said. "I'd love to meet them."

GALEN HELD MY hand as we walked down-campus. He wanted to meet my mom at Descendants Day too, maybe have our parents sit together at lunch. I told him my mom was almost certainly not coming. I blamed her job, not her disdain for the school or the fact that she was the mystery woman who'd vanished from CasTech. He said he felt bad for me that I wouldn't have anyone on campus—which did nothing to get me excited for Descendants Day—then right in the middle of the Girls' Residential Quad, where everyone could see, he kissed me. The kiss was quick, his lips cold, and I didn't do anything out of the ordinary while it was happening. He was beaming as he watched me open the door to Hunter House.

Inside, Lucy sprawled in an armchair. The clicking of her manicure against her phone screen didn't pause as she eyed me. "So the lovebirds patched it up. Are the two of you, like, official?"

"You could say that."

Lucy's mouth fell open into a vicious O of surprise. "Evangeline's going to *die*!"

"Evangeline's immortal," I said.

I was about to head upstairs, but Lucy stopped me. "You didn't hear? All the res houses have meetings called for this afternoon. Someone probably violated the Honor Code at the dance."

The common room started filling with girls. I hung back to look for Taylor in her usual spot, perching on the windowsill that wasn't a seat. She never showed.

Ms. Radtke stood at the front of the room, but she didn't look like her usual self. She was wearing a cardigan with the buttons done up wrong.

Behind me, the stairs creaked. Taylor was sitting on the highest step that still allowed her to see through the railing into the common room. Her knees were pulled almost up to her chin, like she was trying to make herself small, and her hand was curled tight around the carved post of the staircase. I had to drag my eyes away from her.

"Girls, I have some difficult news to share with you," Ms. Radtke began. I knew at once that this was about more than an Honor Code violation. "It is with very profound sadness that I must tell you that Mr. Kontos passed away last night."

It wasn't silence but it felt like silence: the subtle groan of the leather of the fourth-year couch as a girl sat up straighter, the buzz of music someone had left playing upstairs.

"For real?" Evangeline said.

Ms. Radtke was saying something about counseling services and supporting each other and an assembly tomorrow when the stairs creaked again. Taylor was gone.

I didn't wait for Ms. Radtke to dismiss us. I followed Taylor upstairs.

IN OUR ROOM, it was strangely dark. The curtains were closed.

Taylor sat on the edge of her bed, hunched over so her arms stuck straight out and her elbows sandwiched between her knees. Her eyes looked enormous and sad when she looked up at me.

"Are you okay?" I asked.

She rolled her eyes, which I guess I deserved.

"I found him," she said dully. "Like, I found his body. This morning."

"Oh my god, Taylor . . ." I sat down on the edge of her bed without thinking about it, until I *did* think maybe it was weird to be close to her after last night, but then I was already sitting there and I couldn't exactly just jump up again.

Taylor didn't care. She wasn't looking at me, or at the narrow gap that ran between our bodies. Her eyes were fixed on some point across the room. I followed her gaze to the wastebasket; the heel of the brand-new Chucks she'd worn last night were sticking out of it. "He was just on the floor. Blood *everywhere*. Everywhere. And this human woman was dead too."

"Mr. Kontos died of *CFaD*?"

"Yup," Taylor answered, making a popping sound with her lips on the *p*. "Have you ever seen it? The blood's like, not blood colored. It's kind of blackish . . . or maybe that's just because it had been sitting there all night, since the dance. So it was old. Old blood."

Mr. Kontos had been feeding on humans? I couldn't reconcile that with the Mr. Kontos who'd geeked out at chem experiments and unabashedly grinned through every Seated Dinner.

"You never really know people, right? Anyone can turn out to be an asshole." Taylor was making her voice light, as if she had a chance in hell of convincing me she didn't care about this, and suddenly I was so tremendously sad for her—and we were sitting so *close*. Just like that, all I wanted to do was close that space between us and kiss her until she didn't hurt anymore, or if I couldn't do that, hold her while she cried, until she—

What was I *thinking*?

There literally was no less appropriate time to spring a makeout session on someone who didn't like you than right after they'd found their mentor dead. *Obviously*. Taylor didn't need me. She had Evangeline, who was ten thousand times hotter than me, in a terrifying way, and Taylor liked that, terrifyingly hot girls, eat-you-for-breakfast girls. She wouldn't want to just lie in bed with our arms around each other, kissing—oh my god, why couldn't my brain just *behave*?

"If you want to talk—"

Her lip curled. "Don't hold your breath."

"I know, you get hives when anyone tries to care about you." It was supposed to come off as funny, but then I added, "But I'm not just anyone."

"Ha. Whatever, Kath-er-ine."

There was a knock on the door. I jumped up to open it.

Part of me (a very small part) hoped it would be Evangeline.

Taylor needed someone who wouldn't believe her when she said she was okay. Someone who knew that she would deal with being crushed by brute-forcing her way out of it, and that although Taylor was strong, everyone had a limit. She deserved to be with someone who would come to her in this little attic room and hold her. I had my doubts that Evangeline was that person, but if that's who Taylor wanted, I hoped she was.

But when I opened the door, it was to Ms. Radtke. Her black and gray had never looked so appropriate. "Miss Sanger," she said. I stood aside, but Taylor didn't get up. "Miss Sanger—Taylor, I wish you could have been spared what you saw this morning. Mr. Kontos cared for you a very great deal, and I know that the two of you had become even closer recently. I can only imagine that you are feeling very isolated right now."

Taylor darkened. "What's that supposed to mean?"

"Simply that if you choose to reach out, I am here for you."

Closing the door on Ms. Radtke, I turned to Taylor. She'd gone ashen. "What's wrong? I thought that was kind of nice of her."

Taylor's thick eyebrows knit together and her lips parted just slightly (not that I noticed what her lips were doing). "I need to talk to you about something."

"Um, yeah. Sure. We should talk—"

She flushed scarlet. "I didn't mean—"

"Yeah, no, of course!"

"It's about Kontos. Do you remember what we overheard Radtke telling Atherton?"

"That Mr. Kontos was doing something threatening," I said. "I guess she mean feeding on humans."

"No, I don't think so." Taylor worried her lip with her thumb. "Kontos really was up to something. He told me about it, but I promised to keep it a secret."

She looked so heavy as she said it, so weighed down with sadness, that before I even realized it, I was saying, "No secrets."

Her eyes shot to mine.

"I just mean, you don't have to do this alone," I added.

I could see her deciding whether to trust me. I knew it didn't come easy for her anymore. But I hoped she would.

"There's something in his office. A hard drive. I need to get it back before Radtke gets her hands on it."

27

TAYLOR

I'D BEEN TURNING it over in my head for hours. Kontos had lied and lied and lied. He'd claimed he wanted a different future for Vampirdom, where we could be free, but what he really wanted was a future where he could feast on the human blood host again.

Vampires were all the same. They all thought with their fangs.

That just didn't feel like the Kontos I knew. I wanted it to and it *didn't* and that made me feel slimy all over again.

Kontos had made me feel less alone here. He made me feel seen in a way no one else ever had. *That* hadn't been a lie, even if everything else had been.

If that wasn't a lie, what did it mean for everything else? Could Kontos still be a good person if he'd been doing terrible things in secret? And could he have been a bad person if he'd been doing good things in secret?

I wanted the future he'd described: one where Vampirdom didn't have a stranglehold over our lives, where CFaD wasn't destroying humans, where no one would die like Kontos and that poor woman.

We wouldn't get there if Radtke got her hands on that hard drive. I didn't know what was on it, but it was important enough for Kontos to want to hide it. I promised him I would keep it safe. That look of total disappointment on his face when I'd given it back was now seared into my brain forever as our last conversation. I couldn't let that stand.

So that was how I ended up heading up-campus. It was cold and practically night already, the way winter always came crashing down on you after Halloween.

But Kat was a warm presence beside me.

I should not have asked her to come. I shouldn't have said anything to her at all. It felt unfair that she could break my heart on Saturday night then on Sunday act like it had made our friendship closer. I'd vowed to rebuild my defenses twice as strong, but, well, my defenses had taken a serious beating today, and when she'd looked at me with her face somehow made even prettier by worry and said our words—*No secrets*—I didn't have anything left to resist. She'd said I didn't have to do this alone even though *of course I did*. Then suddenly, I just didn't want to.

I wanted to do it with her.

The Science Building, with its hideous molecular design, wasn't yet locked for the night. We slipped inside and headed toward Kontos's room.

"Let's keep an eye out for the human aides this time," I whispered. "Lately it feels like there's always one looking over my shoulder."

As if on cue, an aide holding a broom stepped into the hall and looked right at me. I shoved Kat in the back and we swung around the corner into the next hallway. In a few seconds we were at Kontos's classroom, and before I had time to think about it, I was pulling the door shut and locking it behind us.

"What was that about?"

"I had a bad feeling," I explained. My heart was racing.

When I faced the classroom, my breath caught in my throat.

The lights were off, and the blue-gray dusk was casting eerie light around the room. Well, that wasn't fair. What really made it eerie was the fact that I'd just found two dead bodies splayed out on the same patch of stain-hiding linoleum that I was staring at now. The bodies were gone, but I felt their size and shape and smell, could practically see the blood dried to rusty powder in the crevices between the floor tiles. I wanted to slip right out that door and pretend I'd never come. Instead, I edged my way around the place where they'd lain.

On the desk at the front of the room, a skinny glass tube was set up for a titration experiment. Kontos always geeked out about titrating, as if dribbling a solution into a flask was one of the greatest dramas of our generation. A blunt feeling tightened in my chest: that a man who was supposed to live forever could be so delighted by high school chemistry experiments. "This is going to knock your socks off," he'd say. "By the end of class, you'll have no more socks left to knock." And we would all groan.

He said it about every single experiment.

I blinked back tears, aware Kat was watching me. "It's probably in his office," I whispered.

I stood in the doorway for a moment. His stacks of papers and textbooks, the worn brown leather jacket he loved (because of course he wouldn't have gone for a much-cooler black), that huge bookcase that stuck out from the wall, crammed with DVDs and books. The hard drive was sitting on his desk, its FRENCH CINEMA CLUB label clearly visible. Relief washed over me as I grabbed it and jammed it into my pocket. That should have been it. We should have gotten out of there. But I just *couldn't*.

Kat must have been wondering what the hell I was doing, but she didn't rush me. I sat in the desk chair he'd never swivel again.

Clicked and unclicked pens he'd never use again. Slid open a drawer that he'd—

An envelope was sitting right on top. *Taylor*, it said in his handwriting.

It was completely, utterly stupid, but I started to cry right then, before I even opened it. *Really* crying, like my face screwed up so tight it hurt, the letter crumpling in my hands and my forehead resting against the desk. I had to get my shit together, to stop crying over a liar, but I couldn't get anything together.

This had knocked my socks off; I had no more socks left to knock.

Kat kneeled beside me and pulled me into her. It was all the encouragement I needed to bury my face in her shoulder. I was getting my tears and probably snot all over her coat, but she was warm and solid and *there*. I don't know how else to say it, but it was like just by *existing*, she proved there was a path out of this, that I was strong enough to walk it, even if I was scared and sad and hurt. So I crushed myself against her and I sobbed.

KAT

WHAT WAS I supposed to do—just let her stand there and cry?

TAYLOR

"SORRY." I SNIFFLED when I finally straightened up.

"Look who's apologizing for crying now."

"Fine," I said. "What I meant was, thanks."

She smiled, just a little. Her eyes fell to the letter. "Are you going to read it?"

I sliced open the envelope with that clicky pen.

Dear Taylor,

I see you've been snooping. :)

I'm sorry I'm not here to help you find what you're looking for. That doesn't mean you should stop. Trust yourself. Keep an open heart.

> *With love,*
> *Leo Kontos*

A long, narrow key was taped inside the letter.

"What did he think you were looking for?" Kat asked, examining the key.

"A better outlook on life," I said grimly. "I don't think the key will help. I have no idea what it's to."

Kat slid the letter back into the envelope. "This reads like he was expecting something to happen to him."

"Like multiple organ failure brought on by a mania for human blood?" Kat shot me a questioning look. "He made a habit of killing humans. Atherton told me." Immediately I felt a singe of guilt. In his office, surrounded by his Kontosiness, it felt like a transgression even to think that he'd bite a human.

"Uncontrollable bloodlust just doesn't sound like Mr. Kontos."

"I know," I admitted. "But I saw her, drained and dead, right there."

Kat rocked back on her heels. "So he was chaperoning the Founder's Dance, and right in the middle of it, he goes to his office and, what, he has this woman waiting there? Or maybe she was one of the aides?"

"I didn't get a good look at her face," I said. "But she wasn't dressed like one."

"So not an aide. What was she even doing here?"

"He was probably saving her for an after-dance snack."

"But why feed on her in the middle of the dance, when he could have waited until it was over and taken his time?"

"I'd given him back the hard drive. That's the reason I went at the dance at all. He went to drop it in his office. He must have seen her here and . . . you know. The rest is history."

"So he saw her just sitting in his chem lab . . ."

Suddenly, I didn't want any more of this. "What does it matter what he was thinking and how it happened? He'd probably glamoured her like all the other humans around here, it's not rocket science. It doesn't change the fact that he's dead now."

"This isn't your fault, Taylor," Kat said. "You know that, right?"

"You can know something isn't your fault and feel guilty for it anyway." I shivered. It was almost totally dark now, and even creepier than before. "Let's get out of here."

I was almost at the door when Kat said. "Do you want to take something to remember him by? You have this book too, *1,000 Movies to Watch Before You Die*. I don't think anyone would mind if you—"

There was a grinding sound, like a mechanism turning with a *cha-thunk*. With the book in one hand, Kat swung the overcrowded bookcase free from the wall along a hinge on one side. Behind it was a gray steel door with no handle, only a dark keyhole. Kat crouched to look through it.

"Maybe that key will be some help after all," she said.

——————

THE DOOR LED down a flight of stairs with cinderblock walls. Apparently Kat wasn't freaked out by the discovery of the secret passage, so I was happy to let her lead the way. The stairs ended in a long hallway. The air was cold and damp down here. Overhead, bare fluorescent bulbs flickered, which, when you're in a mysterious underground lair, is horror-movie-level scary. My heart seemed to be trying to crawl out of my throat from the nerves. I really did not want to walk down that hallway. Most especially, I did not want to find out what was behind the door that we were now standing in front of.

"Maybe we shouldn't," I whispered to Kat. "What if it's, like, a dungeon full of humans?"

She looked at me sternly. "If it's a dungeon full of humans, then we should definitely leave them down here undisturbed. I'm sure they're perfectly happy."

She slipped her hand into mine and squeezed.

I tried the door.

The lighting buzzed to life, revealing a windowless room packed with scientific equipment.

Kat and I cautiously circled the room. Nothing dungeony, like handcuffs or cages, or anything that might trap a person here. In fact, there was another door marked with an emergency exit sign, with a couch and, strangely, a coffeepot next to it. Most of the space was full of lab equipment and filing cabinets. Some stuff I recognized from science classes—pipettes, microscopes—but a lot of the equipment looked like hunks of plastic, like clunky old printers or really fancy rice cookers.

It was also obvious that we weren't the first ones who'd been here since Kontos had died. The place looked like it had been pillaged. I counted exactly zero computers. At one lab table, there was a tangle of wires, an external keyboard and mouse, and a rectangle free of dust where a laptop had once sat. A filing cabinet hung open like a gaping, empty mouth. Some of the papers it had held were strewn across the floor.

Kat was examining a machine that looked like an old cash register, except where the money would go, there was a plastic tray that looked designed make one hundred of the itty-bittiest ice cubes ever. "Did Kontos tell you what he was working on?"

"Sort of. He was a reunionist. He was trying to get me to join them. What—why are you smiling like that?"

Kat was eyeing me with an irrepressible grin. "Just thinking of you in a rebel organization," she said.

"I know, it's stupid. I tried to tell him that."

"Are you kidding? If I were starting a rebel organization you're the first person I'd ask to join. You already want to burn everything down."

My cheeks were hot. "I wouldn't know what to replace it with. Kontos never got around to telling me their full plans. All I know is that they want three things: a cure for CFaD, free access to human blood substitute, and the Youngbloods on their side."

"So I guess he was working on the first of those things down here. I recognize some of this stuff." Which, thank god, because I absolutely didn't. "It looks like what they have in my mom's clinic, to test for CFaD." She turned to me, wide-eyed. "It's unbelievable that one person would even attempt that on their own. The Black Foundation has been trying to cure CFaD since the beginning and they have a budget the size of a small country."

She was right: it was absolutely, completely ridiculous to dream you could cure a disease like CFaD on your own. But that hadn't stopped Kontos from trying. My heart swelled at the thought, but I didn't want to cry again so I dropped my eyes to the floor. Whoever had looted the lab had scattered papers everywhere. I nudged one over with my toe.

Human Test Subject 113A
Treatment status: treated
Test results: clotting factor dysfunction virus—negative

The *negative* had been circled in bright-orange highlighter.
I snatched the paper up.
"Look at this."
She inhaled sharply, and I knew I'd understood it correctly.
Kontos had actually done it.
He'd found a cure for CFaD.
We both fell to our knees, gathering the test results from where they'd slid under the worktables and chairs. The same result on every sheet: *negative, negative, negative.*
"How is this possible?" Kat breathed as she shuffled through the results.
"Maybe it isn't." I slammed another metal file drawer closed. I was going through the filing cabinets to make sure we didn't miss anything. "The woman he died feeding on probably came from down here, right? He must have thought she was clean, and she wasn't. Maybe the cure didn't actually work."
"That doesn't explain how he ended up feeding in his classroom, not down in his medical research man-cave, and in the middle of the dance."
I yanked open the lowest drawer, expecting it to be empty like

all the rest, but stuck in the back was a binder. I pulled it out and flipped it open. It was full of plastic sleeves with Polaroid photos of humans, numbers written on the blank white space. They were numbered the way the results had been. 113A, a balding white guy. 124B, a brown-skinned woman with thick black hair. I turned to another page. 154B: a young woman with a nose ring, blue eyes, and blond hair. She was wearing a tank top and a tattoo on her shoulder was visible. I fished the photo out of its plastic sleeve to look at it more closely.

I knew that hair, that tattoo.

I'd seen them on the floor of the chemistry classroom.

"Do you have 154B?"

Kat sorted through the test results. "She's negative. The test is dated last week."

"So maybe she'd been reinfected."

"Or he didn't actually get CFaD from her."

I shook my head. "There was no mistaking what I saw."

"Maybe that was the point," Kat said cautiously. "Think about it: a reunionist claims to cure CFaD, but dies in a way that completely undermines his work. That could be pretty convenient to some people."

"If it was staged, then it wasn't an accident. Kontos wasn't a liar," I said slowly. "He was murdered."

Just then, one of the lights flickered and we both jumped nearly out of our skin. Without further discussion, we hustled back down that creepy hallway and up to his office. But as I locked the metal door and pushed the bookcase back into place, my racing heart didn't slow.

Kontos was dead—murdered—but that didn't mean everything he cared about had to die too.

28

KAT

ON MONDAY, I waited a very long five minutes after Taylor left for her run to call my mom.

Since I'd gotten to Harcote, we'd mainly kept in touch by text, which I knew she hated. I hadn't called her since before I won the mentorship with Victor, weeks ago. But now I needed to talk to her, even if I didn't want to. I couldn't meet Galen's parents at Descendants Day without knowing what her relationship to them had been. Plus, I needed to know for sure whether she was planning to come.

On top of that, I was feeling a little emotional. It wasn't just what had happened the night of the Founder's Dance, or that Taylor and I were low-key investigating a murder, or that the cure for CFaD might be stored on a hard drive in my room. It was also that Mr. Kontos's death had me thinking about my dad. I'd never known anyone else to die of CFaD. The way Taylor had described it—black goo leaking from every orifice—made it impossible not to think about his last moments.

My mom picked up on the first ring.

"Kat? What's wrong?"

I rubbed my forehead. "Why would you think something's wrong?"

"I'm not used to you calling out of the blue," she said icily.

Just like that, any hope I'd had of a reassuring mommy-daughter conversation vanished.

"I wanted to know if you were going to come to Descendants Day. It's in two weeks. My, uh, boyfriend wants to introduce me to his parents."

"I wasn't even aware you had a boyfriend, and you're already meeting his parents?"

"It would be weirder if I tried to avoid them since they'll be on campus. Anyway I *want* to meet them. They run the Foundation for a Cure."

"You're dating Simon and Meera Black's *son*?"

"Galen Black. We met doing that mentorship. With Victor Castel."

"I didn't realize you were interested in spending time with people like that."

"That's kind of harsh. I don't know what they're like. I haven't met them yet. Have you?" I paused a beat, but she didn't answer. "I'm sure they'll ask about my parents and my pedigree when we meet. Obviously, I'll tell them what I can about all that. Then when you meet them someday—"

"When I meet the Blacks someday?"

"I mean, Galen and I . . . it feels pretty serious." I winced. The idea of a serious relationship with Galen—graduating together, having him out to Sacramento, introducing him to Guzman and Shelby—was icky in a way I couldn't pinpoint.

"Now that I think of it, I have met them. A long time ago. I doubt they'd remember, so it's probably better not to mention me."

"Great," I said. "I'll just tell them I'm an orphan."

"*Kat.*"

"Then what *should* I say when they ask about my parents? I have your last name, I'm sure they'll recognize it."

"I went by a different name back then," she admitted.

"What was it—"

"Baby, my lunch break is only so long and I'd rather not spend it explaining to you why I want nothing to do with Simon and Meera Black."

"You want nothing to do with them?"

"And I'd rather you kept your distance too. They're not good people."

"How could they not be good people? They run a massive charity foundation."

"I know," she said darkly. "I have to go, Kat."

"Wait—are you going to come? To Descendants Day?" My voice pitched needfully. "You could see campus and meet my friends."

I knew she wouldn't. I wasn't even sure if I *wanted* her to. Still, it hurt when she said, "I would love to, but the clinic is so understaffed, and we can't afford a ticket right now. But I'll see you at winter break."

TAYLOR

By the time I walked into lunch on Monday, my head was pounding from the sheer effort of ignoring the tidal wave of gossip that Kontos's death had unleashed. We hadn't officially been told the cause, but there were only so many ways an immortal being could suddenly die. Everyone was talking about CFaD.

Kat was at a table in the corner. Her smile as she waved me over made her whole face glow. My stomach leaped to my throat, which was so stupid I wanted to reach into my body and yank it back down to where it belonged. I had just seen Kat that morning. I saw her all the time, more than was probably healthy, so there was no reason for me to lose it whenever I laid eyes on her.

Other than that I was, as ever, completely in love with her.

I grabbed a chair. Kat immediately scooted hers closer to mine and leaned in to whisper, "So I've been thinking about Ms. Radtke . . ."

We'd stayed up too late last night having this debate, getting nowhere. That didn't mean I minded having it again in the Dining Hall, if it meant Kat's hot breath on my ear.

The real problem was, we didn't know who else knew what Kontos had discovered, which made it hard to narrow down our suspects.

To me, Radtke was the obvious choice. We'd caught her directly threatening Kontos *and* we'd watched her poke around his office. Kontos had been stone-cold sure she wasn't a problem. That didn't mean he was right.

"She didn't have an opportunity to actually *do* it," Kat said. "Ms. Radtke was chaperoning the dance all night. Why would she think he'd be at the Science Building at all? And she seems really . . . disturbed by his death."

Across the Dining Hall, Radtke was staring into her bowl of Hema. I had to admit, she was looking pretty morose. Still, I would not feel sympathy for Radtke. "She always looks like that."

"What about this: she doesn't have a motive. Ms. Radtke's a trav. She wants to go back to the old lifestyle, where everyone fed on humans directly. She probably wants a cure more than anyone."

"Maybe she broke into his office to steal it, so she could release it."

"That's a motive for theft, not murder," Kat said coolly, like she was some hot lady-detective on TV.

"But if it's not Radtke, who does that leave?"

Kat's brows knit in concentration. "Basically *everyone*. If CFaD were cured, Vampirdom would change completely. There might not even *be* a Vampirdom. The old ways could return—feeding on humans, no need for us to live where Hema was accessible, no need for Hema at all."

"So you're suggesting Castel."

Kat's eyes widened. "I didn't say *that*."

"You might as well have. He's made a fortune on Hema and all his power comes from it. Vampirdom is practically a monument to him."

Kat shook her head. "He wouldn't just arrange a murder."

"Why not? The guy's perfectly creepy," I said. "He came by the house to see my parents once. It was around the time you left. He kept asking me about going to Harcote, and he had this freaky smile slapped on his face. It wasn't just that." It was the smarminess and cologne wafting off of him. The way he looked me up and down like I was a specimen, another Youngblood in his collection. His tone when he said I was growing up so nicely. "Something's just *off* about him."

"So, to recap, our new criteria for a potential murderer are: an interest in your education, smiling too much, and a failed vibe check?"

I spun my empty mug around. "That's not what I meant."

"Look, I don't think Victor really has a motive. He already has more money than he knows what to do with. If vampires stopped drinking Hema today, that wouldn't change."

"But is it enough money to last him *forever*?"

Kat dismissed this. "I'm sure he has a plan for when a cure is discovered. He's on the board of the Black Foundation, after all."

"Fine," I conceded. "His days are numbered. If he blocks the cure now, it's only a matter of time before it's discovered by someone else. If Kontos could find a cure working alone in that little homemade lab, then the Black Foundation can't be far behind."

"Then why haven't they found a cure already? The Blacks control all the money in CFaD research. My mom once told me that almost every scientist working on CFaD depends on Black Foundation grants."

"Whoever cures CFaD is going to make *a lot* of money off it, right? If the Blacks almost have their own cure, they'd need to stop Kontos from going public with his. It would totally undermine them."

Kat nodded. "Then let's figure out how close they really are."

Behind Kat, a mop of optimally tousled curls attached to the body of a future Junior Executive was striding toward us. "Head's up, it's—"

But then Galen's hand was on her back. He slid it up to her shoulder, and he just *left it there*, casually touching Kat, as he took the seat next to her. And Kat didn't slap it away or tell him off or even flinch. Kat was *smiling at him*. Kat was *asking how his day was*.

Right. Of course. I shouldn't have assumed that the dance—that Saturday night—had changed anything about how Kat felt about the Golden Boy of Darkness.

I grabbed my stuff. "I'm out."

"*Stay*," Kat said.

"Yeah, stick around," Galen added, his arm still slung over her shoulder.

Why would I? With Galen there, we couldn't talk about anything important, and already I felt like my heart had been replaced with a crushed soda can. Then Kat said, "Taylor, come on. Please?"

I dropped my bag back on the floor.

"Galen, I was wondering if the Black Foundation had a timeline for the cure," Kat said. "There's almost fifty years of research. They must be getting close, right?"

Galen tossed his hair back. "I don't know about *close*. It's a very complicated disease."

"You have no idea, do you?" I said.

He glowered at me. It was a very good glower, very black and sullen, I had to give him that. "Of course I do. There's lots of research happening all the time, but most of it isn't public. We don't publish studies that fail, and if we *did* find something, we wouldn't publish that either, because it would be proprietary. Any treatments developed would belong to the Black Foundation."

"Not really a *foundation* then, is it?" I said. "Sounds more like a drug company."

"Everyone does it this way." He didn't sound fully convinced.

"We're not trying to, like, release our own cure for CFaD," Kat said sarcastically, which made me want to kiss her something fierce. "I was just wondering if a cure is on the horizon, what the major developments are—that kind of thing. For Victor's assignment. You must have access to all kinds of insider information. Do you think you could find out?"

He nodded sharply. "Easily."

Before I could make fun of Galen more, Atherton walked into the Dining Hall with the enthusiasm of a youth pastor with some souls to save. The aides paused dishing out Hema or clearing dishes and stood at attention for him. But instead of heading to his spot at the front of the room, Atherton came over to our table.

"Just who I was looking for!" This obviously didn't refer to me; he was beaming at Kat and Galen.

"How can I help you, Headmaster?" Galen said politely.

"I'd like you to give a few remarks at the assembly this afternoon. To help the Youngbloods make sense of these difficult times. Everyone looks up to you two so much as student leaders. A short speech reminding everyone to keep their chins up and fangs sharp will be just the ticket."

"But the assembly's in half an hour," Kat said.

"No worries, Kat!" Atherton squeezed her shoulder, because he was always looking for ways to make me dislike him more. "Everything's prepared, and all you'll have to do is just read a few lines off the cards."

"We'd be delighted," Galen said smoothly. "Thank you for thinking of us."

I had to give this to Galen too: he was brutally good with adults, even adults who looked like teenagers.

Although they were fairly easy to impress when you were always doing exactly what they wanted.

KAT

IN THE GREAT Hall, the mood was somber. Taylor split off to find a seat among the third-years. Galen and I made our way to the front together. It felt like every head turned as we passed by. At the front, we sat next to Headmaster Atherton.

I leaned over Galen to get Headmaster Atherton's attention. "May I see the notes for the speech?"

"They're on the lectern, Kat," he said. "Can't miss 'em."

I frowned at Galen. "We're supposed to give a speech we've never read?"

"It's not the State of the Union," Galen whispered. "You'll be fine."

"I have a bad feeling about this," I said under my breath. "Why did you agree for both of us?"

"I thought it was harmless." He sounded taken aback.

I was beginning to think Galen didn't know what that word meant.

Headmaster Atherton took his place at the lectern. Again, as he had at Convocation, he asked us to stand and release our fangs to recite the Harcote Oath. This time, I did it easily and said the words just like everyone else—with a slight lisp from speaking around elongated incisors.

He began in a somber tone. "I wish we gathered under more pleasant circumstances. But this school year has begun with some upheaval. We're mourning the loss of a member of our vampiric, and Harcote, family: Leo Kontos. The death of any vampire is a tragedy. Especially after we have lost so many of our number in the Peril. Our lives—*your* lives—are a gift."

Headmaster Atherton's fingers snaked over the edges of the lectern. His milky skin was so blotched with pink, he looked like a vanilla yogurt gone moldy.

"When the gift of eternal life is wasted, we must not turn away. Leo Kontos was responsible for his own death. He knew the risk of CFaD exposure, and he decided to gamble with his life. Worse, he did this on school grounds. Leo Kontos's actions disrespected each of you, the school itself, and all of Vampirdom. He disrespected himself. He betrayed our community values. He died pathetic and alone. It was the end that he deserved."

A chill crawled down my spine. The Great Hall was utterly silent. No one whispered to their seatmate, no phone accidentally chimed, no wooden pew creaked.

Abruptly, Headmaster Atherton shifted back to his usual demeanor, of the least-cool counselor at summer camp. "Jeez, that's a lot to take in, right? But don't worry, we're going to get through this as a community. To get us started, we're going to have Galen Black and Kat Finn come up and say a few words about how they're feeling right now."

Galen gave me a reassuring look as we approached the lectern. There was a small stack of papers there, the top one bearing Galen's name.

Galen cleared his throat as he scanned the speech, then he squared his shoulders and began.

"When Headmaster Atherton asked me to say something about how Mr. Kontos's death affected me, I knew exactly what I wanted to talk about. I'm sad, like a lot of us, because I liked him. I thought he was a good guy. That's the thing I can't get over." I knew Galen was reading off cards he'd never seen before, but he sounded so natural. I would never have guessed the speech wasn't his. "Mr. Kontos betrayed our trust. He acted like one person at Seated Dinner or in chemistry class, but he was really someone else. He took risks with his life and he ended up dead." Galen cleared his throat again. "He probably thought immortality made him invincible. But that's not how it works. The Peril taught us that. We come from fangmakers and parents who survived that nightmare. So I guess all of this makes me really appreciate how lucky we are to be here, and to have each other."

As we switched places at the lectern, Galen leaned in and whispered, "See? Not so bad."

I stood at the lectern, looking out at the Great Hall, and for a second I was frozen. I knew that the speech Headmaster Atherton had written for me would be the same judgmental pro-Vampirdom rhetoric that Galen had just read. I also knew that I had a microphone and the attention of the whole school, and I didn't have to say what they wanted me to. I could have talked about Lucy's party or what Mr. Kontos had been working toward. At least, I could have told the truth about how he'd died. My palms began to sweat. Was this the right moment? And where was I supposed to start?

I searched for Taylor's face, as if seeing her would clarify everything.

I found someone else instead.

He was standing in the shadow of one of the chapels, and he was watching me.

Victor Castel.

I took in a sharp breath. The mentorship might have been designed to elevate Galen, but in this moment, Victor's attention was on *me*. Even if Victor had already chosen Galen as his successor, there were a million ways Victor's help could change my life—as long as I showed him I deserved it. Not just during the mentorship, not just at Harcote, but for the rest of my immortality. Unexpectedly, I imagined a moment after the assembly, where Victor was telling me I'd done very well, that I'd impressed him. It wasn't approval I'd ever get from my mom or, obviously, my dad, and suddenly, I wanted it so badly my stomach ached.

I dropped my eyes to the speech and began to read.

"Being at Harcote means something different to me than it does to the other students here. It means a community of people who understand you. My mom raised me outside of Vampirdom.

Our Hema dealer was the only vampire I knew. What made it worse was that I lost . . . I lost my father to CFaD, and both my fangmakers in the Peril." These were my words from the application for the mentorship. They were *personal*. Not something I'd wanted to announce to the *entire freaking school*. I felt used, violated—but with everyone watching me, I didn't know what else to do other than go on. Thankfully, the words diverged from what I'd written. "Mr. Kontos didn't know how lucky he was. He had a community, here at Harcote and in Vampirdom, that supported him and understood him. But he didn't treat that like the privilege it is. He threw it all away. I hope all the Youngbloods realize . . . how lost we would be without Vampirdom."

Galen reached for me as we left the stage together. I barely even realized he was holding my hand until we were seated again. I was numb, my brain fuzzed out and cottony. Headmaster Atherton had tricked me into telling the entire school my family secrets— or what he knew of them—and then spinning them into propaganda. Going to Harcote *was* a privilege, way more than most students here realized, but I'd just made it sound like that meant Youngbloods would always be dependent on it, and on Vampirdom. That wasn't how I felt at all. If I'd learned anything since coming here, it was that both institutions needed some serious change.

"We've got a lot of big conversations about those ideas up ahead, boys and girls," Headmaster Atherton was saying. "First and foremost, let's remember that Harcote is an educational institution. This isn't a place for politics. Any discussion of that nature outside of the classroom is potentially in violation of the Honor Code. That includes *printed* discussions. Any student who has information about that kind of activity should come forward and report it to me. Let's focus on healing and putting our best feet forward for Descendants Day! The Best of the Best, standing together."

As we were dismissed, my skin crawled from standing next to Headmaster Atherton. I wanted to find Taylor, but Galen had hold of my hand again and Headmaster Atherton wasn't done with us yet.

"Not so fast, my favorite student leaders! As the head of our board, Mr. Castel is on campus today, in light of *events*. He'd like to check in with his mentees."

29

KAT

"Why does he want to see *us*, in the middle of all this?" I whispered to Galen as we followed Headmaster Atherton to Old Hill.

Galen shot me a resigned look but didn't answer. As we'd approached Old Hill, his posture had stiffened with that highly pressurized self-control he always possessed where Victor Castel was concerned. It made him look almost like a different person, all his cocksure confidence pulled in close around him like armor. I grabbed his hand and squeezed.

Headmaster Atherton showed us into a classroom where Victor was waiting. His nice suit and shiny shoes made even the spotless classroom feel shabby. He looked different than the man I had met at his house, more powerful somehow, more intimidating. Like you could see the age of him, although you couldn't. He felt larger, bigger, like he exerted a gravitational force that everything spun toward.

Victor eyed the joining of our hands. "Well done, Galen."

As I struggled to keep my cringing internal, Galen ducked his head. "Thank you, sir. Knowing you saw something in Kat, I started to see it too."

We took seats around the seminar table. Victor studied us over his folded hands. "Why do you think I'm visiting campus today?"

I stole a look at Galen. He didn't seem ready to speak, so I said, "You're a trustee, and one of the teachers died. That's what Headmaster Atherton said."

This was the wrong answer. Victor's attention turned to Galen.

"There are four other trustees. Two are my parents. And they're not here," Galen said. "Leo Kontos's death is significant beyond the fact that he was a teacher here."

"Correct," Victor said, very precisely. Shame prickled my cheeks. Galen didn't know anything about Mr. Kontos, not like I did. He'd only guessed his death meant something more because Victor had shown up. Victor continued, "What is that significance?"

What *did* Kontos's death mean? I tried to formulate an answer but my mind kept circling back to the heartbreak on Taylor's face and the heavy look in her eyes when she talked about him.

Victor saw me hesitate. He sat forward and pressed a fist into the table. "Put your emotions aside. Emotional thinking is the enemy of clear judgment. It corrupts the decisions we must make for the greater good of all vampires."

It didn't seem right that emotions were the enemy of logic and judgment. What made you sad or angry or outraged were the things you *cared* about—the things you valued. Replacing that with hard rationality made it seem like values didn't matter at all.

But I shoved those reservations down. Victor was right—I couldn't be emotional right now, and not just because I wanted to impress him so badly sweat was trickling down my spine. I also needed to figure out what Victor knew about Mr. Kontos. Whoever had ransacked the lab knew there was a cure, but whether Victor had that information was still a question mark.

"There are rumors that Mr. Kontos was a reunionist," I said carefully.

"He was?" Galen's face flashed surprise as he cut me off. "But reunionists support integration. How could Mr. Kontos be a reunionist if he died feeding on a human?"

"Evidently, his moral compass was less refined than he had believed," Victor said.

Galen nodded. "Then his death demonstrates that. Mr. Kontos thought humans and vampires could live side by side, but he was preying on them. He was a hypocrite. It will be a blow to the reunionist movement."

"I thought the reunionists were too weak to be a real threat. That's what you told me, Galen," I said. "They can't cure CFaD on their own, right?"

"Of course not," Galen scoffed, and seemed to mean it. He had no idea what Mr. Kontos had discovered.

Victor's face didn't betray a thing. Serious, he trained his deep-set eyes on me. "Kat, on some level, the cure is irrelevant. It's the ideas that matter. The reunionists envision fundamental changes to our way of life. Vampirdom is a delicate architecture. It's a set of circumstances that allow us to live together. It took a crisis that nearly annihilated our kind to create the community the Young-bloods are blessed to be born into. That architecture could crumble. We cannot let that happen."

"But it *is* only a matter of time before CFaD is cured," I pressed. He hadn't given anything away. "It could happen really soon. Especially with the work of the Black Foundation."

"When you're my age, *a matter of time* means something quite different." Victor chuckled at his cleverness. "Every human alive in this moment might be dead before the cure is discovered."

A chill skittered through me. "What will happen to Vampirdom then?" I asked. "You've been asking us to think of the future, so you must have a plan."

He stared at me with that disconcerting intensity. "What would *you* do in my position, Kat?"

I knew what *I* would do. I'd make sure every vampire could get Hema when and where they needed it, as close to free as I could make it, just like the reunionists wanted. I'd create a Vampirdom where I'd only have to hide from Guzman and Shelby if I chose to. But that wasn't his question. Victor wanted to know what I thought *he* would do. I might not have been as suspicious of him as Taylor was, but not one molecule in my body believed that Victor would cave to the reunionists' demands.

"I would make sure there was something else holding Vampirdom together before that happened," I said.

He sat back in his chair, satisfied. "So you understand our goals."

"What do you mean, *our goals*?" I asked. "Who's *we*?"

Victor and Galen exchanged a look that I was pretty sure was an agreement over my stupidity. Then Galen said, "*We're* Vampirdom, Kat. Who else?"

Victor smoothed his tie. "Kat, I'd like to speak with you privately. Galen, close the door on your way out."

Wordlessly, Galen obeyed, and just like that, I was alone with Victor Castel. My mouth went dry. The tentacles of his power seemed to extend from him and snarl around the room, expanding and filling it with pressure. I couldn't remember the last time I'd been alone with a man like this. Victor was hundreds of years old but he looked like he could have been my father, and it made me feel younger and hungrier than I ever had in his presence.

Perhaps he could see that, because he gave me a reassuring smile. "There's no need to be nervous, Kat. I want you to know that how you conducted yourself today impressed me very much. I'm proud of you."

A flutter of shock at his words gave way to a strange, soaring sensation in my chest. Victor Castel was *proud of me*. My mom never said things like that. I could still hear the dismissiveness in her voice when I told her about Harcote—*I'm always proud of you*—like it was thing too trivial to waste energy saying out loud. I knew I had reason to be skeptical of Victor, but at the same time, he felt like the one person in my life who seemed to understand why I'd come to Harcote in the first place.

"I, um—thank you," I stammered.

"It's well-deserved praise. The Youngbloods were moved by your words at the assembly, and your comments in this meeting were incisive. I see a very great deal of potential in you. I know that this opportunity means more to you than it does to Galen."

The fact that Victor had seen that felt like validation, but still, my heart sank. That simple validation was all I could hope for. The seat at the table that Victor had talked about had had Galen's name engraved on it since the moment he was born. It would never be mine. Admitting I knew that was embarrassing, but I couldn't handle Victor pretending otherwise to protect my feelings. "Just so you know . . . I understand."

"What do you understand?"

I bit back a frown. "Galen's your fangborn. You want to recognize him as a successor, but it needs to look legitimate—like he earned it. Otherwise no one will respect him. I'm here because I'm a nobody, to make it look like a real competition. But I think there are other ways I could really benefit from, um, from learning from you. You know, I don't have anyone else to really fall back on, or even talk about my future with . . ." I trailed off.

Victor was wearing a faintly amused expression that made me feel childish, and that made me angry in a childish way. I might have been naive to the ways of Vampirdom, but I wasn't an idiot. I straightened up to look at him directly. "I don't see anything particularly funny about that," I said.

"I'm sorry, Kat, it's not funny. But I don't know where you got the idea that I've chosen Galen as some kind of successor. First of all, I'm not planning on going anywhere anytime soon. Second, Galen has never had my full confidence."

"But all he cares about is impressing you."

Victor rubbed his jaw, dismissing this. "Be that as it may, he's yet to prove that he can be his own man. But you, Kat, you aren't like him. I've been watching you. I can see your drive. I see hints, here and there, of the Youngblood leader you could be, if we channeled that drive in the right direction. Is that kind of partnership, between you and me, something you could be interested in?"

"*Yes*," I said. I wasn't sure exactly what he was offering, but I knew what it meant: the key to the future I'd dreamed of.

"Good. Keep impressing me like you have been, and you'll make my decision easy." There was a nonchalance to his tone, like we'd concluded a business meeting, not an agreement that could change the course of my life. "One final thing: I've heard from the headmaster that your mother hasn't registered for Descendants Day. I'd like to volunteer my services for the weekend."

Surely, I had passed out and now my brain was leaking out my ears. The thought of Descendants Day made me want to crawl into bed and hibernate until spring. After what I'd been forced to admit at the assembly today, it was bound to be even shittier than I'd been expecting.

If I had Victor there instead, I wouldn't be alone. I'd spend Descendants Day with someone there who might actually be proud of me. I just wasn't sure I really deserved that.

I hesitated. "Wouldn't that look strange?"

"Why is that?"

"Because you're Galen's fangmaker. And because I'm . . . I'm a nobody."

"Promise me something, Kat: promise me you'll never say that about yourself again."

TAYLOR

I HAD BEEN staring at my computer for a long time, because that was how I wanted Kat to find me: nonchalantly interneting, completely unconcerned with thoughts of her.

Kat was *dating Galen*. The signs were unavoidable. His touch on her shoulder at lunch. The way their hands had met at the lectern. The looks they'd shared up there, like they were communicating in a secret language right in front of the whole school, as if none of us were there to see it—as if *I* weren't there to see it.

Evangeline was right: Kat was a lost cause. That rock tumbling down the hill to crush me time and time again, as many times as I put myself in its way.

When she came through the door, her cheeks were pink from the crisp fall air, her auburn hair tangled in her scarf, and when she saw me, her hazel eyes seemed to come alive.

"You won't believe what just happened!" she said.

"Omigod! Was it you spewing vampiric propaganda to the whole school? Because unfortunately I had to witness that firsthand."

Her shoulders drooped. "You know Headmaster Atherton wrote those speeches and Galen was the one who agreed to it. You think I wanted to say all that stuff about my dad and my fangmakers?"

"And those lies about Kontos, which you knew weren't true?"

"*Shhh!* There's an aide in the hallway," she snapped. "She might overhear."

Before I realized what I was doing I had grabbed Kat's arm and tugged her into the bathroom. I flipped the shower on. "Now she won't."

Kat's breath was coming in quick bursts. We were standing pretty close together. Admittedly, I didn't consider how small the bathroom was when I came up with this.

"You know Headmaster Atherton wrote the speeches. I *had* to do it."

"No one had a stake to your heart. You could have said whatever you wanted. Like the truth, for example."

"So you get to hide behind anonymity, but I'm supposed to stand up in front of the whole school and come up with some battle cry off the top of my head? Everyone was watching."

"Right, watching you remind us all to be good little vampires. I'm surprised they didn't find crowns for our new king and queen to wear while they addressed their people."

"What's that supposed to mean?" she sputtered, stepping forward. There was barely any space between us.

"Why didn't you tell me you were dating Galen?"

"I—I didn't think you'd care."

My lip curled. She didn't think I'd *care*? "It would have been nice to know that half of this crackpot investigative team was sleeping with the enemy."

"I'm not—he isn't—"

I cut her off. "Do you not remember this morning, when we both agreed that the Blacks had a good motive for wanting Kontos dead? In case you're not aware, Galen is Galen *Black*, which makes him a suspect. By the transitive property!"

"Galen is a junior in high school, not part of some Vampirdom-wide conspiracy, and he's actually not a terrible person."

"He's an entitled ass."

"Which distinguishes him in not one single way from the other Harcoties. Why do you hate him so much anyway?"

I froze. I hated Galen for a million reasons. Some of them I understood: Galen acted like he'd been raised by wolves in a Swiss chalet, he was dating the girl I was in love with, and the girl I was banging had cast him in the role of Husband in her hetero-dreamlife. But the truth was, I had resented Galen long before Kat had showed up, even before things had started with me and Evangeline. That's where the borders of my comprehension got a little fuzzy. Why *did* I hate him so much?

I hated his amazingly good hair, which was a lot like mine but somehow unattainably *better*. I hated the way he was always meticulously dressed but never seemed to have exerted any effort to appear that way—that he looked perfect in a suit, while I'd had to raid the boys' department before the Founder's Dance in the desperate hope of wearing something that didn't make me feel like a corn cob. I hated that he could arch his eyebrow like it was on a marionette string and I couldn't, although I had about a thousand fantasies where I made a pretty girl melt with just a well-arched eyebrow. It wasn't that I wished that *I* had been raised by wolves in a Swiss chalet, but I wanted, just once, to look like I had.

But I couldn't say that. Kat was watching me uncertainly. She knew I was about to lie. "He won't tell me what hair products he uses. Unforgivable."

Kat blew out a breath. "If I tell you that your hair's as good as his, you'll get over it?"

I chewed my lip. "Worth a try."

She locked those hazel eyes on mine. She might as well have put her hand around my throat. "Taylor, your hair is as good as Galen's. Actually, I think your hair is even better."

My lips were pressed very tightly together now, my teeth pressing into my flesh in an effort to hide how entirely this had undone me.

Kat was looking up at me expectantly. I knew she was thinking of him, when I wanted her to be thinking of me.

I *wanted* her.

All of a sudden, it was physically painful, like every muscle in my body cramped up from the pressure of the two of us in that tiny bathroom. How could Kat love me enough to try to make me feel better, even when she didn't understand what was wrong, but still not *love me*? The unfairness of that made even the good things hurt. It had gotten so bad that I couldn't even make her laugh without feeling a brutal twinge of what I would never have from her.

And I thought, for the first time, that I didn't know how long I could keep doing this.

"Better?" Kat asked hopefully.

I shook my head. Then I spun on my heel and left the bathroom entirely, leaving her standing there with the shower running.

30

KAT

IT WAS MID-NOVEMBER now, and every morning the grass sparkled with frost. I was thankful for the preppy sweaters and peacoats the Benefactor had stocked my closet with.

I'd thought that time would make a difference, but the days that had passed since the kiss—the *kiss*—had done nothing to dull my memory of it. I could hardly look at Taylor without thinking about touching her. That day when she pulled me into the bathroom after the assembly, I thought I'd combust from simply standing that close to her. The last thing I'd wanted to do was talk about *Galen*.

Unfortunately, the last few days also hadn't changed how Taylor felt. She was still as pissed about what I'd said at the assembly—which was infuriating because she knew I hadn't meant it—as she was that I hadn't informed her I was dating Galen—which was infuriating because she hadn't told me that she was with *Evangeline*, who was worse in literally every way.

In class, I'd started catching Evangeline staring at Taylor, as if she wasn't just fantasizing about undressing Taylor—she was imagining totally disassembling her. A secret relationship was probably really hot. Although I wasn't sure why it had to be secret. Hopefully because Evangeline wasn't ready to come out, because if any little bit at all was out of embarrassment over Taylor, then I would personally stake her for that.

Lately Taylor had been spending all her free time on tech for Evangeline's one-act, which was in rehearsals leading up to Descendants Day. A nagging little voice in my head kept asking if it was really rehearsals, or if it wasn't something else they were doing together, but it wasn't any of my business. Taylor was too much— too many feelings, too much trouble, too much of a distraction.

I had other things to focus on. Things like Galen. Who was I was still dating.

GALEN AND I met up in the library. The instant we swiped into the Extended Collections, before we'd even made it into the creepy ice cube of the Stack, he spun me around and kissed me.

He'd taken me entirely off guard and it made me a little breathless. I inhaled the scent of him, a very adult cologne and a tinge of Hema on his breath. When I kissed him back, I tried to get lost in it, but then panic-tinged thoughts surged up from the back of my mind.

Do I like this enough? How exactly is kissing supposed to go? Should I be more relaxed or do I seem like I'm turned on, and why am I thinking so hard about this? When will it start feeling good? Why doesn't it feel right?

Galen's hands were all over me, and mine were just hanging like dead weight at the ends of my arms. My hands were supposed to be touching him too, but doing that felt impossibly awkward— touching him *how?* All at once my eyes prickled with traitorous tears. I pulled away from him. It felt like the first correct thing I'd done in the lifetime that had passed since he planted his lips on mine a few seconds ago.

His ash-gray eyes gazed down at me, through lashes so dense he might have harvested them from a baby doll. I was sure he could tell from how stiffly I was holding myself that something was wrong.

But then his lips quirked in satisfaction.

"I've been waiting to do that all day," he said huskily.

My heart sank a little, in relief or maybe disappointment, as I slipped out from where he'd pinned me against the door. "We're supposed to be *working*."

I liked him. I really did. Sort of. The problem was I wanted to like him more, or differently, or—I wasn't quite sure. His little affectations—the arched eyebrow, the gravelly voice—had stopped annoying me weeks ago. I understood them now as some kind of armor, even if he hadn't shown me exactly what they were protecting. That faultless face, all the angles of him just so, as if light and shadow had been invented that they might perfectly highlight the heir of Vampirdom. He had so much but somehow had still never gotten what he needed, and he was happy being with me. He deserved that, didn't he?

But the more I thought that way, the more I heard the quieter voice beneath it, asking: what did *I* deserve?

WHEN GALEN GOT special permission from Headmaster Atherton to leave campus for the weekend, it was something of a relief. Finals weren't so far away, and I was happy to have the chance to catch up on homework. When he got back Sunday night, he texted me to meet him in the Boys' Residential Quad. I pretended not to notice Taylor glowering at me from her side of the room as I buttoned my coat to meet him.

I'd only been to the Boys' Residential Quad a handful of times. It was laid out exactly like the Girls'—four residential houses around a central square—but felt less concerned with being nice. Someone had carved a dick into the trunk of the central oak tree.

Galen came out of his House looking incredibly rakish, with the collar of his black wool coat turned up and his hands buried in his pockets. The wind teased a lock of hair across his forehead. But as he got closer, I saw his forehead was cut with worry lines, and they weren't softening.

"What's wrong?" I asked.

His eyebrows popped up; he must have thought he was hiding it better. He glanced over his shoulder. A few second-years trailed through the quad. He slipped his hand into mine. "Let's walk."

Galen led me toward the sports fields. I tried not to think about Taylor as we crossed the lacrosse field and headed toward where the trimmed turf gave way to trees and behind them the fence that hemmed in the campus.

"You're making me nervous, Galen. Say something."

His shoulders were tensed up to his ears. "You asked me to look into how close to a cure the Foundation is," he began. "Frankly, it was more challenging than I'd anticipated. I should have had access to everything. I'm supposed to take over from my parents someday. Nothing should be off-limits to me. But all of my requests had been rebuffed." He blew out a frustrated breath. "This weekend I went to the Foundation's office myself. They would have to show me what I was asking for or refuse me to my face. But the person they called to explain it to me was my *father*."

"What did he say?"

Galen checked over his shoulder again. It struck me as paranoid, but maybe necessary too.

"Nothing. They have nothing."

"Come on, tell me the truth."

"I *am*. He said they're nowhere near a cure." He choked out a wretched laugh. "It's the Black Foundation *for the Cure*, right? We have all the resources of Vampirdom behind us. You're probably wondering how we could have completely, totally failed to do *the one damn thing we were responsible for*." Suddenly his tone dropped, and he sounded a lot like I guessed his father did. "I shouldn't be telling you this. I shouldn't be talking about it at all. It's *family business*."

He ran his hand through his hair, as though what he really wanted to do was close his fist and pull it out. I grabbed his wrists and forced them from his face.

"Galen, look at me."

With some effort, he settled his frantic eyes on mine.

When he seemed a little steadier, I said, "Explain it to me. What's the Foundation doing?"

"They're not really looking for a cure," he said heavily. "They *are* funding research. But they use that funding to keep the results private. Proprietary. If the study's successful, they never let it be published. It goes into the vault, but they might as well throw it into an incinerator. All the scientists are glamoured into keeping quiet."

"So no research, no progress, no cure," I said. "I don't get it. Don't they *want* a cure for CFaD?"

"That's what I thought! I was proud to be a Black—that my name was going to be synonymous with the cure for this disease. I know my parents were in it for vampires' sake, but the humans were important to me too. That was the mark we were going to leave on the world." He shook his head. "But the mark they want to leave is one of—of sickness, and suffering, and death."

"But why?" I asked. "Why do all of this?"

"My father wouldn't tell me. He said I had to trust him. *The world is complicated*, he said. What's complicated about *curing a disease*? Kat, what am I going to do?"

He was looking at me in this openly painful way that made me want to run all the way back to Hunter House. I didn't know what to do with that pain any more than he did. What I wanted most of all was to find Taylor.

I squeezed Galen's hand. "Take some time to think about it, and you'll know what you need to do."

He sighed heavily. "You really think so?"

"Absolutely," I assured him.

TAYLOR

I WAS ON stage with Evangeline, taping out marks for props, when Kat came storming down the aisle.

"What are you doing here?" Evangeline shouted. "Rehearsals are closed!"

"I need to talk to Taylor," Kat said.

"Can it not wait like one single hour?" Evangeline said.

"If it could, would I be here?" Kat shot back.

"*Taylor!*" they both said, at the exact same time, making my insides convulse.

"It'll only take a second, E, promise." I jumped off the stage where Kat was standing. "What is it?"

She directed a very intense side-eye toward Evangeline.

"Fine, come on," I said.

She followed me to the back of the theater, then up the cramped, black-painted stairs to the tech box.

"She won't hear us?" Kat asked.

"Not unless you scream," I said. "What is it?"

"I just talked to Galen. There's no cure."

"Right, but how close are they?"

"No, I mean, the Black Foundation *isn't looking for a cure for CFaD*. They're actually trying to prevent anyone from discovering one."

She told me everything she'd heard from Galen.

"If the Black Foundation is a sham, then Kontos's cure is an even bigger threat than we thought," I said.

"We have to expose them. I think we should tell Victor."

"Hold up, I don't endorse telling Victor Castel shit."

"Well, we have to tell *someone* and I don't think Headmaster Atherton is a great option," she said.

"Neither is the guy who turned Simon Black, who is Meera Black's fangmaker, and literally *shadow-runs the organization you just realized is a total fraud*!"

"He doesn't shadow-run it . . ."

"He sits on the board and he provides like half their funding. But I'm sure it's a total coincidence that the Black Foundation is hoarding research that would knock Hema off the market."

"I knew you would say that. I just don't think it's *impossible* that the Blacks did this alone. There's literally no evidence that Victor was involved."

"Why are you always defending *dear Victor*?"

Kat's eyes flashed. "Because he's been really supportive of me, okay? He believes in me. I don't want to betray that without good reason. Besides, I truly don't think he would do this. He's—he's nice to me."

I snorted. "You expect me to believe that any man that powerful, let alone a vampire that old, is *nice*?"

She was pacing now, which the box really wasn't big enough to accommodate, and it was putting me on edge.

"We have to go back to basics," she said forcefully. "What we know for sure is that Ms. Radtke told Headmaster Atherton that Mr. Kontos was a threat."

"I've been saying that for *weeks*!"

She suddenly stopped. "What about Headmaster Atherton? He knew Mr. Kontos was doing *something*. And unlike Ms. Radtke, he has a lot to lose if the cure got out."

"Which is what?"

She flung her arms open. "*This*. Harcote and the Youngbloods are his whole world. He talks about it all the time. This school was a dream for him, and being around young vampires—he's really *into* it, you know?"

I grimaced. Atherton tried to slide between authority figure and one of the boys with freakish enthusiasm. Last year the Ultimate Frisbee club had been forced to meet off campus to keep him out of their games. "He's basically been a teenager since the War of 1812. There aren't many other vampires turned so young," I admitted.

Kat seized on that. "*Exactly*. If CFaD is cured, turning is back, and we'd be the last of the Youngbloods. The school will close. He'll lose everything."

She'd made a good point, but I couldn't shake the feeling that it was all a deflection. "So what do you want to do, break into Atherton's office? See where he's keeping the secret files on doing murder during school dances?"

"We can start there," Kat said.

I nearly choked on my own spit. "You cannot be serious. You want to break into Atherton's office?"

"Why not?" she said indignantly, "We've broken into the Science Building. And technically back into Hunter House."

"This is on another level."

"*Everything's* on another level now," she said. "This is for Mr. Kontos. For the cure."

It felt a little manipulative. But I'd promised myself I'd do right by Kontos. I couldn't back down now.

31

TAYLOR

I TOLD KAT I was on board for more breaking and entering, but she'd have to do the legwork to figure out precisely how we were going to get into Atherton's office. I admit, I didn't think she'd be so efficient at coming up with a solution. It wasn't two days later that she called me over to her desk. She had an architectural drawing of Old Hill pulled up on her computer.

"Where did you get this?" I asked.

"The Stack has a whole section for Harcote history. Did you know that Headmaster Atherton actually bought the school in the 1960s?"

"Really? But this is supposed to be the twenty-fifth anniversary," I said. "Why would he buy a boarding school before the first Youngblood was even born?"

"I don't know. But the important thing is, Old Hill is, well, old. It was originally built as a kind of manor-house thing, for the Harcote family, and turned into a school building years later. That was back before central heating. The state-of-the-art thing at the time was building the walls with passageways, so servants could keep the rooms heated without being seen. When the school was set up, they closed off the passages."

"But they're still there," I said.

Kat nodded. "I checked the other day. There's one near the second-floor restrooms that wouldn't be hard to open. It's just hidden behind a painting. That should lead us directly to . . ." She traced her finger along the screen. The passage ended in Atherton's office.

I scratched my eyebrow. "And you think it'll be open on that side?"

"It's worth a shot. Why wall it up there, where the students wouldn't be able to access it anyway?"

"Fine," I said. Maybe it was just the thought of running around inside the walls of Old Hill that was making me uneasy, but I didn't like this plan. "When are we doing this?"

"During the lacrosse game tomorrow. Everyone will be there, and there will be humans on campus so Headmaster Atherton will be extra distracted."

"Aren't you supposed to be at that lacrosse game?" I asked. "Galen's the captain."

She dismissed this with a wave of her hand. "He'll be so focused on the game, he won't even notice I'm not there. Besides, this is more important."

So that was how I ended up hiding in the second-floor restroom of Old Hill until the building closed, so we could heave a five-foot-tall painting off the wall (not as easy as it sounds). Behind it, just as Kat promised, was a small door that blended in with the paneling. It wasn't even locked.

"See?" Kat said, self-satisfied, as she pried it open.

I peered into the passage, goose bumps prickling up my arms. Before me lay darkness, dust, and more darkness.

"If we follow it to the left, there should be stairs we can take down," Kat said.

I pointed at the painting. "And we're just leaving this here until we get back?"

"It'll be fine, Taylor."

I hated every second of the time we spent in those walls. Vampires have good eyesight at night, but this passage was entirely devoid of light beyond what came from our phones, and the walls were close. I couldn't wait to get out of there, but when Kat navigated us to the door she said would lead into Atherton's office, I hesitated. There was a nervous feeling in my guts that wasn't just claustrophobia.

"Are you sure about this?" I whispered. "We'd be in serious trouble if we get caught."

"Since when do you care about getting in trouble?" she snapped, and I felt myself shrink away from her. Not literally—there wasn't space for that—but inside, part of me wanted to hide from her. I did have a right to care about the risks we were taking. They were my risks too, and this was reckless. I'd thought Kat understood that I didn't chase trouble just for its own sake.

"It's Headmaster Atherton," she whispered. There was something unsteady and careless about her. In that moment, I didn't like her at all. "I know it is."

She pressed her weight against the door. There was a creak, then a clunk, and suddenly we were tumbling out of the passageway onto the carpeted floor of Atherton's office.

KAT

I STUMBLED TO my feet. The office was dark. We were alone.

"This is so fucking stupid," Taylor grumbled from the floor.

We were *this close* to solving this thing, so of course Taylor was acting like she couldn't care less. She hated Headmaster Atherton, but it had been surprisingly hard to convince her he even had a motive, because she was so set on Victor. I had my suspicions about Victor too, but I had to weigh them against the person I knew: the person who'd promised to help me, who'd talked about our future partnership, who saw something in me. I couldn't just turn my back on someone who had offered me so much. Plus, even if Victor was at odds with the reunionists, he didn't strike me as the kind to get his hands dirty. It was impossible to imagine him breaking into Mr. Kontos's lab or laying a trap to murder him. Headmaster Atherton, on the other hand, radiated weird energy, and he had opportunity: neither of us saw him during the dance.

Now we just needed proof.

I swung my phone flashlight around the room. I had never been in the Headmaster's Office before. Whatever I'd been expecting, it wasn't exactly *this*. On one level, it was totally vampiric. The beam of my flashlight landed on a creepy oil painting of a bat-monster thing in a tuxedo predating on a naked, porcelain-skinned lady. On a nearby shelf, a cut-crystal award for Excellence in Private School Education was flanked by a dental cast of a set of vampire teeth and some kind of creepy taxidermy bird. But at the same time, the office definitely had something of the atmosphere of *aspiring bro* about it. One corner was cluttered with sports equipment—lacrosse sticks, frisbees from the Ultimate team, a basketball covered in signatures. A dusty gaming console sat off to one side. On one bookshelf I spotted the bright-yellow spine of *Social Media for Dummies*. It might have been the most mortifying thing I'd ever seen in my life.

"I'll take the desk," I said.

"Cool, I'll just . . . randomly poke around hoping to find something incriminating."

I slid open one of the file drawers. "You didn't have to come."

Taylor snorted in response.

I flipped through the files. Taylor was right: I didn't know what we were looking for. Headmaster Atherton wasn't stupid enough to have labeled one of these file folders MURDERS I'VE DONE. But *something* had to be here.

When my vision snagged on a file, it wasn't what I'd expected.

KATHERINE FINN

My heart was thudding in my ears as I flipped the file open. The first page was my application with a note scrawled on the front: *PRIORITY.* That was weird. I'd submitted the application in January and hadn't heard back for so long I'd thought they'd lost it. The next document was my financial aid application, followed by the printout of an email.

To: Atherton@TheHarcoteSchool.edu

From: Castel@CasTech.com

Give Katherine Finn anything she needs. Make it impossible for her to decline. As discussed, I want this anonymous.

—V

I felt the blood drain from my face. *Victor* was providing my financial aid. He was the anonymous donor, the Benefactor who had paid for my tuition and room and board, and filled my closet with clothes, and sent me that horrible dress for the Founder's

Dance. He'd wanted me, specifically, to come to Harcote. I read *make it impossible for her to decline* again and again, but I couldn't make sense of it. It was one thing for him to take an interest in me now, when I'd won the mentorship and he'd gotten to know me. Why would he have wanted me at Harcote before we'd even met?

"*Kath-er-ine*—hello?" My head snapped up. Taylor was shining her flashlight directly into my face. "You find something?"

I crammed the file back into the drawer and pushed it closed. "No, nothing."

"I did."

Taylor was standing in front of an open cabinet. Her flashlight illuminated a tilting stack of laptops, with cables and cords dangling out of them every which way. "Do you think he just raided a Best Buy or—"

"The computers from the lab!" I grabbed the top laptop from the stack. There were holes drilled through the bottom. "He destroyed the hard drives. He probably thought these were the only copy. So he definitely knows about the cure *and* the secret lab."

"You were right," Taylor said darkly. "Happy now? Shit—did you hear that?"

A sound from the hall. I checked the time. "The lacrosse game is only half over."

"Yeah, it's called halftime," Taylor ground out. "My turn for I told you so."

"How can you say that when we found all this?"

"Because if we get caught then *all this* won't matter!"

"We'll definitely get caught if we're going to stand here arguing instead of getting out of here. Come on!"

We launched ourselves back into the passageway. Taylor pulled the door closed behind her and then we were scrambling up the narrow spiral stairs and through the corridor. The instant we got free, I kicked the door closed and together we hung the painting back in place. We were running down the second-floor hall when two figures rounded the corner.

It happened so fast. There was nothing we could do but stand there as Ms. Radtke and Headmaster Atherton walked up to us.

32

TAYLOR

WE WERE FUCKED for real.

After everything I'd been through at this stupid school, I had finally blown the Honor Code out of the water and was about to get punted out the door.

Atherton's acne-pitted cheeks were bright red from the cold at the lacrosse game, and he was wearing a Harcote sweatshirt. He looked more like a student than usual, which was confusing since now I was pretty convinced he was also a murderer. Next to him, Radtke's hair was piled on her head in a frizzy halo. Her lips were pressed into a thin, pale line, and her eyes frantically shifted between me and Kat.

"Good evening, Headmaster, Ms. Radtke," I said in my most polite voice. "Are we winning the game?"

Atherton's rosy mouth quivered. He found school spirit irresistible. "It's halftime. We are up one point."

"Go, Harcote!" I said. "Well, Kat and I were just—"

"Indeed, what *were* you just?" Atherton asked. "What brings you two to Old Hill after hours?"

Kat cleared her throat, stalling. "We were, um . . ."

"These students are members of French Cinema Club," Radtke said. "I have taken over in place of Mr. Kontos. As you are aware,

Headmaster, we are not yet an official club. Still building our membership."

All three of us gaped at her.

"Cinema?" Atherton echoed. "That's out of character for you, Miriam."

"True, I have never quite cottoned to the moving picture, but I feel it is high time I developed an appreciation for the art form," she said. "Miss Sanger is quite the film buff. I've asked them to meet me here to schedule our viewings for the remainder of the semester."

Atherton was wearing a little sneer as he searched us for confirmation that he was being played.

"Headmaster, I believe our business is concluded," Radtke declared. "Girls, with me."

DID I WANT to follow Radtke, my trav nemesis, a walking monument to color-safe bleach, through the halls of Old Hill? I did not. But I had no choice. Kat and I were completely at Radtke's mercy. She all but shoved us into her office and shut the door.

"Sit," she ordered.

We sat.

Radtke stood behind her desk, massaging the paper-thin skin of her knuckles and regarding us with extreme consternation.

"Explain yourselves," she said.

Beside me, Kat was quaking like a frightened rabbit, completely drained of her earlier boldness. She didn't seem prepared for any kind of fight. But if we were going down, I was going down swinging.

Anyway, sometimes you have to be direct.

I raised my chin at Radtke. "We know what you did. You killed Kontos."

"*Taylor!*" Kat cried, but I didn't let her stop me.

"Even if you didn't do it with your own hands, you helped make it happen. I think you're the devil itself," I spat.

Her face sharpened into a sour-lemon look. "I have my faults, Miss Sanger, but I assure you, there are devils far worse than me."

"No, there aren't!" I cried. "Kontos thought you were his friend. He *liked* you, because he was a good person, and you betrayed him." It had started off as a good rant, but now I had that sucking feeling in my chest that was the absence of Kontos in the world, and I hated Radtke so much I could have cried. "You shouldn't even be *talking* about French Cinema Club. That was *ours*. You can't just act like you know what it meant."

"Oh, Taylor," Radtke said tenderly.

"Oh, Taylor, *what*?" I tried to sound indignant, but my voice cracked. My chin was quivering.

Radtke swept around the desk and kneeled in front of me. It didn't make any sense, but her face was the mirror of mine: a broken mess of sadness. She took my hands in hers. I let her. "I miss him too."

This was *Radtke*, the anti-Kontos, the person I'd just accused of his murder, and yet it was impossible to look at her without recognizing it: our hearts had identical holes in them, and they were shaped like a goofy seventies mustache.

"I miss him so much," I managed, but then I was crying harder than I had in weeks, like I hadn't since that day Kat and I had found the secret lab. I'd been fine almost all that time, but maybe grief could swell up out of nowhere once it got inside you. And then the weirdest thing happened: *Radtke hugged me.* She hugged me, and she was crying too. Even weirder, it made me feel a little better, because she knew the same loss I did.

She pulled back and patted her cheeks dry with a lace handkerchief. "I'm sorry to have taken the name of French Cinema Club in vain, but I needed you away from Roger, and Leo always spoke so fondly of your meetings." Radtke straightened up. "I did not kill Leo. We were working together."

"But you're a trav," I said. "Look at you."

Radtke clicked her tongue. "I would have thought that you of all people, Miss Sanger, might be sympathetic to the fact that I don't particularly care if you like how I dress. Or like me at all. I have no common cause with the travs. The travs talk about the traditional vampiric lifestyle, but they're imitating a past that only ever existed in stories. Vampires in their crumbling castles, luring in innocents with their irresistible charm. They've deliberately forgotten how painful the reality was." She smoothed her skirt. "I dress this way because it helps me remember what I had when I was human."

Kat's forehead wrinkled sympathetically. "Those are mourning clothes."

Radtke's face was drawn. "I had a daughter. She was two years old when I was turned. I forced myself never to speak to her again. She died long ago, but she had children, and now her great-grandchildren are having their own children. Frankly, part of me was grateful once CFaD emerged, because it would protect humans from us. Then one of my descendants developed complications of chronic CFaD. I knew I needed to do whatever I could to stop it."

"So you're a reunionist," Kat said.

Radtke *nodded*. "Miss Sanger, Leo and I discussed bringing

you into our group. I don't know how much he communicated to you before his death."

"We found his lab," I said. "We know about the cure."

"His work was stolen before I could retrieve it."

"By Atherton," I said. "That's why we were here, to search his office. He destroyed the computers."

Radtke's eye twitched. "I hope you are both aware how incredibly foolish it was to break into the Headmaster's Office, and how shockingly lucky you are that I was there tonight. But the destruction of Leo's research is terrible news. With the loss of Leo, and the loss of his research, the reunionist cause will be set back significantly. By decades most likely."

"His work isn't lost," I said. "Or at least, I don't think so. He gave me a hard drive to keep safe. I still have it."

Before I quit Climate Action Now! they played a compilation of parts of glaciers calving into the sea—great sheets of ice just giving up and letting go. That was the level of absolute relief that overcame Radtke. It actually caused her ramrod straight spine to sag, ever so slightly. I was worried she might start crying again when she said, with characteristic Victorian restraint, "That is very good news indeed. I'll reach out to my network to organize a handoff."

"There's one thing I don't understand," Kat said.

"Only one?" I asked. "There's like fifty things I don't understand."

She ignored me. "Ms. Radtke, you're not a trav, but you let everyone think you are. Vampiric Ethics is all about how we're superior to humans, how humans are weak. Why would you teach things like that?"

"What I say in class reflects the *curriculum*. Not my personal beliefs."

For two years, I'd ground my teeth through her class, imagining that she was on a one-woman mission to brainwash us with trav ideology. "Let me guess: Atherton sets the curriculum."

She inclined her head. "Roger is very invested in the idea of our separateness and superiority. The curriculum is designed to lead to certain conclusions. I assure you, I wish I could push back on it, but I can't risk my position here. We had constructed the lab in secret, at great expense and tremendous difficulty. Leo's role, as you know, was research. He was brilliant, the very best at what he did, perhaps the only person, vampire or human, who could have developed a cure on his own. My role is as the movement's representative in negotiations, such as they have occurred. It has been to our advantage that I am widely misunderstood. Vampires perceive me as a traditionalist, therefore nonthreatening to Vampirdom. They believe me, for the most part, when I claim I'm merely transmitting a message from the reunionists, rather than one of them."

"We heard you talking to Headmaster Atherton," Kat said. "It was weeks ago—the night the mentorship applications were due. You told him Mr. Kontos was doing something threatening."

Another eye twitch. "That conversation occurred *after* curfew, if memory serves. Victor Castel was the threat I was referring to. His monopoly on Hema is unsafe and unethical. I was asking Roger to relay a message to Victor that the reunionists had found their own cure. We were giving Victor a chance to diversify Hema production first. The movement gave him options: to release the proprietary formula for Hema, set up real distribution centers, sell it at cost and subsidized for vampires that couldn't afford to pay."

"What did Victor say?" Kat asked in a small voice.

"He never said anything. But I think we've received our reply."

I swallowed hard. "Victor Castel killed Kontos, didn't he?"

Radtke's mouth fell into a frown. "Someone certainly did. What we're doing imperils everything Victor Castel has built. His wealth, his empire. Vampirdom itself. I think he'd go to any lengths to protect that."

KAT

MY MIND WAS spinning as Ms. Radtke ushered us out of Old Hill. But I wasn't thinking about the busted computers in Headmaster Atherton's office or what Ms. Radtke had told us about the reunionists, like I should have been. All I could think about was that message from Victor.

Make it impossible for her to decline.

Whatever their motive, he and Headmaster Atherton had succeeded: it *had* been impossible for me to decline. The Benefactor's—*Victor's*—offer was so good, I'd put everything on the line to say yes. Now that I was at Harcote, I depended on him to stay. The dozens of times I'd second-guessed myself to make sure I didn't violate the Honor Code and give the Benefactor a reason to withdraw my financial aid, it had really been Victor I'd been thinking of. On top of that, he'd given me the mentorship and offered to help me build my future—as long as I kept impressing him. He'd somehow known precisely how to slip into the void left behind by my dad and my fangmakers. Even my relationship with Galen bore his touch. Victor had wormed his way into every cranny of my life. But *why*? How had he even known who I was?

As we took the down-campus stairs, Taylor broke into my thoughts. "So back to the whole *I told you so* thing . . ."

"You were wrong about Ms. Radtke."

"I meant about *Castel*," she said. "I told you a thousand times that he's behind this, and Radtke basically just proved it."

I rubbed my forehead. I didn't know if I could find the words to argue with Taylor right now. "She didn't *prove* anything."

"I swear to god, if you defend him right now—"

"Ms. Radtke said she believed he's involved! They asked him to make Hema more accessible and he didn't get back to them. That's not a crime."

Taylor stopped at the bottom of the stairs and gaped at me. "I can't believe you. Does Castel have you brainwashed? Do you have a gross crush on him or something? Him and Galen and all of this mentorship garbage—you can't see what's right in front of your face."

My teeth could have cracked, my jaw was clenched so hard. Taylor didn't have any idea what was *right in front of my face*. If Victor really *was* that evil, what would mean for me? At best, I'd lose Harcote, the future I'd been building. At worst, people might think I'd been in on it. After all, I was his mentee just like Galen, and my mom had worked at CasTech just like the Blacks—that had to be part of whatever was going on, even if I had no idea how.

"I need to think about it, okay?"

"There's nothing to think about," Taylor spat. "He's a fucking creeper in a fancy suit, and you bend over backward trying to protect him."

"Because I'm trying to make something of myself, and he's—he's part of that."

She shook her head, like what I'd said was some great disappointment. "See, that's the exact thing I hate about this place, that it forces you to think like that. You don't need to make anything of yourself. You already *are* someone."

"It's the worst thing in the world to want more, right? You hate it that I want something different for myself and I'm not afraid to try and get it. A closed mouth won't be fed."

"That's the stupidest thing I've ever heard! At least a closed mouth doesn't grovel or beg for scraps."

"I'm sure you'd rather I just didn't give a fuck about anything, like you do. I'm not like that—like you. I won't let you drag me down to your level."

Taylor flinched. "Don't worry. There's only room for one person *on my level*. I'll figure this whole *murder conspiracy* out on my own. You can go back to sucking up to Castel and Galen and Lucy and Evangeline."

"Last time I checked I wasn't the only one sucking up to Evangeline."

"Oh my god, that's none of your fucking business!" she yelled. "You have Galen! What do you even care?"

"Because you are infuriating. You have *always been* infuriating!"

One second, Taylor was glaring at me very intensely, and the next, she wasn't.

She was walking away.

"Where are you going?" I cried.

She turned back. "The room. That we share. And when I get there, I don't want to talk to you. About anything. At all."

"Taylor—"

"I'm done with this, Kat. I'm done with you."

33

TAYLOR

"WHAT ARE YOU doing down here?"

My eyes opened to an unfamiliar ceiling—no attic slope, no Pride flag. The face of Evangeline Lazareanu hovering in the center of it.

My body felt like it had spent the night imitating the posture of a velociraptor: every muscle was cramped. I tried stretching my legs and hit something hard.

Oh. Right. I had slept on a couch in the Hunter House commons.

After that fight, the absolute last thing I'd wanted to do was go back to that stupid little fourth-floor room with Kat, but that's just what I *had* done, because *I lived there*. Every time I'd looked at her, another pinball of weirdly tragic rage set off ricocheting inside me. I'd tried to work. I'd tried to watch a movie. Finally, I'd tried to sleep. But the weirdly tragic rage pinballs had kept brutalizing me. How could Kat have still been so invested in Victor fucking Castel, in Galen, in Harcote? How could she choose all that over me—when I've *been* there, I *knew* her?

I had lain there, completely awake in the dark. I'd been pretty sure Kat had been too. I'd wanted her to break that stupid pretend-sleep silence more than I've ever wanted her to do anything. To explain herself.

To apologize.

To promise she'd stand by me.

The moment I'd had that thought was the moment I let all of it go.

Kat would *never* stand by me—not in the way I longed for, where she loved me like I loved her.

The whole time Kat had been at Harcote, I'd been deluding myself that she was someone she wasn't. I convinced myself that she was putting on a front to fit in, but the *real* Katherine Finn was the person I saw underneath. But there *was* no person underneath, no difference between who she really was and who she pretended to be. Kat had shown me who she was, again and again, and I'd ignored it. I'd been holding onto a fantasy.

Suddenly, I hadn't been able to blink or breathe or physically exist in the same room as her. I certainly could not sleep.

I'd gone downstairs to the commons, grabbed one of the ratty throw blankets, and slept on the couch.

The back of which Evangeline was currently leaning over. "If you don't answer me in the next ten seconds, I'm getting Radtke."

I pushed myself up. Muscles and joints moaned in protest. "I'm fucking *sleeping*, what's it look like?"

"Something wrong with your bed?"

It was barely dawn, but the bluish glow lit Evangeline's pale skin like ice. She looked like an angel—the kind still allowed in heaven, not the kind forced to rule in hell. It had to be early enough that no one else was up, otherwise Evangeline would never have been so close to me.

"Kiss me and I'll tell you," I said under my breath.

Her brilliant blue eyes darted toward the stairs, then she pressed her lips to mine. I leaned up into her. My nose was digging into her cheek, and hers into mine, but I just wanted to be close—like part of me imagined that Evangeline might be the one to pull me out of that sinkhole, if she knew I needed saving.

She broke the kiss. "Someone might see," she scolded. "Your turn."

My turn. As if I didn't feel pathetic enough. I'd already had to barter for a moment of comfort, and the sun hadn't even risen yet. I wanted to burrow into the nasty lint-and-fingernail-clipping-filled crevice between the couch cushions.

"Kat and me had a fight." There was a wicked glint in Evangeline's eye. I gave in to my perverse desire to satisfy her. "It was about Galen and Castel and all that bullshit."

"I did warn you."

I didn't even have the energy for sarcasm. "I know."

Evangeline's brow tightened, her lips pursed. Abruptly, she whisked the nubby throw off me and briskly folded it. "At least sit up, before anyone else comes downstairs. I wouldn't want anyone to see *the girl I've been fucking* moping around like this."

My eyes went wide.

"I looked it up, you know." She raised her chin. "How girls have sex."

Then she swept out of the room, blanket over one arm, leaving me staring after her.

KAT

OUR INVESTIGATION WAS suspended. Not that we'd discussed it. Taylor had barely said two words to me since the disaster at Old Hill.

I spent all of Vampiric Ethics watching Taylor pretend she wasn't thinking about what Ms. Radtke had confessed to us. She was splayed out on the chair: her legs wide and her arm hooked over the back like it was the only thing preventing her from sliding to the floor, and she had sunglasses settled into her hair, although the sun had entered a state of hibernation.

But the longer I looked at her, the less convinced I was that she was pretending. After all, what difference was there between acting like you didn't care and actually not caring? She was always so ready to give up, to let everything drop.

She'd done it to me, after all. We'd left Virginia and I never heard a word from her again; that's how easy it had been for her to believe I'd abandoned her. When I sent her that text telling her not to contact me again, I'd done it after two weeks where I'd checked my phone every five seconds. First I was waiting for an apology for telling her parents the secret about my fangmaker, but then I just wanted her to reach out—we could do the apology part later. But nothing ever came. Eventually I told her off because I thought she'd at least reply.

But she just let me go, like I hadn't even mattered. Now she was doing it all over again. This time, the hurt was different. Now I knew that our separation those years ago was a misunderstanding— a misunderstanding our parents were responsible for—and I'd blamed her for wronging me in a way she never had. The last few weeks we'd built up trust again, and something deeper that I hadn't expected.

My grip on my pen tightened. Even after everything, I couldn't stop thinking about the feeling of her lips against mine.

That kiss was nothing but a rogue wave. It had come out of nowhere to knock me off-center. I would steady eventually. Soon, even.

"Everything okay?" Galen whispered to me.

I jumped. "Yeah, of course."

"So you're going to stare at Taylor for the whole class?"

"I'm not—"

"You must be some kind of saint to put up with her," Galen said.

I forced my eyes to the front of the room. "I *don't* put up with her."

There was a reason I hadn't tried to explain to Taylor what I had uncovered about my mom's past at CasTech or Victor's identity as the Benefactor. She'd leap to judgment, like she always did, before she'd even try to understand what it would mean for me. Even on the (exceptionally rare) occasions Taylor didn't say what she was thinking, her face betrayed her: that cutting quirk in her eyebrow, a little smirk she could never hold back. A version of Taylor lived rent-free in my mind, delivering that little smirk whether she did it in real life or not.

The messed-up thing was that in the last few months, I'd found her judgment almost exciting. It was a kind of freedom, I'd thought, to be yourself like that. But judging everything around you wasn't brave. It was ungenerous and cruel. It walled you off with your misery. It was just like Lucy had said: thinking you're better than everyone else wasn't a substitute for a personality.

It was better that Taylor and I were over. She drew me away from my goals, made me doubt what I wanted—doubt *myself.* I couldn't focus on Taylor's mystery—I had my own to solve.

GALEN STORMED INTO the Stack straight from lacrosse practice. He was still wearing his workout gear. Ever since he'd found out that his family's foundation was more invested in blocking

CFaD research than actually curing the disease, he hadn't been himself. His hair was limp with sweat. He leaned down to give me a salty kiss and I cringed. He stank. When I broke the kiss, he was too agitated to sit down.

I knew Galen wore a crystalline armor. I'd never known anyone so in control of how they presented themselves. If that armor was cracking, something was wrong. A good girlfriend would have asked what was wrong or tried to support him.

I was not a good girlfriend.

So I smiled instead. "Ready for the semifinals?"

He rubbed his temple. "There's no competition until the finals, and barely even then."

"Right, the team's so good," I said.

"We aren't *good*." His voice was thick with frustration. "We're vampires. It's absurd that we play any of these human teams at all because they don't stand a chance. Atherton acts like the athletics program is so strong, like we actually win fair and square. Every year, the team trains like there's an actual fight for us out there, when we've won before the season even starts. When it's bullshit."

"It's just a game."

"It isn't *fair*, Kat. We're telling ourselves that we earned it. That's a *lie*. Don't you think that matters?" He fell heavily into a chair. "Don't answer that. *I* know it matters."

"Is this really about lacrosse? Because you can just quit and join one of the club sports."

He cast his storm-cloud eyes down. His hands rested on his thighs, coiled into fists. "It's not just lacrosse." His tone was raw. "I feel like everything's coming down around me, and all of it's lies. The Foundation's a lie—a lie that my parents and Victor have been telling me my whole life. I keep wondering, when were they planning to tell me the truth? I've imagined it a thousand different ways." He glanced up at me but couldn't hold my gaze. "The worst part is, in every single scenario, I say yes. They ask if I'll lie for them, and I say yes. I let them control me, like I always do."

"You can't blame yourself for their lies."

"I was stupid enough to believe them."

"You weren't stupid. You trusted your parents," I said. "And you haven't agreed to anything yet, have you?"

"No."

"Then you still have time to imagine it a different way."

He scrubbed his hands through his hair, then his expression relaxed and his posture uncoiled. "If my parents knew how we were together, they wouldn't be happy at all that we were dating."

"What do you mean?"

"Since we met, everything feels sharper and clearer. Like feeding on humans, at Lucy's parties, I didn't understand why it didn't sit right with me before. But since I met you, it all makes sense. You make me a better person." He eked out a sad-boy smile. "I really, really like you, Kat."

All of a sudden, I just totally fucking resented him.

This beautiful boy that everyone desired, who *really, really liked* me, was looking at me moony-eyed and telling me I made him a better person—but it made me feel like the air was being squeezed from my lungs. It would never stop shocking me how someone like Galen could be so fragile. Someone who had so much power that the world tilted to serve him, and he simply believed that was how gravity worked.

At the same time, I was Galen's *girlfriend*. I was supposed to help him through this emotional crisis. I knew more about his privilege than he probably ever would. Wasn't it my responsibility to teach him? To be his manic pixie emotional laborer?

I didn't want to be the thing that woke him up.

As long as I stayed with him, the more he'd take from me. Because he didn't know how to be strong on his own. Because I knew I was using him, so I would always feel a little in his debt. Because I would allow him to. But Galen was never going to make *me* a better person. He would never even understand me, although I would always make him think he did.

Because as long as we were dating, I'd be part of that system that kept him the sun at the center of this solar system. I'd watch what I said and how I acted and what my lips did when we kissed and where I looked—even if it felt like I was squelching part of myself as I did it.

I realized it with a sudden, shocking clarity: I would never actually like Galen.

Not the way I was supposed to.

Not the way I liked Taylor.

"Was that too much?" Galen said sheepishly.

I was staring at him, my mouth half open.

Everything was too much. I couldn't spend another second with him looking at me like that—like he was thinking about *loving* me.

"I just have to run. I have a thing—I forgot about it, I'm really sorry." I cursed myself for lying, but I had to get out of there. I shoved my computer into my backpack and was gone before he could kiss me goodbye.

TAYLOR

EVANGELINE AND I met up, in the biblical sense, almost every day that week. It wasn't hard to find an excuse; with her one-act coming up we were in the theater every afternoon or evening.

It had never been like that with us. Never that often. The first time was great. The second time, the next day, also great. But by the fifth time, she was arched against me and kind of panting in my ear—"*Come on, Taylor*"—which usually made my entire body vibrate, but instead there was this abysmal feeling, like the ground had dropped out from beneath me and I was in free fall.

"Don't *stop*," she protested. A strand of her black hair stuck to her cheek.

But I had to stop. I rolled off of her, onto the unclean carpet of the costume closet. Usually being with Evangeline made me feel good. At least *better*. But now it seemed like the more we were together, the less that was true. She never did anything without reason.

"Tell me why, E."

She smiled, sly, and pushed herself up on her elbows. Her shirt was open, exposing her heaving chest. "Is this some kind of a game?"

"No. You've been all over me lately. I'm not saying it isn't hot, but I want to know why."

"People have needs," she said, grabbing for me.

I pulled away from her and yanked my sports bra back on. God, this was difficult. Plus, without Evangeline, who knew when I'd be getting any next.

But every time I kissed her, I thought of Kat. Not just how it would feel if it was Kat instead of Evangeline—but what I would say if I ever had to explain this to her. That Evangeline made me feel terrible and used, and I still went back to her whenever she asked. That she kept me a secret, and I'd talked myself into believing that I didn't care, it was hotter that way. I'd convinced myself that being an ass to her and kissing her at one school dance meant I had some itty-bitty measure of control, when I had nothing.

She sat up and pulled her shirt closed. "Because you know what it's like now. To really *know* you aren't enough. I've watched you chasing Kat. It's the same way I chased Galen."

I shook my head. "You only ever liked Galen for what he is."

"I do like Galen, *and* I like what he is. You can't separate it. You like Kat, *and* you like that she's different. She's an outsider, and you've always felt like one. You want her validation just like I want Galen's." She smiled, horribly. "But you'll never get it, and neither will I. There's always going to be this wound inside both of us." She reached for me again, her black hair falling across her face. "It's the two of us now, you know?"

"E, we hate each other."

She let out a bright laugh. "So?"

It was a genuine question, not plaintive or angry. Like our shared hatred was the stage set, and for the last two years, we'd been acting out a play about something else. Stolen moments of hookups and insults and secret texts and side-eyes. My brain scrambled to reassemble all those scenes into something different. Did Evangeline . . . did she actually *like* me? Was what we'd had a *relationship*? It was impossible to imagine, but I didn't have to imagine it—I could see it on her face. I wasn't nothing to her. Right now, I was everything.

She was a miserable person, and so was I. By some perverse fate, we had found each other in a string of messy, nasty encounters. I was the only person in this whole school that she'd allowed to come close to knowing her. She'd shown me parts of herself that I knew she didn't understand. Maybe I had done the same. In a different world, it could have been a relationship that made us both *better*, instead of letting us be our worst selves. I knew, right then, whatever existed between us in *this* world was at an end. Somehow, the truth of that was kind of crushing.

But crushed or not, I stood up. "It's not the two of us, E."

She smirked at me. "Fine, if you want, we can do the whole *I hate you, this is the last time* thing."

"I don't hate you," I said softly.

Her smirk slid away.

"But being with you makes me hate myself. That wound you said we both have—I think doing this is stopping it from healing, or even making it worse. I need it to get better. I want yours to get better too."

"That was a *metaphor*!" she sputtered. "You cannot leave me for Kat. She doesn't want you and she never will."

"This isn't about her."

"I can't tell if you actually believe that, or if you just expect me to. Stop being so pathetic and get back here."

I really wished Evangeline had not been half undressed and lying on the floor as I said this. I was dumping her, but I didn't want her to feel humiliated. "I'm sorry, E. That was the last time."

34

KAT

I WAS SITTING at my desk, working on a final paper for Ms. Radtke's Vampiric Ethics class when someone pounded on the door to our room.

"Room inspection! Get yourself decent, because I'm opening this door in ten seconds!"

That was Headmaster Atherton's voice. What was he doing here? Room inspections were supposed to be done by the House Steward.

"Ten . . . nine . . . eight . . ."

I launched myself onto my bed and yanked out the magazine I'd stolen from the Extended Collections. I shoved it into the waistband of my skirt, then scrambled to Taylor's side of the room.

"Seven . . . six . . . five . . ."

Taylor was in the library, but the hard drive was here somewhere. Where had she hidden it? I searched her desk, hoping Headmaster Atherton wouldn't hear me sliding open the drawers. Nothing.

"Four . . . three . . ."

There it was, shoved onto the bookshelf right next to *1,000 Movies to Watch Before You Die.*

"Two . . ."

I grabbed it and stuck it up one sleeve of my cardigan.

"One."

When Headmaster Atherton opened the door, I was standing politely in the middle of the room. Beside him was Ms. Radtke, wearing her typical look of mild annoyance. It broke into alarm when she met my eyes. Three blank-faced aides flanked them.

Headmaster Atherton, trapped in that boyish body, for once seemed as old as his many years when he said, "An anonymous tipster reported that *you* were the author of that editorial."

An anonymous tip? The editorial came out weeks ago, and Headmaster Atherton had never found any evidence I'd written it—because I hadn't. Why was he searching our room now?

"This is your opportunity to practice Harcote's values of respect," the Headmaster said. "Did you write that editorial, Kat?"

"No," I squeaked.

"I hope you're telling the truth," Headmaster Atherton said. "Wait in the hall."

"This is my side of the room." I gestured at my desk. "Me and Taylor keep our stuff pretty separate."

"*Taylor and I*," Headmaster Atherton corrected. "The hall, Kat."

I LEANED AGAINST the banister, angling between Headmaster Atherton and Ms. Radtke's figures in the doorway to watch the aides take apart our room. They worked through every drawer in my desk, even flipped through my notebooks. Then they moved to the bed, to search under the mattress, then under the bed frame—as if the school were a jail and Headmaster Atherton our warden. When they finished with my closet, I hoped they would leave. They'd found nothing among my things, since there was nothing to find. *I* was the target of the search, after all.

But then they moved to Taylor's side of the room.

Dread curdled in my stomach. Taylor better not have left any trace she wrote that editorial. I knew there'd be evidence on her computer, but she had taken it to the library. If I could just get to her in time, she could delete it. It would be fine.

Everything would be fine.

Taylor would be fine.

Not that it was my business, whether she was fine.

There were footsteps on the stairs.

"Room inspection?" Evangeline said. "What are they looking for?"

In the past few days, I'd slipped beyond caring about what Evangeline thought. That aura of chaos she carried with her didn't intrigue me anymore. It wasn't hot. It was destruction and cruelty for its own sake—for *her* own sake.

"An *anonymous tipster* told Headmaster Atherton that I wrote that editorial, so now they're searching the room."

Evangeline did a pretty little snort of satisfaction that made me badly wanted to commit physical violence against her.

"The *whole* room." I hissed, so that Headmaster Atherton couldn't hear. "How could you do this?"

"What makes you so sure I did?"

"No one else has shown up to watch, have they? I know you're completely heartless, Evangeline, so you might not have realized this, but when you're dating someone, you're supposed to take care of her—to watch out for her."

"What are you talking about?"

"*Taylor*! Who else?"

"I'm not *dating* Taylor," she said sourly.

Despite what was happening, relief swelled in my chest. "I saw you two at the Founder's Dance."

She brushed her hair away from her face, pretending to be casual. "I don't know what you think you saw, but if you told anyone about it, no one would believe you." She peered into the room, then looked back at me, scowling. "Taylor wouldn't date me even if I wanted her to. She's completely hung up on you, along with Galen and everyone else at this school. But you won't be a problem for much longer."

"You're *jealous*? That's why you ratted me out to Headmaster Atherton. You have no idea what you did."

"Of course I do." Evangeline shifted uncomfortably. I pressed myself against the banister to avoid pushing her down the stairs.

"You are the world's most self obsessed dumbass, Evangeline!"

She put her hands on her hips. "Excuse me, since I'm such a dumbass, you'll have to explain to me what you're on about."

"I *didn't write the editorial*," I said forcefully.

Finally, she understood.

"Oh no—"

"What are you guys doing?" Taylor was unbuttoning her coat on the landing below us. Her curls were wet from the rain. "Is that Atherton?"

I looked up to see Headmaster Atherton at the top of the stairs holding a crumpled piece of notebook paper covered in Taylor's jagged handwriting. "Taylor, come with me."

Her eyebrows tipped up and her lips parted, but just as quickly she gathered herself into something serious and fierce and resigned. It took everything I had not to dash down the stairs to her, put my arms around her, and tell her that I still stood by her. If she was going to be brave, she didn't have to do it alone.

But I didn't.

I just stood there with Evangeline and Ms. Radtke, and watched Headmaster Atherton take her away.

TAYLOR

ATHERTON AND HIS aides escorted me to his office.

That crumpled sheet of paper was covered in my handwriting, words scribbled out and lines crossed through. I shouldn't have drafted the editorial by hand—who *does* that?—but I'm not very good at writing, and doing it by hand helps me think. I should at least have been careful enough to actually deposit it in the trash can, rather than flinging it in the trash can's general direction and hoping gravity would do me a solid.

Not that it mattered now.

"Did you write this, Taylor?"

I opened my mouth to say something snarky. I wasn't going to give him the satisfaction of watching me cave.

But then I remembered what I'd said to Evangeline—that I wanted to heal that wound inside me. What Kontos had told me, about standing up for what I believed in. And although I didn't want to, I thought of Kat. She'd been proud of me for it, even if I'd hidden behind anonymity and then behind her on top of it. I believed in what I had written, and I was done pretending otherwise.

"Yes. I wrote it," I said. "Kat wasn't involved. I did it alone. No one knew, even Max. I told him that it was by a friend, who was going through me to stay anonymous."

Atherton pressed his freakishly pink lips together. His eyes flashed wolfishly, like he had me in a trap. He didn't look anything like the deeply uncool headmaster he usually appeared to be. In that moment, it was disconcertingly easy to imagine him stalking humans like prey.

"This is an Honor Code violation, so the Honor Council is supposed to determine the consequences, right?" I asked. "Are you going to call the other members?"

"Not this time. I have taken this matter personally. I take *you* personally, Taylor. The last two years, you've been nothing but trouble. At every opportunity, you've insulted this school and what it stands for. You've been given warning after warning, chance after chance. Every time, I expected you to fail to improve, and you sunk to expectations exactly. You've never belonged at Harcote." When he grinned, vicious and horrible, he showed the ivory points of his fangs. "Taylor Sanger, you're expelled."

35

KAT

WITH MY NOSE pressed to the front window of Hunter House, I watched Headmaster Atherton march Taylor up-campus through the gray rain. Upstairs, Evangeline had shut herself in her room. I wondered if we could nail the door closed, to stop her and Lucy from wreaking any more havoc.

The inspection had left our room a mess: clothes spilled out and books scattered everywhere. The aides had toppled the carefully arranged tower of shoeboxes that housed Taylor's sneaker collection. Even her Pride flag had been ripped down, although they couldn't possibly have expected to find anything under there.

I couldn't let Taylor come back to this. I grabbed the flag from where it had slipped under the bed and tacked it back up to the ceiling, right where it had been. Then I unfolded the bent pages of *1,000 Movies to See Before You Die*, rehung the button-ups that the aides had ripped from their hanger, and stacked up her shoeboxes.

I sat on Taylor's bed. My side of the room looked still like a tornado had hit, but I didn't move to clean it up. None of that stuff was even really mine.

It was Victor Castel's.

Was anything about me *real*?

My hands twisted in Taylor's sheets.

This was real. How I felt about her. I wanted her safe. I wanted her here with me. It was more than friendship, more than our history, more than all our petty disagreements.

Suddenly it was so simple.

It felt like a door had been opened in me, and behind it lay a new universe. I'd spent the last few weeks feeling like I'd failed somehow, with Galen and with Taylor. Really, I was failing myself. I'd been so convinced that I knew who I was and what I wanted—and I'd spent so much energy at Harcote trying to make those things align—that it felt impossible that there were parts of myself I hadn't yet discovered. Why had I been so sure that it was a failure not to know myself like I thought I did—especially when I'd already been wrong about so many things?

When I let that fall away, this was the truth that remained: I liked girls, and I loved Taylor.

How I'd come to realize that didn't need to matter as much as the fact that I *had*. I didn't know how I defined myself, what label I'd use, how I'd tell anyone, but I could figure that out later. It didn't scare me anymore. It felt exciting.

It felt like *me*.

Someone knocked on the door. When I opened it, Lucy stood on the other side. "Rough day, Kitty Kat?" Her long ponytail swished behind her as she craned her neck to try to get a look inside the room.

"Lucy, if you call me Kitty Kat one more time, I'm going to hack that ponytail into such an absurd haircut, LucyK won't get any spon-con for a year."

Her eyes narrowed. "Truly, whatever happened to asking nicely? Especially when I came all the way up here to tell you Galen's waiting for you outside. He said you're not responding to his texts."

I swiped my phone off my desk.

Hey your room got searched?

You okay? let me know

???

I'm outside Hunter, come down

I'm gonna try Evangeline or Lucy.

"Thanks," I said begrudgingly.
"You're welcome, *Kat*."

IT WAS STILL raining and freezing. Galen was standing under a black umbrella with his dark brows drawn together. He looked like he'd stumbled out of a French New Wave film. I dashed through the rain to him. His umbrella wasn't big enough for both of us, and icy water trickled down my back.

He ran his fingers along the collar of my coat to bring me closer.

I took his hand and pulled it off me. "Don't," I said, crossing my arms.

"What's going on?" His face clouded. "You can talk to me, Kat."

It made my heart ache: Galen wanted to care for me, to support me, to love me. It was the exactly what I'd just called out Evangeline for failing to do for Taylor.

But I didn't want him to.

Galen was so beautiful. Maybe I could forgive myself for expecting my appreciation for that beauty would become something stronger. And I could forgive him for never noticing that I flinched half the time he touched me, that I always broke our kisses first.

And then a small voice in my head wondered, if I wasn't attracted to Galen, was I attracted to boys at all?

I took a deep breath. I didn't need all the answers. What I knew *right now* was that I couldn't keep doing this.

I met Galen's eyes. The irises matched the clouds above us. "I can't see you anymore. I need to figure some things out—things I can't really explain right now."

"We can work it out together. I'm going through shit right now too—this stuff with my family. But we have each other." He reached for me.

"*No*," I said. "I have to do this out alone. Maybe you should too. You don't need me to tell you what's right and wrong. You have to decide for yourself. I'll support you, just as your friend."

"But I'm relying on you, Kat. I *need* you."

I shook my head. "I know you think that. But I can't take care of you when I have to take care of myself."

A pained look crossed his face as he shoved his hand through his damp hair. "I was falling in love with you."

I shook my head. "The truth is, Galen, you don't really know me at all."

I went back to Hunter and left him in the rain.

It was Taylor. It had always been Taylor. And I was going to tell her the second I saw her.

TAYLOR

As I TRUDGED back down the hill, I could barely feel the rain.
Expelled.

After all these years hating this place, I was finally out. I'd leave

Harcote behind, with all its stupid politics and fake people and vampiric ridiculousness. I'd go back home to—to what?

I'd thought about leaving so often, it had never occurred to me what I'd actually lose if I left.

Then I opened the door to Hunter House. While I'd been gone talking to Atherton, the House's entire population had felt the need to study in the common room. The stupid Dent girls gawking at me with a travy curiosity. Lucy flipping her phone around, ready to snap a photo of my destruction. Evangeline had been sitting in the window where I usually sat, watching me with her face screwed up and serious.

Up on the landing, Kat was staring at me.

It hurt too much to look at her. Instead, I shook the rain off my coat and faced the Hunter House girls.

"I'll save you the trouble of starting rumors," I told them. "I wrote the editorial. I don't regret it, but I should never have published it anonymously. I stand by what I said. Atherton expelled me, so after Descendants Day, I'm gone."

I'd barely gotten the words out before Evangeline was on me.

"He can't *expel* you!" she cried. She grabbed my hands tight, practically pulling me against her—right there in front of everyone. I stared down at her manicured nails against my knuckles. "I'm so sorry. This wasn't supposed to happen. You have to believe me, Taylor, this wasn't what I wanted when I—it was supposed to be *Kat*, not *you*."

I kicked myself. I should have known Evangeline wasn't going to let me go so easily. I'd told her I wasn't calling things off with her because of Kat, but her brain wasn't wired to believe it. Kat had Galen; Evangeline couldn't let her have me too. Her plan to get Kat out of the picture had hit the wrong target.

I squeezed her hands. "I'm not mad, E. It's okay."

"It is *not* okay!" Her voice wavered like I'd never heard it, as if she might cry—over *me*, over something she'd done wrong. "You belong here. I *need you* here."

"Um, you need her?" Lucy said tensely. "This is Taylor Sanger. You can't be that surprised they finally kicked her out."

Evangeline dropped my hands and turned to the room, as if she'd just remembered we weren't alone. Then she summoned herself into that glorious avenging demon I knew so well. "I'll be surprised about whatever the fuck I want, Lucy. They can't expel her for speaking her mind. That's, like, fascism. Taylor's the only person at this school who's even halfway interesting, and we've all been terrible to her." Then she turned back to me, and the demon fell away again. "*I've* been terrible to her."

It wasn't that I didn't appreciate Evangeline's apology. I did. A lot. But there was a lump in my throat, and all of these eyes were on me. It was one thing to fess up to the editorial; It was another to act out a soap opera in the Common Room. Over Evangeline's shoulder, I could still see Kat, on the stairs, like a sphinx between me and the sweet relief of a minute alone to process this.

I couldn't be here.

So I turned around and went back out into the rain.

I SAT ON the bleachers and stared out into the lacrosse field. The rain had slowed into a thick drizzle. My eyes kept going to that midfield line. My brain kept going to Kat. I had tried to forget about her. I'd tried to be her friend. I'd tried to push her away.

None of it had worked.

It wasn't fair that I had to lose her again.

But at the same time, she wasn't mine to lose. She never had been.

Below me, the bleachers clanged. A damp figure in black was hiking up her oversized, muddied skirts to climb toward me. By the time Radtke made it to the top, she looked like a soggy black cat.

"I'll talk to Roger," she said. "It is technically a breach of protocol to expel you without convening Honor Council."

I shrugged. "It won't matter. He wants me gone."

"Yes, he does," she agreed. "I'm sorry it's come to this, Taylor."

I picked at my cuticle. I wanted to say something snarky to her, to demonstrate that I didn't need her condolences. But I couldn't think of a single thing. Had I even lost my ability to antagonize Radtke?

"Why were you so hard on me, if you were secretly on Team Kontos?" I asked.

"I wasn't only hard on you. Enforcing the Honor Code is my job. It's made me unpopular with all the students. But most of them only have to be told once before they bring themselves into line. Not you. Every time I've warned you of an Honor Code violation, it's only made you want to do it more. You remind me of myself before I learned patience." She smiled at the horrified confusion on my face. "I admit I may have watched you quite carefully, but it was in hope that I would catch your little acts of rebellion, instead of a less sympathetic audience."

"Atherton?"

"Atherton," she agreed.

I set my head in my hands. Water dripped into my eyes. "He gave me until the end of Sunday to leave. I'm banned from anything Descendants Day–related, except teching Evangeline's play."

"What are you planning to do with that time?"

"Nothing. I'd leave today if I could. Get it over with, instead of spending two days acting like I don't know everyone's talking

about me. I'll probably just watch movies in my room, although—"
My room would be full of Katherine freaking Finn. I glanced
sideways at Radtke. "Things are kind of awkward in the room."

Radtke brushed raindrops off her skirts. "If you want my advice," she began primly. I did not actually want her advice. She'd
probably want me to meditate on the virtues of friendship or
something. "You could simply tell her how you feel. You're leaving
the school, and who knows what could happen before you see Kat
again. If I were you, I'd leave it all on the floor."

I gaped at her. "I don't think you understand . . ."

"Taylor, I have lived ten times the years you have. Do you really
think I cannot comprehend homosexuality?" She huffed with ex
asperation. "Even if I couldn't, the way you look at Kat makes it
clear how you feel about her."

My cheeks went hot. "If it's obvious, then why say anything? I'd
only be giving her a chance to reject me, and if that's how it's going
to be, then I'd rather skip it."

"One day you will realize that if you want something—if you
really want something—you have to pursue it. You owe yourself
that. Yes, it is risky, and embarrassing, and sometimes painful to
care, but you will never get what you want if you cannot ask for it.
You're immortal, Taylor. But that doesn't mean you have time to
waste."

36

KAT

TAYLOR WAS GONE.

Again.

She was always running away, leaving before she could be left. She made it impossible for anyone to actually stand by her.

There was nothing I could do but wait for her to come back.

I was staring out the window in our attic room, watching the rain and holding the inside of my cheek too tightly in my teeth, when the door swung open behind me. Taylor was soaked through, her hair plastered to her face, and she was pale from the cold. My heartbeat stuttered as it hit me like it never had—or maybe I had never let it—how utterly beautiful she was: the soft cleft of her chin and how her lips swelled into a perfect Cupid's bow, the gentle rise of her dark brows, the gold that glimmered in her eyes. A gust of cold air had followed her into the room, but my body was flushed with heat.

"Taylor, I—"

She cut me off. "I have to—"

"No, me first," I said. "I've been thinking about what I want to say to you for hours. I came to Harcote to try to be a different person. That was what I wanted, and I thought it made sense. But I ended up losing track of who I really was. I did a lot of things I regret. But the one thing I don't regret, that I *never could* regret, is you.

"You're the only person in this whole stupid place who makes me feel normal. Like I'm being the person I'm supposed to be—I mean, who I really am. You've always seen right through whatever I pretended, whatever lies I told.

"So that's why I decided that if you're expelled, I'm leaving too. I know that doesn't sound like it would fix anything, but we can figure it out. Maybe you can come stay with us in Sacramento. You'd really like my friends. And basically everybody's queer there." It sounded so stupid when I actually said it, when I'd imagined it as this grand gesture—the two of us, *together.* Taylor was just standing there, with her mouth a little open and this look on her face like I'd left her adrift at sea.

I stepped closer to her. Closer was better.

"I can't survive here without you. I don't understand now how I ever thought I could. I don't even understand how I spent the last three years believing I hated you. You're my center. I'm not leaving you again."

Her whole body was pulled taut, like something I'd said had hurt her and she was straining not to let it show. She scratched her eyebrow, then crossed her arms tightly across her chest.

"You mean, as friends, right?" she said carefully. "You want to be with me as friends."

"Taylor!"

But she rushed her words out over mine. "I need you to tell me if it's just as friends, because I can't take this anymore. I promised myself I'd say this, and I don't know how you're going to react and maybe you'll hate me—but I'm leaving anyway and I don't want to regret never saying it." She squeezed her eyes shut tight for second, then let out her breath and locked her eyes on mine. "I'm, like, completely in love with you. I always have been."

"I—"

"No, don't say anything. Just for a second, okay?" Her eyes glistened with tears, but slowly there was this look of relief, something lighter about her, like she'd been carrying this weight for too long and finally set it down.

My heart thundered in my chest. I could feel it all over my body. "Always?"

She nodded. "I know that's a lot, and I know—"

"Taylor—"

"—you're probably completely freaked out, but—"

"Taylor, listen to me! That's what I was trying to say," I cried. "I think—I think I might be completely in love with you too."

"You—what?" Her eyes were as wide as I'd ever seen them, the whites visible all around the irises. "What about Galen?"

"I broke up with him. You said it yourself, I don't even like him."

She was staring at me, her lips slightly parted. She seemed so completely defenseless and vulnerable, it was almost scary. But then again, I felt that way too.

I added, "And *I* kissed *you*, remember?"

She shook her head. "That was a mistake. You apologized."

"Not for the kiss, for surprising you. Then you were so upset, I was sure you must not have wanted it, and then I thought you were with Evangeline. But that kiss wasn't a mistake. To be honest, I haven't been able to stop thinking about it."

"Kath-er-ine." Her voice was low and rough, and it drew my name out the way no one else did. It lit a fuse inside me, flinging off sparks that threatened to catch. "I haven't either."

"Say my name again." My voice had gone low too.

"Kath-er-ine." Taylor's lips curved into a grin, crooked and hungry. "Can I kiss you?"

"Please."

But she didn't, not right away. First, she shrugged her wet coat onto the floor. Underneath, her button-up was soaked, plastered to her. I let myself take in how it clung to her body, the curves and planes and swells of it. Heat bloomed through me, like I'd never felt with any boy. I didn't want to be thinking about boys right now—I never wanted to think about boys again, not when there were a thousand other things I needed and all of them right here: I needed to take that shirt off her. I needed to press my skin against hers. I needed her to hurry up and kiss me.

Taylor cupped my cheeks in her palms. I tried not to shiver. She eased her fingers into my hair. The look on her face, it was almost painful, but a kind of pain I recognized as the surreal pleasure—*finally, finally, finally*—of getting what you wanted and not believing it was real. I slid my hands over hers, meshed my fingers into hers, and still, for an eternal second, I thought she wouldn't do it—that she'd run again.

She leaned in and kissed me.

Her lips against mine were warm and soft, her kiss was tentative, gentle—as if she was testing whether I really wanted this. Or maybe whether *she* wanted it. But the same instant I thought to worry about that, I was already kissing her harder, leaning into her, my tongue tracing her lips.

Heat ran from my where my fingertips touched her, down my spine, and into my core, a magnetic pull that made me want to crush myself against her, so that not even air would come between us.

It was real *desire*, strong and hot and true, and nothing like the paltry feeling I'd called by that name before.

I slid my hands over Taylor's arms, gripping her muscles under the wet fabric of her sleeves—then, surprising myself, pushed her up against the door. I ran my palms up her torso, feeling the ridges of her ribs, the seams of her sports bra. She tipped her head back, and I turned my mouth's attention to her jaw, her neck. The darkest little corner of my brain, the last bit that remained operational, wondered if I wasn't doing this wrong, if she wasn't supposed to be taking the lead or if kissing a jaw wasn't a thing—but then Taylor curved her body up against mine and *moaned* softly. I'd never heard a sound like that before—a sound that slipped inside me, made my heart tremble.

The thought that she was enjoying this as much as I was—that made my very foundations shake.

Always, Taylor had said. She had *always* wanted me.

I pulled back to look at her. Her pulse flickered in her neck. She was watching me, dark-eyed, her mouth slack.

"Was that okay?" My breath was short and quick.

"Yeah," she whispered hoarsely. "Very okay. Really, really good."

I smiled and wove my fingers into hers. "Bed?"

Her eyebrows popped. "You sure that's what you want?"

Was I? I had never been this person before, the one who pushed to take clothes off or find a bed. Maybe I should have felt nervous now, but I just wasn't.

"If this is too fast, we can slow down. Whatever you want," I told her. "But I want you, Taylor. I'm sure of that."

37

KAT

I WAS IN the auditorium with the Descendants Day Committee of Climate Action Now! discussing the presentation we were supposed to be giving during lunch on Sunday. I'd volunteered to make the slideshow in the probably futile hope that the presentation might talk about something real.

My mind was not in it at all. Back in our room, Taylor was packing. I knew she would be packing because I was gone, and she wasn't getting much done while I was around. My cheeks warmed remembering the last two days. I couldn't believe I had once wondered if I just didn't like hooking up all that much. Because now I knew that I really, really did.

It had taken a while to convince Taylor that I'd been serious about dropping out and having her move back to Sacramento with me, but once I did, she had firmly rejected the offer. She understood that Harcote meant a lot to me. It hurt my heart to think about everything we wouldn't share now: cozy winter nights together, holding hands around campus, the scandalized stares of the other Harcoties.

We flipped through the slides I'd made with pictures of oceanic plastic and landfills.

"We don't want the presentation to be too depressing," one of the leaders said. "Our fangmakers and parents will all be there."

I rolled my eyes. "Right, they deserve a happier vision of climate change. I'll swap these for, like, baby birds getting rescued from an oil spill."

I had not been serious about that idea, but everyone liked it anyway.

I felt a hand on my shoulder: it was the pointy-faced vampire who had greeted me on Move-in Day. "Kat Finn," he said. The nasal drone of his voice gave me goosebumps. "You have a guest in the Visitors' Center."

HARCOTE'S VISITORS' CENTER was a vine-covered cottage near the front gates. It was twee enough that you hardly noticed it was actually the security office that processed all campus guests, especially humans who visited campus during the occasional open houses and sports events the school had to give to maintain its public face as an elite prep school.

When the vampire opened the door onto the waiting room, my mother was standing there.

The instant she saw me, she rushed up and hugged me.

"Mom, what are you doing here?" I said with my face crushed against her shoulder.

"I decided to get here for Descendants Day a little early! I wanted to spend some extra time with my baby."

"You told me you weren't coming."

"Surprise!" There was a rattled, shaky energy to her. Her eyes kept darting to the vampire who'd brought me here. In turn, he hadn't moved his beady eyes from us. "I've got a hotel room in town so you can come spend the night."

A hotel room? "But we don't have overnight privileges right now."

She smiled in a way that didn't look totally like herself. "I'm still your mother, Kat. I still have the power to sign you out."

AS MY MOM tensely maneuvered her rental car through Harcote's gates, I texted Taylor, although I didn't know what was going on myself. Was my mother *kidnapping* me? Then the gates swung shut behind us and my mom let out a breath.

"God, does it always feel so oppressive there?"

"More or less," I admitted. "Where are we going?"

"Home," she said. "I'm taking you home."

"You are not!" What about Taylor—if I left now, I didn't know when I'd see her again. Mr. Kontos's research and Ms. Radtke. Descendants Day—Galen and his parents. Victor, and whatever it was he wanted from me. We had almost figured out how everything was connected, and now my mom was taking me *home*? "You can't do that!"

"What I cannot do is let my daughter sit through a weekend with the Blacks and *Victor Castel*." She practically spat as she said his name. "I cannot lose you to him. When you were admitted here, I tried to convince myself that they wouldn't concern themselves with you. I was a fool."

"What are you talking about?"

"It was a mistake to let you come to this school, and I'll be paying for it for a long time."

"If you don't stop this car right now and tell me what's really going on, I'm going to open the door and fling myself into the road."

"*Kat.*"

"I'll do it! You know I'll live!"

She pulled over in a rest area off the highway a few miles from campus and turned off the car. It had started raining, fat drops splattering on the windshield.

"I know you used to work at CasTech," I said. "I found a picture of you in the archives, *Meredith Ayres*."

"Really?" she huffed. "I thought they'd destroyed any evidence of me."

"That's what you have to say? You told me you'd barely had contact with vampires when the truth was, you knew them all—the Blacks, Victor Castel! You were at CasTech from practically the beginning."

"Not *practically* the beginning. Victor and I had the idea for a blood substitute together."

I flinched away from her. "What are you talking about? Victor invented Hema, everyone knows that."

"Kat." Her voice was flat. She was giving me a familiar, hard look, the face she used when she needed me to be serious and stop acting like a child. "Victor and I set up Castel Technologies together. He changed the name to CasTech later, he thought it sounded more *modern*." She rolled her eyes. "No accounting for taste."

I had never really thought about Victor Castel before he was the savior of Vampirdom—before CFaD or Hema. Before Vampirdom had existed to save.

"You spent thirty years with him and never told me. Why?"

"You have to understand, Kat, that I left as soon as I could. It wasn't always what it is now. *Victor* wasn't always what he is now. I didn't see things changing until it was too late."

"You're talking about the money he's made from Hema, right? The fact that as long as CFaD's around, CasTech will make millions off of Hema."

"Yes, I suppose that is what I'm talking about," she said slowly. I knew that wasn't the whole story.

"Me and Taylor—" Despite this moment, I blushed. My mom's eyebrows rose at the name but I ignored it. "We found out that the Black Foundation isn't working on a cure. They're actually trying to *stop* a cure from being discovered. We think Victor might be involved."

"He *might* be involved? I don't think Simon Black has made a decision that wasn't calibrated to please Victor since the day he was turned. Then again, it's been ages since he's needed to."

"What do you mean?"

"I mean, at this point, their interests are the same. What's good for Victor is good for the Blacks, and vice versa. Victor is the reason that the Black Foundation exists in the first place."

I wasn't sure I understood. "Like, he had the Blacks to set it up, to make sure a cure wasn't discovered."

"That's true, yes. But what I meant was, Victor is the reason we need a cure *in the first place.* He's the reason CFaD exists. He developed the virus. In a lab. At CasTech."

"That can't be true," I stammered. "CFaD jumped from bats to humans."

"Bats, to humans, to vampires." She clicked her tongue. "I told him that was a little on the nose, but then again, if he really cared about my opinion, he would never have done it in the first place."

My eyes felt big as saucers as I stared at her. I could barely breathe, let alone speak, and even if I could have, what would I have said? The world felt flipped on its head: Victor Castel, the engineer of a deadly virus, and my mother, his—his *what*?

"Believe me, Kat," she said. "I didn't think it was going to hurt anyone—not in the way it has. You have to understand that."

"I'm not understanding anything until you explain it to me from the beginning."

MY MOM AND Victor had shared a dream—they really had, at first, she assured me. Being a vampire was isolating. When you were turned, you left your whole life behind—your family and friends, your profession and your religion and eventually even your name. Everything that made you *you*. What you got in exchange was bloodlust, immortality, better night vision, and a few other vampiric traits that were nothing to complain about, but hardly compensated for the gaping hole in your life and sense of self.

She and Victor were lonely. They knew other vampires had to be lonely too: isolated, skulking around in the dank caves and dusty castles that travs fetishized. They were ashamed of the need to hunt or of enjoying it too much. If vampires could come together, things might be better. But a concentration of vampires led to trouble, once they got hungry. On top of that, if the point of a vampire community was to recapture some of what they'd lost as humans, the body count had to be kept in check.

What they needed—what *all* vampires needed—was freedom from the need to feed on humans. They needed synthetic blood.

World War II had just started, and it had ushered in huge advances in hematology. Victor and my mom devoted themselves to researching what it would take to develop a substitute. A blood replica that could transfuse into humans was incredibly complicated, but recreating the components of blood that vampires need to survive was more basic. They had a testable prototype in fifteen years.

"The first time we tasted it, we weren't sure what would happen," she said. "Had we gotten everything right? If regular food made us sick, what would this do, if we were wrong? Could it kill us? It was just the two of us in the lab together. Victor brought champagne flutes. You know, Hema has additives to make it more blood-like. Coloring, flavoring. Without those, it looks like chocolate syrup and tastes like—well, nothing good. We toasted and then I remember the feeling of the glass on my lips. How unfamiliar that was, to be drinking from something *cold*."

"Mom, ew!" Thinking of her sucking blood from a human was only very slightly less gross than thinking of her having sex. "I know a little of what happened next. You couldn't find a way to distribute Hema to other vampires. That was in the late fifties, right?"

She nodded. "You have to understand, Victor is highly intelligent. Highly strategic. But he had failed to anticipate this. This is his blind spot: he's so enamored of his own genius, he can't imagine anyone failing to recognize it. He wasn't just disappointed. It wasn't even about the fact that he'd nearly exhausted his personal resources—and far more of the Blacks' resources—in service of this project. He had spent years fantasizing about the community of vampires that he would bring together. Long before we tasted that first prototype of Hema, he had started speaking about his idea of *Vampirdom*. When vampires didn't recognize what he had done for them, it was simply unacceptable. He told me once he felt like he'd been stabbed in the heart—not that he remembered how a flesh wound felt at that point.

"The idea that we might have children, as vampires, was his too. I told him he'd never get vampire women to agree to it, and he said we'd see about that." She paused, her face dark. "He can't have them himself. Not all vampires can."

There was something in her tone that gave me pause. "Mom,

were you . . . like *with* him?" She glared at me like I was being a prude, which meant yes. "Ew! What about *my dad*?"

"I met your father later, and he was the true love of my life. But Victor and I were together for many years. At the time I thought I loved him." She shook her head. "That wasn't love, not even close."

"How long? What about all those years you told me you spent alone?"

She swatted my arm with the back of her hand. "Don't distract me. The point is that Victor had invested everything in this fantasy of Vampirdom. And what did it amount to? Nothing.

"He obsessed over it. It made him intolerable to be around: one minute he wanted to be consoled, and the next, he'd be enraged that he was in a position to be consoled." She flexed her hands against the steering wheel. "I'll admit, I was glad when he started spending so much time in the lab again. Eventually I learned his plan: if he could create a disease that would prevent vampires from feeding on human blood, then they'd have to depend on Hema to survive. Vampirdom would be a reality.

"I should have stopped him, I know that now. To say that it's my biggest regret hardly expresses the guilt I've had to live with. But the truth is, for a long time, I didn't think he would actually *manage* it. Even after he infected bats with the virus and released them, it was ten years before we heard of the first vampire death. That's when I finally understood that he'd opened Pandora's box."

"But it's not like you *helped* him, not like the Blacks."

"Even if I didn't have a hand in the virus itself, I knew what he was doing and I turned a blind eye. We all played our roles. The Blacks, the engineers and scientists he collaborated with . . ."

The personnel list, all those early employees marked "deceased." "None of them survived the Peril. Victor killed them, didn't he?"

Her face paled. "Not directly. He cut them off from Hema. Victor didn't want to worry about keeping them quiet about the virus's origins forever."

I swallow around the knot in my throat. "What about you? Did he . . . did he try to—"

"Kill me?" She shrugged. "I did my best to make it hard for him. I ran, and hid, and saw his face everywhere. I thought I'd managed to disappear, but really, there's no escaping him; I know that now. If he'd really wanted me dead, I wouldn't be here. I think I meant too much to him to kill at first, even though he hated me for leaving. It wasn't until I had you that I had a little bit of security. Victor thought his fangborn would—" She stopped herself.

"His fangborn?" My stomach clenched. "Mom, what do his fangborn have to do with me?"

The stillness of that moment was excruciating, like in those films of atom bombs going off, the way time seems to pause between the detonation and the destruction.

She drew in a deep breath and forced herself to meet my eyes. "You're his fangborn, Kat. Victor turned me."

I got out of the car.

It was too small, the air pressing down on me, and before I'd even thought about it, I was fifty feet away, standing in the rest stop parking lot. But I couldn't feel the cold rain or the wind whipped up by the semis barreling down the highway.

Victor Castel was my *fangmaker.*

My mom's fangmaker hadn't left her for dead in a ditch. She hadn't spent her life as a vampire adrift and alone. She'd spent it with Victor Castel, as his fangborn and his lover, until she'd been willing to die to escape.

And I'd run right into his arms at Harcote.

I'd come up with a dozen different explanations for Victor's interest in me: I made Galen look good and I worked hard and I was just enough of an outsider.

All along, it had been because I was . . . I was *his*. Like Galen had said.

Victor had known that all along.

My stomach turned, remembering how Victor had made me promise I'd never call myself a nobody. He must have hated to hear me say that.

I thought I'd defied the odds getting into Harcote and getting the mentorship, but I hadn't defied anything. Just like Galen, I hadn't realized that the deck was stacked in my favor.

And *Galen*. Had he known all along? Was that why he'd wanted to be with me? I remembered that gross look of approval Victor had given Galen when he'd held my hand.

His two Youngblood fangborn, together at last, ready to do his bidding.

That's what I'd been doing, hadn't I?

"Kat! Baby, stop!" The rain soaked my mom's hair as she ran across the asphalt to me.

"He paid for all this, you know—my tuition, my uniforms, the flight out here." There were tears on my cheeks, mixing with the rain. "He gave me that mentorship. He made me need him, and I fell for it. I—I defended him. Every problematic thing Taylor called out, I had an excuse for. I thought Galen only resented him because he's ungrateful. I *trusted* him! I wanted his approval! I've done every single thing he wanted me to—and he's a *monster*! What does that make me?"

"Baby, no. This is what Victor *does*. He's had centuries of practice manipulating vampires, and you didn't know he was dangerous. That's my fault. I should have told you. I thought if I kept the truth from you, I could keep you away from all this sickness and death. Away from *him*. That's why I never wanted you to come to Harcote. I wouldn't be able to protect you here. When you texted me about that mentorship with him—oh, Kat, I don't even know how to explain that feeling. Like I'd lost you."

I hugged her tight. It wasn't enough to make up for the weeks of distance Victor had put between us, but it was a start. "You haven't lost me. I'm right here."

She brushed tears from my face. "So you understand why I'm taking you home."

"No," I said. "I can't leave now. You've heard about the reunionists, haven't you?"

38

TAYLOR

RADTKE WAS GIVING Kat's mom a tour of campus, and Kat and I were along for the ride.

That's how it was supposed to look.

Radtke had said this was the safest way to talk without being overheard. Leave your phone behind, stay out of buildings, keep moving, watch for anyone following. This was the real sneaky spy shit. Radtke was legit.

"I had to beg my mom to come back here," Kat said to me. The icy rain had cleared, and now her hair shimmered red in the sun. A strand slipped into her gorgeous face, and I could not believe that I wasn't kissing that face right now. The muscles in my hand were cramping for not holding hers, for being close to her and not touching her. Just then she hooked her pinkie around mine and glanced up at me with this impish glee, like she had been feeling the exact same thing.

A blast of euphoria assaulted my brain, forcing my own face into a goofy—and slightly inappropriate—grin. It was surreal how *good* I felt with her. It made everything before feel dull and gray and sad.

I'd spent two years at this school, and who knows how many before that, hiding. Not that any *straight* person would have de-scribed it that way, but they couldn't hear the voice in my head that second-guessed and analyzed every little thing I did—or wanted to do. What were the consequences? Was it worth potentially getting hurt? That's what felt gently tragic about the way Kat hooked her finger around mine: she seemed to do it completely without agonizing over it. It was this same ease when she'd kissed me after the Founder's Dance that had made me so angry—no, not angry. That feeling had been sadness, that I couldn't do anything without approaching it like a military maneuver. But maybe, with Kat, I could change.

"Did you tell her—about us?" I asked Kat.

"Not yet. She's got a lot on her mind. But I'm not worried."

When we got to the lacrosse field, I flipped my hand around and slid it into hers. When Kat smiled at me, her eyes glinted like amber, and she was the most beautiful person I'd ever seen.

Ahead of us, Radtke and Kat's mom stopped near the far goal and turned to wait for us. I saw her mom notice us holding hands and my guts clenched up.

Kat's grip on my hand tightened too.

But then her mom just *smiled* and turned back to Radtke. She didn't even mention it.

"It's incredible to speak to you," Radtke was saying to Kat's mom. "This conversation has confirmed suspicions we've held for years about the origins of Hema and CFaD. Now, I have a discovery to share with you. We have successfully developed what we believe to be a cure for CFaD."

Cue the fireworks, right?

Not right.

Kat's mom's face melted into a look of terror. *"No!"*

"Mom!" Kat cried. "You work in a *CFaD clinic*. You've always wanted a cure."

Kat's mom had her shoulders hiked up to her ears and her

arms crossed, like she wished she could cave in on herself. "I *do* want a cure. There's been so much suffering. But you don't understand Victor. A cure threatens everything he's built. Vampirdom. Hema. CasTech. He won't allow you to simply tear that down."

"When we tell Vampirdom the truth about CFaD, what he wants won't matter," Radtke said.

Kat's mom gave Radtke an absolutely scathing look. "He can make it matter."

"Ms. Radtke, you told him in September that there was a cure, but after the attack on Mr. Kontos and his lab, Victor must think he's dealt with it for now," Kat said. "That means he believes he has time to come up with other strategies. He told me that he has at least one contingency plan for when the cure is discovered. But what if it's something even worse than CFaD?"

"Does it matter?" I asked. "I mean, are we seriously considering sitting on *the cure for CFaD* because of what Victor Castel might do? People are suffering everywhere. Vampires are dying. And this is Kontos's legacy. We can't just cave to Castel because he's rich and scary."

"Forgive me if the idea of facing Victor Castel chills me to my core." Kat's mom pulled her jacket closer around her. "I've spent so many years hiding from him. *Running* from him. He wanted me, then he wanted Kat." She looked at me and her face softened. "I can never repay your parents for what they did for us."

"My . . . what?" I stammered.

"Your parents gave us a safe place to stay for years, when Kat was at an age where she needed stability."

"Are you telling me that *my parents* knew about this?"

"Certainly not all the details, no. But they knew my fangmaker had been abusive and that I'd struggled to get away. Your mother understood. I'd known her for decades, and she'd always hated Victor."

"Wait—you mean the Sangers knew that Victor was your fang-maker the whole time?" Kat asked.

Her mom nodded.

"Then why did they make us leave?"

She shook her head. "They didn't. Victor came for you."

"When he visited the house," I breathed. "The same winter you left, but I couldn't remember if it was before or after you'd gone."

She nodded. "He'd come to make sure Kat went to Harcote the next fall. We were lucky she wasn't home. Your mom told me that night and we left. You girls were so close. We couldn't let that be the link that allowed Victor to find us. Your mom and I agreed to discourage you from staying in contact."

I let that settle on me. Kat and I had realized weeks ago that we didn't know the full story behind why she and her mom had left, but without another explanation it hadn't done much to close the wound I'd had for years—the guilt that it had been my fault. I didn't even know where that certainty had come from. Maybe blaming myself was the only option I'd had.

But it wasn't me at all. It was Vampirdom's Number One Jackass.

"At least, it seems that bridge has been repaired," Kat's mom said with a faint smile.

Kat flushed a beautiful, brilliant scarlet.

WE WATCHED KAT'S mom drive away.

Radtke's jaw was set as she turned to me and Kat. "Now, don't you do anything rash. Remember, you're to carry on as if you know nothing and nothing has happened."

That was the plan. We didn't want to find out what Castel would do when he realized he was backed into a corner by the reunionists. Now that Kat's mom was back in the picture, reverse-engineering Hema wasn't an impossible task. We needed to tread carefully. The first step was for Radtke to get Kontos's research into the hands of her contacts—off campus. That was supposed to happen during the distraction of Descendants Day. *Our* immediate task in Operation Revolution was to avoid raising suspicions. For Kat, that meant hanging out with Castel as if she didn't know he'd nearly forced vampires to extinction to make us dependent on Hema, or that he was her fangmaker, or that he was the Benefactor who'd sent her to the Founders Dance dressed like Jessica Rabbit. By comparison, I had a very chill day ahead of me: I was still teching Evangeline's play but other than that, my expulsion excused me from all Descendants Day activities. I just needed to finish packing.

For some reason, as we left Radtke at Old Hill and headed to the down-campus stairs, that felt surprisingly depressing. Kat was finally by my side, things were okay with Evangeline, and even though Kontos was gone, I was beginning to think I'd found the part of myself he'd always seen. The part that *cared*. Now I had to leave all that behind. It wasn't fair.

Kat's hand found mine. I wasn't expecting that. Below us, Harcoties were wandering from the residential quads to the Dining Hall, so I squeezed her hand once and let it fall.

"Too much?"

"No, it's just . . ." I jutted my chin toward the quads.

"I don't understand. You're leaving."

"I know," I said. "But you're not."

Kat had said she wanted to leave Harcote because I was, but

that was ridiculous. She'd been telling me all along that the opportunities here meant more to her than they meant to me. She
deserved to stay—at least as long as she could. (Radtke had promised to look into other ways to fund her tuition, just in case.)

"I'm not going to make you fill my spot as the Token Queer," I
said.

We were at the bottom of the stairs now, near the Dining Hall.
Kat spun around so she was standing in front of me, in order to
glare at me, very ferocious. "First of all, you *know* there are other
queer kids here. Just because someone isn't ready to come out or
maybe isn't totally out to themselves doesn't mean they're not
queer. And second, when was the last time you managed to make
me do anything I didn't want to?"

God, she was amazing, how she was staring up at me like she
could kiss me here, in front of everyone. Still, I did not expect her
to say, "I'm going to kiss you now, okay?"

My lips parted in surprise. I managed to nod. Then she leaned
in and kissed me.

It felt like I'd been stripped naked. It was painful to care about
someone, but that had nothing on how terrifying it was to let
someone care about you, to stand outside the Dining Hall and let
anyone who turned their head see how much I loved Kat—how
much she loved me. But I forced my eyes to close. We had so little
time together, I had to savor each kiss.

Kat broke away. Behind her, everyone pretended they hadn't
been watching us. Maybe nothing was wrong with that.

"I don't care who knows," Kat said.

"Me neither." I grinned as I laced my fingers into hers. "But it
sucks that we only have one more day together, and you have to
spend it with Castel."

Kat grimaced. "I know. But we have to pretend like everything's normal."

"You don't feel right about that either, do you?"

"No," she admitted. "But what choice do we have?"

KAT

I KNEW WE'D helped achieve some major progress: Radtke would get Kontos's research into safe hands today, and the reunionists would put together a plan to release it. Eventually, humans suffering from CFaD would finally get the help they needed. With my mom involved, an alternative to Hema was suddenly possible too. But still, as I stood in the chilly morning mist on the lacrosse field waiting for Victor's helicopter, it was hard to feel like we'd won. Especially when the thought of spending the rest of the year without Taylor made me want to run back to the room and barricade the two of us inside.

Beside me, Galen scanned the clouds. The circles under his eyes looked unusually dark. We hadn't spoken since I broke things off with him. I had to assume he now had an idea why. My cheeks warmed, remembering how I'd kissed Taylor outside the Dining Hall last night.

With a distant whirring, the helicopter emerged from behind the trees.

"I need to thank you," Galen said suddenly. "You've made me realize a lot of things—things I should have thought about before."

The helicopter buzzed closer to the ground. The wind battered us, plastering Galen's curls to his forehead. I wasn't sure I heard him right when he cried, over the sound, "I know you'll do the right thing."

"What are you talking about?" I yelled, but it was too late. The helicopter had set down on the field and the door was open. Simon and Meera Black and Victor Castel were striding toward us.

DESCENDANTS DAY WAS the least-festive occasion I could have imagined. It began with an assembly in the Great Hall, where Headmaster Atherton was so excited about the school's twenty-fifth anniversary, I feared his head might pop right off his body. After that, our families and fangmakers sat in on shortened versions of our classes. I led Victor through Old Hill, participated in a "debate" in Ms. Radtke's class with him beside me, and, in the science building named after him, explained what Mr. Kontos had taught us about titration. I kept a deferential smile slapped on my face, reacted to everything he said like it was a pearl of wisdom. I was pretending to be someone else, but it felt different this time—more like I was playing a character and less like I was trying to change who I was.

Everyone gathered in the Dining Hall for lunch. A chill ran through me as I looked around the room. These vampires were the oldest and most powerful, the ones who'd not only survived the Peril, but who'd lived for decades or centuries before that. Victor and the Blacks kept mostly to themselves, although we shared a table with Lucy and Evangeline. Lucy's fangmaker was a woman as thin and angular as a fashion illustration, with a shock of white in her otherwise black hair, wearing a complicated, armor-like jacket; she would have looked more at home in *Vogue* or at the International Criminal Court than a high school cafeteria.

Evangeline bore a strong resemblance to her mother, who was just as pretty and looked nearly as young as her daughter; the clearest difference between them was that Evangeline's mother didn't seem interested in contributing to any conversation. I'd expected Carsten's fangmaker to be some kind of Viking lord, but he turned out to be an extremely creepy Emperor Palpatine-looking dude wearing a tattered robe; thankfully Lucy had dumped him so he wasn't sitting with us. The Dent twins, Dorian, and their parents fawned over their fangmaker, who was apparently the same person: a rickety-looking woman with a blond bouffant a foot high, huge fake eyelashes, and extremely pink lipstick. She hadn't retracted her long, stained fangs the whole time she'd been on campus. Nowhere near that lady, the school's few Black families sat together, looking uncomfortable. At a table in the corner, Taylor nursed her Hema with the handful of other students whose ancestors hadn't made the trip. I wished I'd been with them.

The a cappella squad was performing a few songs. Climate Action Now!'s presentation was up next; I was not looking forward that. Max Krovchuk was winding his way through the Dining Hall, dropping the newest edition of *The HarNotes* off at each table.

Max placed a stack on our table, then shot a self-serious nod to me and Galen before dashing away. I grabbed one. It wasn't *The HarNotes* after all, but a leaflet printed on copier paper.

The Harcote Renegade was printed at the top.

I smirked. Of course Max had set up his own publication. After the scandal with the editorial, the paper had been placed under Headmaster Atherton's direct supervision; nothing went to print anymore that he didn't sign off on.

Then I read the headline of the leaflet's only article.

FRAUD AT THE BLACK FOUNDATION, CFaD SCION SPEAKS OUT:
An Investigation by Galen Black

I couldn't believe what I was reading. I stared at Galen, my mouth agape. He was studying the table, very intently with his lip held tightly between his teeth. Silence had fallen across the Dining Hall as Harcoties, their parents and fangmakers, the whole of the vampiric elite, read Galen's words.

"What is this, Galen?" Simon Black was saying. "Some kind of joke?"

Galen lifted his chin. "It's the truth."

"It's no such thing," his father snapped.

"But you told me so yourself, Dad," Galen said with that ever-present composure, the faint pinkness in his cheeks the only sign of alarm. "*This is our family business.* You said that. *Our duty to Vampirdom,* you called it. *Curing CFaD doesn't fit with our goals.* Those are your exact words. The Foundation exists to make sure we depend on Hema or we die. Isn't that right, Victor?"

Victor was staring at him with a look of total, burning hatred, as if he was fantasizing about driving a stake into his fangborn's chest right then and there.

"Is the boy unwell?" Victor forced out.

Meera Black leaped up and grabbed Galen's arm, pulling him out of his chair. "Yes, yes, my son isn't well. His mental health—he's struggling!"

Headmaster Atherton skittered about among the tables, snatching up copies of *The Renegade.* His aides fanned out around the Dining Hall to collect unread copies. But then Headmaster Atherton tried to grab a leaflet from the hands of Lucy's fangmaker, who said something to him so arresting that Headmaster Atherton backed away with his hands up and his aides stilled.

None of this had stopped anyone—including me—from reading the leaflet. What Galen had written was persuasive. He'd used his access to the Black Foundation to gather a lot of evidence, and the way he'd laid it out made the conclusion clear. As Meera began trying to drag Galen from the Dining Hall, some of the vampires rose from their chairs, the leaflet clutched in their fists, demanding an explanation.

When Simon closed his hand around Galen's other arm, Galen stopped resisting. As his parents hauled him out of the Dining Hall, Galen looked back at me.

He was wearing a defiant smile.

With the Blacks gone, the energy of the room zeroed in on Victor Castel. Unhurriedly, he rose, sliding a copy of the leaflet into his suit pocket. "I'm as shocked by these claims as you are. The Blacks were close associates and trusted friends"—it chilled me to hear him speak of them in the past tense—"but there will be a full investigation into these very serious accusations. Vampirdom deserves a cure for CFaD. Justice will be done."

With that, Victor summoned Headmaster Atherton and stormed out of the Dining Hall. As they headed toward Old Hill, I grabbed Taylor.

"Pretty ballsy for a Timothée Chalamet knock-off, right?" she said.

"Yeah—and it changes *everything*. This is exactly what Radtke and my mom wanted to avoid happening. This isn't some anonymous opinion piece: it came directly from *Galen*, his little prince. Victor can't sweep this under the rug. He'll blame it all on the Blacks."

"Even if he doesn't disband the Foundation, he'll have to make at least some of their research public—some of the good stuff that Galen says they've been hiding."

"That means the timeline to the cure just got a lot faster. Even worse, Victor's just been *humiliated*. He's not going to let that stand."

Taylor ran her hands through her hair. "What should we do? Radtke's still off campus handing over the files, but this seems like a really good reason to throw the old plan away."

"We have to stop him from leaving campus," I said. "Things are only going to get worse once he gets in that helicopter. But how?"

"How?" Taylor's lips quirked into an off-kilter grin. "*You're* how. Ask him not to leave. Castel is obsessed with you, Kat. He basically spent years strategizing about how to get you to Harcote, so he could hang around with you at Descendants Day just like this. He's literally only here because of you."

"And Galen."

"No, he offered to come for *you*, to stand in for your family," she said. "Anyway, I don't think he cares about Galen anymore."

She was right. After this, Victor wouldn't care about Galen. Victor had spent years molding Galen into an obedient successor, but he'd never respected Galen for doing what he was told. Now that Galen wasn't so obedient, he stood a chance of actually becoming some kind of leader for the Youngbloods, but Victor would never trust him again.

Galen was dead to him. The loss would sting, but Victor would heal fast enough.

Because now he had me.

For the last few weeks, he'd been testing me, training me,

preparing me in the same way he had Galen. He had never been keeping me around to make Galen look good. He had always wanted me—his fangborn—for himself. Now that Galen was out of the picture, he needed me too.

I gazed up at Taylor, with her curls tumbling into her face and her eyes bright.

"*Kath-er-ine*, don't look at me like that. You're only allowed to kiss me once you have a brilliant idea."

I leaned up on my toes and planted my lips on hers.

39

KAT

I WAITED FOR him at the lacrosse field, where the helicopter sat. I worried if I'd be able to pull this off. I worried about what was happening to Galen. I worried if this would work. My phone buzzed.

You got this my vampire queen

I had to bite my check to keep my composure as Victor Castel emerged from the path from up-campus. Headmaster Atherton was beside him, like a kitten dogging the steps of a pit bull.

"Kat, run along to your activities. Mr. Castel's visit has been cut short," Headmaster Atherton said.

I didn't even look at him. Actually, his buzzing made it easy to square my shoulders to Victor, cutting Headmaster Atherton out of the conversation entirely. "Victor, you gave me an assignment—assessing threats to Vampirdom. One of those threats has emerged."

"Mr. Castel is very busy—" Headmaster Atherton began.

Victor raised his hand and Headmaster Atherton quieted.

"Well?" he said.

"One thing I've learned from your mentorship is how important it is to control who knows what." I cut my eyes to Headmaster

Atherton, who was red-faced and still hovering a little too close. "I know a place we can speak privately."

Victor studied me, his face unreadable. I tried to match his stony expression. Which is to say, I tried very hard to look like his fangborn.

"Lead the way."

THE DOOR SUCTIONED closed behind us. The darkness beyond the glass walls of the Stack gave the impression we were floating in space. I was totally alone with Victor Castel—the man who'd engineered the Peril that led to my father's death, who'd turned my mother, who'd crafted every circumstance that had led me to this point.

I fiddled with my phone. "There's no reception and Headmaster Atherton never installed Wi-Fi. Plus the air in here is barely oxygenated, to prevent fires. None of his aides can spy on us. We can speak freely. Your archive is this way."

Motion-detecting lights flickered to reveal the CasTech Archive. I put my phone facedown on the same table Galen and I had worked at.

"Galen has put you in a difficult position."

"The Blacks acted of their own accord," Victor said smoothly. "I would have stopped them had I known."

I smiled to reassure him. "I told you, it's just the two of us here. We don't need to pretend that Simon and Meera Black have ever done anything of their own accord. Galen hadn't either, until this. It must hurt, after you've given him so much. I mean, you had to work for everything you have now, and Galen's barely even aware of what he has to be grateful for. I understand why you never respected him."

Victor massaged his knuckles, his brow furrowed. "Respect is earned."

"Exactly," I said. "Galen was never going to be what you wanted him to be. You've always known that. To lead the Youngbloods like you lead Vampirdom, he has to be his own man. If he's his own man, you can't control him, and now you can't even trust him. The problem is, you've treated Galen like a protégé."

"Did you make me come down here to criticize Galen's upbringing?"

"That's only a problem because you don't need a protégé. You need an *ally*. Someone who wants the same things you do. You need me. Isn't that why you brought me here?"

A smug grin inched across Victor's face, making his deep-set eyes glitter darkly. "You figured it out?"

I nodded, pulling in a deep breath. "The financial aid, the mentorship. I'm so grateful, but at the same time, it feels like a waste. I should have always known that you were my fangmaker."

His eyes widened. For a disturbing moment I thought he might move to hug me, so I kept talking.

"I'm the ally you need now. I've spent my life outside Vampirdom, so I understand why we need it to stay strong. That's what you want too. But the Youngbloods think I'm different. Independent—because they don't know how you've been watching over me. You've seen how I've risen here in just a few months. I can lead them. I'll lead them exactly where you want them to go."

He was watching me, barely blinking, like he was seeing me for the first time. "Kat, I . . . I admit I didn't think you were ready. I didn't realize you *knew*."

"I suspected, but my mom only just told me."

He shook his head. "I should never have let your mother leave. I would have brought her back, but then she took up with that man, and you were born. You should have been mine, but I was forced to watch you from afar."

His words scraped along my insides like a shard of ice. I burned to tell him that I never had been and never would be *his*, but instead, I said, "Until I applied to Harcote."

"I would have found a way to you."

I did not want to hear any more about that. Even if I did, we were running out of time. Evangeline's play was starting soon and we needed to be in the audience.

"We don't have time for emotional thinking right now," I said. "If you want me as your ally, there's something I need first."

"Anything. Anything for you, Kat."

"I need to know what really went on. I don't mean the Black Foundation. I mean Hema, and CFaD. I figured out most of it, but you covered your tracks so well. There are a lot of missing pieces. If you want me as a partner to navigate what Galen's done to the Black Foundation, I have to know the truth." I gazed up at him, full of gratitude. "You're my fangmaker. Everything I am, I owe to you. Trust me: I would never betray you."

TAYLOR

SITTING IN THE tech box in the theater, I couldn't stop bouncing my knee. Evangeline's play was starting in fifteen minutes, and the rows of seats were filling in below me. I tried not to think about how Kat was in an underground book-cave, sucking up to the greatest vampire-killer of all time. Instead I tried to think about how this was my last moment at Harcote—my last time teching or seeing all these stupid Youngblood faces. Soon it would be like I'd never even been here.

There were footsteps on the narrow stairs. I jumped out of my seat and flung open the door.

It was Evangeline.

She looked radiant in her Joan of Arc costume. Her hair was tucked up under a pageboy wig and she was wearing a chain mail shirt: battle-ready in the hottest way possible. I hadn't seen her since her outburst at Hunter House; lucky for her, between me and Kat coming out and Galen's exposé, the gossip cycle was pretty packed.

"You should be backstage!" I said. "Someone's going to see you."

"I wanted to check that you knew what you were supposed to be doing," she snapped.

"Oh jeez, I've never seen a light board in my life, please explain." I rolled my eyes. "Of course I know what I'm doing."

"That's not really it." She played with the edge of her chain mail. "They're really making you leave?"

"My flight's late tonight."

"I can't imagine it here without you. After what Galen did, things aren't going back to how they were before. I should never have talked to Atherton. I thought Kat wrote the editorial and I was so jealous of her. I never even really thought about what it actually *said*."

I raised my eyebrows. "And?"

"I told Lucy if she ever has another one of her *parties* again, I'll leak the photos I have of her feeding on humans. I've probably got hundreds. It'd be a cancellation so quick not even vampiric charisma would get her out of it."

"Aw, E." I grinned. "I knew you had a conscience somewhere in there."

"Yeah, well. Surprise! I should get back down there." She didn't leave. Her eyes darted between me and the floor. Then she took a quick step forward and wrapped her arms around me. "Goodbye, Taylor."

She slipped back down the stairs and was gone.

I put my headset on and scanned the theater. It was five minutes from curtain and the stage manager called places. Below me, the seats were mostly full. A funereal figure swept down the left aisle. Radtke looked up to catch my eye and nodded exactly once: she'd handed off the hard drive successfully. No doubt she'd heard what Galen had done. The last thing she'd want to be doing right now was watching Evangeline's one-act. But hopefully Radtke had the stomach for one more surprise.

Hopefully Kat would make it here to give it to her.

At two minutes out, as I was about to dim the house lights, Kat and Castel came down the aisle. Atherton had saved an empty seat next to him, but only one. He practically shooed Kat away so he could be alone with his buddy Castel. I wasn't sure if that was a good or bad sign. Then I saw Castel look to Kat, as if he was asking her permission. She gave him a perfectly gracious smile, and only then did Castel sit.

That was when I knew: we had him.

I brought the lights down all the way, the curtain opened, and I turned the spotlight on Evangeline.

A minute later Kat burst through the door to the box and practically tackled me in a kiss—or she would have, if the mic from my headset hadn't been in the way. She knocked it into my teeth.

"Ow!" I whispered. "Did you get it?"

She nodded and handed me her phone.

"It's cued up," Kat breathed as I plugged the cable in. "Evangeline's gonna kill us for messing up her play."

"Luckily for us, we're the ever-living, never-dying," I said. "You ready?"

"Kiss for good luck," she whispered.

I pressed my lips to hers.

Then I pressed play.

40

KAT

THE WHITE SPOTLIGHT glinted off Evangeline's chain-mail shirt as a maidservant, played by Carolina Riser, attended to her on stage (yes, actually). Suddenly, Victor Castel's voice filled the theater.

"The problem with vampires is that most of them spent so many decades worrying about where their next meal was coming from that their minds have gone dull. I gave them a gift with Hema, and they were too stupid to realize its potential."

"Which was?" my voice said.

"Vampirdom. A society where we can be free from our pathetic dependence on humans. Vampires are superior beings. We deserve to be allowed to embrace that superiority. But it takes a visionary to imagine a different future, and to make that future a reality."

"That's where CFaD came in." I peered down into the still-dark theater. Victor was clutching the armrests, his back rigidly straight. He understood what was coming.

"CFaD was my idea—perhaps my finest idea." I cringed remembering the pride that had radiated off him, the smug satisfaction to finally brag about his terrible accomplishment. *"You can't imagine how difficult it was to get it exactly right. Creating a virus was something that, at the time, humans were barely capable of. To develop that technology, then to tailor-make a disease transmitted*

through humans that was fatal to vampires? CFaD is a work of art. It's a shame that so few understand that."

"What a freaking monster," Taylor whispered. Her eyebrows had crept up to the middle of her forehead.

"That's not the worst of it." I shivered, knowing what he'd say next. The wolfish look on his face as he'd said it.

"So you knew that CFaD would kill a lot of vampires."

"Did I know? Their deaths were the point. The necessary cost of progress. CFaD turned out far better than I'd hoped. Look at my position now. Vampires worship me. They look to me for every decision. Every meal they take fattens my wallet. And the Youngbloods— a whole generation of vampires, with no humanity, indebted to me. I have to credit Roger Atherton for setting up this school: he understood that if there were going to be Youngbloods, we'd need to make sure they thought like we did."

"And the cure for CFaD? You know the reunionists have one."

Gasps of surprise rose from the theater below us.

In the recording, Victor scoffed. *"Don't worry about that. The Blacks, clearly, can no longer serve their purpose for me, but I have other strategies, other diseases, other allies. And now I have you."*

I mimed gagging for Taylor.

"Everything I've done has led to this point: Vampirdom belongs to me."

I hit pause, and Taylor raised the house lights. The vampires in the theater had heard more than enough. Some were still confused or wondering if this was some kind of joke, but others—the fangmakers, the oldest vampires—understood that it wasn't. They were on their feet, yelling at Victor and hemming him in. Victor had stood and was offering some kind of explanation with his hands up—as if this was just another situation he could manage away. Somehow Headmaster Atherton had slipped out of his seat and vanished.

The Youngbloods—the Harcoties—didn't know what to do. Evangeline and Carolina were still on the stage, their faces slack with confusion. Ms. Radtke made her way to the front of the theater to try to wave them off into the wings.

Then Victor moved into the aisle and took the tiniest step toward the emergency exit at the front of the theater. It was a critical miscalculation. Max Krovchuk's father—a bald-headed man so enormous he looked like a real-life supervillain—grabbed Victor's arms and pinned them behind him.

"What do you think they going to do to him?" I asked, transfixed by the scene.

"Hopefully something bad," Taylor said, turning to me. "What did he mean about Atherton and the school . . . Atherton was in on this from the very beginning, wasn't he?"

At that moment, the door to the box swung open.

Headmaster Atherton's figure filled the doorway.

TAYLOR

"OF COURSE I was *in on this*, you idiots." Atherton twisted the deadbolt, locking the door behind him. I stood up, and Kat followed. "Victor would take credit for turning the first vampire if no one stopped him, but he doesn't do everything himself. You heard him say that the school was my idea, but *I* was the one who saw the potential of the Youngbloods. *I* saw we needed our own vampire youth!"

"That's why you bought the school before the Peril even started," Kat breathed.

"So you were obsessed with Youngbloods before they even existed? Not something I'd brag about." I tried to sound like my regular snarky self, but I had a serious lump in my throat. Atherton was wild-eyed, and he had us alone. I looked down at the theater: no one was paying attention to what was going on in the tech box behind them.

"*Shut up*, Taylor!" he roared. I couldn't help it, I flinched. "You can never keep your stupid mouth closed, can you?"

"Headmaster—" Kat cut in.

He slapped her across the face.

The force of it flung Kat into the wall, and she sank to the floor. I dove to her side, putting my body between her and Atherton. My heart was thundering in my ears as Kat mumbled, "I'm okay."

"You ungrateful bitch," Atherton cried. "Victor was prepared to give you *everything* and you spit in his face! The two of you have done nothing but try to destroy what the older generations built for you. You have no idea how lucky you are, that you'll never have to suffer like we did. You have no appreciation for the sacrifices we made, just so you can have a nice high school experience!"

I got to my feet. "Harcote is *your* playground. The only place on Earth you really don't have to choose between being a teenage boy and a five-hundred-year-old monster."

"I built Harcote for the Youngbloods!"

"Liar," Kat said as she pushed herself up. "If you did it for the Youngbloods, then why aren't they all here? There have to be dozens, even hundreds, of Youngblood vampires who could be here, but aren't. What about them?"

"Harcote is an elite institution. It's for the Best of the Best."

"Exactly," Kat said. "You *want* the school to be exclusive. You set the tuition and make sure there's no financial aid. You know there are barely any BIPOC vampires here and you haven't done anything about it. You practically go out of your way to make queer students uncomfortable and you run around calling us boys and girls like nonbinary people don't exist. The school's nothing but a fucked-up fantasy."

"And you've been using it to brainwash us with your toxic ideas about vampire supremacy," I added.

"Leo Kontos was the one doing the indoctrinating! I've never done anything but educate Youngbloods—until you came along and tried to ruin everything I'd created."

"Your little empire was ruined anyway," I said. "Kontos found the cure."

"His *cure*?" Atherton snorted. "I took care of that. I took care of him too."

"You killed him?" I murmured. To suspect it was one thing, but to look at Atherton—a scrawny, frisbee-loving immortal boy-man—and to hear him admit it was another.

"Is that so hard to believe?" he roared. "Leo was attacking the foundations of Vampirdom, of everything we've worked for. He had the audacity to do it right under my nose. I knew about his lab, his experiments. Your little nighttime excursions."

"I knew it!" Kat cried. "You use the aides to spy on us!"

Atherton's lip curled in disgust. "Of course! It would be ridiculous not to! Nothing goes on at my school that I don't know about."

I waved at the chaos in the theater below. "Except for this, right?"

Atherton lunged forward. Kat and I leaped back but there was nowhere to go. We were crushed against the back wall of the box. Atherton was so close I could see the pits of his ancient acne scars and smell the metallic tang of Hema on his breath.

He reached into his jacket and pulled out a syringe. A crimson liquid filled its chamber.

The world narrowed to the point of that syringe. I found Kat's hand and gripped it in mine.

"Is that . . ." Kat began.

"Infected blood? Yes, it is. So perceptive, Kat." Atherton snorted out a horrible laugh. "All it took to get rid of Leo was a little of this. I drained the woman myself to set the scene. His cure really is incredible."

Kat pushed herself in front of me, and I clung to her shoulder. "What are you doing?"

"Victor Castel's my fangmaker," Kat said. "When he finds out—"

"Don't you understand? That doesn't mean anything now! You just made sure of that." Atherton's too-pink lips pulled back into a vicious grin. "No one is coming to save you now."

Our backs were literally to the wall. There was nowhere we could go. Atherton may have been scrawny, but he was tall, and he had centuries of vampiric strength on us. Below us, with the theater in chaos.

He was right.

I pulled Kat toward me and wrapped my arms around her. Hers slipped around my waist and she buried her face in my shoulder. I pressed my own cheek into her hair and one last time, breathed in the smell of her jasmine shampoo. This completely sucked, but if I had to die young, at least I had managed to get a few things right before I did.

It happened so fast: Atherton heaved toward us, the syringe in his fist. Its point was headed for me first, I was sure of that. I held Kat tighter, for the last time, and squeezed my eyes closed.

A tremendous crash filled the box. My eyes flew open. Time

seemed to slow. Inches from me, Atherton was frozen in space. His arm was raised, the syringe was nearly at my shoulder, but his body had stiffened, stopping him mid-movement. His face was a hard mask, fixed in the anguished moment before a scream. Suddenly purplish, spindly capillaries burst through his blotchy complexion, like cracks spidering through glass.

Kat shoved her weight against me. We tumbled to the side, out of the syringe's path, just as Atherton keeled over into the wall. He hit it face-first.

A long wooden stake protruded from his back.

At the other side of the box, the door that Atherton had locked had been kicked off its hinges, the wood scattered in thick splinters across the floor.

Radtke was standing in the doorway, her crow-colored figure sprinkled with pale woodchips. Her hair had toppled off her head and she was out of breath and she had a fist full of shards from the door, ready to hurl at Atherton's back.

She opened her hand and let them fall.

On the floor between us, Atherton was dead.

41

KAT

STILL IN MY pajamas although it was nearly noon, I grabbed a mug of Hema from the microwave and hopped up on the counter. I'd heated it too long—the first sip burned my tongue. The California sunshine streamed in through the front windows of the apartment so bright, it was hard to believe it was December. I didn't miss upstate New York at all.

I'd been back home for three weeks. After what happened at Descendants Day, it didn't make sense to keep Harcote open. So many parents had decided on the spot to take their kids home that the school probably would have closed anyway, even if Headmaster Atherton hadn't died. The first thing that Ms. Radtke had done as Interim Headmaster was decree that the last two weeks of the semester were canceled and we could take our finals from home.

Ms. Radtke hadn't had much competition when it came to temporarily taking over Harcote. Most of Headmaster Atherton's closest affiliates, like the vampire from the Visitors' Center, tried to skip campus, only to be apprehended by Max Krovchuk's fang-maker, who began patrolling the grounds before the drama in the theater had even ended to prevent that happening; he was actually a pretty terrifying guy. It wasn't that hard for Ms. Radtke to prove that she'd only been playing the part of Headmaster Atherton's ally, since she'd just staked him to protect the two students who had brought Victor Castel down. Plus Taylor and I both stood up for her.

The second thing Ms. Radtke had done as Interim Headmaster was close the school—at least for the rest of the year.

The Harcote School was an institution built on exclusion, exploitation, and actual death, Ms. Radtke had announced, from the use of glamoured humans as servants to the abysmal lack of diversity among the student body to the ideological curriculum. If the school was to continue to serve Youngbloods, it would have to be in a very different form: open to everyone and built on the premise that vampires and humans were inherently linked. Ms. Radtke had been honest that she wasn't sure that kind of reform was possible. That was why she'd encouraged the parents to enroll their Youngbloods in regular human high schools for the next semester instead of going back to their private tutors. It was a clear signal that our isolation from humans wasn't going to last.

So now, three and a half months and a lifetime after I'd first left, I was back in Sacramento.

Even if Harcote did reopen, I wasn't sure if I could go back. After all, my no-longer-anonymous Benefactor was being held by a vampire tribunal and his assets had been seized. Vampirdom didn't have a functional justice system—given what I'd seen of the Honor Code at Harcote, that didn't surprise me—so everything had been a little ad hoc. Victor and the Blacks, along with a few others, were being held in a roadside motel near Harcote, just because it was the most convenient place to keep watch over them. Given the scope of what they had done, vampires from across the country and around the world had come together to work through the crisis—including vampires who'd been excluded from Harcote and from the boundaries Victor had set for Vampirdom. They didn't just organize investigations into Victor's various crimes or debates on appropriate punishment for people responsible for so much evil. Suddenly, there were real, open discussions about Hema access and educating Youngbloods and life after CFaD. For the first time, vampires were talking about what a more just Vampirdom could look like. It made me smile to imagine Victor locked in his dingy motel room while his beloved creation evolved past him.

I took another swallow of Hema. It had cooled to the perfect temperature.

The pile of blankets on the couch shifted, and a groan emerged. Taylor stuck her head up, her curls rumpled and the imprint of the pillow marking her cheek. I broke into a grin.

"Hungry?" I said.

She rubbed the sleep from her eyes. "Starving."

"Then come here."

Taylor rolled off the couch and padded over to the kitchen in her socks. It was her third day here. She'd taken her finals at home, then flown out to spend the winter holidays with us. With my mom starting a new job as chief scientific officer of the Leo Kontos Foundation—formerly the Black Foundation for a Cure—we could actually afford to host her.

Her parents were happy to let her come. Taylor hadn't told them that we were girlfriends, exactly, but she thought her mom suspected, given how many times she'd said she was glad that us girls had patched things up.

I'd missed her terribly during those three weeks, but at the same time, it wasn't as bad as I'd expected. Having her in my life at all, knowing she was there and understood, wanting her and being wanted in return—even having her far away was so much better than her absence. I'd even forgiven my mom for making Taylor sleep in the living room, because finding her here in the morning was like seeing the first sunrise after a lifetime of night.

Taylor was still half asleep, mussing up her hair so it was standing up on its own. I put the mug down and pulled her into me, so she was standing between my legs and I could nuzzle my face against hers. She sighed happily, her fluttering lashes tickling my cheek.

"You know I have morning breath and this is technically gross, right?"

"I don't care," I mumbled against her lips. Then I kissed her.

TAYLOR

I SAT IN Kat's car, chewing on my thumbnail, bobbing my knee.

"What even is bubble tea?"

"It's this drink with tapioca balls in it."

My nose wrinkled. "And you suck the balls up through a straw?"

"Come on, it's not like you're going to be drinking it. Shelby and Guzman are obsessed."

"It sounds terrible," I said, squinting into the sun setting across the parking lot from behind my sunglasses.

"Taylor."

"What?"

She reached across and rubbed my shoulder. "It's going to be fine, okay?"

I tried to let her touch reassure me, but still, I worried my nail against my lip. "You say that but . . . what if it's not?"

Was I delighted to be in Sacramento staying with Kat, who was still, unbelievably, my official girlfriend? Yes, I was fucking elated.

Did I want her to teach me to ride an electric scooter and make out with me in a movie theater and drive me around in her car (which was really hot, for some reason)? Yes, incredibly, overwhelmingly yes. Did I want her to introduce me to her friends? Intellectually, yes.

But actually, in real live reality? Kind of no.

My brain was locked in a battle over which anxiety would reign supreme.

It was embarrassing to admit, but it had been years since I'd met humans my own age—since before my fangs had come in—and I was nervous. I didn't believe humans were that different from me, and certainly not a lesser species, but I'd spent basically my whole life being told that they were. Would I accidentally treat the humans badly? Would I even *know* if I'd done that?

On top of that, Guzman and Shelby were Kat's *best friends*. She'd promised they would love me, but that wasn't up to her. Two years at Harcote hadn't quite conditioned me to expect others to be friendly and accepting. Kat had only come out to them when she'd gotten home a few weeks ago, and I knew they were really eager to meet the girl responsible for their friend's big queer awakening, but that still left a million ways for me to disappoint them—and Kat, by the transitive property.

Maybe that was the root of it: it wasn't just humans, or Kat's best-friend humans, but Kat's *queer* best-friend humans. I could feel my shoulders creeping higher in spite of Kat's touch. The truth was, I'd had almost as little contact with queer people as I'd had with humans. What if I didn't fit in with them? What if I wasn't queer enough, or in the right way? On the one hand, I knew that was ridiculous—I was who I was, regardless of their opinion—but on the other hand, most of my idea of what being gay was came from movies, TV, and the internet. How well I matched up with those ideas didn't matter at Harcote, because no one at Harcote paid attention to that kind of stuff. I mean, even I had been guilty of assuming the entire student body was straight when I had firsthand evidence of the opposite. (And who knew what was going on in the Boys' Quad? Probably something!) Here, in the real world—the human world—there was an actual LGBTQ+ *community* to fit in with.

Kat squeezed my arm. "Do you not want to do this? We don't have to."

I pushed my sunglasses up. "No, I want to meet them, it's just . . . there's a lot that could go wrong, you know?"

"You mean, in addition to the three thousand other things that have already gone wrong?" Her hazel eyes were bright. "Then I guess we'd just have to deal with it."

I bit my lip. She was right, but still, part of me wanted to run. I tried to think of what Kontos would say. He would tell me it was okay to be nervous, that this fear was a sign that I really cared. That wasn't anything to be embarrassed about. Kat was worth the risk of getting hurt.

"You know what, I am pretty curious about this bubble tea thing," I said. "Let's check it out."

A FEW HOURS later, I could barely remember what I'd been worried about. Guzman and Shelby, who were sitting in the back of Kat's car, were awesome. I still wasn't used to the feeling of being around people like me—of being able to hold Kat's hand or even kiss her if I wanted without worrying about comments or weird looks. Well, Guzman and Shelby didn't hold back on the comments and weird looks, but they were teasing, playful, affirming.

"I can't believe you guys went to school with LucyK," Guzman was saying. "I'm so bummed all her accounts have been on hiatus. Was she as cool as she seems or *cooler*?"

I didn't know if it was because of Evangeline's threats, but Lucy had gone radio silent when Harcote shut down. Her fangmaker, who was leading the investigation into Victor Castel and the origins of CFaD, might have had something to do with it.

"Neither. A lot less cool," Kat said. "She's actually pretty problematic. I can't exactly explain it right now, but let's just say, I wouldn't be surprised if she gets canceled. I'd just unfollow."

"Seriously? That's so lame!" Guzman cried.

I twisted around in my seat. "Lucy's done some messed-up shit, but there's one thing I have to thank her for, and that's tricking Kat into switching rooms. That's how we ended up rooming together."

Shelby shot Guzman a look. "Oh my god, they were roommates!"

"She didn't trick me, okay?" Kat protested. "She *asked*, and I agreed. Don't forget I saved you from living with Evangeline too."

Kat straightened up in her seat.

I caught Kat's eye. "You did—you totally saved me too."

The downside to having friends like Guzman and Shelby was that they were as attuned to Kat's little emotional shifts as I was.

"So who's Evangeline?" Shelby asked. "What kind of a name even is that?"

"Taylor's ex," Kat said as she turned off the main road.

Kat didn't totally love that my relationship with Evangeline had evolved into a kind of friendship. We texted almost every day. Kat said she trusted me, but Evangeline was a low-key monster. A friendship with someone like that, given our past, felt dangerous.

I didn't disagree, but I knew Evangeline in a way Kat didn't. Evangeline had only just started to accept the parts of herself that she'd shared with me, when, like Lucy, she'd been taken to task. Her ultra-ancient father had ordered her off to Romania to spend the rest of the year, and possibly the rest of high school, in his castle; no American public school for her.

"She's only *kind of* my ex. We were just hooking up," I said, suddenly embarrassed. "She was really in love with the guy Kat was dating."

I didn't know what Kat had told her friends about Galen, but before they said anything, the car passed a sign that read EL DORADO HILLS COUNTRY CLUB. Kat asked, "You have the key, right, Shelbs?"

KAT

WE SNUCK AROUND the back of the Club. Months of lifeguarding had won Shelby the key to the back gate. It was already ten o'clock, and the temperature had to have been in the fifties, but the Club stayed open all winter, so the pool was heated—not that the cold would be much of a problem for me and Taylor.

We followed Shelby around the side of the building to the pool and watched them roll back the cover to reveal the steaming, turquoise water below. Taylor came up behind me and circled her arms around my waist, her nose nestled in my hair, and Guzman excused himself to go help Shelby.

"You don't need to feel bad for him, you know," she said. "He did what he did on his own."

"I know," I said quietly. "But I still do."

Since Galen had exposed the Black Foundation for what it was, his life had been chaos. His parents weren't able to take care of him: in addition to living in that motel-prison, they'd basically disowned him. He didn't have any family, or anywhere else to go, so he'd ended up staying at Harcote, under Ms. Radtke's care. We'd texted a little since school ended, mostly me checking in, so I knew he was struggling but didn't want to talk about it. To be fair, that's what I had always wanted—for him to do the right thing by himself, to stand on his own—but I strongly suspected he hadn't gotten over the fact that I'd left him for the one person at Harcote whose hair was better than his. Even still, it was hard to let go of the feeling that I could have, maybe even should have, done more for him.

I spun around and faced Taylor. "I don't want to think about that right now. I've been waiting years to swim in this pool."

Behind us, I heard a splash. Guzman had cannonballed into the pool, and Shelby dove in after him.

I stepped back and pulled my sweatshirt over my head and dropped it on the ground, then my T-shirt. Taylor's gaze snagged greedily on my bra, my collarbones, my neck. She reached for me, but I stepped back to hold her eyes as I unfastened my jeans. "In the pool," I breathed. "Come on, let's get in."

Taylor stripped off her jacket and flannel, down to her sports bra, then I was the one looking at her hungrily. She kicked off her sneakers, then her chinos. She was beautiful, she was perfect, and she was with me. I shivered a little as I reached for her hand. Together, we jumped and plunged into the water.

THE END

ACKNOWLEDGMENTS

I conceived of the idea for lesbian vampire boarding school at a time when I was utterly burned out on creative work, temporarily living in Russia, and going through a lot of, you know, personal growth. I had never read a single book about vampires, but I was too exhausted to come up with a more original fantasy element. Because drinking blood is icky, I created a world where vampires couldn't do it. As it turned out, early 2020 was a weird time to begin working on a story about a pandemic disease. This book wouldn't be in your hands without the encouragement and hard work of many people.

The team at Razorbill and Penguin Young Readers has been tremendously supportive of this book. I kept waiting for someone to say no to my ideas, but it feels like no one ever did. My editor, Ruta Rimas, trusted my vision so completely that I actually had a hard time accepting it. I am so grateful that she has always understood what I was trying to achieve—and let me know when I was not achieving it. I'm also very appreciative of the work of Casey McIntyre and Simone Roberts-Payne.

Jayne Ziemba, Krista Ahlberg, and Abigail Powers made sure this thing was legible; I am sorry I don't know how to spell or use commas or capital letters.

Kristin Boyle, Maria Fazio, and Rebecca Aidlin did an incredible job with design. When I was planning this project, I wanted to write characters cool enough for Kevin Wada to illustrate, but

I never thought that would actually happen. I am so blown away by how he brought Kat and Taylor to life even better than I'd imagined them.

Felicity Vallence, Bri Lockhart, Vanessa DeJesús, and others at Penguin Young Readers have done amazing work making sure this book reached its readers and I'm very grateful for that.

Stephanie Kim, my agent, has been a steadfast advocate and ally, and I'm so glad that fate threw us together. At New Leaf, I'm thankful to Veronica Grijalva and Victoria Gilleland-Hendersen, my foreign rights agents, and Pouya Shahbazian and Katherine Curtis, my film rights agents. I'm also, as ever, grateful to Jennifer Udden for plucking me from the obscurity of the slush, even if she's transitioned from agent to full-time friend.

I'm very thankful to Andrea Contos, Cale Dietrich, Kelly DeVos, Jessica Goodman, Jennifer Iacopelli, and Cameron Lund, and all the other early readers and reviewers, for their support.

Amanda Zadorian allowed to me ramble about queer shit and the romantic dynamics of characters she had never met in the cocktail bars of Moscow, the breweries of Kaliningrad, and the frozen streets of Nizhny. She also made sure I didn't fully descend into an emotional black hole during my fieldwork. This book would not exist without her, and I am a much better person for her friendship. She wants you to know that one of the fantastical elements of this book is that Taylor's off-the-rack suit fits without alterations.

I'm so grateful for the friendship of Kylie Schacte, her unending supply of excellent craft advice, and her willingness to respond to my chaotic text messages at all hours of the day. Writing this book during the isolation of the pandemic was hard, but Kylie was the one-woman writing group who got me through it.

Devi and Stephanie, thank you for cheerleading this book and me every step of the way. I'm so lucky to have you in my life. Erin Miles let me commandeer her apartment as I wrote this proposal in early March 2020 and again in November 2021 as I finally wrote the epilogue. Ashraya Gupta sagely advised me early on that having Kat kill all the bad guys would not be a satisfying ending, and she was right. I'm also grateful for Katie Reedy, who I can feel raising her eyebrows at me even as I write this. Zander Furnas, Joe Klaver, Blake Miller, Steven Moore, and Mike Thompson-Brusstar have stuck with me through so much, including somehow finishing my dissertation while I was working on this; thank you for always having my back.

I never know how to properly thank my parents, Ann and Ronald—words never seem enough. My sister, Alissa, you are my favorite person. Thank you for your unfailing love and enthusiasm for everything I do.

Thank you to Adrienne Rich for writing "Compulsory Heterosexuality and Lesbian Existence."